THE
PHONE
SWAP

Lia Louis is an author from Hertfordshire, the United Kingdom, where she lives with her partner and three children. She has written five novels to date – *Somewhere Close to Happy* (2019), *Dear Emmie Blue* (2020), *Eight Perfect Hours* (2021), *The Key to My Heart* (2022), *Better Left Unsent* (2024) and her new novel is *The Phone Swap*. Lia's books are enjoyed around the world and have been translated into over sixteen languages.

THE PHONE SWAP

Lia Louis

ZAFFRE

First published in the UK in 2025 by
ZAFFRE
An imprint of Bonnier Books UK
5th Floor, HYLO, 105 Bunhill Row,
London, EC1Y 8LZ

A CIP catalogue record for this book is
available from the British Library.

ISBN: 978-1-80418-275-8

Also available as an ebook and an audiobook

1 3 5 7 9 10 8 6 4 2

Typeset by IDSUK (Data Connection) Ltd
Printed and bound in Great Britain by Clays Ltd, Elcograf S.p.A.

The authorised representative in the EEA is Bonnier Books
UK (Ireland) Limited.
Registered office address: Floor 3, Block 3, Miesian Plaza,
Dublin 2, D02 Y754, Ireland
compliance@bonnierbooks.ie
www.bonnierbooks.co.uk

For Bubs.
My brother. My best mate. Thank you for believing in
every dream I've ever had.

Part One

[*Research Port // Excerpt saved by: Allie Lake*]
'*The Atlantic puffin, for example, builds trust with a monogamous partner through routine and consistency. But trust in monogamous humans relies a great deal on emotional intimacy: being fully seen, and loved, in spite of, and because of, who we truly are.*' – Rossiter, Tyler (2024, June 19) *The Evolutionary Roots of Monogamy and Connection in Humans*

Day 1 of 21

7:43 A.M.

Allie Lake's diary (via CloudLink Drive // The Lake Dock *new*)

Oh my God.

I've just got home from the airport, and I've lost my phone.

Genuinely lost it.

I don't mean that it might've fallen down the back of the sofa or something, either. I mean that I've actually left it somewhere. The plane, I think. The plane's the only thing that makes logical sense. Because, even worse, I've accidentally picked up someone else's phone. Can hardly bear to type that sentence because how on earth does that even happen?

I never lose things. Yet, here I sit: my phone, definitely lost, a stranger's in my hand instead. An accidental swap on the flight . . . I think? Maybe?

Argh. I don't know.

Can't currently think in a straight line. Keep retracing my steps.

- Left work in Bermuda yesterday afternoon. Arrived at JFK. Boarded my flight to London.

- Phone died an hour into the flight. I had no charger pack. Lent it to another researcher who had hours until her flight home to Berlin and wanted to call her kids.
- Swapped seats with serious-faced man in a pink baseball cap and sunglasses who needed legroom. (Suspect number one?)
- Was happy with new location of window seat but then kept being woken by fidgeting man beside me who was constantly checking his phone and slotting it into the back of the seat. (Deduced eventually that he was waiting for a game to hatch a dragon, but suspect number two maybe?)
- Landed in UK and took a taxi home.
- Pulled out phone, momentarily forgetting deadness. Muscle memory. (Otherwise known as: moderate phone addiction I'm definitely in denial about.)
- Realised that while it was the same phone with similar black case, it had 67% battery and my PIN did not get me get past the wallpaper – which was a plate of tagliatelle. My wallpaper is not tagliatelle. (It's that meme of a photo of space, saying, 'You are here, worried about your council tax bill.')
- Proceeded to panic more than I'd intended on taxi's back seat.
- Called airline on grumpy driver's phone. Hung up when driver's messages trilled and trilled in my ear and I felt adequately haunted by endless Simply Red hold music.
- Got home just now. Called airline from my sister's phone and spoke with yawning customer services

agent who filled out a lost property form and asked me to 'pop the other phone back to the airport' as if the airport is a little shop in the village and not fifty-plus miles/one grumpy driver away.

And now, am just sitting here. In my stuffy loft-bedroom. Wondering what to do next and driving myself a bit mad about how such a thing even happened.

Maybe I was really tired from the red-eye and simply picked up someone else's phone by accident? Dragon Man? Slipped it in my bag when preoccupied? Easily done when the plane you're on suddenly smells like fried fish without explanation, and you're actively dreading landing and going back home to June House and your sister for six months. She's gone all-in, as Sian always does, on the whole turning-Mum's-farmhouse-into-a-bed-and-breakfast thing. I pulled up to find she's painted the front door Pepto-Bismol pink ('branding purposes' although am very unclear as to what she's branding it as). It's on a hotel booking app. There's a (also berserk pink) website now, which is all a bit 'out there' for my liking. Have even arrived home to a real, human guest – 'Clive', in room number three, downstairs. Bricklayer. Owns a van with a stuffed Honey Monster hanging out the grille. Recently thrown out by his wife. And rusty foghorns for sinuses, by the sound of him through the floorboards.

All pretty disorientating.

Just yesterday, I was in Bermuda. Peacock-blue sea and sunscreen, my only focus: checking one last time that all the new gull chicks were tagged and logged.

Now I'm back home in sleepy Stought writing my diary on my old tablet because I need to talk it all out. Well. Type it all out, at least. I keep saying I'll give up writing here, but it's still too much of a comfort to stop. Mum set up this shared drive for us a couple of years ago, so she could read this diary while I was working away. Her way of keeping in touch with me while I was in Bermuda. Me, elbow-deep in field research, her, propped up in bed, her usual rust-orange tea, just as excited as me with my findings and bird data. Sometimes I imagine she's still somehow reading this. Would be nice if she was, if only for the fact she was the tech-savvy one in this family and would probably know exactly what to do. (Hi, Mum. In case you are somehow, even though the idea is quite ridiculous.)

Regardless, this helps. Writing. Retracing. Making a plan. Because I NEED to get my phone back. That's assuming I even can. And if I can't, then what? It feels like my whole thirty-one-year-long life is on that phone. I'm confident my cloud will have a lot of it, but I can't seem to get into it without the two-factor authentication code, which maddeningly goes to the phone itself, so I'm without all of it. Banking. Photos. Research data the university will want ASAP. Messages. Memories. Mum's last voice notes are on there, days before she died. Years-old farming games we'd play together. Our scores, our messages, frozen in time.

My sister shook her head when I told her I hadn't used an authenticator app, and hadn't 'fixed' my Find My Phone. (Cannot tell her I disabled it because she kept tracking me while trying to rope me into stressful

DIY projects at the house, texting stuff like, 'Your phone says you're not at work, but at a jacket potato cafe?')

Iris has been far kinder. But she's my friend. She has to be. I texted her from my sister's phone, which I'm permitted to borrow while she gets herself 'breakfast service ready' (whatever that is).

'Oh, Allie,' Iris texted. 'What a twenty-first-century hell. Losing a phone is like waking to find you have no pancreas or something!?' She also says I should keep calling my phone because someone might have it and pick up and 'most people are nice.'

Optimist. ('Er, all realists are optimists to the cynic,' she'd say.)

Anyway, I've called loads, but no answer. Straight to voicemail. Phone clearly still very dead.

And there's no point texting, because even if it was switched on, unlike a phone call, without the PIN, a stranger couldn't even view it, let alone respond.

There must be a way I can put a visible message on the screen, though.

I just need to find a way and fast, before Sian arrives to take her phone back, when I'll be back to being stranded in analogue wilderness. Which is far worse than real wilderness. I've done real wilderness for work and, as much as I don't like it, at least there, you get the technicolour sunrises and a large animal-to-human ratio which I find favourable. You even get patchy satellite internet and group chats with colleagues on obscure collaborative apps like TeamSync.

Maybe I could use TeamSync now?

No unlocking needed for TeamSync. As far as I remember, anyway. Helps to not have to contend with PINs and facial recognition when you're a muddy scientist, typing in all weathers, up a mountain.

Hmm. Could that really work?

I could message myself from my tablet, and if anyone ever switches my phone on, they'll see it. Hopefully reply.

Not a minute too soon, either, because my sister just arrived to take her phone back, 100% 'breakfast-service-ready'. Which is . . . just her in a chef's hat.

Yes. Sian, in a tall, *Ratatouille*-style chef's hat. To serve our single guest, who's only here because his wife kicked him out for buying an OnlyFans model something from her Wish List. (A Just Eat voucher, for record-keeping purposes.)

'I need to get a recipe from my Pinterest for croque madame,' she even said, like we have a fussy French monarch sleeping downstairs and not a trucker with a penchant for cereal box mascots. 'Clive in room three is stirring. I can hear him blowing his nose.'

7:45 A.M.

Milo from Allie's phone to Allie's tablet via TeamSync: Hey Allie, I have your phone! And it seems, you may have mine!!??! Yours is safe and well with me. So sorry. We must've straight up swapped, I guess. Somehow????

Allie: Oh my goodness! Hello! I can't tell you how thrilled I am that it's been found. Thank you very, very much for texting back. Where did you find it?! I can't believe it!

Milo: It was in my pocket, but no clue how it got there! ☺ Thought it was mine until I charged it up and saw it wasn't!! Same phone. Kinda crazy, right? Were you on the JFK to Heathrow flight? 🌚

Allie: Yes! The 22:01 JFK to Heathrow, two days ago.

Milo: Ahhh, there we go!!! Knew it had to have been the plane. We probably sat near each other or something?

Allie: Not sure. I was seated in A3 in the bulkhead row, then I swapped with another passenger to business. Row L?

Milo (via Allie's phone): 😲😲😲😲 Holy shit!!! I'm the dude you switched with!

Allie: OMG! Really!?

Milo: Ha, yeah!! Wow.

Allie: Well, thanks. I enjoyed the window seat.

Milo: Thank you for being so cool about it!! Was kinda embarrassing. I still can't understand how we switched phones, though 💀 I mean, I'm on my third replacement passport of the year, so not sure why I'm shocked!!

Allie: How about when they came to get your bag and jacket? Our stuff was everywhere and so was everyone else's. It was chaotically disorganised.

Milo: Yeah, I guess!! Jeez, this is so crazy, though. Also, what is this app we're using?

Allie: An app I use for work. I had to message via something that could be accessed on my lock screen.

Allie: Are you still there? Am very happy to travel to you to swap back. How close are you to Heathrow?

Milo: Hey, sorry Allie!! I'm actually in Romania right now. I'm American but here for work.

Allie: Oh, goodness, Romania? Will you be returning to the UK at all?

Milo: Yeah, heading to NYC with a layover in London in three weeks. I could FedEx your phone? Trying to figure out how I can make this work . . . .

Allie: Ah. Yes. Hm. I'm not sure I trust my phone being posted. There's so much of importance on it. I know that may sound paranoid, but at least now, the phones are both currently accounted for. I'll research alternatives.

Allie: Could I just have an address of where you're staying for logistical purposes?

Allie: Hello?

Milo: Hey, yeah, sorry for the wait, I'm here. Can we just take a second, Allie? It's all good, but I'm not 100% comfortable with that right now.

Allie: Not comfortable with?

Milo: Just the whole giving my exact location deal. It's just a work rule kinda thing 👻

Allie: I see. A town or city name for now would be fine.

Milo: Yeah, still can't say!! So sorry, Allie, I know this sounds whack! ☺

Allie: Whack?

Allie: Sorry, it's just you have my phone.

LIA LOUIS

Milo: I know, I'll figure it out!! It's complicated, but I can't give out specific location details for work purposes. Nobody's supposed to know where I am . . . 😬

Allie: If you're concerned about identity for some reason, I hardly remember you. (Not meant at all rudely, but reassuringly.)

Milo: Oh yeah? Well . . . ouch? 😄

Allie: ??????

Allie: I'll be in touch shortly with options that rectify this situation ASAP. I just really, really need my phone back, and I know you must want yours too.

Milo: Well, mine's new, so pretty sparse and I've been trying to curb my screen time, so I've gotta admit this feels a little like divine intervention or something! 😄

Allie: I see. Conversely, mine is not sparse and has sentimental value. I recently lost my mum. There's a lot of her on it. Hence why I worry about it getting lost. I'm hoping I can access a lot of it on my cloud but am having login problems currently.

Milo: I'm so sorry to hear about your mother, Allie. Let me figure something out 🙏 🙏 🙏 My name's Milo, by the way.

Allie: Thanks, Milo. Google says 'onboard couriers' are a thing. People who personally courier your package on a domestic flight. Perhaps you could research this on your end too? Happy to wire money for costs.

Milo: Da doamna!! 🕑

Allie: Sorry?

Milo: Romanian for 'yes ma'am'!!!!

Day 3 of 21

2:09 P.M.

Allie's diary (via CloudLink Drive // The Lake Dock *new*)

Good news is someone has found my phone.

Bad news is that the 'someone' may be a bit of a clown.

His name is Milo. (Allegedly.) And he's in Romania. (Also, allegedly.) And he won't (and can't) tell me any more than that. Both concerning and understandable. We are strangers, after all.

The only reassurances that he isn't some sort of phone-ransom-pulling scammer are:

- a) He seems a bit too silly.
- b) Have offered to wire this man money, and he isn't interested.
- c) While he seemed reluctant at first, he now appears to be working off his own back on 'an assistant' to fly to the UK to execute a phone swap. So perhaps he really does mean it when he says it's just that he *can't* tell me where he is.

Iris thinks he's a spy.

I think he's a contract killer. (Though, a contract killer with a squirty flower slotted into his lapel, maybe.)

Either way, he has my phone, and if he's to be believed and this isn't some kind of bizarre scam, it's looking likely I could have it back in a day or two. Phew. I need the notes I have on it for a formal review I have next week at the university with Peter, a program manager at Terrarium, who are funding us, and my supervisor, and it needs to go perfectly. The three-year grant for Bermuda is coming to an end, and while most data is backed up, the data I recorded on voice memos isn't. Argh. At the time, it felt like a no-brainer. Needed to count colonies, keep both eyes on the birds, but now it seems like such a ball-drop. There're already rumours they're looking for reasons not to renew the grant, but telling them the research they're kindly funding for us is stuck in Romania with a spy/circus hitman does not say, 'Please keep funding my project, I'm a responsible bird biologist.' Worried a lot about this with Iris earlier on a TeamSync video call, and she had a – respectfully – ridiculous suggestion.

'Why can't you and this Milo bloke have a little trust?' she asked. Honestly. 'Get him to send your stuff?' She looked so at ease, of course. Lounging in that cluttered, sun-smoked camper van of hers. She's in Wales with a small research team on what she's calling 'a bug hunting extravaganza', and she glowed with it – sun-kissed. Mud-dusted.

'Iris, you think he's a spy,' I reminded her, and she said, 'Why can't it just be a genuine accidental swap, though? Between two normal people and not you and some highwayman.' 'Highwayman' made me laugh. A

17

lot. A package getting lost in the post is 'pretty unlikely' she told me. Then, 'Worst comes to worst, you just hold on to the phones until he flies back. Or, like, lock down your bank and stuff, then get him to send you what you need for work. Right?'

Wrong. Surely, surely wrong.

And I told her so, as she ran through non-scary scenarios like a calm detective and I argued back about data and identity theft, all the while changing Clive in number 3's bedsheets. He's a surprisingly neat guest, Clive. (Messy, OnlyFans-marred marriage aside.) Just a sketch of a dalmatian on the back of an envelope and a tube of Trebor mints on his bedside table. Very civilised.

Iris was a bit thrown by it, saying, 'It is *so* strange watching you fluff pillows,' and, 'It's like seeing a politician in jogging bottoms or something. A dog in a pair of shoes.' Then she asked if I was doing OK with 'all this your-mum's-house-being-a-hotel stuff? 'Cause it feels weird for me and I'm just watching.' And I laughed. Said I was fine. Pretended that it definitely did not feel like the end of a pencil was being pressed against my heart.

Because, truthfully, everything feels wrong.

Mum's lovely June House as a pink, taxidermy-filled 'boutique' B&B. She wanted it to be a retreat once – rooms for women and children for respite, like the cottage was for us. Not like this though. But Sian won't be told. Coming home since Mum died is hard enough, but now every time I do, the house has changed more and more. Mum's decor: now gone. Her bedroom, lifeless, like a film set. But it's worse now there's a weird, pretend-feeling reception desk in the living room and strange, smiling guests – we have two more now – stalking the corridors in branded pink robes like in-patients in an appendicostomy ward.

And I wish we could talk about it. But neither me nor my sister are good at talking. I shut down, and Sian avoids speaking about Mum as if she's shamefully incarcerated rather than having died suddenly of a heart attack, and too soon. This house creaks with all the unsaid things between us sometimes. I often fantasise that she reads this diary, somehow. To air it all. To remind her this house was given to Mum and us as children as a safe place and it's served its purpose, so maybe, as painful as it would be to say goodbye, we should let it go. Maybe then I could ask her to stop buying tacky taps shaped like elephants. To quit foghorning this very distinctive old house across the internet – because if Dad ever happened to see it . . . Thing is, she probably wouldn't believe it anyway. How horrible the elephant taps are, nor how callous our absent dad can be when he wants to be. She's only three years younger than me but there are things she doesn't remember – wasn't privy to – like I was when we were kids.

Then there's my lost phone, plus Milo's, dinging unfamiliarly with notifications, which only adds to this whole 'wrong' feeling, although the few I've happened to see previews of seem pretty regular and boring, and not phone-swapping fraudster fodder. Iris believes I'm overthinking. Weighing myself down with it all.

'Nobody ever won a prize by shouldering everything by themselves, Allie,' she texted when we hung up. 'It's totally fine to take a little risk and open up.'

'Iris, are you asking me to lean on the contract killer?' I asked.

'I'm saying talk to me if you need, amigo,' she replied. Then, 'Hold your hands up to your supervisor about the lost research. Find a way with Milo. (P.S. Contract killing is probably pretty trustworthy work anyway.)'

I thanked her, promised to confide in her, and said that I'd lean on Milo as much as I'd ever lean on a stranger who was in another time zone and in possession of my phone.

Just enough to safely get it back to me.

*

2:13 P.M.

Milo via Allie's phone to Allie's tablet via TeamSync:
Hey!! I've got news!!! An assistant called Sierra lands in Gatwick at 10:16 tomorrow morning to pick up a journo. Flight number: FO1908. ⚠ I'll give her your phone and you could meet her with mine at arrivals??? Hold a sign or something? Really hope this works Allie!! Kinda starting to need mine now too. So much for 'divine intervention' haha. Glad we could get through this!! – M

*

2:17 P.M.

Allie's diary (via CloudLink Drive // The Lake Dock *new*)

Not so much of a clown, after all, it seems. Milo's solved it. Have confirmed formal review with Terrarium. Big phew. Panicking is an unproductive pursuit, but I admit, I was actually starting to . . .

6:34 A.M.

Allie via TeamSync Messenger for tablet: 'DIGITAL DISRUPTION: A major outage on IT systems world-wide has caused chaos for travellers today, with over 1,500 flights cancelled, so far. Although rumours of malicious attacks have been circling on social media, it has now been reported that the global disturbance was caused by a security update . . .'

*

6:59 A.M.

Milo: Ah, shit.

Allie: I know.

Milo: This is the worst luck!!

Allie: I really don't know what to do now. I have such an important meeting in the morning, and I've lied and told them I had everything ready. But some of it is on my phone.

Milo: I hear you, Allie! Ironic, but shit's going badly over here and I need a couple things from my phone for work. Thought I had it all locked in, but I'm big-time messing up without them. Such a pain in the ass . . . Feel like I'm getting my karma for the divine intervention smugness!! 🙁

Allie: Sorry for the delay there. I had to speak to my friend. Need all the advice I can get.

Milo: No worries.

Allie: Perhaps we can safely help each other. There must be a way.

Milo: Could we? 🤭

Allie: Mm. I don't even know what I mean really. This whole thing is really difficult. I've spoken to my phone company and they're helping me recover my cloud info, but they can't tell me how long it might take, due to security and so on. They say it could be days. Really thought I had the whole two-factor security stuff sewn up, too, but it turns out I definitely am not as tech-savvy or organised as I thought.

Milo: Oh man. Ditto, if that's a comfort!! So what can we do here?? I'm actually up a mountain right now!!

Allie: Gosh, really?

Allie: Hm. What if we could ascertain that we're genuine and send what each other needs? Is that quite insane? It is, isn't it? I just really don't know what else to do.

Milo: You have my whole-hearted word that I'm genuine!! ⚠ But hey, I feel the same. This is weird and kinda unnerving if I'm honest!

Allie: Agreed.

Milo: So, OK, you're saying we'd send each other things from each other's phones? Is that right?

Allie: Yes. Swap PINs. Bloody hell! That's nuts, isn't it?

Milo: Yeah. Shit. I guess we'd have to though?! Jeez, I don't know.

Allie: What if we traded information, and confirmed we are who we say we are? We could cross-check using Google if information exists about you online (i.e. social media) and then video call each other? Does this sound like something that would work? I admit, apart from this, I have no other ideas. Video call would help me feel a lot more comfortable. If we felt safe and OK after speaking, we could go from there.

Milo: I think that could work. And yeah, info about me does exist online!

Allie: Me too.

Milo: But also, this feels pretty crazy, Allie. Even for me, haha 😃

Allie: I know. It does seem a little less so when approached from an odds perspective, though, which helps.

Milo: Odds perspective??

Allie: Well, the odds of me losing research data and jeopardising funding are higher than the odds of you not only being a world-class phone scammer, but one who has orchestrated a real digital outage/planted another phone for so far unknown reasons.

Milo: Hahaha, wow OK, that's true. And sort of somehow reassuring . . .

Allie: My friend Iris said we should have some trust in humanity.

Milo: I love that. I'm all about that! 🙏 🙏 🙏

Allie: My sister says we could secure insurance from each other that could destroy one another's lives should we decide to use the access to each other's phones for evil.

Milo: Well, shit. That's dark!

Allie: I know. And anyway, surely the insurance is, destroy mine and I'll destroy yours?

Milo: I guess you're right! But again. Dark?!

Allie: 🐨

Milo: So . . . Are we definitely gonna do this, then? 😃

Allie: Currently out of other ideas, so, yes. Why don't we gauge how comfortable we feel after the video call?

Milo: Deal.

Allie: Suddenly very nervous . . .

Milo: Same. Super weird feeling right? OK so, I'll start I guess? My name is definitely Milo.

Allie: My name is definitely Allie.

Milo: I'm 30.

Allie: I'm 31. I'm a scientist.

Milo: Seriously? I'm an actor.

Allie: Interesting. Known?

Milo: Ummm, yeah! At least I hope to some!!

Allie: Ah. Is that why you can't tell me where you are?

Milo: Yeah. NDA! Filming right now. Top director. New writer trying to make a mark. Pretty intense.

Allie: I see. That makes a lot of sense. The apprehension, the weirdness, etc.

Milo: Yeah, the weirdness will just be my organic state, Allie 😁

Allie: Ha. And what's your full name? Mine's Allie Lake.

Milo: It's Milo Ford 🙂

Allie: OK. I've not heard of you.

Milo: How many times can a dude say ouch in one week? And why did I use such a smug emoji? Regrets. But, yeah, that's me. I do mostly movies, some TV.

Allie: Well, it shouldn't be read into. I don't watch a lot of TV or films. And if we're doing specifics, I'm a biologist. I do mostly seabirds.

Milo: Oh, whoa, cute shit! Love birds. So, do you mean you care for seabirds?

Allie: No, I work at a university. I work in conservation.

Milo: So you're out there saving the planet for us assholes and I'm jabbering about 'cute shit'!?! I apologise!

Allie: Some of the time, it definitely is 'cute shit'.

Allie: Anyway, I think we should google each other now, then video call to confirm identity. Are you able to do that?

Milo: Yup, got a laptop. I need to be clear though, Allie, that I still can't tell you where I am, I'm sorry.

Allie: Understood. Googling now.

Milo: Feel you should also know Google Images is a wasteland of every cursed pic ever taken of me. Can't get those things removed either 😄

Allie: Done.

Milo: Done over here too!! Found your university profile. You sound like a genius.

Allie: Ha. Thanks. When are you available to video call?

Milo: Right now? Sooner I can get my stuff, the better! My call time's in an hour and then I've gotta run, but I have Zoom if that works??

Allie: OK to Zoom. Just trying to log in. Meantime, a question of my own, if I may?

Milo: Sure!

Allie: Do you have a trailer? Or is that just a Hollywood myth?

Milo: Hahaha, not a myth, you totally do get trailers! Gotta be special enough, though . . .

Allie: Ah.

Allie: Sending username now.

Milo: I sounded like an asshole, reading that back.

Allie: Ready to call when you are.

Day 5 of 21

9:54 A.M.

<u>**Allie's diary (via CloudLink Drive // The Lake Dock**</u>
<u>***new*)**</u>

In an unexpected turn of events – and by far, one of the most uncharacteristically irresponsible things I have ever, ever done – I have given a stranger my phone's PIN. A stranger who happens to be a Hollywood actor.

That's correct. An actual, real-deal Hollywood actor. He's on IMDB and has fan pages and everything. It's ridiculous, isn't it? Totally ridiculous.

Milo the Clown/Contract Killer is, in fact, a thirty-year-old New Jersey-born actor. Occasional model of designer swimwear, and owner of incredibly brown eyes and an almost preposterous amount of wavy shiny hair, both of which had been obscured by the sunglasses/cap combo (which now makes sense). I admit I only allowed myself to google him for three minutes because it felt relatively inappropriate to delve any longer. Plus, I mostly wanted to screen him for any historical, weird phone-related (and non-phone-related) crimes, and his crime slate is clean. I did, however, find out he was first cast as an 'immortal' in a movie franchise called *Day Falls*, a moody cult

30

teen werewolves and warlock thing, and that made him known. Then he played 'Vex' in a TV show called *Brothers,* which has just won two Emmy Awards, and that made him famous. He recently left *Day Falls,* and it was clear from even from my cursory search that he's pissed off a lot of fans. (From what I can gather, they feel *Day Falls* made his name, but he quit mid-filming the third movie and 'sold out.') There are also articles on ad-filled gossip pages of him helping out at a dog shelter, throwing parties at a beach house and infuriating anonymously quoted neighbours, and also an interview with an ex and *Day Falls* co-star, Sara Santi, in which she delivered one line about him, but a pretty scathing one. Something like, 'He left the movie and then me.' She also called him 'self-conscious', 'smoke and mirrors' and, as a boyfriend, a 'man who cares only about himself.' (Ouch.) The article then sent me to another about his swimwear campaign, quoting him as saying, 'If my ass be the food of love, play on.' An eclectic mix, yes, but nothing criminal. Thankfully.

And despite how incredibly irresponsible this sounds as I type it out, I do believe giving Milo Ford my PIN was the right decision. If only for the fact he helped me log in to my cloud (which I've now locked down properly) and sent my research voice notes over, and my meeting this morning went as well as it could've. My supervisor was pretty bleak after, full of stories of funding cuts from similar projects, but I really think when Terrarium look properly at my data, they'll keep supporting us. At least, I have to believe that as a matter of survival.

This whole phone swap incident is working for Milo too, I think, although I have since learned he has less to lose than I have, as when he said his phone was sparse, he meant it. New number, new phone, he said. A 'spiritual clean slate,' he called it, which sort of made me want to scoff. Still. It's at least helpful to him too. He's playing a British soldier and 'totally bombed' his first scenes after nailing them in rehearsals, months ago, so I had to send him a twenty-two-minute sound file from his dialect coach and a video of him reading lines in what looked like an old garage. I did ask whether there was a UK luvvie contact somewhere who could help once the planes are back on track, and he replied with something like, 'Kind of want to avoid anyone who knows me finding out I'm losing phones and accents right now, Allie,' and I told him I understood. I made clear, actually, that I would feel more comfortable if we kept this arrangement, within reason, as close to just us as we can. Keep the circle small. Tell nobody. Keep the phones safe, in our respective homes, for privacy. He agreed.

Meantime, we spent time turning off notifications for things we can access ourselves now and we've agreed to switching the phones back in person in just seventeen days when he's back in the UK for a layover. Until then, we are to simply act as 'phone secretaries' – Milo's term, penned on video chat. And it was interesting, the video chat. I thought I'd feel exposed, but when he blinked onto the screen, I felt only a huge wave of relief. It was definitely him. The Milo Ford from Google.

'It's you!' he laughed. He was less polished than his red-carpet poses on Google. Scruffier than I'd expected;

thick, brown hair skewed as if nervously yanked to one side, prisms of creases covering his white T-shirt. But definitely the same Milo. Self-conscious, *definitely* arrogant, but an enthusiastic type. A 'feeler', I think. (He said that his new phone and number felt like 'a rebirth or something' and that the video call was 'a true solace'.)

'Well, if you're ever at all concerned,' I said, 'we could always have regular check-ins like this to maintain comfort and trust.' I told him I saw it on a programme once about police and undercover informants. Milo laughed; I think he thought I was joking. I was not. 'Spies do it,' I explained.

Smilingly, he said, 'And actors and scientists now too.'

Yes, I told him.

Whatever gets us through the phone swap. A responsible plan to see us through this potentially very stupid, irresponsible decision made out of mutual desperation.

For just seventeen days.

And really, that's what I keep saying to myself. Even in all my alleged cynicism, what could possibly happen in just seventeen days?

Day 6 of 21

10:09 A.M.

Allie via Milo's phone: Morning. Some screenshots of notifications you've had today:

Allie forwarded [screenshot]
Bunty's Coffee: Black card member alert: Scan your app at any Bunty's Coffee worldwide today and receive your fave drink free all July long!

Word!: Milo, your word of the day is 'fortuity'. Meaning: A chance incident that is mostly beneficial.

iMessage from Jameson: Dude, you ghosting me? How's the movie? Just finished a 24-hour gaming stream. I'm soooo knackered. Think I broke YouTube, though, so that's good, ahaha. Anyway, hope you're staying whole!! :-) Always proud of you, friend. If anyone's got this, you've got this. Clean slate this shit. J xx

*

12:56 P.M.

Milo via Allie's phone: Hey, thanks for forwarding these, Allie! Just got back to the apartment. A half hour ago I was dressed as a 1940s soldier yearning for his lost wife, now holding a scientist's smartphone, haha. Life, huh?!! Could you text Jameson back for me? Tell him to check his emails. Literally my only means of comms right now! ⚠

Allie via Milo's phone: Hi! Sure.

Milo: Also, an app keeps springing up with super over-active flame emojis saying something about 'count your chicks'??? Need me to do anything?

Allie: Oh, that's good news. No, Count Your Chicks is my website.

Milo: Website? Cool!! What sort of website?

Allie: It's time-lapse wildlife cameras where people can watch the birds we track in Bermuda and other places, and count them for us. It still won't let me log into it here unfortunately, so it might keep going off for now. Starts panicking about security and being logged into another device.

Milo: I love that idea!!! Can I go see? And what does counting do?

Allie: Yes, go ahead. I had 22 members last I checked, I need all the eyes I can get, ha ha. And counting helps us track population numbers over time.

Milo: Currently looking at puffins in Scotland. This is super cool, Allie!! Do you travel a lot?

Allie: Mostly in spring/summer. I suppose I'm home and away equally as much! It's mostly always about the breeding seasons.

Milo: Same. Save for the whole breeding thing 😄

Allie: Ha. Relieved to hear this.

Milo: Also, feel free to pick up the coffee. They sent me a black card, but no Bunty's over here!! 😣 Nearest town here has no electricity. Seriously!! Like, real Dickensian shit. No stores or restaurants. Probably a good thing, though. Curbing my caffeine right now.

Allie: Curbing caffeine AND screens? Life is tough enough as it is, I say, Milo. We all need a bit of balance.

Milo: Ah, but I'm not a man of balance, Allie 😄

Allie: Ha. Well, I've never actually been to a Bunty's, so maybe I will. Their big neon yellow sign always reminds me of one of those 'biohazard' warning signs. People disposing of blood and stuff? Probably why I've never been in.

Milo: . . . I thought it was a little honey bee? Not anymore, I guess!!?

Allie: Sorry about that.

Milo: I mean, chances are high you might hate it with my drink!! It's an interesting one? You've gotta tell me if you do, though. I'm a big boy, I can take it.

Allie: Am expecting biohazardous waste, so the bar is low.

Allie: Also, Jameson has just replied. Just said: 'Oh yeah? Thank u kind stranger :-)'

Milo: Haha, thanks!! 'Kind stranger . . .'

Allie: You're welcome. Kind stranger.

Milo: Ahhh, look at us! 🌚 We're really phone-secretarying away here, right???

Allie: And only 16 more days to go!

Day 7 of 21

10:01 P.M.

Allie forwarded [screenshot]

With Gratitude: *'Don't lose your streak, Milo! Spending just five minutes practicing daily gratitude is scientifically proven to promote better sleep, improve physical health and instill healthy habits!'*

9:55 P.M.

Milo via Allie's phone: Just shooting this over. Hope you had a nice day, Allie!! Night ☺

Milo forwarded [screenshot]

ResearchPort: Allie, you may want to read recently added scientific paper 'Space and the Arctic – A most unlikely relationship'.

Count Your Chicks: Two New Member Sign Ups! AcerSpark and R29201.

9:19 A.M.

Allie's diary (via CloudLink Drive // The Lake Dock *new*)

It's fascinating how fast something becomes routine. Birds can be like this, but humans can be extra skilled at it. We settle in, quickly adopt something new until it feels like something familiar. Like hotel rooms that feel like home after just one sleep. It's the same on the field, when my home is suddenly a musty dorm in a research station, or an Airbnb with mismatched mugs. A sub-conscious search for safety, perhaps. A longing to make things feel familiar, and undangerous.

That's sort of how things are with Milo and me, and this whole strange phone arrangement. It's fast becoming familiar. Something that is just simply part of my day.

I wake up. Make a giant mug of tea before Sian drags me into the surrealist art installation that is the June House B&B breakfast service and we make stilted, hollow conversation (about anything other than anything that really matters, like Mum, or the fact I'm worried that June House's new Instagram page is growing, and someone who knows Dad might see).

I then check Milo's phone. He does the same for mine. We then keep an eye on them throughout the day, almost like you would your own, whenever we're home, as we've promised to keep them safe inside, for safety purposes, and then check again before going to sleep. The last few days have started with a good morning to or from Milo, and most days have ended with a goodnight.

It's interesting how much you can learn about someone from their phone, too, even if it is a 'spiritual clean slate'. I scoff, but I get it. I can't imagine how busy a person's phone can get after their career 'blows up', like his has appeared to. My worst nightmare, to be that visible. Regardless, it's still a window in.

His apps tell me he likes words and reading; motorsport and cooking. Multiple habit trackers keep reproaching him for not logging data for weeks, which tells me he's likely flaky, but has high expectations for himself. (His ex called him 'work-obsessed' too, which tracks. Not that I believe things I read on trashy websites.) A shopping app keeps alerting him to air drying clay and crochet yarn.

He also loves coffee. A lot. He has a brew timer app (who knew such a thing existed?), coffee recipes and numerous take-out apps prompting him to order his drinks ahead.

And I'm actually about to redeem his favourite drink. There's a Bunty's opposite campus, so I thought I'd catch up on some emails in there, before I go into work. With Milo Ford's drink. Redeemed on Milo Ford's (with permission) but contained in my own reusable cup, and all while Clive sets me up with a

spare phone back at June House – he fished an old
iPhone out of the footwell of his van, and promised
more than once, concerningly, that it would be 'wiped
clean. Fully, Allie. Trust me.' (Sian flapped, of course,
reminding me guests should *receive* a service, not the
other way around, but I ignored her.)

It's weird, though. This feather-blending of mine and
Milo's lives. Me and a perfect stranger.

And it's nice too, that it's working.

Milo's even sending me updates from my nesting
cameras. Plus, today he sent an 'on this day' memory
photo of me and Mum, both holding the (hilariously
bad) rum swizzle cake she'd made me to celebrate landing the Bermuda funding, three years back.

I thanked Milo for sending it. 'A sign?' he texted with
a praying hands emoji, and it made me smile.

OMG.

The barista just called me for my coffee.

'Milo?' she called, and I had to say, loud and clear,
'Yes, that's me.'

*

11:03 A.M.

Allie via Milo's phone: [image description: Allie
drinking coffee in Bunty's – mousy hair pulled back in
a ponytail, wearing yellow shirt dress, small seashell
charm necklace around her neck. She holds a purple
reusable coffee cup]

42

Allie: Double shot, no milk, but two pumps of candy-floss syrup, one pump of mint, AND whipped cream . . . Excuse me?

Milo via Allie's phone: Oh man, I warned you!!!

Allie: I think I like it.

Milo: Holy shit, seriously???? 😨

Allie: Yes.

Allie: Yet it makes no sense. It's too bitter but really sweet. Like Santa Claus with a machine gun or something.

Milo: Hahahaha. Seriously!? I've never met anyone who likes it!

Allie: May change my mind a few more sips in, but so far, I'm enjoying.

Milo: Hahaha, keep me posted. Also, you've had a voicemail from 'Terrarium'. You don't seem to have visual voicemail, with a play button and stuff? Should I call later and play it to you?

Allie: If you're not too busy?

Milo: Nah, free at night until night shoots start!! I can call at like, 9 Romanian time? (7 your time, I think?)

Allie: Thanks.

Milo: First spy debrief scheduled!

Allie: Ha. Yes. Will add your drink to the agenda.

Milo: Your drink too now, Allie. ☺

Day 10 of 21

8:35 A.M.

Direct message from Iris via TeamSync: UMMMMM, DID I JUST READ YOUR MESSAGE RIGHT? YOU VIDEO CALLED!? FOR TWO HOURS? I THOUGHT IT WAS TO HEAR ONE VOICEMAIL? OH MY GOD, ALLIE, CAN YOU HEAR ME SCREAMING ALL THE WAY FROM WALES?! 😩😩😩😩

Iris: SCREAMING I TELL YOU!

Allie: Ha ha. It was just a very nice conversation.

Iris: A very nice conversation? Err, a two-hour video call with a gorgeous man is not normal for you! Don't you be fobbing me off with 'a very nice conversation' cop-outs . . .

Allie: I'm going to lose this tablet if you carry this on.

Iris: But you never spend two MINUTES talking to someone unless you really like them, let alone two hours! And to Milo Ford no less! 😊

Allie: Also going to give Just Eat Clive's temporary phone back too . . .

Iris: But this is sooo exciting, amigo! I'm levitating in this bloody van with my porridge right now!

Allie: Currently hanging both devices out the window.

Iris: Do you fancy him?

Allie: For goodness sake!

Iris: Well? Are you attracted to this man? 😶😶😶😶😶😶

Allie: Iris, this is a man who, yes, is very nice, but is probably trying to keep me on side.

Iris: Answer me . . .

Allie: I'm essentially the minder of his personal phone. I could let it slip to the nearest gossip page and probably make a much-needed few quid, if I wanted to. It might be sparse, but it's his after all. (I kid. Obviously. May not be kidding if we don't hear about the funding soon, though. Got the real fear about it.)

Iris: ALEXANDRA HELEN LAKE!!! Just answer the question! Do you fancy Milo? 😶😶😶😶😶😶

Allie: Bloody hell, OK.

Allie: (a little bit?)

Iris: !!!!!!!!!!!!!!!!!!!!!!!!!!!!

Iris: OMG OK, why am I now sure that this is it for you!?

Allie: Absurd.

Iris: But maybe this is why you're allergic to dating! You were subconsciously waiting for this. You're going to fall in love with this man.

Allie: 'This man' is someone who could likely date any person he wants, Iris. And 'this man' is in the mountains keeping a low profile wanting to pass time between scenes.

Allie: I can guarantee he's thought nothing more of it.

*

10:03 A.M.

Allie forwarded: [screenshot]

iMessage from Ben: Yoooo, Jameson was just telling me you're coming all undone cuz this Allie chick LIKES your crazy coffee order and you talked all night!?! Are we sure she's deffo a real person and not like AI? You're just the sort of romantic motherfucker that'd get attached to AI.

iMessage from Ben: Oh shit. Didn't realise Jameson meant you were emailing and not texting. Sorry!! She can probably see this. Hi Allie lol.

Day 11 of 21

9:45 P.M.

Allie forwarded [screenshot]

iMessage from Skylar speakeasy: when r u and those hands back in new york?

8:45 A.M.

Allie's diary (via CloudLink Drive // The Lake Dock *new*)

Ever since our two-hour video call three days ago, I've not heard much from Milo. I've received odd notifications from him (my sweet subscription box renewing, and Count Your Chicks sign-ups). I also forwarded him those messages from his friend Ben, which I've spent more time analysing than I'd ever admit. Because 'undone' could definitely be regretful. But 'undone' could also be positive. Excitement that we get along and I like his coffee. Milo's response offered no insight either. He first said, 'Ah, shit, wish strangling friends across an ocean was scientifically possible. Haha! And it's just my two buddies who know. And Sierra who signed an NDA for the movie. So you still have my word!!'

I suppose less comms makes sense now I gain more and more access to my digital life. Plus, I reason that he's very busy and on set a lot.

I even said this to Sian, who has been mostly avoiding me since I told her offering spa days at the B&B was a terrible idea (due to the fact we have no spa), but she seemed in the mood for chatting after I offered to help with breakfast service. I toasted bread. She organised eggs in a saucepan (and all while wearing an *actual* Wee Willie Winkie-style sleep cap, for the morning's breakfast theme: 'Breakfast in bed', God help us. Next Wednesday, the theme is: woodland. Am scared she's going to ask me to dress up as a shrub and cover me in miniature pastries).

'I know you think creative work is frivolous,' she said, and I interrupted to say I wouldn't quite say *frivolous*. But I couldn't think of another word. *Lighter* work, maybe. Whimsical. At the superficial end of jobs, if pushed. She carried on though. 'He's probably deep in his work. Obsessive. Creative work takes so much *personal* energy.' Then she smiled down at her pig-shaped, for some reason, egg cups, and I realised she was comparing her breakfasts to Milo's movie.

And Milo probably *is* too busy to be worrying about my phone. He's signed an NDA. He's working with an award-winning writer, a trailblazing, record-breaking director who has a journalist there, in Romania, currently writing an exclusive biographical piece about her. Of course he won't always have the time to send screenshots of texts from Amazon unable to find my house, tucked away in the village, or hourly bird camera updates with his usual, 'Damn Allie, starting to love checking up on these guys' messages.

But I also think that something has shifted after that video call.

I would never of course say this aloud to anyone because it sounds nonsensical.

But I felt it.

Hung up and simply stared at the tablet on my bed in front of me like it was a piece of smouldering coal on the duvet. Perhaps he felt the same. A little blindsided, like me, after that out-of-nowhere deep-dive chat about family and distant fathers and those specific intense memories of summer days you have as a child, and all while making hot chocolate (me) and waiting for catering to deliver dinner (Milo). We talked about Mum. He lost his own mother, ten years ago, to cancer, and he was so open in the way he spoke about it. ('I still can't say died. It's simply not something she would've ever done.') We talked about Dad. 'Estranged as estranged can be,' I told him. I was fifteen when we left. He doesn't know where we are. We as good as hid. The broad strokes. And I was surprised really, that I just gave it up to him. Dad's chaos and alcoholism that blights every childhood memory like an ink smudge. But then, Milo did the same. Said his dad was a king-like figure in his childhood, now crippled with arthritis, living in a luxury retirement village Milo pays for, and disapproves of every single thing he does, even the success. 'Think I'm still waiting for him to love me,' he said.

It was strange. Different.

Because I don't do this.

Whether conversations with strangers at wedding tables, blind dates with friends of friends, neighbours in front gardens at dusk, slippers on and wheeling in recycling bins, even heart-to-hearts with friends . . . I try to hand over parts of myself, settling a ripe peach of it in people's palms. But I retreat. Every time. Envisage it being pulverised in a scrunched fist.

But the call with Milo . . .

Maybe it's something about the face-to-faceness of a video call. Nowhere to hide. No making excuses, no drifting off into another room. You can do that at a friend's barbecue. You can't do that on a video call.

It was just us, faces lit by screens.

And what's weird is, twelve days ago, I didn't even know this man existed.

And in nine days, we meet to switch back, then I likely won't hear anything from him again.

*

Forwarded by Allie [screenshot]

Milo's phone: *Word! – you haven't added a word for a while! Tap now to add a word. Have you heard a new word recently? Add it to 'Milo's List!'*

Day 13 of 21

8:56 A.M.

Forwarded by Milo Ford:

Instagram DM from Dr Andrew Gaines: Hey, Allie, this is my new profile! Spoke to Iris last week and she said you lost your phone so thought I'd DM! We also talked a lot about you ☺ Mostly about the golden days of our first field trips and how you always had a backpack full of Cup a Soup. Hehe. She said you're having funding woes. Maybe we could get together? Strategise? Pizza? Andrew x

*

Milo via Allie's phone: Morning, Allie!! ☺

Milo: I'm sorry for the delay in messaging. Night shoots have been kicking my ass!!! I might need your help later. I've gotta log in to something to pay rent for my dad's retirement place but it needs me to verify by putting a text code in? It gives me like 60 seconds to enter it, so do you mind if I call later and you hand it over?

Milo: Last up, the screenshot from Instagram! It's asking me if I want to accept his request? Do I keep Andrew in the holding pen or release the dude? 🤔

Allie via Milo's phone: Hi. Sorry, I've been downstairs helping my sister erect a 5-foot-tall pink gnome statue for the dining room at the B&B. I feel rather haunted after the whole thing. And yes to calling. No worries.

Milo: Cool, thank you!! A giant pink gnome sounds awesome by the way!

Allie: It isn't. I hate it. Keep thinking it's an intruder. Dreadful for the amygdala.

Milo: Is it too early in the secretarial relationship to mention I have a 6-foot statue of a brown bear in a cowboy hat in my kitchen in NYC? That I love so much I crocheted him a scarf?

Allie: I believe it's always too early to mention this. (Though I'm impressed with the crochet.)

Milo: You're the only who is 😄

Allie: As for the Instagram DM. You can ignore it and switch off the notifications.

Milo: Noted, Captain Lake. I'll send him and his 'hehe' on his way to look for someone else to date.

Allie: Ha ha, I meant I can message him from here. I have access now. And he's an old friend. We dated for five seconds once, but we were young and stupid. I don't really 'date', as a rule.

Milo: Oh yeah?

Allie: Yes.

Milo: OK . . . ?

Milo: Gotta admit, sometimes I leave silences hoping you'll fill them with stuff!! Media training trick. People generally fill silences if you give them the space to . . .

Allie: I see.

Milo: You don't.

Allie: Ha. I suppose I tend not to talk for the sake of it.

Milo: I know. Find it kinda fascinating because I totally do.

Allie: Maybe the whole leaving silences thing doesn't work via text.

Allie: I certainly had enough to say the other night, though, anyway. Two hours! Gosh.

Milo: On our call?? Yeah, I could've talked for much longer. Was genuinely pissed I had to sleep. By sleep I obviously mean stare at the ceiling playing poker with all my millions of thoughts like all good insomniacs do!!

Milo: But I had a really awesome time.

Allie: So did I 😊

Milo: 😊

Allie: Oh, also, you've just had more messages from Skylar speakeasy. More enquiries about where you and your hands are.

Milo: Damn, sorry about that, Allie!! 😁

Allie: It's fine. I just imagine you arriving at JFK wearing giant foam fingers.

Milo: Hahaha, is that right?

Allie: Could I also ask, what's your 'Word!' app? It's very insistent.

Milo: Ahhhh, yeah, it's literally the only thing I ever keep up with. I'm a word nerd I guess? Collect the cool and interesting ones as I come across them or whatever. Feel free to take a look. I kinda miss it!! Keeps me grounded.

Allie: That sounds interesting. Maybe I could add some for you?

Milo: Sure!! Actually, if you head over to 'new list', you can shoot me a link and we can share a list? Only if that wouldn't bore you to death of course.

Allie: Deal.

Milo: Better go. Needed in costume!! Still OK to jump on a call tonight for the credit card thing?

Allie: Sure.

Milo: You'll have to swear you won't take my code and go shopping though.

Allie: Well, I was going to buy a silly giant bear in a cowboy hat for my kitchen.

Milo: In that case, Allie, take all the money you want!! I'll crochet it something.

Day 14 of 21

8:21 A.M.

Forwarded by Milo [*screenshot*]

Zoom: How are you finding our service? Rate last night's call – 9:02 p.m. outgoing video call via tablet, to Milo Ford – duration: 02 hr 47 m

Milo via Allie's phone: What're we saying, Allie? 5 stars? ♥ Also, did you realise it's only a week until we meet?

*

10:09 A.M.

Allie's diary (via CloudLink Drive // The Lake Dock *new*)

I do not know what's happening.
    I spoke with Milo for almost three hours last night.
    Three.
    Whole.
    Entire.
    Real.
    Hours.

And it was meant to only be a few minutes. Just a code, which we solved within moments of him flickering onto the screen with thick hair, wet and tangled from the shower, wearing a strange, holey-on-purpose brown jumper that nobody normal would ever look good in.

'Hey! Here she is!' He grinned. 'Captain Lake, secretary of my phone . . .' I keep thinking about the grin. Conspiratorial. Cocky. Liquid warmth.

We talked about work – mine and his. He showed me a prop he'd accidentally taken that belongs in the pocket of his costume. A fake wallet, holding a fake photo of his beloved fake wife. I showed him the gnome, which he studied like a museum relic and said, completely unironically, 'Ah, wow, Allie, he's a beauty.' It even made me warm to it a fraction. Then he showed me the sunset from his balcony. Sky dimming peach and gold, that same sun still wide awake and blinding out of my own window. We watched together for a few moments in silence.

But then the conversation just . . . kept going, and going.

Songs that make us feel.

Obscure fake names Milo uses at hotels.

Favourite type of mug (for some reason).

Rain.

Inventing a time machine.

This diary. (Which again, I so easily gave up to him and told him about.)

And then he talked about *Day Falls* – all that stuff in the articles I found. Him leaving last year. Pissing people off. I could tell it was still raw to him. He went all shiny-eyed and I didn't know what to say.

'I had to leave,' he said. 'Hardest thing I ever did, but it was survival in the end.' He said he's used to people talking about him, that 'to be known is to be content with being misunderstood', but the backlash hit him really hard. Fans were enraged. Writers had to scrap full scripts. For a while, his Instagram page was 'like a pocket in space and time where I could go to read the worst things I think about myself'. He mentioned the ex too – the 'he left the show and then left me' ex. He said her interview seemed to send him into some sort of 'trending worldwide' orbit. But the truth was, he left to go to rehab. He said he considered going public with it, but that the reaction to it can be either good or bad. You gain support, or lose it. Forever seen as something different than who you are. Sometimes getting 'outed', he said, works better.

'Fuckin' benzos for me,' he told me with a sigh. Prescribed initially for his insomnia. 'Then they just made me make bad decisions.' I keep shuddering with guilt because I think – no, I *know* – I froze as he spoke. I don't always know what to say at the best of times, but . . . it's just Dad, isn't it? Rehab. The fallout. The language Milo used, reminds me of everything back then. But he's better now. Called it 'a blip'. 'And OK, now I don't sleep, but I've got Bunty's to keep me awake,' he laughed, and I said, 'And you don't even have that now!'

We started saying goodbye, then. But somehow, instead . . .

We ended up watching a film together.

It was all so random and silly. He said he was going to eat ramen and watch *Roman Holiday*, because watching old films with old actors shrank his anxiety; said 'it's humbling, the way a museum is.' His worries are nothing new. He's not special. Just another person.

I told him I hadn't seen it. Then he said I was welcome to join and I thought he was joking. But he sent me a link and I laid on top of my duvet, turned off my bedroom light, and together, we just . . . watched *Roman Holiday*. We laughed at the same lines. He pointed out tiny things about the dialogue – the way it felt unscripted and real – and we talked a little about fame. He said he loves and loathes it, equally. And yet, a part of him chases it.

I ran downstairs for toast.

Milo made ramen in a giant mug covered in acorns, added extra seasoning, tasted, added more, and I found myself watching him, and thinking, plainly, what on EARTH is going on here?

I'm watching sunsets with a man I've never met.

We're eating meals and watching films together.

We're adding words to a shared list. ('Surreptitious', 'perfidy', 'tryst'.)

He's reading science papers that ping up on my ResearchPort. ('Yoooo, puffin beaks glow in the dark? WHAT?')

It unnerves and delights me how much I enjoy having him around.

Because in seven days, Milo will hand my phone back to me, and I'll give his to him. He will go back to his life, and I'll go back to mine.

And this will stop.

And I realised, as he sat listening to me, a hand flat to his chest, screen lighting his face, that I don't think I want it to.

Day 15 of 21

12:11 P.M.

Forwarded by Allie [screenshot]

Milo's phone: *Word! – 'Melifluous' was added to 'Allie and Milo's list!'*

Allie via Milo's phone: Interesting word choice.

Milo via Allie's phone: Right? It means 'pleasing sound' in relation to something musical. Or a voice . . . ☺

10:03 P.M.

Milo forwarded [screenshot]

Notification from Calendar on Allie Lake's phone: New event – Table booked 7 p.m. at The Cricketers with Andrew Gaines – accept?

Notification from CloudLink: Someone logged into 'Allie Lake's CloudLink' on a tablet in Stought, Gloucestershire, was this you?

Day 17 of 21

10:17 P.M.

Milo via Allie's phone: Nothing to report today Captain Lake! Hope you're good.

Milo: Feels weird to be going to sleep without one of our three-hour talking marathons, hahah.

Milo: Should probably say goodnight now.

Milo: But I kinda hate when there's no news for us to send to each other!!

Milo: And I probably shouldn't say this but I'm gonna. Because the simple truth is, I saw how golden the sunset was again tonight, and you were the only person I wanted to show it to.

11:50 P.M.

Allie's diary (via CloudLink Drive // The Lake Dock *new**)**

The funding has been cancelled.

Bermuda is over.

I know a part of me was expecting it, but I can't actually believe that's it. Was out with Andrew and Iris, and the email just landed, as a wood-fired Hawaiian pizza was slid under my nose and a Katy Perry song blared. 'Unfortunately,' it said, 'funding is being redirected to projects that align with Terrarium's current focus.' What does that even mean? What about my birds? My tern chicks? My *cameras*?

Andrew told me he had some ideas on how to raise the money, that he'd call me today, and Iris hugged me in the booth and assured me something better would come along. I could hardly eat after that, although I pretended I was fine. Squashed my pizza closer together so it looked like I'd eaten, because the whole thing erased my appetite.

I told Sian when I got home. She said she was sorry, but then told me I'd made too much noise coming home. 'Guests,' she said. 'You seem to forget them.'

I hate this B&B.

I hate what this house represents.

I miss Mum. So much. And she loved the Bermuda conservation project as much as me. She followed it religiously, excitedly, *proudly*. It feels like a part of her too which makes this so much more painful. It's been almost two years now, since she died, and I still feel like I'm nowhere close to being able to go even a day without remembering suddenly and it feeling, on the best days, just deeply *strange* and hollow, and on the worst, totally unbearable.

And now I'm stuck here.

Alone in my room.

And I am alone. Truly. Aren't I?

Andrew's got a girlfriend now, was saying things like, 'We found a lovely little place for tapas,' and 'We're trying to find a new series to watch.' Iris is going to the Arctic wilderness where there's no internet with two other researchers and a handsome meteorologist who keeps making her playlists.

I'm scared of the wilderness.

I'm scared of staying here.

I'm scared of being a 'we'. Because Mum was an 'I' once. An 'I' who wanted so much. She used to talk about going to Fiji for Christmas; wanted to sign up for an archaeological dig. When she was twenty-one, she went to California with just a backpack. Then she met Dad and became 'we'. A 'we' that turned into chaos and lies and holding doors shut with her whole body as the other half to her 'we' banged to get in and cried secretly so her daughters wouldn't see. Then just mere years after gaining freedom as an I, she died. All of it, the pain, and the hope for 'someday', whipped away as if by the wind.

That's why I'm scared. Of dating. Of love. Men. Ripe fruit placed on palms. Dating men. Becoming a 'we'.

And Milo?

No. I'm not scared of Milo.

I want to call him, actually. It's all I want to do right now. See his face, linger over all those deep things he says without reluctance.

Is that weird? It's weird, isn't it?

But then, is it? We've spoken for hours over the last couple of weeks. Hours and hours and hours.

I miss him when we aren't speaking.

Oh, Christ, how ridiculous. I've never even met this man.

I'm going to text him.

No, I won't. No. I'm going to have a bath and not text him. It's almost midnight for goodness' sake.

Day 19 of 21

12:03 A.M.

Allie via Milo's phone: Hello.

Milo via Allie's phone: Hey!!!

Allie: So sorry if I woke you/you're busy.

Milo: Already awake!! Just reading and googling the meaning behind my fear of owls. So awake. Not busy. And still with strigiformophobia!! That's the word for it. Haha.

Allie: Ha. That made me smile. (Because you're googling words. Not the phobia itself.)

Milo: Good. Wish I could see it. I love your smile.

Allie: ❤

Allie: Milo, would you talk to me? Thought I could type this out in my diary, send my thoughts out to the ether, but I think I need to talk to someone. To you.

Milo: Of course. I can call? You can keep us (me and this batshit book I'm reading) company. It's aliens and bears and also . . . crop circles and this intense love story. I went in hard at the sci-fi section at this weird book shop in Queens. Worried I purchased a curse 😊

Allie: I'd love that. But warning, I'm a bit weepy tonight.

Milo: Good. Be weepy with me! And warning, I'm in bed and wearing the most terrible pink shorts. Love pink. Always buy it. Always look like a dick in it!!

Allie: You'd like our B&B. Everything is bloody pink.

Milo: You inviting me over?

Allie: Maybe.

Milo: I'm going to need a yes or no answer to that question, Allie. You do realise we meet in just two days!

Allie: Am more aware of that than you think.

Milo: Calling now 😊

*

10:12 A.M.

Milo via Allie's phone: Good morning, Allie ♥ I hope you slept well. I didn't want to hang up, but you were asleep. You looked super peaceful. And beautiful. Can I say that???

Milo: Too late. Said it. Would say it again.

*

11:01 A.M.

Allie's diary (via CloudLink Drive // The Lake Dock *new*)

I was up till 3 a.m. talking to Milo again. (Five his time.)

We talked.

I cried.

He read to me.

And then . . . something happened. Something I can't even think about without my face burning and feeling as though my whole body is sinking into hot bath water.

He was reading to me. (The most obscure book I have ever come across.) Then he started saying he wished he was with me, reading this beside me, that he wished my head was against his chest, that his hands were beneath the blanket . . .

Gosh.

His voice. It was low and rumbling. I could almost feel his breath tickling my neck; like he traced every inch of me with words or something.

It was unexpected. And . . . sounds dramatic but, probably one of the most beautiful thing I've ever experienced.

I like him.

I really, really do like him. And this is *something*, isn't it? This is what people talk about when they meet someone, and it's like there's suddenly a tear through normality.

I just never expected it. And I can't even tell you what I expect next, with Milo.

Milo Ford with his ruffled hair and grey T-shirt and sideways smile and the hand he always places on his heart when he listens.

And I keep thinking about something he asked me. Softly, as I was falling asleep. Something nobody has ever asked me. 'What is love to you?'

I didn't think I knew the answer. But then I said, 'Action.' Not words, but showing it.

I asked Milo the same thing. He said, 'To me, it's a whisper. Like . . . It's an "I love you" in a silent moment, with nobody else to hear it.'

I started to drift off to sleep after that as desperate as I was to stay awake, in the moment. I keep remembering things he said, like strange, muddled memories. But as I slipped into sleep, all I remember is him saying, 'I hope I get to hold you, Allie Lake.'

Day 20 of 21

11:23 A.M.

Milo via Allie's phone: Hey!! It's Wrap Day here!

Milo: And Allie day tomorrow!!

Allie via Milo's phone: I feel really quite nervous. Which is so stupid, isn't it?

Milo: I think it's fuckin' cute that you're nervous.

Allie: I'm sticking with stupid.

Milo: I haven't even read any more of my book because it feels wrong that you won't get to know what happens next, even though, let's be real, there's not a motherfucker on earth that understands this book. 😄 Even the Goodreads geniuses are out of ideas!!

Allie: Maybe you can read some more to me in London. And we can NOT understand it together.

Milo: I'd love that!! 🖤 I wanted to arrange staying near to you for one night before I need to fly home. But I didn't want you to feel pressured to see me.

Allie: Tomorrow night?

Milo: Every night.

Milo: Haha, man, that sounded dumb.

Allie: No, I'd really love to. I'd love if you stayed and we could see each other properly. No phones or video calls. To mark the end of this.

Milo: Except . . . it doesn't have to end.

Milo: Does it?

*

11:22 P.M.

Milo via Allie's phone: You're probably asleep, and don't be mad, but I told my friend Julia about you. She's invested in us meeting tmw!! Can't stop thinking about you!!

Milo: I'm at home! Came back to text you.

Milo: I keep saying your name. Even aloud to myself. Think it's my favorite sound. ❤❤❤

Milo: I lied . . .

Milo: Your voice is my favorite sound

Milo: The way you say 'Milo.'

Milo: Also the way you say 'interesting' and 'completely' for some reason??? Hahaha.

Milo: Anyways. Goodnight allie lake ♥

Milo: Counting down the minutes to you . . .

Day 21 of 21

5:02 A.M.

Allie via Milo's phone: Today is the day! ☺

Allie: I know it's early, but I wanted to be the first to text . . .

Allie: I wish I could say I was more relaxed, but my stomach is in knots. My insides are a big giant twisted pretzel, or something.

Allie: But I'm excited to see you, Milo.

Allie: Counting down the seconds to you . . .

*

11:00 A.M.

Allie's diary (via CloudLink Drive // The Lake Dock *new*)

He won't pick up my phone. He always picks up and he is not picking up. I hope he's OK. Maybe it's a mountain thing and he's driving through that town with no electricity? Trying not to panic but something feels a bit weird.

*

1:43 P.M.

Allie's diary (via CloudLink Drive // The Lake Dock *new*)

His flight's about to leave. But he hasn't messaged me or called me and I'm starting to feel uneasy. Something isn't right. I just know something is wrong.

I'm supposed to be leaving for the hotel near the airport soon. I just hope he's there when I get there.

But what if he doesn't show up?

I told my sister and she looked at me, shrugged and said, 'Well, maybe you've been scammed.'

Gosh, knowing Milo, this feels like a crazy thing to suddenly think, but why isn't he answering?

*

3:47 P.M.

Allie's diary (via CloudLink Drive // The Lake Dock *new*)

It's been hours. Where is he? Why was he ignoring me? I don't understand. I'm so confused and my heart feels like it's going to combust from the disappointment.

But there must be an explanation. We were both so excited for today. Everything was fine. Completely fine.

I just called him and got my own voicemail. All I could think to say was: 'Milo? Milo? Where are you?' And I'm scared I'll never know.

Declaration: Every single word you have been reading is a transcript that was published by Verified Insider, but originally leaked on the 'anongoss' forums by user29382901. Allie Lake's diaries were originally published via a public CloudLink drive called 'The Lake Dock *new*'. These have since been taken down.

Thank you for visiting The Everything Milo Ford Fan Page. We forever ship Mallie!!!!

HOLD THE LINE! Phone Leak Reveals Milo Ford's Romance With Ordinary Everywoman, Allie Lake, and Fans are Going Wild!

Actor and *Brothers* star Milo Ford has spent the summer falling head over heels for ordinary 31-year-old scientist Allie Lake – a love story that has had fans firmly glued to their screens.

Ford and Lake met when the pair accidentally swapped phones on a flight from New York City to the UK three weeks ago, with Lake going home to Stought, Gloucestershire, where she lives with her sister, and Ford on to Romania to film *Sharp Hearts*, a secret project directed by Oscar-winning Tilly M. Tandy.

While it was planned that they'd meet in person to switch the devices back when Ford eventually flew back to his New York home, their romantic plans were thwarted when multiple of texts and personal correspondence appeared on an anonymous forum, appearing to belong to Milo and the unassuming scientist. It's unclear whether they met to execute the switch, but the leaked messages have now been read by thousands.

The messages begin with the pair swapping and relaying important notifications, but slowly blossom into more personal, deeper exchanges, with Ford declaring, 'I saw how golden the sunset was again tonight and you were the only person I wanted to show it to' – one of many quotes that have quickly become affectionately shared internet memes. Verified Insider were the first to publicly report on the story.

While Lake has been tight-lipped about the romance, Ford has been taking it all in his stride. Just last week, Milo appeared as a guest on *The Really Late Show*, and strode onto the stage wearing a T-shirt with his own meme on: his face photoshopped on a water-sodden Colin Firth's, a still taken from the famous 'lake scene' from the 1995 adaptation of *Pride and Prejudice*, with a text to Lake underneath it in faux-subtitles.

'Yeah, well,' he laughed, entering the studio. 'You've gotta laugh at it, I say.'

Ford then talked openly and emotionally about his long-frowned-upon exit from *Day Falls* and his split from Sara Santi, as host Joey Benedict asked if he was doing OK. Ford admitted he was happy and healthy, and he addressed his fans to let them know how much he loved them, which garnered an eruption of applause.

'I think we're all a little obsessed with Milo Ford being a romantic, you know?' said Joey to audience laughter. 'So, is that it then? You're open to normies? Are the normies across the land allowed to rejoice?'

Ford laughed. 'Yeah, why not?' he said. 'It's open season over here.'

'So, you're single?' pressed Joey, to which Milo replied, 'You asking me out, Joe?'

Lake, however, has so far been less good-natured about the leak, opting for a single post on her website, that simply said, 'A reminder that I am a human being and not fiction to be feasted upon. While I truly appreciate the messages of support, I ask that you direct this energy into something important and real.' Lake then shared links to conservation organisations and charities. She went on to say, 'I'd like to be known for the research I and other scientists conduct through these amazing organisations. Not an apparent publicity stunt I was not privy to, nor a stranger I will neither see nor speak to again. Thank you.'

While it looks like it's the end of the road for Ford and Lake, fans have expressed both relief and disappointment on the viral Verified Insider post. 'Omg yesss, does this mean we now have a chance with milo ford? someone find me his next flight details,' commented one, to over 1000 likes, while another added, 'Oh, this sucks, they seemed to really like each other! So, did they ever meet? What even happened? I'm dying to know!'

Part Two

Two Years Later

Chapter One

Allie

I meant it when I said it two years ago.

It was basically a vow. Both a logical and relief-inducing promise to myself, the world, and time and space. *I will never see or speak to Milo Ford again.* Because a) Milo was the very last person I ever wanted to see or speak to again, and b) Milo was the last person I was *likely* (from an odds perspective) to see or speak to again. After all, why would I, a British scientist now working at a small, extremely remote Arctic research station in Norway, ever be in a position to see or speak with a privileged, American Hollywood actor? We live thousands of miles apart, both in location and lifestyle. Worlds apart, as the saying goes.

And yet, I'm here.

Somehow, *I'm here.*

Crouching in a musky research station dorm that has been my home for almost two years next to my best friend's bed, internally freaking out. Because it's been 732 days since I have spoken to Milo Ford, and that counter – and I can't *believe* I'm about to say this – might be about to be reset to zero.

'*Iris?*'

Iris doesn't so much as stir.

It's 8:30 p.m. in the depths of the relentless polar summer, the sun a constant never-setting spotlight here, and just an hour ago, Iris took herself off for an early night.

Back when everything was normal.

Back when we had just eaten dinner in the station canteen and our only worry was whether we had packed enough energy bars for our expedition tomorrow.

Iris is already asleep of course, and deeply. Classic Iris. Tired, so sleeps. Fancies learning how to act, so joins an am-dram club in the UK, makes friends, enjoys it, says no more.

'Iris,' I say again, closer to her face this time, leaning onto her bed in the gloom. '*Iris—*'

That does it. She sits up like a Halloween vampire in a coffin. 'Allie, what the – what the *hell*?!' Her hand flies to her chest as if to stop her heart catapulting out into the tiny bedroom.

'Sorry, sorry, sorry, *shh shh*!'

I'm kneeling next to her bed like I'm praying or something (and at this point, it couldn't hurt).

She's in fleece pyjamas covered in miniature Christmas snowmen even though it's May; her oil-black hair in a bun on the top of her head, a pink sleep mask now resting on her forehead, two cartoon eyeballs printed on each soft pad.

'Something's happened,' I say to her. 'Or about to happen and I . . . I don't know what to do and – I don't know if I've just got the wrong end of the stick or . . . But . . . I don't think I have. I mean, I *hope* I have—'

'Allie, what's going on?'

'I can't believe I'm about to say this.'

'Oh my God. What?' She grabs for her glasses on the bedside table.

'And the thing is, I might be wrong, or it might just be that they have the same *name* or something, or—'

'Allie, what are you talking about?'

'Milo,' I blurt. 'I think . . .' I can hardly get my words out. I can barely face saying them. 'I think Milo is coming here.'

Iris stares at me, as if waiting for a punchline. '. . . Milo?'

'I . . . I saw his name. On a sheet on Oliver's desk. You know . . . The visitors who are coming to stay? The people coming to do the YouTube documentary thing.'

A totally pointless explanation because of course Iris knows of the documentary. All of us at the station do. Oliver, our principal investigator keeps talking about it, but news here, at the very remote Brimcote station, near Svalbard, Norway, travels fast, regardless. Our station and the surrounding settlement has a permanent population so small, we could all fit into one double-decker bus, but, in summer, visitors can triple that, and we're always interested in who, what and why.

Scientists make up a lot of the numbers, or station workers arriving at the base to work in the kitchens or in medical, but occasionally, like today, people arrive to film. This is something that always causes rumbles of either irritation or excitement among the team, especially when, like now, details are embargoed until they land. I am mostly part of the irritation group, and I've been quite relieved to know that when the 'influencers' land to film their documentary for a climate campaign, Iris and I will be a boat ride away researching on the field in Cote Rock, gathering data, looking in on some of my colonies. They're mostly always pleasant, filmmakers and YouTube do-gooders, but last year, one group filmed some scenes of a space movie here, and not only was it like an Apple store had exploded, some of us found the director meditating cross-legged in the computer room wearing furs during the tiny window of internet time we get here.

Iris wiggles on her glasses. 'The visitors,' she repeats, half asleep. She checks the time, almost as if she's doing a sanity check. Is Allie sleepwalking or suddenly very feverish and in need of the emergency chopper? (I wish it was either.) 'I – I thought they were coming tomorrow?'

'The flight changed.' I jabber. 'But there were waivers on Oliver's desk, Iris, and it said his name. Milo Ford. Milo is coming here.' I face-plant her duvet. *Milo is coming here* ricochets around my brain, like a tennis ball.

'Allie, are you—'

'Serious? Yes!' I peel my face away and glance up at her. Stray hair falls over my face like cobwebs. 'I saw it. Milo Ford. Emergency contact and waiver.'

'But – I mean, it's not *that* unusual of a name—'

'I saw the other one and it said J Merritt. Jameson? Jameson, his best friend, Jameson. The influencer. The Watch Me Try The Worst-Rated Restaurants in the US guy—'

'Oh. *Oh.*' That seems to have convinced her. Her eyes widen like shining coins in the dark. And there's something unnerving about it. Iris is always a steady ship. 'See it as it is, not worse than it is,' is one of her sayings. But even she looks haunted. '*Jesus,* Allie.'

'I know.'

'This is . . . And they're actually coming here? *Now*?'

'Yes.' I swallow. 'It says J Merritt. It says Milo Ford. Milo who leaked the screenshots of our entire relationship and laughed about it on TV.'

As if she needs reminding. Iris lived every awful moment with me, back then, after the phone leak. She was there. It was Iris who called me the day Milo and I were meant to swap phones back and asked me if I'd checked social media. It was Iris who drove at full speed to meet me at the airport after Milo had finally got in contact, and we'd agreed to still meet, both of us – or so I thought – wobbling on the line. It was Iris who force-fed me sweet tea to stop me shaking. It was Iris who spotted two paps at arrivals, so met Milo's location assistant, Sierra, outside a tiny WHSmith to swap the phones so I didn't get caught on camera. It was Iris who tried to convinced me, too, after, that nothing fishy was going on; that Milo hadn't, somehow, for some reason I did not understand then, expected this leak. And it was Iris who'd been wrong.

'Bloody hell, Allie.' Iris stands up on the bed now, reaching her hands high, as if summoning some sort of Arctic god from the skies to help us. She accidentally thumps them against the ceiling. If she's hurt, she isn't showing it. Instead, she brings her hands into a ball at her chest and stares down at me, now standing.

The room is quiet and hot and smells of warm wood, in the same way a sauna does, and sunlight tries to push its way through the gap around the square window's shutter. The walls warp in my vision, like a fish-eye lens.

'Jesus, you must feel . . . Bloody hell . . .' Iris's words evaporate.

'I know. It's . . . I have that odd feeling. Like I'm not really here.'

'And they're definitely coming today? Why?'

'I don't know. I mean, well, clearly to film a documentary.'

'Yeah,' Iris nods. 'Yeah. *Yikes*.'

'And logically, it has to be a coincidence. Right?' I say. 'Or a ploy for – who knows what reason? Gosh, I don't even know what I'm talking about.'

Iris swallows, eyes darting, like she's reading invisible lines in the air. 'How're you doing? You look pretty mad, to be fair.'

'Absurd,' is all I say. 'This whole thing . . . And like, I feel like Polly should've known, or something. She's our supervisor. You know? Saw his name and warned me. Got me an emergency bloody helicopter. Hidden me in a bunker.'

Iris tips her head to one side, half sympathy, half oh-come-off-it-Allie. 'Polly may be our supervisor, but Oliver did all the admin for the documentary.'

'But surely he'd have *mentioned* his name to her, she's been talking about it—'

'This is Polly. She would never remember a name you probably mentioned once. She still owns floppy discs. Her favourite celebrity is *Jason Donavan*. As for Oliver, he doesn't exactly follow celebrity gossip. Unless it's whales at the center, of course—'

'But . . .'

Iris stares at me. *You're being unreasonable, amigo,* is right there, in the silent raise of the eyebrows she gives me.

I know what she's thinking. That it may have been huge to me, the leaking of our messages. But like most viral moments, the world and everyone else forgot it – or should I say, forgot *me* – quicker than it even happened. As for Polly, the only world worth knowing, to her, is this. Out here, in the Arctic, where she knows more puffins than celebrities. Polly knew why I took the job here, for her project – I *needed* it, to escape what felt to me like the glaring of the world's spotlight. But Iris is right. She never cared why I came here, just that I did.

'I'm sorry,' I say.

'Don't be.'

'Just . . . The whole thing's ridiculous. Totally ridiculous.'

And it is.

Milo Ford is coming here.

To my place of work. To the *Arctic*. Thousands of miles from home. In remote no-man's-land – somewhere so far away, they say it's the closest thing to space, to life on an uninhabited planet. That's why this place was perfect. Terrifying, but perfect. Another planet is exactly where, after Milo, I wanted to be.

'I mean, I won't have to see him,' I say, little fingers grasping at flimsy straws in my mind. 'We're going to Cote Rock tomorrow. For four whole days. Just you, me and Lars.' Lars is one of our boat captains here. I'm almost tempted to go and find him – convince him to break rules, take us now, before they land. He'll be in the research station's canteen. Beer, peanuts, pack of playing cards, like an uncle on Christmas Eve.

'Uh-huh. Deffo.' Iris nods. 'Although, you probably *will* have to acknowledge him.'

'Well, what's that? A second?' I try to take my first deep breath of the last fifteen minutes. 'I can do that. A nod, or similar. Right? I can nod at someone, right? For the sake of my supervisor? For science? A nod is nothing.'

'Million per cent,' Iris says, sinking back down to her knees. A warm hand slips over my shoulder. 'Are you OK?'

'No.' My voice cracks, vocal cords bending like a guitar string. 'I don't want to see him.'

And why would anyone in this situation want to? I trusted him. Not only with my phone, but with who I was. For the first time, I pressed a finger to the jabbering mouths of all those scared voices inside of me, cracked open the door to my life and let someone see inside. Ripe peach, placed in palm. And then he squashed it to coulis. Blew the door off the hinges. Invited the whole world in to have a long, good look at the result. I almost sadly and passively let them, too. Because, at first, I really thought we'd been victims of some sort of hacking. The final phone call we had the night of the leak, him in a London hotel, me, spooked by paps and in June House's kitchen, Sian silently making tea, the air thick with that palpable charge of your world having changed suddenly.

'I'm sorry this shit happened,' he'd said down the line. Warmly. Familiarly, like all those phone calls before. 'We'll talk tomorrow. My publicist Sue is working on it.

She's a genius. OK?' He even said, 'I hope I can see you, Allie. I can't believe how close we got to it today.'

Then – that was it.

The publicist called, and her genius plan was . . . for me to come to the hotel and be seen with Milo. 'Play it,' she said with you've-got-the-job! enthusiasm. 'We can go all serious on this or we can play it. Things like this have worked very well in the past. It could be lucrative for you both.'

That's when it landed. That's when I blocked him. He'd done this on purpose and leaked our messages. He'd used the phone swap – used *me* – for publicity. 'Outed' himself. Elevated his profile. Garnered sympathy and adoration. Took back control.

I couldn't believe it.

'I hate that I'm now dreading even leaving this room,' I groan, moving to sit next to Iris on the bed. 'I was so excited for the expedition, to look in on my colonies. Hang out with Lars, you. Now I just feel completely rotten.'

'Erm, excuse me, mate,' says Iris. She pushes her face against mine. Her cheek is cool, and she smells like the lavender facial oil she pats on every night. 'This is where you work. This is *your* place. We bloody love going to Cote Rock and this is your research. Your birds. And it's important. Really important.'

'I know . . .'

'So don't let anyone dump on that. Whether influencer or knobby celebrity or first love—'

'He was not my first love.'

No. First love would be silly.

And, in hindsight, the *whole thing* was silly, thinking I might be feeling real things for Milo Ford over texts and video calls. It wasn't real. I was simply grieving and vulnerable. Certain birds for example, who lose an egg, will find a rock, or pebble, or similar, and they care for it, like an egg, to cope. That's what Milo was. Milo Ford was a pebble. A fake egg of a man.

'Well, potato-potahto,' Iris pffts. 'This is your territory. They're just . . . I don't know. Luvvies without a clue in the world? Remember that—'

Someone taps on the other side of the door.

I sigh, meet Iris's kind, brown eyes in the gloom.

'You're good, amigo. I promise.'

Then she gets up and pulls open the door.

Polly Sitaker, our supervisor, stands there, pink-faced, exhausted and perpetually contented.

'I've been looking for Allie – ah!' She puffs. 'Our visitors are about to land and I wondered if you'd do me the enormous favour of welcoming them with me?'

Then

The last six months for fast-rising star Milo Ford may
have been a litany of awards ceremonies, glossy cover
features and once-upon-a-dream acting roles, but he still
suggests, in a text that ends in two exclamation points,
that we meet here: a slit-in-the-wall dive in Brooklyn
that boasts pizza and karaoke. A building I walked past
twice because the neon sign flashed with only a third of
the letters and a dead pigeon splayed on the ground by
the entrance like a horror movie doormat.

'I love these places,' says Milo when he arrives. Late
by an hour. Tossing out a well-rehearsed apology. Eyes
tired, but utterly beguiling. 'I don't feel lonely in a place
like this. You get everything here. Old dudes who've lived
here too long and seen too much. Bus drivers on lunch.
Starving musicians. Occasional lost tourist. Real life. You
know? Helps me connect to my own.'

And I spot my moment.

'And how is it,' I ask, 'your real life?'

Ford's heavy-lidded brown eyes look up from the
menu in his hand at that. He quirks a smile, and so do I.

93

We, of course, *know* what I'm getting at. I mean, sure, I want to know how he really is. Is he well? Is he still benzo free? Do *Day Falls* fans still want his head on a spike? But, mostly, I want to talk about his viral text-romance with Allie Lake, a biologist he met on a flight. A text romance leaked online that not only had people (yup, me included) holing themselves up in work bathrooms to binge it, like a juicy boxset, but that established him as something of a Hollywood lothario overnight.

'I thought this would come up,' he says, easily, and I cut straight to it – *Have you been hanging out? Did you ever meet Allie Lake?*

'No,' he says. 'No, Allie and I didn't actually ever meet in real life.'

The romantic in me's heart drops to my ass. The realist in me scoffs, wants to paint 'love is a lie' on a brick wall somewhere. 'And will you meet?'

'Ah.' Milo laughs – it's an exasperated laugh. Guarded. An if-only-you-knew laugh. 'I don't know, man. No. No, I can't think of why we would now. And is it sad? Yeah, maybe, but it was a moment in time. You know? But no. To answer your question, Allie and I never met. And am I happy about that? Yeah. Now, I think I am.'

Chapter Two

Milo

This cannot be happening.

There is no way.

And yet – it's her, all right.

It's really her.

Allie.

And I mean it for real this time. This is not like all those times I *thought* I saw her – the back of another woman's head in probably every single airport I've been in since we met; hearing her voice in the line at Bunty's; or when I've picked up an unknown number, trying to sell me Wi-Fi or eco toilet paper, and for a split second, the woman on the other end has sounded like her . . .

No. No, this is *for real* this time. No mistaking and no mirage.

Allie Lake stands in front of me. The woman who betrayed me; who sold me out.

In the middle of the Arctic. Just a measly few hours from the North Pole. Seriously? She's supposed to work at a university in Sheffield. A new one, as of the last two years. She's not supposed to be here. I checked. More than once. Totally chalked it up to paranoia.

Except . . . she is here, *not* in Sheffield, and she's looking at me like I'm a pumpkin crammed with TNT and she's just waiting – hoping – for the thing to explode.

'Hey!' Jameson is beaming next to me. The man's all, 'Oh, the flight? It was awesome!' and 'So humbled! So super humbled to be here!' and me – as good as a wax figure.

What am I supposed to even do? This isn't just awkward, this is – agonising. Unbearable. This is beyond anything I could ever craft into words. *Vexatious*. There. Learned that one yesterday.

We've just endured hours of travel. New York to London, London to Oslo, Oslo to Longyearbyen and *then* a chopper to this station. I haven't slept. I'm wrecked. All I've been thinking about for hours is hot food and lying down in something bed-shaped so I can read until my thoughts dissolve and I can get some kind of rest. But now – now I just want to get the hell out of here. Every fibre of my soul wants to turn and run.

How is this even happening? Jameson said this was a documentary for polar climate research. *Why* is Allie here? She does birds. In Bermuda. In *Sheffield*.

Oh, shit, we're moving down the line. Handshakes and witticisms, out on the snow, just a hundred yards from the helicopter that brought us in. Allie stands just a metre from me now and I'm opposite a woman called Polly, who wears a giant smile, and all while a choir in my head chants, 'What the hell? What the hell?' on repeat.

God, it's weird here. Even without the woman who betrayed me. We're in front of a large grey, angular building that sort of resembles an aircraft hangar mated with a visitor centre at a nature reserve or something – the sorts of places you'd gather in, as kids, on a rainy school field trip to look at insects in petri dishes – but all that surrounds us is ice and snow, and jagged glaciers so breathtaking, my brain is trying to file it under 'stage play backdrop.' It's unreal. Totally freezing cold. Like the moon or something. Wilderness overpowering man. Yet I can't even fully digest it. Because of her. Allie.

'Polly!' Polly's grinning, introducing herself. She's a round sunbeam of a woman and I'm nodding like an ass, laughing at absolutely nothing, shaking Polly's excitable hand. I'm so close to Allie now. So close. This all feels so impossible. Not even twenty-four hours ago, I was waking up in my bed in New York, suitcase hastily and messily packed, texting my coffee order to Jameson, who was on his way in a cab to pick me up for the airport. Now I'm here. Snow. Cobalt, crystal ocean. Allie Lake.

Fuck. How do I even play this? I mean, this is a huge place, right, so maybe I don't have to play anything. Maybe she'll greet us, but I won't even see her after. It's like a whole village in itself. Little Scandi lodges scattered across the land, cinnamon-brown slats, like those miniature railway villages you get in Macy's windows at Christmas. She'll be busy, have places to be. Also, is it delusional to think she may not even recognise me? Or if she's even noticed? She hasn't looked at me yet. Not even for a millisecond.

Filled with shame probably.

Good. As she should be.

We move down the line.

Polly introduces me to Iris – whoa, *Iris*. Allie's *best friend* Iris.

I keep trying to get Jameson's eye, try to convey, 'Man, what the hell?' without words, but he's completely oblivious. Of course he is. He's wanted to make a documentary like this his whole life.

Ah, shit, now it's us.

Finally, inevitably, us.

Just me and Allie, face to face.

I never thought I'd ever be here, with her. Even with the googling paranoia, knowing something like this was her world, knowing I only care about this stuff because she woke me up to it, had me wanting to sign every dime I ever earned over to it. But she said she'd never do something this remote; that it wasn't for her.

But who knows what was ever real? The phone swap – 'The Leak'. The ill-famed leak showed me I shouldn't take any of it as gospel. I've been so careful since. Vetting every decision I make, every person I let into my life like I'm a damn FBI agent.

Yet somehow, here we are. Two years later.

Two jackasses in the Arctic in neon coats I only bought because a stylist on a shoot said anyone worth anything is wearing them at ski resorts and I thought 'Well, if that's what *real* people are doing, then I'd better too.' And so continues my endless search for true love and acceptance in anything except myself . . .

In this case, a coat.

And I'm . . . discombobulated, looking at her. Those serious eyes that always look like they're holding back oceans or something. The pursed, pink mouth, the pixie point of the ear her hair is pushed behind.

But mostly, I'm mad.

After two years, I'm still mad.

'Hi,' she says. Short. Snipped. We're now opposite each other, and her eyes dart up to meet mine, and slide quickly away. I thought it might be shame, but she actually looks furious – I'd even say *apoplectic* – that she's being forced to confront me.

Irritatingly, despite myself, somewhere, deep inside me, a dumb animal part of me reacts. A warm zip through my body at the invisible friction of her huge, blue eyes on mine. I can't believe it's really her.

'Hey,' I say. 'I'm uh, Milo. Nice to meet you.' Dumb, but it's clear we're playing the 'pretend we don't know each other' game and I think that might be for the best for now. Although I've never been that good at improv.

There's a lot of nodding, a lot of surface-deep, mind-numbing questions about flights and how cold it is. Jameson really, amazingly, does seem totally dumb to it all, but he's not of this earth right now. He's in full excited Jameson mode, my two-year-old romance leak far from his mind. Iris, though . . . She *definitely* knows. She keeps staring at me. Not with curiosity – no. Like someone who is *pissed*.

Fortunately, then, Polly leads us towards the research station. It sits on the snow like a space shuttle.

Allie trudges next to me. It's just us.

Should I say something? I don't know. And what do you even say to a woman you haven't spoken to for two years because she betrayed you and leaked your personal text conversations across the world for money and a fresh start? Are we really pretending we don't know each other? Should I . . .

'Allie—'

'No,' Allie responds, quiet but harsh.

'N-no?'

She folds her arms, eyes unblinking. 'Whatever this is,' she whispers out the side of her mouth. 'I'm not interested. Weird entertainment, an apology—'

'An *apology?*' I whisper back. 'For what?'

She scoffs. 'I'm not talking to you anymore.'

'I didn't do anything, Allie.'

'Yes, you did.'

'I didn't. You did.'

'I did not—'

'Come on stragglers!' calls Polly. Allie thunders ahead. Is she for real? The *audacity* of her. She leaks the phones and thinks *I'm here to apologise?* God, I wish I hadn't said a single word. How the hell am I going to deal with four days of this?

The station is warm, air that smells of mealtimes and bleach. It's interesting. Kind of like a spaceship and a hostel, rolled into one. Is this where Allie lives now, then? Does she have her own place here? One of those little wooden huts outside? Do I care? I don't know. No. Maybe?

I've wondered a lot about her over the last two years, sometimes think about our calls from her bedroom. Always low-lit, like rooms at nighttime in the fall. Slanted wooden beams of her mom's old farmhouse; plants and novelty picture frames. The tiny village she'd show me glimpses of through the window. Now I know nothing about her life. Well. Except she's as blunt as ever. That 'no' was so entitled.

But did I ever know anything real about her? Really?

'I'll get you some food, then show you to your rooms,' says Polly. 'How's that sound? And then I'd like to sit down and run through a slight change of plan for tomorrow, if I may be so bold? God help us all, but I've been thinking. Hard.' She gives a big grin.

'Absolutely,' replies Jameson, practically pulsating with excitement, like a full water balloon. He's been waiting for this. Counting down to it, kneading my shoulders, like you would an athlete, like we're preparing for a race, saying, 'This is going to be awesome, man, trust me.' Preparing for a fight would've been more accurate.

To think we'd planned this, looked forward to it. An evening of musing on New Year's resolutions, Jameson pacing his house in pyjama pants, saying, 'We need to start doing the things we talk about, Mildred. You're happier, healthier. You've had your healing. This is the year me and you *do* something,' turning into this . . .

Then Polly turns to Allie, who's straggling behind, blue eyes wide, wide circles, her face now totally inscrutable.

'Allie, could I bend your ear?' Polly asks.

'Mm?'

'I've had an idea. About your expedition tomorrow?'

And I watch, in real time, the colour drain from her face, in a way that is intangibly familiar to me. The way you know, when you really know someone, that something has 'happened' and you're just yet to be brought up to speed. And I hate that, for a split second, the dumb animal wants to stride in and ask if she's OK.

But then they're walking away, Polly directing us to a weird hospital-like cafeteria, and a man greeting us with a handshake so hard, I can feel his fingers long after he's released me. But all I can think about is Allie Lake. And the fact she's here, and I'm here.

Four days.

I can't do four days here. I almost laugh at the notion.

Jameson grins obliviously at me. 'This is so sick,' he says.

'We need to leave.'

'Huh?'

I lean in and whisper, 'We need to leave, Jameson. Now.'

Then

'Working with the Wild' live podcast recording transcript excerpt

Dr Marie Power: We're now moving to the Q&A part of this live podcast episode, coming to you live from the Women in Conservation and Nature Conference in Bristol, and I know a lot of hands are itching to be raised, so does anyone have any questions for Allie Lake or Dr Stewart? Uhhh, can we get a microphone to . . . Oh, yes, Cliff, our lovely sound engineer is on his way [audience laughter] We love Cliff! OK. You, please, with the pink dress . . .

Audience member: Hi. Hugely enjoying this conversation. And I hope you don't mind that we broach this, um, but I know a lot of us women are wondering. Allie. How are you?

Allie Lake: [silence] I'm fine. Thank you.

Audience member: I saw the message on your website. About Milo Ford. We probably all did. I firstly wanted to thank you for speaking out and redirecting the attention

103

to the work so many of us do. I just think it's so common-place for women to be scrutinised and whittled down to their appearance, their dating history, their flaws. Even women like you. Women who are changing the world.

Allie Lake: It . . . I . . .

Dr Marie Power: I agree. I'm sure all the women here understand being under scrutiny. Like, how was it for you? How did it *feel*? If you didn't mind speaking to this . . .

Allie Lake: [pause] Um. Well. It was . . . obviously very difficult. T . . . Traumatic. Which probably sounds overdramatic or overblown, but . . . it was. I'm a private person. Those were my messages. My personal diaries.

Dr Maria Power: Talk me through finding out that everything was *out there.*

Allie Lake: Oh. Er . . . Yes. Gosh, it felt . . . like the most horrible dream or something. A nightmare. Just. Yeah, I try not to think about it. It's still obviously quite recent. Should we move to other questions? I can see there are lots and . . .

Dr Marie Power: Did you get any warning?

Allie Lake: That it was going to leak? No. We spoke the night before, everything was normal, we'd planned to meet the next day, to switch back our phones, then the day of the swap arrives . . . Sorry, this is really off topic, I'm conscious that we're—

Dr Maria Power: No. I think this'll help so many of us. A roomful of women supporting women.

Allie Lake: Right. Yes. Well. Milo suddenly wasn't picking up the phone, then my best friend called and asked me if I'd been on social media. I . . . don't really remember much after that. Other than almost being sick. Then *actually* being sick on the Heathrow Express.

Dr Maria Power: So you just open up your phone and there it all is?

Allie Lake: Correct.

Dr Maria Power: And you don't for certain know exactly how?

Allie Lake: [silence] Um. No. Well. No, I'm not really comfortable . . . talking about that.

Dr Maria Power: Of course. So, did he eventually get in touch?

Allie Lake: Yes. By that point it was out there. I was panicked. He seemed to be too.

Dr Maria Power: And then what happened?

Allie Lake: We agreed we'd meet. Carry on as planned. Swap the phones. Meet in real life. Finally.

Dr Maria Power: And did that happen?

Allie Lake: No. My friend ended up collecting my phone from an assistant and by the following day, I'd made the decision not to meet him. Which was difficult. I felt quite torn, wondered whether I'd made the right decision. But then he did the show.

Dr Maria Power: A TV show?

Allie Lake: Yes. Days later, he went on TV and laughed about it.

Chapter Three

Allie

'No. Sorry. Absolutely not.'

Polly stands gazing at me hopefully in the corridor next to the canteen, old mascara dotting the end of her sandy lashes, completely blind to the fact she's just asked me the worst thing I could possibly be asked in this moment of my life. Can Milo and Jameson come with us to Cote Rock tomorrow? A tiny, tiny, inescapable island?

'No?' She laughs. She's waiting for me to laugh, too, slap my thigh, say, 'Haha, just kidding, Polls! Had you there for a minute though, didn't I?'

Instead, I stutter, 'I j-just think it's a bad idea. The fieldwork on Cote Rock is really important and Iris and I have really planned everything we need to do when we're there—'

'Oh. Well. Of course I understand. That's why I suggested I come too. Shoulder the load.'

'It's a lot of physical work as well,' I carry on, desperately. 'Plus, the tents and the . . . the weather, and no showers. We've only planned the trip for three people. It's me, Iris, Lars . . .'

The fluorescent lights and shiny floors seem to stretch then contract like a beating heart as I stand here. This cannot happen. I cannot let this happen. Milo and Jameson can*not* come with us on our expedition. It's bad enough they're here, at the station, but to follow us to what is essentially a rock you can walk the breadth of in six hours . . . No. *No*. Absolutely not. Plus, you need to be prepared. Prepared to be exhausted, to be vulnerable, and I don't want two – *strangers* with a camera witnessing us being exhausted and vulnerable, just for them to cut and edit us so even more witnesses can watch us as entertainment and not humans, all while shovelling popcorn into their judgemental mouths. I've been there, thank you. I don't ever wish to be there again.

'The thing is,' Polly says gently, holding her hands together at her chest, like a priest might. 'Everyone agrees it'll help. That it'll be the best use of the opportunity. For awareness. For donations. Oliver even said it himself and that man's ego means he never acknowledges the dwindling interest in our area of work.'

'Celebrity endorsement rarely helps long term, Polly.'

'I'm the last person to understand all of the internet stuff, Allie, you know that. But even I'm not sure I agree with you.' She says this in a gentle, careful way. Her whole demeanour has the feel of *I like you and I know your heart's in the right place, but I'm afraid to say you're talking a barrel of absolute shite.*

'Just think. It'll be a real fly-on-the-wall video about what we really do,' she carries on. 'Isn't that what we always talk about? Making this accessible to the public. That if only everyone knew how important and real our work is for humanity, the world would change. Look at Count Your Chicks. Yes, you don't have the users you'd like, but the people that do know about it help hugely.'

My heart sinks then. She looks so full of hope and how could I tell her no and tell her why? It would sound selfish. And I know she's right. Sweet, too-good-for-this-world Polly. I think of my regular users – SunshineGirl23, Magic_ Garrett, AcerSpark, logging on just to count for the good of the birds, for the good of all of us. This could reach so many. But how am I supposed to agree to this? Four days. With Milo Ford on a giant rock in the middle of the ocean?

'But what if I don't want to be filmed?'

'You won't be filmed. If you don't want to be. I said I'd happily be interviewed, and Iris doesn't mind either.' Of *course* she doesn't. 'The birds and bacteria are OK with it too!' She chuckles. I don't.

'Right.'

Polly steps forward, places her fingertips lightly on my forearm. 'I'm sorry if it feels like an intrusion.'

And it does, more than she knows. Because viral really was the word for what happened last time. Something that took hold, covering the world like a rash, until it faded away just as fast. A story people, bar a handful of fanatics, have forgotten . . .

I haven't.

I haven't forgotten.

Because it changed my life, meeting Milo. The leak. It changed it inside and out.

But this is work, isn't it? This whole thing is bigger than my silly relationship – if you can even call it that – with a celebrity I was forced to interact with for nineteen dizzying, confusing days. This is about something that really matters. This is not about me. Or Milo. It's about what matters most to me.

'The medicals?' I ask quietly.

'Of course. Both passed.'

'We'll need extra pen launchers and camping equipment and . . . It's a *lot* to suddenly organise, Polly. The Bay hates it when we just show up without warning, needing supplies. It's almost nine at night—'

'I'll organise it all.' Polly places her hand on the shoulder of my jacket. 'It'll be worth it, Allie. I really think we'll come back feeling like we've done something important.' She smiles. 'And all you have to do is your amazing job . . .'

As I shout after her that we leave at 8 a.m. sharp, no excuses, Iris emerges from around the corner of the corridor, like someone sliding from the wings of a stage.

'*Fuuuuck*,' she mouths, and it is the only word that could ever describe what's about to happen: four whole days in the wilderness with Milo Ford.

Fuck indeed.

Chapter Four

Milo

'I mean, this is fate,' Jameson grins. 'You do know that, don't you?'

He's wearing the same sleep attire he's been throwing on since we were teenagers – a Chelsea Football Club jersey and baggy shorts – and pacing this tiny oddball room we slept in like a tiger trapped in a cage. It's got a wooden bunk bed, an empty G-plan 1960s desk, and the smallest closet I've ever laid eyes on. It reminds me of a room on a sleeper train. Even a garden shed or something. It's kind of cool, though, and the view through that little porthole window – it's unbelievable. A whole ethereal universe. A sky so pastel blue, it looks like a fresco or something.

In here, though, it's another story. Not so much the room, but the situation. My own mind.

'Like, if you looked fate up in the dictionary, this would be it.' This has been Jameson's melody for the last nine hours. Playing it over and over like a one-hit wonder everyone grows to hate. *Fate. Destiny. More fate.* Because how else can you explain it? We make a New Year's resolution to finally do our project – our something-important-and-real our something-bigger-than-us movie – and after Gabby, Jameson's assistant, approaches charities and organisations proposing a twenty-minute impactful YouTube documentary, two reply, and he chooses this one because, 'Well, I chose it for penguins, then realised that's *Antarctica*, which is actually like, the opposite direction, haha.' And I agreed to do it.

I've never spent a single moment in any kind of real wilderness, but since entering recovery, I've found comfort and healing in putting myself into unfamiliar situations; ones that prompt me to really stop and think, gather my bearings. Animal shelters. Museums. Memorials. Anything that connects me to something bigger than me. But now, of course, I just feel like an asshole. A stupid Hollywood gimmick who'll rock up for a few days like a child on a field trip, then disappear back to my apartment with a concierge and its own sushi bar.

'Jameson, can we stop now,' I ask, 'with the fate?'

'But didn't you always hope this would happen?'

'No.'

'Don't believe you.'

'Dude, are you hearing yourself?' I unroll a T-shirt from my suitcase. What do you even wear out here besides the coat and all those thermal socks we bought? Why did I bring a vintage Prince tour T-shirt to an Arctic research station? And how emblematic. A prop representing the fact that we should not have come here. I had to Wikipedia search the Arctic before we came, for God's sakes.

'Like, this is Allie,' I carry on. '*Allie* Allie who sold me out. Who literally used me.'

'Yeah, I heard you, man.'

'I don't think you did. It's just, it's *Allie Lake*? On an island, in the middle of the Arctic circle and now we've got to go to an even smaller island with her with no escape, no *internet*. Like, what did they even mean by this is a radio silence area—'

'It stops interference—'

'—And all the while you, you're getting all poetic about fate—'

'Uh, you're usually the one who's poetic about fate,' Jameson says with a laugh.

I stare at him.

Jameson holds his palms up – two giant basketballer's hands – in surrender. His curly hair bounces, then settles. 'I know. I know,' he says. 'I get it, I do. It's really her. But . . . can we just take a sec? Like, how do you *feel*?' He stops, then shakes his head, bursts out laughing. 'Sorry, but this is – it's two years on, and here you both are. End of the world. Or beginning of it. Two summers later . . .' He's enjoying this. From the second I told him, he's been enjoying it, and now he's thrown his art hat on. He's in documentary-maker mode. This'll be gold dust to his creative mind. The jackassery in that, 'How do you *feel*?' If I didn't love him, I'd punch him in the face.

'She's supposed to work at a university,' I say, throwing another shirt back into my bag. Shirts. Why did I bring so many shirts? 'I checked before I came here. Blamed *paranoia*. Laughably.'

'Is that so?' asks Jameson. He's wearing that giant Pac-man grin on his face. So much of Jameson's optimistic, romantic personality is in that Pac-man grin – has been the whole time I've known him. Jameson was born in London, but his parents divorced when he was eleven, and his mom remarried a dude from New Jersey. They moved in three doors down from me and my parents, and while Jameson stayed in London with his Dad, he came over to the US to visit every summer. Jameson literally appeared in my front yard one afternoon when we were twelve, and said, full-Pac-man, 'Hiya! I'm Jameson, do you fancy hanging out?' He admitted years later that he'd actually heard my dad yelling at me over the fence and felt bad for me. A friendship born out of pity, I always say. He says, 'Fuck you, dude, I fell in love with you.'

'Well, that's what the internet says,' I reply. 'That Allie works at a university in the UK. Not the goddamn Arctic.'

'Oh. Dude. Surely you and me both know not to trust anything we read on the internet.'

Jameson chuckles for longer than I'd like him to. And I get it. I'd be the same if this was happening to him and I was just a bystander. It's funny, right? It's *fun*, knowing your best friend is stuck on a remote island with the woman he's never been able to haul his ass into getting over. The one he coached me through forgetting, trying to glue me back together again over Cokes and karaoke sessions. (Always 'Perfect Day' by Lou Reed or 'Breaking Free' from *High School Musical*. No in between.)

'Personally, I think this could be brilliant,' he says, adjusting something on his GoPro. 'Like, this is the stuff of life, my man. We've wanted to do something like this forever. Me making a real doc. You, doing something important. This is life and love and nature and everything *connected*—' He brings the camera to his face. 'How are you really feeling?'

I sit on the edge of my bed, drag my hands through my hair, scrunching my fists to relieve some of the pressure.

'Don't film me, man.'

He ignores me. 'There must be a part of you that feels intrigued, no? Seeing her again. You're about to have breakfast with the woman.'

'No.'

'No?'

I turn my face towards him. 'The woman traded me in, Jameson. Used me. For money for her project. Money I'd have given her.'

'So you *say*.'

'So the evidence says.'

'What evidence?' he scoffs.

'Uh, all the screenshots were from her end. We talked the night of the leaks and arranged to meet at my hotel, then she cut me off, didn't show. No explanation. I go to her house because I'm worried and—' I stop. Going back over this is pointless. 'You know all this. Don't act like you don't know this story just as well as I do.'

He mimics me in a whiny voice, then says, 'Yeah, but *you* had her phone, though.' Jameson has never bought, completely, that Allie was the one behind the leak. He always hoped we'd reconcile somehow. He's like that; thinks everything and everyone can be redeemed. *Love conquers all.*

'She had access to her cloud, J.'

'Oh, cloud, blah blah . . .

'Can we just stop? Look,' I say standing. 'I'm still in yesterday's clothes. We need to shower, we need to get ready for . . . whatever awaits us today. Which I'm hoping is somehow convincing a helicopter pilot to fly me out of here. Or a spaceman to rocket me out of earth's orbit. There're space people here too, right?'

Jameson drops the camera to his lap. The chair is like something from the nineties. White, rough plastic; waffle-holes in the backrest. It creaks beneath his long limbs. It's like we're at summer camp or something. 'Milo, you've got this.'

'I really don't wanna do this, though.'

Jameson lets out a hissing sound, like air escaping from a tyre. 'Well, you've got to. Even if you just do it for me.'

And he knows I will. Because Jameson is Jameson. This man has been there for me through everything. Slept beside me at the hospice when my mother died. Cleaned up my tiny, horrible rental, filled my fridge, cooked for me in the weeks following. I barely acknowledged him, sleeping every night on the couch. He's treated every rehab visit I've undertaken in my life with optimism. He wrestled the phone out of my hand when Sara's interview went live and she said that line – 'He left the movie, then left me.' 'Let the world think you're a prick!' he shouted, pulling the phone from my ear. 'You know you're not a prick; I know you're not a prick!' Jameson is always there, one ear to the fence.

'Come on.' He jumps up. 'Let's get started.'

'I'm going to be stuck with a woman I can't stand for four days. Come here to help fix something and there she is, my biggest mistake . . .'

Jameson smiles to himself. 'I mean, it's a great hook. It's a love story.'

'Love story,' I scoff. 'Nah. It was just phones.'

And at the exact moment Jameson leans and opens the door, there she is. Allie, in the corridor, walking past our room. She freezes. She's in a rose-pink dressing gown, wet hair waving across her face. She stares at me. In her hands, a neat pile of folded clothes, bottles of shower gel, shampoo, lined up on top. Her pale, smooth legs are bare from just below the knee.

Our eyes meet. And for a second, neither of us moves.

Jameson smiles at her, a warm neighbourly smile, and she stiffly returns one. Then she takes off, footsteps in flip-flops disappearing down the corridor.

Jameson shakes his head, an exasperated laugh puffing out of him.

'Just phones,' he says to himself. 'Nothing but phones.'

Then

Milo orders for us from the dive's biblically thick menu.
A meat feast pizza, a cherry soda for me, and a pint of
water for him, that he downs like he's just completed a
triathlon. An old episode of nineties sitcom *Just Shoot
Me* plays on a small, retro TV above the bar. It's muted,
but in it, Finch is getting married.

It's clunky, but I tell him I was kind of hoping for a
wedding. A happily-ever-after for him and Lake.

Milo laughs, good-naturedly, signals to the waiter for
more water. Ford is one of those people, I think, that
you'd describe to your friends as someone you can say
anything to.

'Yeah, no, that's . . . I'm afraid your hopes are going
to be dashed there, Laura-Lee. Sorry.' He gives a sideways, melancholic smile. 'I don't know. The leak struck
a match. I thought it would burn out. But . . . turns out
we were extremely flammable. And my heart still feels
a little sore.'

I'm ashamed to admit it, but I let slip an 'aww'. 'I just
mean it's a shame,' I clarify. 'Heartbreak sucks.'

'But is it? Is it really a shame? It's better to know before any more time is spent, right? But I was definitely all in. Very ready to meet with her, and so was she. Or so I thought. Woke up, and I'm blocked. On everything.'

'Out of nowhere?'

'Yup. As far as I knew, she was coming to my hotel. Ah.' He holds both palms up now, a napkin screwed into a golf ball in the palm. 'Anyway. Probably already said too much. I might be a jackass, but I'm not going to talk about her publicly. Shall we uh, [laughs] get back to talking about the new movie now?'

Chapter Five

Allie

Milo and Jameson enter the canteen like they're about to stride onto the stage at Wembley Arena. A boyband moonlighting as an Arctic rescue crew. What on earth are those *coats* for? If not to trigger a mass flurry of visual migraines.

Polly pogoes up from the table beside me. 'Sit, sit!' she beams. 'We have baked oatmeal, and we have coffee. Oh, and two different types of tea. Mint and . . . is that English breakfast? I can't think.'

Polly is so excited this morning, she's practically crimson with it. Sometimes, she reminds me of Mum – Mum *after* we moved away from Dad, that is, when every morning was like waking up on holiday – a decade-long, pent-up breath, released. It helped, being around her when I first began working here. Someone who reminded me of Mum, who checked in on me like Mum, and all in a place that gave me the quiet space to grieve, properly. Polly's hardy but warm. The type to keep trudging on with a smile on her face, never quibbling, because, yes, life can be tough, but it can always be tougher. I normally find her comforting to be around. Not today, though. Today, despite the crimson excitement, I just feel territorial. Icy. Because I hate how the canteen feels different suddenly, with Milo in it. No longer the sanctuary it slowly became for me. It feels unsafe. And this is what it's going to be like, isn't it? Four days with him stuck here.

Jameson grins out multiple 'hello's and 'good day's (yes, really) and Milo utters a single, gruff, 'Morning.' His brown eyes are dark and serious, and he avoids looking at me, thanking Polly for the oats as she hands him a steaming slab in a bowl.

'Allie's favourite,' she smiles. 'Gustav, our chef, cooks up a favourite of the team's before an expedition.'

He plonks down opposite me, clearly totally unmoved by the oat-based anecdote. Thick, wavy hair dangles over his face and he swipes it away.

'Morning,' I say. The word barely comes out.

'Hi.'

He looks down at his bowl, away from me – he's looking *anywhere* but at me. Of course he is. Hopefully he's wracked with shame. Being here opposite me, being reminded I'm a real person he chose to use as a prop to elevate his flailing image. From sell-out and love rat to healed romantic who loves his fans.

I don't look at him either. Because, despite myself, all my ghost feelings are reacting like the past two years didn't happen. His face. It's almost unbearable to look at. He's too . . . *real*. And somewhere inside of me, there is a choir of dormant emotions that don't know what's good for them, saying, 'It's really him. It's really Milo!'

Worse is that he hasn't changed, except for being a little rougher. More stubble. Longer hair. (Both of which suit him, annoyingly.) He's that same Milo who comforted me across airwaves and mountains, on that small screen in my hand. Sleepy and bed headed. Night after night, that handsome face beaming into June House, a time zone away, making me smile so much my cheeks stung.

The ghost feelings would do well to remember it was the same face that laughed on *The Really Late Show*, too, that posed seriously and pouting on a shoot for a magazine two months later, where he, while shirtless, held a bloody red rose between his teeth, using us, my heartbreak, to further his career.

'Well, we certainly won't lose you two in those colours,' chuckles Polly. 'Isn't that right, Allie? They're extraordinary, your jackets.'

Extraordinary is one word. They're walking highlighter pens.

'Hell yeah!' Jameson laughs, mouth full of oats. 'Like little rays of sunshine, us.'

Milo smirks. 'The idea is to be visible from space. If we get lost. Which, I say, is highly likely for two assholes without a clue.'

A wave of low chuckling travels around the table.

'Mm,' I say. 'It is a bold choice.'

He glances up at me, gives a half-smile.

'Albeit a potentially dangerous one,' I add.

'Sorry?'

Ironic, that apart from his ham-fisted attempt at conversation yesterday, this is one of the first proper things Milo has said to me: *Sorry*.

'I just . . . the colour,' I say, clearing my throat. 'You may not get lost, but . . . you may die.'

The table falls silent.

Ah. It really wasn't meant to come out like that. Like I was delivering a doomed prophecy at the start of a horror movie.

Iris, who has, as always, not spoken a word while her first coffee is consumed, lets out a big laugh of surprise. Jameson appears to be hiding a smile behind his spoon.

'Sorry, I—I just mean . . . bright colours? Bright colours can attract predators. Bears. Sometimes. Rare, but – still.'

Milo's eyes flick from his bowl, to me, narrowing slightly with amusement and irritation all at once. Were they always this brown, his eyes? They're quite ridiculous. Like . . . caramel or something. Are they contacts? I bet they're contacts. Milo Ford is a hundred per cent the type to wear coloured contacts he doesn't really need. He's the type to wear a neon orange designer coat after all. (And to model swimwear and smoulder into a camera, surrounded by a thousand messages in bottles bobbing on the ocean, probably setting us back another hundred years in conservation. I'd seen that particular image last year, suddenly, on a train station ad. I'd frozen. Couldn't finish my crisps after.)

'And there I was thinking your oatmeal special might be the thing to kill me.' Then he smiles, places that hand on his chest and says, 'I kid. This is great. The oats. Not the death by bear stuff, but – thanks, Allie. Appreciate the heads-up.'

Polly and Jameson laugh – Jameson's born out of friendship loyalty, I'm sure, because it's not even funny. Iris pretends she didn't hear. And I say nothing else. Yes, they're just oats, but how dare he even jokingly insult *my* oats? I remember arriving here, just six weeks after the leak, mid-darkest polar-night, just a few researchers left, eating by candlelight in the cafeteria, and I could smell something spiced and warming. It was these – these baked oats. Someone placed some down in front of me. It'd felt like an embrace. I had felt so alone until that moment. It was a single spark of light in the dark. And now Milo has gone and ruined that too.

We finish our drinks and breakfast, and Polly runs through the plan; we're to meet in twenty minutes outside. They'll take the equipment over to Lars, on the boat, and I will take a snowmobile to pick up a rifle and meet them there. She runs through safety too, suggests Milo and Jameson pick up boots from the storeroom in the station, and, only if they want to, jackets as well. Jameson asks Iris about the bear and bright clothing thing. She shrugs, says, tactfully, 'Well, my girl's not wrong, it *can*, but I've never known it to happen. You're safe with us.'

Polly also reminds them of the radio silence rules, that phones and Wi-Fi-connected devices should be switched off. Milo's eyes find me then, in the group, and irony chuckles into the room like a clown. We only met because of phones. Now we're somewhere we can't use them at all. Not for rich actors to call for an emergency helicopter, nor for uncomfortable scientists to text their sisters with, 'YOU WILL NEVER GUESS WHO JUST LANDED HERE!' Not that Sian would probably say a lot anyway. Weirdly, I felt compelled to reach out to her when Milo landed. That yearning for family that happens when things are rough, regardless of whether the ties are unsevered or not. We barely speak these days, since the diary leaked, since selling June House, but I think a message like that would have even Sian look-ing past everything she read about herself and biting for more information.

'Oh, and while we're here,' Polly says. 'I thought it might be good to pair everyone up? For safety purposes. Rare, but bears, and the like. There's an equal number of us, so . . .'

My mouth opens, like a goldfish. No. *There's no need*, queues up in my throat. *No, no, we can just all move as a team. Let's stick to working in a team!* But nothing comes out.

And before anyone can say another word, as though Milo and I are caught in the crosshairs of a gun that's about to go off, there it is. Of course it is. Polly says our names, together, and it's like a remnant from another universe where the leak never happened.

'Allie and Milo,' she says. 'You can be together.'

And like it's nothing at all, Milo nods politely at Polly. 'Lead the way,' he says to me. Then, 'Captain Lake.'

Then

<u>'Working with the Wild' live podcast recording transcript excerpt</u>

Dr Maria Power: Was it real to you?

Allie Lake: I want to say yes, very much so, but I think it's more accurate to say that I *thought* it was real. I was too close to it, to really see it truthfully.

Dr Maria Power: What do you mean by that?

Allie Lake: I . . . I don't know. You can be taken in by something sometimes. I think successful men often keep women around just to watch them bathe in their own light.

Dr Maria Power: So, are you saying that's what you believe it was?

Allie Lake: I believe some people place more importance on how they're perceived versus who they actually are. And I think my messages were useful for a very *watched* and 'in the spotlight' person's image. I think my feelings were useful. My heart, if you will . . .

126

Chapter Six

Milo

Allie and I have not spoken a word to each other since the whole bears and coats deal. Nothing.

And in a scene I thought I'd never wind up in, we are right out here, on the snow, a short distance away from the station, by something they call 'the garage' but which is more like an auto-repair shop with Disneyland-blue wooden slats. This place – it's truly something. Breathtaking. Almost . . . divine in some way; the way the sun never leaves, the total white-blue expanse and boundlessness of it, the jagged white of the mountains, like thick, crumpled copy paper. The edge of the world. Earth before humanity. It's why the buildings – the lodges, the station – look out of place. A Coke can that should've been edited out in the background of a period drama.

Allie jangles keys in her hand.

She's prepping a blood-orange snowmobile we've got to ride, and we've got ride it *together*.

I still can't get past Polly partnering us off. I almost laughed out loud when she said it, but instead I just pretended I was totally OK with the whole thing, just in case Polly thought I was an asshole, and Allie and I just silently allowed the awkwardness in like a sour smell through an open window.

Everyone else though – they seem just fine. Peachy. Polly's with Lars, the dude who's sailing us to the island, and Jameson is with Iris, who seems to be cool with me. She keeps shooting me warm – albeit *slightly* apprehensive – smiles, and she and Jameson are getting along like a house on fire, because, well, this is Jameson and he'd obviously get along with a week-old dinner roll. From what I can remember from everything Allie told me, Iris is the same breed. I wonder what she thinks of all this. If she even knows the truth: that Allie sold the story for Bermuda, and squashed the B&B she hated as an added bonus. I imagine she skipped away from that giant pink gnome. I do wonder about Sian, though. Do they still talk?

I check up on the Bermuda project sometimes, too. It's thriving. The B&B closed literal weeks after the leak. To me, it couldn't be more obvious how the leak happened; those dominos falling in that order. Money secured for Bermuda suddenly. B&B sold. But Allie probably feigned innocence. A glitch. A hack. She skirted around bullshit about my image once, on some weird podcast that beat the last gizzards from my heart at the time. But friends are blindly loyal sometimes. Iris would probably just believe her, hold her hand. Unless you're Jameson, who'd have always preferred to believe it was wood sprites or something. Bad fairies.

Allie hands me a helmet. 'Can you take this, please?'
'Sure.'

Then she hefts her own helmet up from her side, holding it the way someone might hold a bowling ball. 'Helmet on.'

'Yes, ma'am.' And as I say it, I'm reminded of the first time we ever texted and I almost want to say it in Romanian, like I did then. Of course I still remember how to say it. I always remember the small details. The actor in me can't help himself; collecting them like pieces of humanity, in fiction, and reality. A crack in the voice on a particular word. The way someone orders their eggs. A laugh when you're not expecting it. But we're worlds away from when we first texted. In every single way there is.

I slip the helmet over my head and Allie puts on her own.

'Visor,' she says.

'What?'

'Pull the *visor* down.' And before I can do it, she reaches over with her hand and slides it down over my eyes with a hard clack. 'We're running late. We can't keep wasting time.'

'Heard,' I say, but God, she is being stick-up-her-ass self-important right now. As if it's my fault I don't know how to work a snowmobile or know whatever helmet protocol this is.

I can feel myself slipping into wanting to strike up a two-year-old conversation I've been having in my head with her. *Why did you do it? Why didn't you just ask if you needed help; needed money? Was any of it real? Were we? I really thought it was the best thing I'd ever had.* Because how can we just *not* acknowledge the fact we're here together? It feels ridiculous not to mention it. Unbearable. And I want to, but I swallow it back down.

Doesn't help that I can't stop sneaking glances at her either. She is, annoyingly, totally beautiful. Even more so than I remember, and I remember that pretty damn clearly.

'OK, so, snowmobile rules, for safety,' Allie says, muffledly. Apparently, Allie finds it *very* easy to not acknowledge the fact we're here together.

'All right.'

'I'll run through the basics . . .'

'OK.'

'And we'll have to move quickly because we're running out of time. Jameson and Iris are already at the boat.'

Eerily, we planned this, back then; loosely, the way you do during whispered, midnight conversations. Things that feel half-plan, half-daydream. Our friends meeting. *Us* meeting, as a foursome. At Jameson's farm. Or touring us around June House; all the pink, the gnome décor.

'Allie . . .' Her name drifts from my mouth. I knew it would at some point, but I was hoping I might be able to keep it in a little longer.

She stops, mid-running-through-the-basics. 'Yes?'

'I . . . I uh.' I lift up my visor. 'I . . . Before we go, I just wanted to say that . . . I really didn't know.'

Allie freezes. Behind the clear glass of her visor, her round blue eyes blink just once. A strange tinge of irritation I recognise – like I've messed up and forced someone to break character mid-scene. 'Know what?' she asks, coldly.

'That you were here. I just wanted you to know that. That I really didn't know.'

She says nothing. Regardless of this whole horrible thing, her betrayal, this will be as shitty for her too.

130

She'll be embarrassed. And while there's a part of me that thinks, *Good, actions have consequences*, I don't want her to think this is how I do things. Showing up out of the blue, two years later, like, 'Time to pay for what you've done!'

'Right,' she says. '*OK*, then. Sure.'

Oh. But her *tone*.

'What's that supposed to mean?' I ask.

'I said OK, Milo.'

'No, but . . . but you said it like you don't believe me.'

She gives a harsh scoff, moves past me, starts to pull at a strap holding her backpack in place on the rack at the back of the machine. 'Milo, I'm working. We have a lot to do, I don't have time for this right now.'

'No, I know, I just . . . wanted to acknowledge it,' I explain. 'Because I'm finding this hard and weird and intense and confronting and—'

'*You're* finding it hard?'

I stare at her.

'I haven't done anything wrong,' she says, harshly.

'And I haven't done anything wrong either.'

And now *she* stares at *me*, unblinking, nostrils flared, as if she's holding back a gazillion words she wants to drown me in. Then she says, jaw tensed, 'Snowmobile rules.'

I swallow down my irritation and instead nod, like a scolded dog.

She continues, talking in the tone of a bored store clerk, and I listen, but all I can think about is how it *is* tough, being here. Not just having to face her, this woman who as good as sawed through every fibre of trust in my body. But having to . . . *look* at her. It's harder than I thought it ever could be. Equally, it isn't easy looking away either, from those familiar, lost eyes, that impy little quirk that means one of her eyebrows is always slightly cocked, as if she's always got a little attitude that makes me sort of want to piss her off on purpose—

'Milo?'

'S-sorry. What?'

'Hand,' she grumbles.

'Hand?'

Like a robot, I put my hand on hers, two cushioned gloves, one on top of the other.

She jolts it back like I just poked her with a hot skewer. 'W-what are you doing?'

'You said hand—'

'I said when the snowmobile is *moving*,' – she lifts the visor – 'I'll be communicating with my hand. *My hand*. And we like you to mirror back with your left hand, so we know you're aware.'

'Oh. Sorry. It's just . . . jet lag,' I say.

'So, this,' she continues, holding her hands in a wave, then closes her gloved fist, 'it could mean something on the track. So, I'll be braking, so brace.'

'Right. OK.'

'Why are you saluting at me?'

I laugh. Plainly because it's such a stupid, farcical sentence. 'No, I just . . . I don't know, I don't want you thinking I'm not listening.'

'I can make my own mind up,' she says. 'I can think whatever I choose to.'

'. . . OK?'

'And Polly isn't stupid, by the way,' she adds, and it's released in one rushed sentence as if she's been dying to say it. 'Jumping in like that, when she paired us up. Acting like you were totally fine with it, leaving me to look like the one who wasn't.'

I hold my hands up at my sides. 'I was being polite, Allie. Keeping up appearances or whatever. I thought you might be grateful.'

'*Grateful*? Oh, right, *thanks*,' she scoffs, giving a taut, false laugh. Then, she says, 'Keeping up appearances,' as if only to herself.

'*Yeah*, keeping up appearances,' I say, folding my arms. 'Saving face, or like, keeping my composure, in case Polly—'

'You were spinning the narrative, you mean?' she shoots at me.

'I mean, I keep asking this, but what? Like, are you being serious right now?'

And her face. It's smug and angry all at once. Like I'm a bear who's walked into a trap and while that delights her, she's now got to deal with the pain in the ass of cleaning it up. What would she prefer? For me to *not* keep up appearances and stand up over Gustav's oats and announce this to everyone? Remove her mask like it's an episode of *Scooby-Doo*? *Attention please! Allie Lake betrayed my trust and sold my personal messages to a gossip column to fund her own project! Do you really want to be eating oats with this woman?*

'It's just you seem to want me to know you really didn't know I worked here, and if you had, you wouldn't have come here, and oh, of *course* I don't mind being paired with Allie. I'm a nice guy. I never do anything wrong.' She sighs. 'I'm not playing this fake game.'

I shake my head, tip it towards the sky. Despite myself, a hot ball in my chest aches, that she thinks that about me. 'Fake game? Allie, why would I come here if I knew?'

'I don't know,' Allie replies. 'Accolades? Praise for a serious documentary that's going to *help the world*, and screw how uncomfortable that might make me feel because look at what you're set to gain? Or, I don't know, some weird quest for my forgiveness to help you feel better?'

'*Your* forgiveness? I want *your* forgiveness?' My jaw clenches like a rusty hinge. I'm an actor. I get sticking to a story, getting into a character, but Jesus Christ. She is playing this like even she believes she didn't do it.

'Yes,' she says.

'For what?'

She laughs then. It's a real, angry, exasperated laugh. 'Well, the awards are certainly deserved,' she says. 'I almost believe, listening to you now, that you didn't leak the messages.'

Wow, she *is* sticking to the story. But that's what they say, don't they? If you want to lie well, believe it yourself.

'Allie, you know I didn't leak the messages. Two years have passed. Just admit you did.'

'Milo, you know I didn't do it, because you did.'

'It doesn't even make any sense.' A scoff bursts out of me. 'What was it you said? That I leaked them to help my *image* because what better way than to leak all of my stupid romantic messages? That's the line you're sticking with?'

She shrugs, sharply. 'I'm not sticking with anything, Milo. I just think, as a motivation, that makes a lot of sense, yes. You talked a *lot* about that on our calls. What people thought of you.'

'A *lot*?'

'Yep. About how everyone was angry at you after *Day Falls*, that interview which blew up your Instagram page, probably lost you roles, what a *bad* boyfriend you'd been painted out to be—'

'I know you think it's a watertight narrative you've created for me,' I bite. 'A motivation, as you called it. But really, if I wanted to *help my image,* I think I might've been able to come up with a better, more simple way than leaking my personal messages to a woman I met online.'

Her nostrils flare. 'Well, you seemed to come out of it looking just perfect,' she says.

'Oh yeah? So I should be thankful?'

Oh, she's *really* pissing me off now. Because has she forgotten? She used to tell me she wanted to send her diary to her sister, that she sometimes left the document open, wanted everything out there. She used to tell me there was nothing she wouldn't do for her job; that her project in Bermuda was all she had. She even said to Iris – and OK, jokingly, but even so – she could hand the phone in, make some cash. I don't think she ever expected her messages to Iris to be part of the deal. But, regardless, she looks guilty. She knows she is. And she's scared, so she's throwing it back to me.

'Yes,' she says again. 'You did just fine, so why complain?'

'Oh, so it all worked out.'

'For you,' she says, wobblily. 'From where I'm sitting. *Day Falls* fans loved you again. Actors apologised to you publicly. People commenting and fawning over how romantic you are. All looked great and continues to, from where I'm sitting.'

Is that what she's telling herself? That she might've betrayed me, but I benefited, so I should lighten up, or shut up?

'You have no idea what you're saying, Allie.'

'I think I do.'

'Well, maybe you should pass that on to my father, huh?' I say. I try to steady it, but my voice wobbles now too. I'm angry. 'He doesn't think I came out *looking just fine*, but I don't suppose we have time to get into that now, right? We're running late. This is your work.'

For a second, Allie stares at me, her eyes wide. The corners wilt, just a fraction, with something that could be – no, *is* sympathy, as far as I can tell. Her eyes shine and I almost feel sorry for her. I wait for her to probe. Her mouth opens to speak. Instead, she clears her throat and says, 'Yes. We are running late.'

She continues on, robotically, about staying seated, about keeping my feet on the rails at all times, and as she speaks, I feel like I'm listening to her with my head dunked under water. How the hell will we get through four days of this?

'Let's go then,' she says finally, and she hops onto the snowmobile. A petite nimble leg thrown over the seat, straddling it. I get on behind her. I can smell her hair. Watermelon. Of course she smells like watermelon. Annoyingly that feels very Allie. And that makes the stupid dumbass animal part of me think about her legs last night. Bare and smooth. Those eyes that stuck to mine – wide with anger and judgement, like she was marking my every move, like an assassin. It's stupid. But despite the anger, there's an unspoken something else here too, in fleeting tiny moments. Chemistry. The same chemical make-up that was there two years ago. Confusing, because for two years I've been telling myself it wasn't real . . .

Below us, the engine rumbles into life.

'Hold on,' she says and as I ask, 'Is it like a motorcycle? Do I put my hands on your waist, or—' she cuts in like I'm hovering above a full bathtub with a plugged-in toaster.

'No, Milo. No,' she says. 'You have handles for that. OK? Please hold the *handle*s. Do not hold me.'

Chapter Seven

Allie

I should not have done that.

I'm at work. I'm being paid to do a job. I promised myself I wouldn't go there and let Milo hijack what I'm here to do, and yet somehow, it just exploded out of me.

But I just couldn't help myself. It's so hard trying to gulp down all these things I want to say; all these things that have been proving, like dough, in my mind for two years with nowhere to go. That I really sympathised with rehab. I understood how hard it must've been for him to find a way to properly broach it and tell everyone the real reason why he left. But why did he have to use me to do it? To relaunch himself as some bettered, wholesome romantic with a juicy scandal I never consented to. Just so he could be seen in the way he wanted to be seen. Even the coat – that bloody coat. It's all so pretentious.

But still, his dad.

That mention of his dad and the way his voice shook slightly, the way a sharp jaw muscle pulsed beneath smooth skin. In that split second, I saw him. *Him*. The Milo I knew back then, who hurt deeply because of his dad's cold disapproval. Because he'd planned for a son who wasn't Milo – who carried on the family carpentry business. Traditional. Modest. Humble. Ever since, he'd been trying to prove why he was worth loving, and, more than anyone, I understood that. And I saw it, there, in his eyes. The Milo I trusted; the one I'd been myself with. The Milo who had not only liked what he discovered, but celebrated it. And for a long time, I've chalked it up to a stage play I mistook for being real. That Milo being charming and conjuring a feeling of trust is just what people do sometimes, to get what they want. Plus, the man *pretends* for a living. I'm sure he's done the same with hundreds of other women since me. Iris sometimes keeps me posted, mostly when she's drunk.

'Don't you google him? Because *I do*,' she'll slur, and then it's all, 'A model called Karma allegedly dumped him and it was the week before Cannes, but they were never photographed,' and, 'According to Dating Who, he hasn't been in a long-term relationship since Sara, but fuck me, the man's been seen with a lot of mysterious strangers who all have legs up to their earholes. Do you think he's OK?'

I'm grateful now, though, that I can only hear the bumbling engine of the snowmobile; jolting and bumping over lumpy, ice-topped terrain. I can just pretend he isn't even here at all. I can pretend I can't feel him, his warmth behind me, a contrast to the cold that bites my cheeks; that I'm not dreading the next few days, seeing him, reminding myself not to relax for a second, into that low, familiar, comforting voice—

Gah.

Shit.

I brake so abruptly, that I'm thrown to one side, and I'm mortified that a shriek bursts out of me. The

Bay! I almost forgot, foot to the floor, to stop at the bloody Bay.

The snowmobile comes to a powerful lurch of a halt.

Milo's arm has slid around my waist.

Oh, God. *No.*

We stop. Silent on the snow. Wind whooshes, ever present, like distant panpipes. A kittiwake swoops overhead.

His arm stays there like a tight, strong bracket.

Between us, there is total, total silence.

Then, '*Shit.*' Milo breathes. 'Are you OK?'

'Fine.' I wriggle away, like a cartoon mouse from a cat's fist. 'Sorry. I . . . I should've warned you. I messed up. I didn't realise we were here.' *Was too busy thinking about you and your stupid voice and shamefully drove right past it.*

'It's all right.' I hear the click of his visor. He lets out an amused whistle. 'I didn't have you down as a loose cannon, Captain Lake.' There's a smile in his voice.

'Didn't *have me down*?' I ask, clicking the kill switch to 'off'. 'How would you know?'

'I'm just saying, from what I *do* know about you—'

'Which isn't a lot.' It makes me bristle. Adrenaline, perhaps, and the fact it's what they do. That false over-familiarity. Dad used to do it. Leave us, come back, feign 'turning his life around' but breath still tinged with sour alcohol. He'd bring toys we no longer liked, sit with his arm around us in cafes, smiling at waitresses, all, 'Ugh, yeah, hard work with these two,' as if he hadn't been AWOL for two Christmases. The smiling along was exhausting. It's why it was a relief his father, my grandfather, a kind but stiff factory owner, discreetly gifted us June House, and we disappeared to it. An elaborate but bleak apology present on behalf of a son who baffled him.

I jump off the snowmobile. I want to run it off, or something; these thoughts of Dad, of Milo . . .

We're parked outside The Bay, the main research centre here. It sits large and authoritatively on the ice – a weird mix of shiny, corporate glass and angular lines, like a space-age greenhouse, and the older parts of the building in Scandi cladding. It's where the fire service operates from, the nurses, and also where we pick up important supplies that we don't store at our smaller station. Flares, weapons . . .

I make my way to the entrance. I'm hoping to walk it off. That arm around my waist, the smile in his voice at my ear. Who does he think he is?

'So, what're we doing?' he calls behind me, catching me up.

'Walking.'

'Ha. No, I mean, what is this place? Polly said supplies?'

'I need to get a gun,' I tell him. 'From the store.'

'Whoa, a gun? I thought that was a joke. So, we're talking, like, an actual *gun*?'

'Yes, Milo. A gun. That's what a rifle is.' I pause at the entrance, the first of two air-locked entryway doors, but I don't elaborate any more.

Inside, I leave Milo in the carpeted reception area, gazing out of the large, square windows at the distant ocean, and pick up my rented rifle from the store. A grumpy man called Paulo hands it to me, says nothing. The red pen he asks me to sign the paperwork with keeps running out.

When I emerge, Milo is holding a tiny camera and tracing it in the air, as deftly as someone might burn and wave around sage. At the sight of me, he stops filming – *good* – his feet still on the mud-brown carpet. Music plays from behind the reception desk. A German-speaking singer. A piano. Old silver tinsel left over from Christmas hangs over the reception computer monitor.

'So. Is this when I get shot?' Milo laughs, but I don't. 'I mean, we had a briefing on polar bears yesterday at the airport, but – I dunno, I just thought guns were a last resort or that this stuff doesn't really happen, or . . .'

'It rarely happens,' I say, 'but it does sometimes. Polar bears see us, and, well, they don't want us here, frankly. This is their world. So, we have to be prepared. With guns. Especially when some of us are intent on goading them with fluorescent colours.'

'I don't want to kill no polar bear.'

'No?' I say, looping my arm through the gun's strap and hoicking it onto my shoulder. 'How noble of you,' and I walk past him, to the exit.

'Actual full-blown rifle,' I hear him mutter to himself. 'OK. Sure. *Cool.* Yup. Why not?' Goody-goody Milo. Mr Idealist with his faux warmth and 'good prana' and gratitude lists and '*Who me? Date a normal woman? Grace her with my presence? Of course! It's open season! I'm a romantic! I'm nice! I would never kill a polar bear either! I love animals! Cute shit!*' And cue roars of approval from the crowd . . .

Outside, we both stand by the snowmobile. I adjust the rifle, double-check the safety catch is on (it is) and pull out my walkie-talkie. I radio Polly a small update.

There's silence as we stand next to each other, and I'm grateful for it. I can ground myself, remind myself of my place here. It's my favourite kind of day here today. Squinting bright. Miles of undisturbed snow ahead, like an enormous, clean rippled silk sheet. Not a soul in sight. Chest freezer-cold. It used to frighten me. The nothingness of it. Then it just became safety.

Today, though, with Milo here . . .

'Waiting for them to radio back,' I say.

Milo nods. 'Allie . . . can we . . . I don't know. Talk about earlier?'

'I'm not sure that's a good idea.' Why does he want to keep *talking* about this?

'I disagree.'

I raise my eyebrows.

'No, I just mean – I should've kept my head. Kept this professional. I promised myself I would. Regardless of . . . everything.'

'OK,' I say. 'Me too. At least we agree on that.'

'And I don't really want any of this clouding the doc. This is work. Like . . . this is Jameson's dream.'

I sag a little with something inside. Relief. Work. I know what I'm doing with work. We can just keep this to *work* until it's over and he's gone. 'Agreed. And me either.'

'Cool.'

Even more silence now. A long, icy breath of wind. We stand here on the snow, nothing and nobody for miles, a clean, propless stage. Milo and me, under the spotlight of the polar sun. The radio in my hand is silent.

'And I am sorry about your dad, Milo,' I say. 'Whatever happened. I'm sorry about it.'

'Yeah.' Milo brings his hands to his head, laces his fingers and cradles the back of his beanie hat. 'Yeah, he stopped speaking to me.'

In spite of my anger, my heart sinks. 'Completely?'

'Yeah. Cut me out. Well. He actually picked up a call last week, so maybe we're moving forward? I dunno. But . . . he cut me off. Even my cheques?' He puffs out a dark laugh. 'I guess he read the shit I said about him. He hates that kind of thing. He's private. Hates people knowing his business, you know? So, he took the opportunity to go full Disappointed Father.'

'Gosh. I'm – sorry, Milo.'

'Yeah . . .'

A breeze whooshes by us, menthol-cold and sharp, but I feel confused. Because I feel sad for him. Perhaps he didn't think it through; thought his dad wouldn't see. Maybe he was too fixated on the story of us getting out there, all romance and fun, that he didn't consider the real-life, *true* implications. And of course he didn't. He didn't think of me, did he? How *The Really Late Show* felt to watch, how the publicist's words down the phone to me broke my heart, my own father getting in touch, my sister, heartbroken from losing June House so suddenly . . .

I radio again.

'They're probably loading the boat,' I say. 'Maybe we should just go .'

'It's crazy,' says Milo. 'Like you have to radio just to hear another human.'

'Mm,' I reply. 'It's a lot to digest.'

'You said you'd never come here.'

The words land hard, like javelins in the ground at our feet.

I stare at him. 'What do you mean?'

'No, it's just . . . you were working in Bermuda.' His brown eyes crinkle at the corners, in what could be faux-concentration or anger. 'I remember you saying you couldn't do what Iris did. The remoteness, the cold, the no internet—'

'Well, people can change their minds.'

'Yeah, but from Bermuda to here, I just . . . There's change and then there's . . . *whiplash*. I just wondered why the sudden pivot.'

The gall.

What's he even saying? That I can't complain because I don't keep to my word anyway? Is that what he tells himself to sleep at night? *Oh, yeah, I might've made us public, but she's full of shit about not liking cold places, anyway!*

'I'm not talking anymore,' I say.

He holds his hands up, in surrender. 'I just asked a question—'

'This is R1,' comes Polly's fuzzy voice over the walkie-talkie and thank *goodness*. 'Schedule slightly delayed but all team members en route to boat. ETA five minutes. Do you copy, R2?'

I bring the receiver to my mouth with relief, like it's a glass of wine (and gosh, I wish it was), tell them we'll be there at roughly the same time.

'We need to go,' I say, and I look up to meet Milo's eyes. 'And, for the record, I didn't want to come here. I had to. I had no choice.'

He looks at me like I just pushed him hard in the chest. 'You had no choice?'

'Correct,' I say, and my teeth are so firmly mushed together, they ache. 'After the leak, people bombarded my university. They – crashed my website, filled my DMs, emailed the station in Bermuda, some even came to my house to take photos, which . . . I mean . . . and most people were just excited, whipped up by a weird viral moment, I suppose. But . . . Some people were awful. Like, really, really awful. And I had no one.'

Milo hasn't blinked. 'Allie . . .'

'So, I needed an out. Polly needed people here for the polar winter and it felt like the only choice I had. I had Christmas here alone. The sun didn't come up for six months. I knew nobody. But it felt safe. It *is* safe, to me now. That's why I changed my mind. That's why there was *whiplash*.'

His Adam's apple bobs. His eyes glisten and his mouth opens and closes. 'Allie, I . . . I didn't realise that.'

'And why would you? You're protected from it, aren't you? Publicists. Fans. Magazines. TV hosts . . .'

He reaches a hand up, towards me, then stops and lets it hang back at his side. He clears his throat, eyes dropping to the floor. 'I'm . . . I'm really sorry, Allie. That must've been so rough. I didn't . . . I didn't know.'

'What, and if you had, you wouldn't have done it?'

He stares at me then, gently, tips his head to one side. And something about it – something in it – makes me want

146

to cry. Because of his familiar kindness. Because it's Milo. His softening eyes, his comforting voice. Because this really *was* my escape, and now the very thing I was escaping has landed here with me. And I almost – *almost* – believe that he didn't do it, looking at him. Which is ridiculous. Totally ridiculous. Of course he did it. And if he didn't, then why else would the publicist have called? Why *else* would he have gone on TV and laughed about me? And if he didn't do it, then who did?

No. No. Not this again. I packed this *well* away, deep, deep into the attic of my mind two years ago. I can't start unpacking it all again, start wondering who did it, if not Milo. Hacking. Passwords being taken. Someone stealing my phone somehow . . . No. No. Milo did it. The simplest answer is often true.

'I'm not doing this here,' I tell him. 'I just want to be clear, Milo. This is my place of work.'

'I understand,' he says gruffly. 'We'll just shoot footage as agreed, and we'll leave.'

'Good,' I say.

'Good,' he says, eyes flashing, and for a second, they fix on mine – serious and beautiful – and something that feels like hot sunlight travels down my body.

'Let's go,' I say, climbing onto the snowmobile. 'And, um, contact lenses. Sub-zero temperatures can cause eye irritation when wearing them, so I suggest you remove them. We won't have the means to treat irritation on Cote Rock.'

And Milo, helmet poised above his head, suddenly smiles; a slow, wordless 'nice try'. 'I'm not wearing contacts, Allie,' he says. 'But thanks.'

Then

Milo leaves his crusts.

I order dessert.

Which feels like a nice time to talk about the now; the future. 'I'm just focusing on work,' Milo tells me. 'There doesn't seem to be a downside to that, you know? I'm reading a lot, I'm spending a lot of time with Jon [Malik, director of *Crush, 32 Figures . . .*] trying to learn everything I can, I'm reading an awesome script of a play right now and I think I'm going to take it . . . Like, I'm just sort of smothering myself with it. Which – I don't know. Is that healthy?' He laughs, stirs his drink – fresh ginger tea with honey from a sachet that looks like it's lived at this restaurant since the Spice Girls were number one. 'There's no room for anything else.'

I tell him I'd wager it being healthy. Because he seems OK. More mature than at our last dalliance – a drunken wrap party in Romania, at which I almost lost a shoe (the less said about that, the better). He's quieter. More poised. The messy hair and five o'clock shadow of an overworked married father, but the dewy skin

148

of a perfectly ripe apple. The hydrated face of a man who's working a lot but has no time to party anymore.

I tell him this. He laughs throatily. 'Me, a married father.'

Not on the cards then?

His mouth twitches. He's been pretty discreet with romances since Lake, the world having to settle for occasional blurred pap shots of him eating or walking in Central Park with mystery women, all smiles and autumn trench coats.

'Ah. Things don't really get off the ground there these days,' he says.

'What do you mean?' I press.

'I don't know. I guess sometimes you meet someone who sort of shows you what you really want. And once you've felt it, you're always searching for that same thing, and nothing measures up. And until it arrives again, you're just kind of . . . at sea? That's where I am. And I'm cool with staying here, I guess.'

'So, Milo Ford is at romance-sea? Waiting for his boat to come in?'

He laughs, brings tea to his lips. 'That's me! Bobbing around at sea, hoping that boat might find me again.'

Chapter Eight

Allie

We're at sea now, Milo, me and the rest of the team, on our way to Cote Rock. Lars, my favourite of the boat captains at the station, is taking us there, and for half an hour, I've been sitting with him at the controls, watching him gaze easily across the water like it isn't the jagged, unpredictable Arctic circle he's navigating, and instead, a swan-shaped pedal boat on a still lake at a theme park. He vapes. It smells of sweet shop cola bottles.

'Another day . . .' He smiles through a bushy, iron-filings beard, rough, weather-beaten hands on the wheel of the boat. 'And what's the news with the young squirts we've got today?'

'*Squirts*,' I laugh.

'Saying what I see.'

I like Lars. There's something grounding about him. He's worked here at the station for as long as I have been here. He's a boat captain – used to ferry rich people around the Arctic on cruises, then took early retirement at sixty, missed it, and came here – and he is one of those people who's just 'happy with his lot'. He's stoic and hardy. There's something cowboy-ish about him too. But he's also the first person to weep when an animal is injured. His soul, he says, lives here.

'They're here to film a documentary,' I tell him. 'For YouTube. But in partnership with our funding organisation.'

'So TV stars?' he asks, unimpressed. His voice is deep, with a thick Norwegian twang.

'Sort of,' I reply. 'One's a big YouTuber, one's . . . an actor.'

He reverse nods, a jut of his hairy chin. 'The one with the hair looks familiar,' he mulls. 'Thought it might be another *Star Wars* moment.'

I laugh. Lars is referring to when one of the *Star Wars* movies was filmed by another research station on Skellig Michael and there were *so* many puffins there that they couldn't edit them out so they just CGI'd new little creatures in. Something about it amused us all. Puffins: inadvertent film extras.

'No *Star Wars* problems this time. It's to raise awareness, et cetera . . .'

'Right, right,' he says. 'And they're good guys?'

'The squirts? They're OK. I don't really know. Pass.'

He laughs out of the side of his mouth. Lars wears a gilet and a short sleeved T-shirt around the clock, which is unheard of out here, sailing through glaciers, trudging across ice. But Lars doesn't feel the cold. A girlfriend once took him to Rhodes. 'The heat's like being skinned alive,' he said.

'Eh, it'll be OK,' he says. 'Plus, if it bags you guys some cash, win-win . . . correct?'

And he's right. *That*'s what I must keep coming back to. It's for something more important than me. I watch the mainland now, getting more and more speck-like in

151

the distance, the path leading to it spiked with glaciers, like dinosaur teeth. A solid one degree centigrade. This is not about me. This is not about Milo.

It feels like it, though, sitting here, a tangle of feelings weighing down my skull. A child's mismatched mud pie of them. I keep thinking about his father. I keep replaying, over and over, those warm, sympathetic eyes that held mine tightly when I told him why I came here; the way his hand reached towards me, the tip of the head. For a moment, he was just . . . Milo as I knew him. Milo who would never do anything to hurt me. Milo who would've never betrayed me in any way – gosh, what am I saying? That it wasn't *him*? No. He laughed on TV. He posted *memes*.

We chug along, ice water like sharpening knifes against the boat, and I turn to look over my shoulder. I keep doing that. Like I keep looking to check it's true, because what a ridiculous situation we're in. But much is the same. Polly chats to Iris on a bench on the wooden deck. Jameson films. Milo observes, arms folded, with that smile. He really is striking. In that way movie stars often are. It's quite distracting. He's unusual looking. Full lips, a mouth that slants when he smiles, sleepy, cognac-brown eyes that absolutely are not contacts. I wish I'd never bloody said that; he *liked* that I said that. His ego, stroked. His hair is pushed hastily to one side in a floppy, messy quiff, and it's hardly attractive being out here in thick giant coats and hats and boots that are more armour more than shoes, but somehow, Milo manages it. Even in that silly neon-orange jacket.

Shit. He's seen me looking. I swoop back around.

I must remember why I'm here; stay grounded. My puffin colony. My auks. The spring hope of new eggs. It'll be better once we moor up, organise camp, start the real work. At least, that's what I'm counting on. We have a lot to do in a short space of time, and while Milo and I might be partners, Cote Rock is about working as a team.

'Allie? Uh, Polly?'

I glance over to Captain Lars. 'Yes?'

'Looking at where you guys want to camp, it isn't very wind sheltered.' His eyes squint to the tail of the islet of Cote Rock, tapering off into the water in the distance. 'The wind isn't set to be too bad, but I think it's better to be totally away from it. Start as we mean to go on, yeah?'

And now everyone is looking at me. Polly, Iris, Jameson and Milo. They're looking at me in that way people look at authority figures. This is why I have to keep this together. Polly is our supervisor, but this is my expedition. Letting anything get in the way is negligent. I need to throw my mud pie of feelings over the edge of this boat, let it slowly disintegrate deep, deep beneath, with the cod.

'Where do you suggest?' I ask.

'Just around the other side on the beach. It's sheltered by a hill. I think this would be better. The only thing is, we will have to dinghy our way over.' Lars gives a wonky smile. 'My boat won't be able to go right to shore. Too rocky. We'll have to do a couple of relays for the equipment.'

'Oh.'

Polly approaches, hands on hips. 'That'll be OK,' she says cheerily. 'Is that OK with everyone?'

There's a chorus of sures and nods. Milo, who leans casually against the side of the boat, looks over his shoulder at me a moment longer than everyone else.

'Yeah,' he says. 'We can all put Jameson's newfound muscle to good use, right?' Milo laughs, and Jameson slaps his back, says, 'Erm, haven't you just stopped some insane training regime, Mildred? After *you*, babygirl. Please.'

Everyone laughs. And I find a smile, despite myself, forcing its way onto my face too.

I turn back around to the mountains. They stare back at me like stoic, immovable father figures. 'Sod all to do with us,' they silently say, as I hear Polly call, 'We'll stick to our pairs, OK? Two people to a dinghy.'

Chapter Nine

Milo

I'm with Allie.

On a tiny boat.

In the Arctic Ocean.

There're three dinghies, and each pair was assigned one, plus a shit ton of equipment to balance in the bottom, and now all six of us are sailing to shore away from Beefcake Lars' big-ass boat (I'm sure Allie would roll her eyes if she heard me call it that, correct me with the right name, be all self-important and, 'Actually, that's a world-renowned Big-Butted Boat. *Not ass*. You mustn't say *ass*. You'll die in the camp if you say ass').

Speaking of the 'camp', it seems to be just . . . a beach? A gnarly, untouched beach. I'm not sure what I expected, but even calling it a beach is a stretch, because that is not what it is. It's more like a layer of cement-dark sand, still half coated in snow. I've camped before. Mom and I used to go when I was young. Campsites with picnic tables and showers; just a few miles away from home and Dad's eternal crankiness. But this is . . . real-deal shit. Wild camping. In *snow*. The sort of camping you watch on TV kicked back on your couch with an extra large meat feast pizza, while saying to your friends, 'Yeah, screw that, I'd rather stay alive and stay here.'

Wish I was on my couch right now actually. The atmosphere on this boat is so suffocating, I feel pretty sure some of this fancy science equipment would pick it up, measure it on a graph, like the sharp red spikes of a seismogram. Maybe Jameson and Iris can already see it from land. An angry, smoky red haze.

They went on this nightmare first, except it doesn't seem like a nightmare for them; Iris's head was thrown back with laughter the whole way, Jameson non-stop talking and filming. They're already on land setting up, erecting two huge white tents that sort of look like those ones from *CSI*.

Lars anchored his big-assed boat, and now he and Polly sail in another dinghy, just ahead of us, weighed down with all this *stuff* but still slicing through the water as if it's nothing. Until we reach the shore, it's just us. Allie and me. In a tiny boat, on the coldest, darkest-looking water I've ever been close to, weighed with our own heap of stuff. Oh, and painful silence.

Silence.

Silence.

More damn silence.

I clear my throat. Allie's eyes, round, blue, slide to me, then back to the horizon again. Serious. They're always so serious.

I sigh. I stretch – *shit*.

OK, I don't think she noticed that I stretched a little too far back then; almost socked heads with the ocean—

'Careful,' she sighs.

'Sorry.'

Sorry what? Sorry I almost . . . fell in? Died?

Are there things that kill here, in the water? Polar sharks or something. There are whales, right? Killer ones? Things in the sky I know about these days, thanks to Allie, but I don't know about shit in the water. Not sure Allie would've thrown me a lifebuoy, so I feel I should've probably become acquainted. Bit late for that now though, I guess.

'So, like, uh . . . will we just . . . be there?' I ask, and I wince. But since the snowmobile, I *want* to talk to her more. I keep going over and over what she said about coming here – about her DMs and fans and her Christmas alone and . . . it made my blood run red-fucking-hot, despite the ice cold of the arctic air, could feel my veins practically popping in my forearms. I wanted to say, 'Well, that's the name of the game when you press publish on your life for your own gain!' But, equally, I wanted to wrap my arms around her, pro-tect her. Because maybe she underestimated it. Maybe she underestimated the backlash of being celebrity gos-sip when she chose to leak everything. It can be more brutal than you could ever describe to someone. Being so exposed and picked apart that your mind begins to warp and you start to believe what literal strangers who only know you from a movie and a blurred photo of you at an LA coffee shop are saying about you.

'Sorry?' she huffs.

'Oh, I meant the camping? Will we just be setting up . . . just – there? Like, on the pebbles and ice and sand and stuff?'

'Do you mean, the beach?'

I laugh. 'Well, yeah.'

'Yes,' she shrugs. 'No hotels here, Milo.'

'Ha. No?' What a smart mouth. 'Shame. That's all a guy like me is used to. As you said, I'm going to die out here probably.'

'I didn't say that,' she replies.

'No?'

'No.' She looks down at her gloved fingers; splays them like a starfish. I glance behind her, to Polly, who watches us and then quickly grins and waves like she's been caught. Maybe there really is a red haze around us . . .

'I didn't say exactly that,' Allie carries on. 'You won't die – so long as I'm with you, anyway.'

'Are you absolutely sure you can promise yourself that? You've got four days of me.'

And for the first time in eighteen hours, warmth washes over her face like a passing sunray, and there's the tiniest, tiniest smile at the edge of her mouth; as if she's holding in laughter, and I feel . . . I dunno – high on it. Like I've won something. Cracked a code. (Dumb animal appears to be firmly in control right now.)

The feeling fades fast, though. A swift retract, like a mark in the sand. I think about the station – that clinical cafeteria, the strangers trudging the corridors, the wilderness that surrounds it. I hate knowing she came here alone. But . . . it didn't need to be this way. I told her to just give me a second. I told her we'd come up with a plan, that I'd speak to my publicist. She seemed . . . tentatively all right with that. We even talked about meeting the next day, before I flew back. That was when she blocked me. On everything. Erased me like I never, ever existed. Then the website statement. Then, weeks later, the goddamn *podcast.*

'Does this feel weird to you?' I ask, despite the fact I know she really wants me to shut my mouth. 'That this is the first time we've actually met. It does for me.'

'Yes,' she says quietly. 'Everything aside, seeing you . . . it's weird.'

'Jameson said it's like something on TV.'

She gives a single nod.

'*Catfish* or something . . .'

Her head snaps up. '*Catfish?*'

Ah, fuck. Words. This is what happens when, despite extensive media training, you're always fighting the urge to fill every gap with words without thinking. Rogue words make their way out. Stupid ones that piss people off.

'I obviously didn't mean—'

'What? That I'm not what you expected *online*—' She rolls her eyes.

'That's not what I meant. Especially about you—'

'It's fine, Milo. I wasn't actually being serious.'

'You *are* what I expected.'

'I was kidding—'

'*More* even.'

She says nothing to that, but her chest rises and falls beneath her coat.

Ah, shit, what is this, an endless ocean? Because, of course, we've got a huge hunk of silence once more. She pulls on her hat, adjusts her hair under the edge of it. Her face is pink and flushed.

'And, like, there were things I didn't notice, of course, online,' I carry on. Because I don't know when to shut up. Because I feel responsible and guilty for her flushed face. Because my clueless inner animal is a galloping rogue . . . 'Didn't notice on camera, I mean.'

'Milo, stop talking.'

'Like – I – I didn't realise you had that – little thing?' I gesture to my own mouth, tap an index finger above my top lip.

She raises her eyebrows. 'Little thing?'

'The . . . the little line above your lip.' I swallow. *Shut up, man. Shut up.* 'W-when you smile. You can't see everything on video chat, I guess.' It's like a second smile, I want to say. But I don't, because she looks mad again. And it makes me want to say, *Oh you're mad? Yeah, well, me too, gorgeous, but I'm the one who was betrayed here and I'm trying to be a grown-up.*

We move across the waves. The motor of the boat seems to be making a weird humming sound now. And that's all there is for what feels like an age. Increasingly loud humming. Sloshing of waves. Distant laughter from the shore. Allie's eyebrows knitting together.

'All good, R2?' crackles Iris's voice on the walkie-talkie, laughter around the words. 'Alive and well?' And the way she says it – it's an inside joke vibe, if ever I heard one.

'Confirmed,' Allie says, humourlessly.

'Hot Shot Actor still on board, present and correct?'

'Confirmed,' says Allie again, flatly.

'Unfortunately,' I say. 'Go on. There's still time to add an *unfortunately* on. I don't mind.'

'Why would I need to add an unfortunately on?'

'It would be easier to be rid of me, right? Nothing to explain if I've accidentally fallen overboard, had a little rifle accident. It's a heroic way to die, so I'll take it.'

Allie barely reacts, save for the tiniest eye-rolling whatever-you-say smirk.

She moves to rest her chin on her hand, arms tight and close to her body. Sandy bangs fall over her eyes and she squints, moves them with her fingers, which my body reacts to; finds cute.

Stupid. The body is a stupid, disobedient machine, stuck in the 'back then'. Back then, when were so close. Back then, when I'd listen to her sleepy voice, her breath catch in her throat when we talked at 3 a.m. The memory makes my limbs tense. Back then, we were – at least, I *believed* at the time – moments away from . . . *something*. Everything.

And here we are.

Nothing.

Strangers.

In the arctic. Me and Allie. Victim and perpetrator. Right?

Allie suddenly jumps up, leans over the boat.

'The . . . the motor,' she says, with more feeling than I've heard her show ever since we got here. 'It's . . . oh my God, it's blown.'

'Are you kidding?'

But she's not. She wouldn't kid – and least of all, with me – and we're now stopping completely. Polly and Lars are tearing forward in their boat, but we aren't. We're just here, bobbing in icy, icy waves. I bet it's a-thousand-knife-edges levels of cold. I bet it's deep.

'Are there whales in here?' I ask. 'Like, killer ones or . . .?'

Allie says nothing. She radios over. It's all weird language I don't really understand, but then she mutters, 'We'll have to paddle.' Then she says a hefty, 'Fantastic.' Paddle?

'We'll have to do it the manual way.' She leans over me, untying an oar . . . Oh, God, an oar? I don't know how to *oar*, is she serious? She's squashed against me, we have no choice, this boat is tiny, and we are drowning in equipment.

'Here.'

She passes me an oar, then begins untying another.

'We've got to row our way over?' I ask.

'Yes.' She brandishes her own oar with a sigh. 'The engine's failed. Happens. It's because of the ice. So, we need to paddle. Together. It's better that way. Preserves energy.'

She sits in front of me, her back to me.

'It's called sweep rowing,' she explains. 'Where you have one each. We have to make sure we're synchronised. Thankfully, we don't have far to go. I'll count: one and two . . .'

'Three?'

'No.' She tuts. 'One and two, and on two, you row. In *this*' – she demonstrates – 'direction.'

'OK. Yes, captain.'

Within moments, Allie and I are rowing. You seriously could never write this shit. I'm saying nothing, and Allie is just repeating 'one and two, one and two' like she's testing a mic.

'We're doing OK, right?' I add.

She just nods, while repeating one and two.

'Look, I know this has been hard. But, I was thinking, people work with people they don't get along with, people they don't like, all the time, right? So, maybe, we can actually do the whole professional thing—'

She scoffs a laugh. Then says, '*Feather* the oar, don't dunk it—'

'I am.'

'You're not—'

'*Jesus*,' bursts out of me. 'When're we going to stop this shit?'

Silence. Allie's 'one, two' stops. The boat stills.

'What?'

'Like, I'm trying. OK? And I don't have to. You know? *You* did this.'

'Me? What is this, stick to the story no matter what. Nobody's listening here, Milo. No newspapers, no press, no fans . . .'

'Stick to what?'

'Your well-crafted story.'

'*I* don't have a story,' I laugh.

'No?'

We don't paddle. We don't move. We're just bobbing, oars still in our hands. Her hair bristles in the wind in front of me.

'You seemed firmly in your story when you went on TV,' she says, wobblily. 'In that stupid meme T-shirt of *my* messages, laughing about it—'

'What else was I supposed to do? I was hurt.'

My shoulders sag. I do regret *The Really Late Show*. It felt cheap to capitalise off it. But I wasn't thinking.

I was . . . drunk. In total denial that I even had another problem, because, 'Hey! At least it wasn't benzos!' Everything felt like it does on alcohol. Doable. Like nothing. And I leant into it. My publicist, Sue; my agent, my buddy Ben, all telling me to lean into the discomfort and betrayal, and own it like it was mine. 'Play it like a damn tune, I say,' one of the producers had said. The show had the meme T-shirt waiting for me in costume. Screw it, I thought. Allie had her money. She had what she wanted. What about me? Everyone seemed to be eating it up anyway, and yeah, I guess it was the biggest temporary injection of external validation I could've ever hoped for. Especially after Dad. Especially after Allie erased me from her phone (and life). I wanted the fawning. I wanted to be the good guy.

'What does it even matter to you?' I ask her. 'You did it. You got what you wanted.'

Allie looks up at me. Her eyes are watery. 'Stop,' she says. 'Please just . . . tell the truth. Admit it. It's just us here.'

'Admit what?'

She laughs, tearfully. 'That you leaked the messages. I mean, what does it even matter? It's done. Nobody cares anymore—'

'*No*,' I say. The boat bobs on the waves. The waves have turned us at an angle. I dunk in the oar and swoop through the water to turn it again. 'No, I won't because I didn't.'

Allie is silent, stunned.

'I mean, what even is this, Allie? Did you forget? Are you so enmeshed with the story that you just believe it? We were meant to meet. Remember? Then you're *blocking me*. On everything. Out of nowhere.'

Allie's shaking her head. 'No,' she says. 'I blocked you because I didn't want to do what you wanted me to. What your publicist suggested.'

I freeze. This feels . . . weird. Like the world has suddenly frozen.

'What? My pub— my publicist? Who?'

She turns and looks at me. 'Your publicist,' she repeats. 'You told me you were going to speak to her. Then she called me. Sue Lewis or whatever her name was.'

My heart falls through my body. 'What? W-when did this happen?' Sue wanted to talk with Allie. I remember she took her number down, but – she never picked up.

'You said to bear with you,' she says, voice wavering. 'I *was* going to meet you the next day. Then she called me, said you'd confided in her about everything . . .'

'I did, but . . .'

'And she said to roll with it. To come to the hotel, to lean into the attention, because everyone was invested and we could both gain from it. I was already getting messages and people had turned up to take selfies out-side of June House, and I just thought . . . fuck you. So that's why I blocked you.'

I shake my head. 'Allie, that – that shouldn't have happened . . .'

'You orchestrated it.'

'What are you saying? You – you didn't leak it? You think it was me?' *Is* this not a story she's sticking to, or playing dumb? Did she really not do it? Shit. I feel like I'm gonna throw up.

'I said I wasn't doing this here,' she remarks, sitting up straight and angling her paddle back into the water.

'And I heard you,' I say, quietly. 'But . . .' My voice falls. 'Do you really not know how it happened?'

'You know I don't.'

'And neither do I.'

She says nothing.

I stare at her. I can't think straight. No. No. I feel blindsided. I can feel it, that familiar, old squeeze of panic in my throat, where the world feels unpredictable. A tiny, old spark blinks within me. A habitual yearn to mute it with something – a drink. It burns out as quick as it happens. But this is . . . heavy. Something I've known as fact, something I've believed for two years . . . there's a crack suddenly running through it.

But what about the funding money? She had none, then she had it all. Her old friend, Andrew. He's a funding strategist. Works with newspapers – the type of newspapers that slam people like me for wearing the wrong suit to a gala. I looked him up. Everything pointed to it being Allie. Her cooking this up, between them. But now . . .

'Research,' she says firmly. 'Filming. You're meant to be here to research and help and film, right? Why don't we just go back to agreeing that you do your job and I do mine.'

'Fine,' I reply, even though it's the last thing I want to do. I can think of nothing else to say. I feel like there's a piñata above us and we just took a first bat to it, released a flurry of lies and truths and I don't know yet what's what. Because if Allie didn't leak the phones, who did?

'One and two,' starts Allie again, and together, in tandem, we row closer and closer to land.

Chapter Ten

Allie

I have never looked forward to stodgy camp couscous and salami more. I'm hungry, and we have spent the entire day in Cote Rock, setting up the camp, which takes a lot of energy and time. And that's on top of the extra energy given to actually getting to the island with nothing but oars and rage.

First there's our temporary lab for Polly and Iris's bacteria, and our sleeping quarters, which we've partitioned off to separate us – Polly, Iris and me – from Jameson, Lars and Milo.

That's a strange feeling. Knowing nothing but a tarpaulin sheet will separate Milo and me tonight, as we sleep, but I'm grateful to not have to sleep in the same space as him. I can't even imagine that.

Building a camp with him was hard.

Sitting here, around a crackling, smoking campfire, eating couscous and salami – an easy-to-store wild-camping favourite – opposite him, harder.

The dinghy – unbearable. Something happened on the dinghy, too. And now, for the first time in two years, I feel real doubt. I feel doubt that he did it. And that frightens me. Because . . . what does that even mean? And what about *The Really Late Show* and the laughter? What about the interview and magazines and the memes about it he posted on Instagram? But then, if he didn't do it and he really believed it was me . . .

Ugh.

I don't even know.

And what's harder, is there's no space to think.

He's everywhere.

I work, Milo is there. I set up the lab, Milo's voice is there, floating over from the shore like a familiar song. I eat dinner, Milo is *there*. The quicker I can finish this meal, the quicker I can go to bed, crawl into my sleeping bag, hope that I survive both polar bear attacks and the sheer amount of *dread* seeping into my skin, that feels like poison, and this day can end—

'Who fancies a little *getting to know you* session?'

Oh, no. I look up from my meal. We're sitting in a loose, straggled circle on a mat at the entrance of the tent. Polly is beaming with her question as she stands with her own empty camping bowl.

'I, um . . . We should rest?' I start to say, through chews, but it's of course lost amidst a chorus of 'sure!'s and 'yeah!'s. Jameson and Milo are sitting opposite me beside empty camping bowls, bottled water in their hands. Milo doesn't appear to react.

Iris, from beside me, nudges me. 'It's all good, amigs,' she whispers.

We've barely found the time to chat, Iris and me. She's been talking a lot to Jameson and his camera, directing them both, as if his GoPro is another person, with her finger across the horizon, but she keeps checking in with me. In her last check-in, she said, 'I just need you to clarify you're not going to, like, dinghy off when we're all asleep.' Then, 'I know you're in hell, but I have to say, I'm going to take Jameson home with me in a little jar.'

Polly slaps her hands together, stands authoritatively, like a teacher at the edge of the circle. 'Who's heard of the human knot? Come on, Lars, you've heard of the human knot, right?'

Lars laughs, sitting with his leg cocked, wrist resting on top of it, a bottle of Mountain Dew hanging from his fingers like a beer. 'I'm a knot *expert*, baby.'

Iris leans into me. 'It'll be OK,' she whispers. 'Think of the doc. I really think it'll be worth it.' She's hook, line and sinker, isn't she? She's even speaking like them: 'doc.' But that's Iris. Had her heart broken more than anyone I know, but still loves people. Attaches to them. Borrows little parts of them. Trusts them because not trusting feels worse. But I know she's right. Jameson has millions of followers, and Milo, the enormous reach of Hollywood. It really will raise so much money.

But this is some unknown game called the human knot. I can't imagine the human knot has ever benefitted a single human soul. Unless the human knot consists of being bent into a pretzel and thrown out to sea as an act of euthanasia.

'It's a great ice breaker and a lot of fun,' continues Polly. 'I played it at a family reunion last year, back in Canada, and it even thawed my grumpy wife.' Did she just look at me? Blurred at the corner of my vision, I can feel Milo looking at me too. We haven't spoken a word since the dinghy. And now I'm the person in the group who needs *thawing*. Great.

Polly explains the rules, which sound both simple and agonising. We have to stand in a circle and hold two mystery hands, at random. Then we simply have to unknot each other without dropping hands. But we can only make a move when we each answer a question about ourselves. 'Like truth or dare, without the dare part. And if you don't want to answer, you can't move.'

Within moments, Iris is collecting up the dirty camping dishes and rinsing them in the ocean – bears sniff out food, so it's important no old food is near the camp – and we're all making a standing circle. The campfire smokes and cracks behind us, and the sky, despite it being 8 p.m., is still light, but thick with cloudy, thunderous gloom. It feels like an early autumn evening back in the UK. But unlike an autumn evening, the sun simply won't go down here. A party guest who never wants to leave, still drinking on the lawn when the bin men arrive, and the neighbours leave for work.

Milo stands two people away from me, Iris and Lars between us. If I aim over to the right, I should avoid his hands altogether. I feel uneasy about our conversation on the boat. The way he said, 'I was hurt.' I know how that feels. I often wish I hadn't done the podcast. It was live, it was unplanned, I felt I couldn't just walk off stage in front of all these amazing, supportive women. But I was hurt too. Even Sian told me once, and harshly, that it was a mistake, but once she'd read my diaries, she was out to say anything that would hurt me as much as she was, and I understood it. I would often say I wished she'd see them, so we could air everything, but I still wish we'd had a conversation. Sat at June House's kitchen table, months before.

Mum used to make us. A proverbial banging-together of our heads. Instead, I'm only left with regret about the way things unravelled, in the end, with my sister. June House. The B&B. Her moving away. All of it.

'Ready?' laughs Polly, as Iris leans in and says to me, 'Breathe through it, amigo.'

There's a chorus of agreement and then Polly makes sure the neon coats are turned inside out to their dark insides so we're all wearing similar colors, and so we're all standing facing away from one another. Close your eyes and grab hands, she orders. Hold on. Whose hand is that? Do I have one of Iris's? Jameson's? Please let these hands be Polly and Jameson's. This one looks a bit too big for Polly's . . .

'Is that yours?' Jameson laughs over to Milo. 'Squeeze once for yes.' Then everyone squeezes and there's an explosion of laughter.

'You'll never know, dude,' says Milo with a giant smile in his voice from behind me. That smile. Even the sound of it . . . stirs something in my stomach. It's still such a ridiculous smile. The sort of smile punctuated with a 'ding!' in a cartoon.

Polly's up first. Iris asks: 'What's the most embarrassing thing you've ever done?'

Polly bursts out laughing. 'Oh, damn,' she says. 'Erm. OK, once, I showed up for training at a job and one of the trainers was my *ex-girlfriend*, Nahla. I was totally terrified things would be awkward so I wrote a note that said something like, "I'll pretend I don't know you. Let's keep this to work and keep our relationship out of it," or something like that, but I put it on the wrong desk, and I had to watch, in real time, as another trainer unfolded it in front of everyone.' Her story makes us all laugh. She unknots a little, facing into the circle now.

Then it's Lars' turn. 'Um, are you married?' asks Polly, and they both burst out laughing.

'She is asking me, this,' he sniggers behind me, already making a move to unknot himself, which turns me slightly to the side, 'because I've been married three times. A number that's set to rise!'

Everyone laughs again, and for a split second, Milo glances over his shoulder and we lock eyes almost as if by accident, and we're laughing together. And it feels so – normal. Nice. As it always was. I'm surprised by that; that in small, millisecond glimmers, it feels safe with him. Familiar. Like I'm sharing space with someone I've always known.

Jameson goes next – Milo asks him his favourite childhood memory, and as Jameson tells an anecdote about him and Milo getting trapped in an old greenhouse in a heatwave, all because he was hiding from a girl he fancied, I somehow now, in trying to shift myself from an uncomfortable position with Lars' leg somehow twisted around mine, have Jameson's arm across my chest. He is essentially hugging me from the side.

'Hello,' says Jameson. 'Kind stranger.'

'Hello,' I reply. 'Kind stranger.'

And he gives me the most shit-eating, enjoying-every-moment-of-this, schoolboy smile.

Iris takes her turn, confesses she went to a psychic once who told her she would marry a farmer she is still waiting for.

'Extra fact,' I comment, my arms stretched now, across the circle. 'His name was Sorcerer Duncan.'

Milo laughs loudly at what I say, which, despite myself makes me laugh too, and as we try to unknot, Jameson is now beside me, Polly has her back to us, and Milo is stuck hugging Iris, who has the total giggles. Poor Lars seems to be sinking to the ground. OK, perhaps this game was not the disastrous suggestion I initially thought it to be.

'All right, Mildred,' announces Jameson. 'Your turn. Uhhh, what's the . . . OK, OK, I've got it. What's the most romantic thing someone's ever done for you?'

Oh. I had not expected that at all. Nor how I'm interested, for some reason, to hear his answer.

'Jesus . . .' Milo laughs. 'Seriously?'

Jameson and Iris are both giggling. I'm so hot for some reason, I worry my head might explode. Mostly because it seems everyone – even Polly – has glanced over at me. Lars might, if he wasn't splayed out on the floor, all arms and legs, like a praying mantis.

'Um . . .' I glance up at him. He actually appears to be a little *embarrassed*. Shifting eyes, chewing the corner of his mouth.

'Maybe he has too many to choose from,' teases Polly.

'Maybe he has none,' I mutter under my breath.

'Sorry, did you say something?' Milo meets my eyes. He's two people over from me, an arm stretched across the circle. There's a tiny quirk of his mouth.

'I just . . . I have pins and needles, so can you just hurry up and answer.'

'Yes, do it for Allie,' says Jameson. 'I mean, she can answer if she feels she might know.'

Iris is now in a fit of giggles. Little shits, both of them.

'OK, OK,' says Milo. The circle falls quiet. 'I think it's got to be: she let me read her to sleep. And – yeah. It was . . . the best.'

He smiles, looks over at me. As everyone coos and swoons, I look away. There's a warm buzz travelling up my body and I don't even want to acknowledge it.

We unknot some more, and the group are suddenly freer, most facing outwards, but Milo and me . . . somehow, suddenly, we're in the centre of the circle, just inches between us, opposite each other.

A hand squeezes mine. Iris grins over at me. I squeeze back.

'Your turn,' Milo says, voice low, opposite me. The campfire crackles. Waves crash. This is quite unbearable. I want to run. Equally, I don't want to move from looking at him. His voice. His honeyed eyes. His mouth. Him.

'I've got one,' says Lars. 'What's your one-pass celebrity crush? You know. A celebrity you'd kiss if you could.'

Oh my *God*.

Lars is asking me this because of an inside joke. He once told me he paid £120 to meet Helen Mirren at Comic-Con and hoped she might fancy him. She didn't, but they had many photos taken together and she signed his cigarette lighter. I had then told him I didn't have celebrity crushes. Luckily Lars is just as oblivious to my viral moment as Polly. 'That's some crazy bullshit, Allie,' he'd insisted. 'Everyone has one!'

The circle falls quiet.

'Bloody hell, Lars,' I say, embarrassedly. 'I told you, I don't have one.'

'False!' shouts Lars. 'She's not telling the truth.'

'I am,' I say. 'I don't have celebrity crushes and Lars doesn't believe me.'

'Not even when you were younger?' asks Polly. 'When you were a teenager? Not wanted to plant one on one of . . . I don't know. The New Kids On The Block?'

'Ha. Bit before my time, Polls.'

Everyone stares at me. Milo's Adam's apple bobs. My face burns. Iris's hand squeezes mine, comfortingly.

'I . . . find it hard to fancy strangers,' I say. 'Or think about kissing them.'

Jameson laughs. 'OK, but what if they're a celebrity but not a stranger?'

The atmosphere is taut, like a stretched bow. The fire pops. Wind hums.

'Well,' I say, 'then that would change things. But – that wasn't the question.'

I look up to meet Milo's eyes, and his mouth lifts, in a tiny half-smile, eyes glinting with . . . something. My heart thump-thumps. Then, without waiting, I make a move, and then Lars apologises, says he has to move, too, regardless, because he has cramp, and we're unknotting again, people are laughing again, Lars straightening his arm and striding in front of me, and Jameson pulling Milo across the circle. The taut bow of an atmosphere, loose again.

We answer more questions.

Ice is broken.

When the game is over, I'm holding two hands. One is Polly's. The other, the one who squeezed mine, was Milo's.

Then

Extract from article on e-Paper: Love on the Rocks! Monogamous birds can actually divorce (seriously!) – a report by Gillian Goggins

. . . Scientist Alexandra Lake, a seabird biologist, recently reported that she was surprised to find two puffins from a colony in Svalbard, in other separate burrows, apart, for the first time in eight years.

'It's rare, but it's the same as in humans,' she explained. 'Promiscuity, for example, shows the other bird that their partner's commitment isn't rock-solid.' Long-distance migration also contributes: bird pairs arriving at destinations at different times. 'Trust and synchronicity,' Lake says. 'It's important to them. In the way it is to humans. We hope it's true love, but it doesn't always work out. Timing's off, trust is eroded . . .'

And what about Alexandra? Does her work help or hinder her own relationship with love? Does she take her work home with her? 'Ah,' she laughs. 'Well, I'm not as lucky as some of our lovely puffin couples! But I suppose I could say we've all at least been close once.'

Just once? 'Just the once for me. And that's the great thing about ecology and why it helps us understand ourselves. We're all connected. And everyone can relate to that right? Being close to becoming something with another, had the timing just been right, had the trust not been fractured . . .'

Chapter Eleven

Milo

The thing about Jameson? He sleeps. He sleeps any-where and *everywhere*. Constant, never-setting sun? Freezing cold tent, dressed in five layers? Potential polar bears? Yup. Jameson Merritt still sleeps. I'm guessing everyone is sleeping right now. Polly, Iris and Allie, on the other side of this plastic-sheeted wall. Beefcake Lars won't be – he's outside with a gun and flares on bear watch, making tea after tea by the fire. I keep hearing him clear his throat. I'm trying to join them in sleep, lying beside Jameson on a mattress, listening to nothing but his breathing and the waves outside, but this mat-tress is the same depth as a slice of bread and my eyes are like goddamn unblinking craters – to be expected, I guess, after a day of emotional boot camp.

We tried to talk it over, Jameson and I, when we came to bed, but we can't really talk without being overheard. We resigned to talking in mimes and hand gestures, fran-tic eyes and scrawling in the air.

'The chemistry!' Jameson mimed earlier. Then held up his camera, did the OK sign with his hand. *'Perfection naturelle.'*

I'd rolled my eyes at him.

But I get it.

There's a lot of . . . everything between Allie and me. Anger. Distrust. Shame. Especially since the dinghy. It's killing me. Do we really actually blame each other? Could it actually be that Allie didn't do it? And if she didn't, then what *really* happened back then?

And I feel it too, despite it all. Something that's warm. Something big and alive that I feel in my body like an energy of its own. An electrical charge. Something I could've sworn dissipated with the leak. Lifeforce, cut. But – it's still there. Like an old phone in a drawer you swear no longer works, but springs back into bright life when plugged in. That's how this feels. It was dormant until we came together again.

'Do you still like her?' Jameson whispered, and I shook my head.

'We keep arguing.'

'Oh, and that celebrity crush thing?' He fell back into his sleeping bag, laughing. 'Fuuuuck.'

I nudged him with my elbow. 'Shhhh!'

The Human Knot was – a lot. It definitely melted away some proverbial ice, but I probably shouldn't have said the reading thing. It's true though, and I think . . . I wanted her to know that. I want her to know that to me, for a moment, it was real. Regardless of what she chose to do with those moments, how real they were to her, I remember them – replay them in my mind sometimes, that night on the phone, like a favourite chorus. Then there was the way those innocent blue eyes found mine, through the haze of woodsmoke, when she answered her question, said, shyly, 'Well, that changes things.' A second-long pulse between us,

180

of a secret knowing. I squeezed her hand. She squeezed back. And maybe this is me just being a jackass who always feels like things'll work out, but I felt sure it might've been real to her too.

Jameson and I talked a little more – mostly about footage and tomorrow's shots, and about how much he 'bloody worships' Iris, then Jameson being Jameson grabbed the back of my head, said, 'Love you, bro' and mashed a kiss on my forehead. And that was that. Zipped-up sleeping bag, weighted eye mask: *See ya*. Out of it. Two sardines in a can, one dead to the world, one still writhing around, mouth throbbing from the hook.

I can't switch my brain off. It's like a darkroom in there, with a movie reel of everything Allie and I have talked about in the last twenty-four hours, spinning and spinning, and a single light, projecting them all.

The snowmobile was hard.

The boat was *really* hard. But illuminating. The publicist and that call she told me she didn't make. Allie blocking me for reasons that, if true, I totally understand.

And the human knot – holding her hand like that, and knowing it was hers I had in my grasp from the start . . .

And really, where do we go from here? I am totally crammed with questions.

Is it that she was responsible for the leak and she'll die trying to cover her ass, even though I would never *do* anything. Sue her. I decided way back then, I wouldn't ever do anything like that. For her. She was desperate. I was heartbroken, I was angry, but people do a lot when they're desperate, and I did not externally suffer because of it, Allie is right.

Or is it that . . . she didn't leak the messages? And for two years, we've each been consulting our own well-read but untrue lists of why each other is an asshole, crumpled and aged, but held onto, like goddamn evidence.

My crumpled list: the leaked screenshots were from her end. She said herself that she could do it 'for a much-needed few quid'. I'm not sure why exactly she'd have gone on record saying that to Iris, but it sounded like a joke between friends, and many a true word said in jest, right? Then there's Bermuda. Going from unfunded, to fully funded, within the same twenty-four hours the leak happened. An easy few grand for those messages, slid over like dirty money from some soulless gossip site. Not to mention, she told me she wanted her sister to know everything. The diaries saw to that. Then she blocked me. Talked about me publicly after saying she was a private person.

And if you were to look at Allie's list – let's say she didn't leak the messages and fully, ridiculously, suspects me, she'd say: I laughed about it on TV, even wore a meme T-shirt, and how goddamn callous. Allie would also say I was worried about my image (I was) and that I wanted people to know I was a good guy. (I did. Still do. Working on it.) She'd say the messages showed that. That all the cover shoots and interviews after proved I was basking in it, as planned.

But I would never have done that to her. A showmance. A tell-all interview. There are other ways, if she really believes that I'm the type of guy to do that. I would never have hurt her. I was *falling* for her—

'Milo?' A whisper. 'Milo, are you awake?'

'Yeah?' I whisper back.

It's Allie.

There's a tap on the sheet. It's directly next to me. Is she literally on the other side of this sheet? Jeez, that's close. Not even a half-inch of material separating us while we sleep. Aren't we technically sleeping next to each other? The thought makes me swallow.

'Tap back,' she whispers.

Despite myself, I tap back with the knuckle of my index finger. What is this?

'I'm here, Allie.'

'Hold on.'

There's silence.

Then – a weird rustling. And, under the sheet, through a tiny sliver of a gap, a note is slid through. Maybe it's her crumpled evidence list. Title: Milo Ford is an Asshole by Allie Lake.

I take it, unfold it, quietly. I can hear nothing except the paper in my hand, and the angry, sheet-metal roar of waves.

'I'll pretend I don't know you,' it says in black ink. 'Let's keep this to work. Keep our relationship out of it? A.' There's a single 'x' too.

A smile spreads across my lips. Polly's Human Knot story – she had to work with someone she used to date, she said, so wrote her ex a note.

I stare at the writing. Small, looping. 'Our relationship.' There it is again. That *something* deep and low in my gut. That hot, electrical surge. Is she feeling the same as me? Did that whack to the piñata have her thinking all the same things as me? Is this where the pages of the story come apart at the spine? And if it is, what's the truth? What's the real story?

I lean to Jameson's backpack at our feet, unzip a pocket at the front, take out one of his sharpies. Blue.

'At least you got the note to the right guy,' I write. Then 'Deal. M x'. And I'm sure it's cool to send an 'x' back. It's not like it's meant as a *real* kiss, right? Brits love an 'x' as a sign-off.

I post it back.

Chapter Twelve

Allie

Today will be better. This is something I'm chanting silently to myself this morning, as I stand outside the tent. It has to be better. I've been given no choice – I've been told off by Iris. Something that rarely happens, but when it does, it must be heeded. Because Iris never disagrees with me unless I *am* in the wrong in some way, and that means – like always – she's probably right.

Last night, I'd laid down in my sleeping bag and, as Polly snored, Iris had turned to look at me – her head twisting in her bed like a haunted doll.

'What is it?' I'd whispered.

Her eyes went wide and she looked over at slumbering Polly. 'She asked me what was going on,' whispered Iris. 'She worried there was something she was missing. That, I don't know, Milo had upset you or was making you uncomfortable—'

'Oh, shit.'

'I know.'

Then she'd reached over and pushed hair out of my eyes, gently. The gesture, after the intensity of the day with Milo, almost made me cry.

'Look. This was always going to be a bit of a reckoning. You know? This knobhead that allegedly did the unthinkable.' Iris often says allegedly about Milo. It annoys me normally. Last night, it didn't so much. 'But you've got to be professional, Allie. It's quite obvious you two are . . . at loggerheads. Or obsessed with each other.'

I put my middle finger up at her when she said that.

'But just – try to get along with him. Try to push this aside, yeah? Polly's Polly, but she's essentially your boss, mate. Don't let this . . . *thing* overshadow your job.'

And I knew she was right. You'd have to be pretty brainless to not pick up on the fact that there was *something* amiss yesterday between Milo and me. So, Iris passed me some paper, I dug out a biro, and I wrote what Polly had said during the game – Iris said she wouldn't be surprised if that story was for my benefit. Within minutes, I'd passed it to Milo and he'd passed it back, and Iris had fallen asleep like she always does – like someone turned off at the mains.

It helps that we have a lot to do today, here on Cote Rock. On today's itinerary is checking on my little auk colony on the south-side, conducting an observation, then checking for egg presence. Iris will be collecting samples from that end of the island too, Jameson will have various things to film, and Polly and Lars will be staying at camp together. As for Milo, he'll be shadowing me.

I'm always better when I have a quest.

I'm always better when I have my work to immerse myself in.

That's the best thing about this job. There is always a quest, a mission – and a mission that's more important than just me.

*

'So, where're the pancakes around here?'

There it is. A ridiculous, bad joke delivered with that charming smile of his and a croaky, deep morning voice. My first post-note test. To keep this to work; to act as if Milo is someone I met just yesterday. Polly falls for it. She laughs, touches Milo's jacketed arm with a motherly hand.

'Oh, it's energy bars, instant coffee and a little Arctic air instead here, I'm afraid, Milo.'

'Arctic air. They probably charge three hundred dollars for that in the city.' He grins, takes a cereal bar from Polly's hand, and thanks her (a flurry of ma'ams and thank yous and awesomes. *Charm charm charm).*

We're standing just outside the tents, in brilliant morning sunshine. Steam rises from the ground; the large white sun thawing the hardened ice at our feet, and just a little way from us, Iris crouches next to a fire with Jameson; she's chatting to him and he's nodding, listening intently, camera videoing the fire. She pours from a metal camping teapot; the familiar ding of metal spout on metal camping mugs resonating in my gut. Iris always makes me tea, every morning. Regardless of whether we're at the station, or in the field. It's one of my favourite parts of the day. Something about that first sip. Slowly waking me up. I can't put up with much until that first sip . . .

'Good morning, sunshine,' Milo squints over at me. Another test. Post-note but pre-first-tea. He's standing, open-shouldered, an arm as a visor against the sun, head cocked to one side. His hair is full bed head. Glossy and thick, all hands-just-run-through-it. Exactly how it was on our very first debrief video call, sleepy and bare-chested . . .

I pretend not to hear him. I know we said professional, but *sunshine*?

'I *said* good morning, sunshine,' he repeats as Iris and Jameson join us.

'Oh, sorry, you're talking to me?' I say. 'Good morning, *Milo*.'

Polly chuckles nervously.

Iris watches us, hands me my tea. I can almost hear her, as if via telepathy, 'Remember the rules, amigo.'

'And how'd you sleep, Allie?' he asks. 'It was Allie, wasn't it? I'm so lousy with names.'

I freeze – is he having a laugh? I blow into the mug, steam unspooling like ribbon into the air. 'Like the dead,' I reply. 'You?'

'Wish I could say I also slept like the dead. Like a . . . polar bear got me? The gunwoman on my team, fast asleep . . .' He grins and I can't help but smile. I press my lips together to try to stifle it, but it comes unwanted. Polly seems delighted I'm not scowling. 'But, unfortunately, yeah,' he says, as if to the group, 'characteristically, classically *bad*.'

'Aww,' coos Polly. 'Poor you, Milo.'

He looks very bright for someone who has been awake all night, though. Probably all that . . . what is it celebrities do? Botox? Collagen? Beef fat? My sister used to swear by some sort of beef fat. Maybe still does. Ugh, and is it silly that sometimes I would give anything to know the answer to whether she uses bloody beefy skincare or not? I miss Sian. A lot. We

188

had a stifled phone call last month – I called her at
the holiday camp she's working at in Norfolk – but,
as always, since the leak and leaving the cottage, she
seemed to want to get me off the phone fast. My heart
hurts when I think about her. The themed breakfasts.
Clive. Even her gnome. It was all so misplaced, but
she was trying. She was grieving too. And I've offered
many apologies. She's just not ready to accept them.

'I'm used to no sleep,' Milo carries on.

'Really?' asks Polly.

'Unfortunately.'

'An insomniac, then?' I ask, pointedly, and he smirks
at me, bites into his energy bar.

'Mhm,' he speaks between chews. 'Always awake.
Sometimes panicking. Sometimes reading obscure novels.'

And despite myself, that sends a little thrill zig-zagging
through me. *Stupid.* I'm only doing this to show Polly and
Iris I'm trying, so why is my bloodstream full of lightning
bolts? But this is what has always been the hardest. Worse
than the whole leak thing, the whole betrayal of interviews and memes and screenshots from *my* phone and
cold publicists, is that I know Milo. Or thought I did.
Or, maybe, know parts of him that *are* real. I know he
doesn't sleep. I know coffee shop ambience helps him drift
off because his mum always held dinner parties downstairs and he'd fall asleep, listening. I know he has hob-
bies he's too afraid to say aloud – crafts. Karaoke. Words.
Even I still collect words because of him . . . Pernoctate.
That's one I learned last week. Means 'to stay up or out
all night'. And what are you supposed to do with all that
fondness? All that *like* that feels like a ball of energy that

can't be dispersed. It's why I was so sure the leak had been a mistake. A crime even.

Until the publicist.

Until the audience, laughing. What felt like the whole world, laughing. Then the fallout. My old university, in Gloucester, asking me to take some time out, that the attention they were getting, that the Bermuda project was getting, was making a mockery of it. They'd received donations, for the funding, but I had to sit it out. Then, my sister. Dad finding us. Us having to face him again. Sober now. Yet another new family now. Transformed, apparently, but not quite enough to not want what he was owed from June House. A polar winter, alone . . .

'Allie?'

I clear my throat. 'Yes. Sorry?'

'Would you . . .' Milo moves in. 'Leak break? *Partner*.'

Leak. Is he joking? 'Oh. Yeah.'

And now, another test: we have to accompany each other to the bathroom.

On fieldwork like this, we have to get creative. A bathroom becomes a 'section' of the island. We erect what's essentially a windbreaker, and we 'go' behind there. There are bottles of water there too, for cleaning our teeth, and the rules are, we can't do anything unless a partner is nearby, within reason, with a rifle and bear-scaring flares. This is the kind of thing that has lit a fire behind Jameson's wide, hazel eyes. Everything is different. From the landscape and the total absence of night, to toilets and teeth brushing. Iris must've recorded at least an hour of conversation with him last night, as I hid in the tent and pretended to sleep early.

We crunch along. The gun taps, taps, against the zip of my jacket pocket with my step, like a steady beat. I'm trying to think of how to start. Of what to say, now it's just us two.

Nice. I promised Iris I'd be nice . . .

'Thank you for the note,' says Milo. Of course he speaks first. Milo always does. Decent opener too.

'Yes. I . . . wanted to apologise,' I say. 'Because when you said about being professional, on the dinghy, that was . . . the smart suggestion. And the right one.'

He nods. 'I'm glad you think so.'

'So, we keep this professional?'

'Yeah,' says Milo. 'Keep it to the doc. The work.'

'Exactly.'

'Because this is not exactly a warm and comforting place to start extracting confessions and truths—'

'I don't have any confessions,' I jump in.

Milo stops, and replies, warmly, 'We said professional, right?'

'Yes. Sorry. OK. Agreed. Plus,' I say. 'You're an actor, right?'

'Right,' he smiles, slowly.

'So, I'm sure, between us, we can just pretend it didn't happen. That we're strangers, just for the next three days. Well, actually, I suppose we sort of are. Factually speaking, we never properly met.'

'No?'

'No.'

'Hmm.' Suddenly, Milo swings around and looks at me. Intense liquid-brown eyes, the edges narrowed. A total, total smoulder, worthy of a magazine cover. He strides in front of me, boots crunching on icy sand. 'Hello.' He holds out a hand.

'Um. H-hello?'

He leans in, voice low and raspy, as if telling a secret. 'I'm in character, Allie. As Milo who doesn't know you at all.'

'*Oh*. Oh, OK—'

'My name's Milo. It's so nice to meet you.' His voice is low and husky; like he's slipped into some sort of smooth, sultry version of himself. 'And you are?'

I stare at him and then can't help it – another smile takes over my face. I don't even try to stop it. He takes my hand, eyes fixed on mine, all caramel and concentration.

'Hi, Milo. I'm Allie. Allie Lake. It's nice to meet you too.'

He shakes my hand then, squeezing a little, and I realise it's the first time I've ever touched him, skin to skin. Last night, even if one of the hands *was* Milo's, there were gloves between us. All that intimacy, all that closeness back then, and yet, this is the first time. And despite myself, I can't help the goosebumps.

'Great,' he says. Then he releases my hand; drops it as if it's a hot rock, and tucks his hands into his pockets. 'I mean, you could work on your fluidity. Really embodying the fictional circumstance, you know?'

'I thought I was fine.' And I'm trying to pretend I'm not just a *little* wounded by his critique.

'Fine doesn't win awards.' Then he laughs, a wonky slice of white teeth. 'But yeah, feels better. Right?'

'Yeah.'

'Like . . . the prana feels better.'

'*The prana*,' I repeat, and he grins slowly.

'Oh, I'm still so down with the prana.' And the grin irritates and amuses me all at once.

I'm not just going to forget, I want to say. *This is just an arrangement. A note.* But, instead, I gesture to the makeshift bathroom.

'Off you go then,' I tell him. 'I'll stand by with the bear scarers. Then we need to make a move.'

Over my shoulder, I meet Polly's eyes. She smiles.

'Why, what's today's plan?' calls Milo.

'An hour hike,' I say. 'To check on auk nests. We need to climb a cliff.'

'Uh, who needs to climb a cliff?'

'Us,' I tell him. 'Me and you. *Partner.*'

Then

THE STOUGHT STAR – HISTORIC JUNE HOUSE
UP FOR SALE

Only two years since its launch, June House, a local boutique bed and breakfast, will be closing its doors. Owners and sisters, Allie and Sian Lake, inherited the farmhouse from their mother and have spent the last two years turning it into a thriving business in the heart of Stought, which has over 200 five-star Trip Advisor ratings, but it is now up for sale with local estate agency, Waller and White. The cottage is a grade two listed building and has a rich history, dating back to 1765, and was once the second home of famous modern sculptor, Elizabeth Willings. It goes on sale with a starting price of £549,000 and the website boasts a 3D tour for interested buyers.

'It was a wonderful childhood home for me and my sister and will always hold happy, safe memories for us,' owner Allie told the Star. 'But unfortunately, a recent change in circumstances means we can no longer keep it. We knew this moment would come someday, but it feels somewhat premature and both of us are truly devastated to let it go.'

Viewings can be booked by calling Bradley at Waller and White.

Chapter Thirteen

Milo

Looking for bird eggs doesn't exactly sound like hard work, but, as default, I'm finding anything out here hard work. This shit is tough. I've just finished a movie that I had to train really hard for – six hours a day in the gym, nothing but eggs for meals – but this is a different kind of – what's the word? *Endurance.* Yeah. Perfect word for it. Endurance. We're running on little sleep, it's endlessly cold, we're weighed down in these bulky, heavy clothes and there's nothing here. No people. No familiar sound of planes in the air, no distant traffic. And the sun . . . It's like the day never truly ends and we just have to pretend it has, with shutters and eye masks and obeying the digits of someone's watch.

We've been walking, so far, for almost an hour. Allie and me, Iris and Jameson, and we're only just coming to a stop, right by the crashing, foaming ocean and a teetering rocky cliff, grassy and snow-covered, that seems to stretch into the clouds, scaly, like a dragon. Jameson and Iris crouch ahead of us, investigating what looks like a pile of rocks, Jameson in his own version of heaven, gazing through the camera lens more than he's looking through his actual eyeballs, quizzing Iris as if she's in a chair on a late-night talk show. They make a great fieldwork duo, both of them so relaxed, they're basically lying on invisible magic carpets, floating through their lives.

Allie stands a few feet away, watching, surveying all the time, soaking it all in. Every now and then, she'll see something in the air as we walk, and the tiniest quirk of her mouth tells me she's seen something she likes. Her whole face transforms; eyes softening, pink mouth lifting. It's like . . . even her skin brightens? Like, now. She's got binoculars at her eyes, and she's nibbling her bottom lip and her skin damn-near *glows*—

'What?' She's dropped the binoculars and she's looking at me. 'What're you looking at?'

I swallow away a laugh. 'Nothing, just . . . why is Iris so interested in rocks?' I manage to deflect.

'It's what's beneath them that she's interested in.'

'Ah. Bugs?'

'Yes, bugs,' she says. 'And bacteria. We can tell a lot from the bacteria that survives here, in the climate, in the circumstances.'

'But . . . Is it stupid to ask why?'

'No, not stupid,' she says, brightening. 'I suppose you could say, you're just as much as what's under that rock as you are a man standing in front of me. We're all connected.'

And right now, I wish I could slip the little handheld camera out of my backpack, film her speaking, her serious eyes, her creamy skin, freckly under the high, blue sky. She has no idea how interesting she is, how photogenic . . .

But no. I'm not about to pull a camera out on her. Especially Allie Lake. And Allie Lake with *a shotgun*.

I'm grateful we're here and not stuck in yesterday, though, with the atmosphere you could slice, like a razorblade through an apple, every word, every look, like an edge of chipped glass. This is better. It's awkward, of course. A whole cloud between us full of words I keep wanting to take a pin to, let them rain down on us, once and for all. I want her to tell me again that she didn't do it. But Allie has even smiled at me today, and damn – it's nice to see that smile. So, for the time being, we'll obey the note – well, try – and the words will stay there, for now, caught, like fish in a net.

'*Allie?*' calls Iris. She's shrugging off a backpack, dropping it at her feet.

'Uh-huh?'

'I think this is the one,' she says. 'I'm happy to stay here, collect some samples. Then you guys can . . .' Her sentence dissolves and Allie holds a hand up in a wave.

Jameson swoops the camera around and gets us both in shot.

'No,' Allie calls simply, assertively. 'No camera on me, please. I don't want to be in the shot.'

'Sorry, Allie,' calls Jameson, giant Pac-man grin. 'Really sorry. I'll cut you out!'

I don't mean to, but a laughs fall out of my mouth.

'Sorry?' Allie twists to look at me.

'Nothing,' I say. 'S-sorry.' My ego, of course, wants to ask: would it be so bad, being photographed with me? My old self wants to ask why it would be so bad when she was quite happy to publicise our conversations? But I know that's unfair. Especially since I'm now slowly, slowly not so sure that's even the truth. Which is . . . beyond crazy. I've

197

lived for two years believing she did this. For two years, I've been walking around with that as a hard, real, horrible truth.

Allie stares at me, taken aback, but says nothing.

But I guess I feel defensive for Jameson too. We're here to do a job. We're here to make a video. We could really help. And she's so self-sufficient, I don't think she believes it.

'We need to go up there.' Allie gestures to the cliff casually. 'We need to be on lookout, so we should gain some height. I need to conduct an observation of my auks from a distance too.'

'What? What do you mean we need to go *up there*?' I gaze slowly, up to the cliff.

'It's where my auk burrows are,' she explains.

'Up there?' God. It'll be like scaling a dragon's *back*.

'It looks worse than it is,' she says. 'Plus, this one goes up in stages. See. Mound by mound? We just need to be at the top of this first mound to be on lookout.'

But that first mound is the height of a suburban house, I want to exclaim.

'Uhh. OK?' I say instead.

Heights. Jameson told me that, apart from the chopper, there would be no heights. I *hate* heights.

'If you don't stop, if you just keep your eyes focused on the top, keep going, no hesitation, it's easy. The studs in the boots will help. Short strides, light feet . . .'

She steps away from the mound, and positions herself like an athlete does, to get a run-up.

'We're going now? I . . . I'm no free-runner, Allie. Like – do we not have equipment?'

'No,' she says simply. 'And you don't need to be a free-runner for something like this, you just need some ba—' She stops, clears her throat. 'You just need to go for it.'

'Were you just going to say . . . *balls*?'

'Perhaps,' Allie replies.

'Huh. Well, balls I have, Allie. Last time I checked, which was this morning, so . . .'

She doesn't give anything away. Her face: neutral. 'OK, so you'll be able to do it, then, won't you?'

'I'm uh . . . I'm . . .' *afraid of heights*, I finish in my head, but I just can't say it out loud.

Then, like she hears my thoughts, she drops her hand down to her side, tears off a glove, and holds out her hand to me. I stare at it. Not falling for that one again.

'We'll go together. You won't stop if you think you'll take someone else down with you. So . . .' She shakes her hand, as if I need help locating it.

'Well, forgive me for not taking it right away,' I tell her. 'Last time I did that, the girl recoiled like my hand was a spider crab. Happened on a snowmobile. Recently actually.'

Her shoulders sag.

'Just . . .' Allie grabs my hand. 'Short strides. Light feet. Focus on the top.'

Something tightens low, low down in my body when she squeezes my hand; warm skin, fingers tight, entwined. Then she says, 'Go,' and we do.

Short strides, light feet, focus. Short strides, light feet, focus. Her hand grasps mine, and it steadies me. It's steep and windy, and I don't look down, concentrating only on Allie's hand. And, of course, she's right. It takes no time at all, and suddenly, we're at the top.

Whoa. We're – OK, we're high. My heart feels like it's been attached to a car battery. But it definitely looked worse than it was. I probably rolled down hills this high when I was in kindergarten, right?

And man – the view.

'Jeez . . .'

'I know,' says Allie softly. We both seem to notice, at the exact same moment, that we're still holding hands. We drop them in unison.

Stretches of mountain, grey-teal, like paintbrush-water, ice cascading the glaciers like that thick powdered sugar you get on funnel cake at carnivals. The type you scoop onto your finger and dissolve on your tongue from the bottom of the bag. It's the sort of view that makes you want to write, boil it down into words. Take a photo. That yearning to document something; hold onto it. Encapsulate it. The illusion that you can create something better, or just as good as the moment itself, so you can always access it. But, of course, you can't. It's the present moment, right? That's what all the gurus and therapists say. It's the now that matters. This view, this silence. This great sky. Me and Allie. Just our ragged breaths, our beating hearts . . .

I look over at her.

She's oblivious, looking too, at the stretch of everything in front of us, mouth open, the corners of her pink lips upturned just a little into a quiet smile. I wanted to kiss Allie Lake more than I wanted air once – ah, shit.

But I can't help it. I liked this woman so deeply and now she's right beside me. Where do you even begin? What do you even say? Because I want to say so much. I've written this woman a thousand letters in my head, written *poems* about her, for God's sakes; I've also imagined angry conversations with her, full of how could yous and why me—

'Milo,' she says. 'Is this one of your silences? *If you leave a silence, people fill it,*' she mimics with a smile.

'Well, if it was, it just worked on you. For the first time.' I laugh. 'And no. No, not this time. You seem pretty content to be silent, so I'm . . . *behaving* myself.'

'That might be so,' she says. 'But, also, you're not here to be silent, remember? You're here to do a job, and I'm doing mine, so you should feel free to do yours – whatever that turns out to be.'

'Ouch?' I straighten. '*Whoa*. Damn. Not said that in . . . two years?'

She, smirks, bringing binoculars to her eyes. I don't know how she can look into those things. I like my eyes right on the floor up here – a little memo to the brain that it's all good, we have steady ground beneath our feet.

'I know you don't agree with what we're doing,' I say. 'The doc.'

She breathes out, drops the binoculars. 'It's not that. I just think there are other ways, I suppose, without—'

'Two dickhead celebrities attached?'

'*Two* dickheads?' she deadpans.

It almost gets me – I almost apologise for being unprofessional, saying dickheads. 'Ah. You mean you can only see one, right? Ouch. Again.'

For a while, we say nothing. Allie watches birds, scrawls in a notebook – rough flight traffic numbers, she says distractedly, as she observes, serious, counting in her head. And up here, high up, adrenaline pulsing, that part of me that's untethered, all heart and no logic, has gathered. I sort of want to reach out and gently push her hair behind her ear. I want to be closer to her. And yeah, yeah, what about the professional agreement? What about *everything*? That part is still there too, shaking its judgemental head at me. But right now, it's weaker than the brainless animal part that wants to be near her, finally. Touch the soft skin of her face, run my thumb across her jaw, her bottom lip—

A bird cries above us, and I recognise it, by the call. And before I've even thought about it, the excitement of it, of recognising the sound, takes over. 'Ivory gull,' bursts out of me.

'Huh?'

I follow it across the sky. 'All the white. Ivory gull.'

I tip my face away from the sky. Allie is gazing at me, pink lips parted. 'That *is* an ivory gull,' she says, practically beaming, despite herself. 'That's . . . *Well done*.'

'Ha. Yeah.' I smile. 'I'm more of a bird guy than I was, I guess?'

Because of you, I want to say. I read about them because of you, never scroll by a picture of them, still check the cameras. But I don't. Instead, I wave back to Jameson, who's filming the horizon, down on the ground.

'Does it feel less scary now? Being out here?' I ask her.

'Yes,' she replies, thoughtfully. 'Probably the opposite now. It's one of the only places I feel genuinely safe.'

And now I leave an intentional silence. Something warm pools in her eyes, like a dawn sun, and I will for it to stay there. It's like I've put in the right combination code; drawbridge lowering.

'It's like . . . awful things can happen. Hearts break. People leave, people die, you lose things, and I can feel totally alone, but this . . . it just continues. I think . . . I think it's the only thing I depend on.'

And there she is.

Allie.

Captain Lake.

This is the Allie I met. This is the Allie who lives in my head. This gun-wielding, seagull obsessed ('there's no such thing as a seagull really, Milo'), stubborn, gorgeous genius. This is who I worried wasn't real. But it's her. And if it's her, was it this Allie who smashed my heart open like a crab apple on the highway? Is it possible I really was wrong? Is there something else – someone else – to blame?

'Is there nothing for you to depend on back home?' I ask. 'On earth.'

'I don't know,' she says, quietly.

Down below, Iris and Jameson laugh, the sound carried on the wind.

'What about you?' she asks.

'On earth? Ah, man,' I sigh. 'Uh – work, firstly? It's the North Star of my life, I guess. Just – being able to chip away at humanity. Find another layer you didn't know existed in you because you stepped into the soul of this other person. Getting at what it is to be a person in the world.' I look up at Allie and she smiles at me. 'But

I used to think other things were the work. Everything outside of myself, I guess? That's the shit you shouldn't depend on.'

'Like?' asks Allie.

'Accolades. Parts. Reviews. Photos. Cash. If this director thinks this, and that co-star has that. My damn hair. Fuckin' . . . *jackets* . . .' I laugh. 'It's kind of why we wanted to do this. Be somewhere none of that truly matters. Create something *where* none of that matters.'

'Mm,' she nods. 'Nobody cares about you here. I meant . . . the birds. The things that live under rocks, of course.'

'Sure. The *ivory gulls* are what you meant.'

Allie smiles then, carries on watching, writing things down, and I watch Jameson setting up a tripod. And right now, I feel like – it's worth it. If someone had told me I'd be thinking this yesterday on the dinghy, I'd have laughed. But all of it feels worth it – the heights. The aching legs. Cold-cold bones. The bad camp food. Even the confused throb of sitting here so close to Allie but feeling a whole solar system apart from her. She used to fall asleep next to me. She used to send me photos – selfies and those whacko breakfast props and themed clothes Sian bought . . .

'How's your sister?' I promised myself I wouldn't try to catch up, but it's like a drug or something. The more she shows me, the more we talk, the more I want to know. The greedier I get.

But instantly, I wish I hadn't asked. If asking her about this place was the right combination, this was the wrong one. She looks at her lap. 'Um, she's . . . She has a job at a camp now. A holiday camp? Has her own caravan there. She works a lot. Entertainment, lifeguarding, all that.'

'She lives there?' The diary. The diary floats to the top of my mind like scum I wish would dissolve. It appeared to just be found, by fans, hours after the leak. Published in a public drive under Allie's name. It's another thing on my crumpled evidence list – another thing that made me totally sure I'd been screwed over by Allie. Because she used to talk about showing Sian the diary because they found it hard to talk these days, stopping the whole bed and breakfast venture. The themed mornings. The gnomes. How Sian was bad at talking and so was she. 'Wow, so . . . the bed and breakfast. The farmhouse . . .'

'June House.'

'Yeah. That's it. You're . . . so it's done?'

She looks at me sharply. 'Done?'

'No, I just meant . . . I know you hated it and—'

'It was a bit more complicated than hating it, Milo. I didn't hate the house, I just . . .' She stares out across the sea, runs her fingers the wrong way along a small white feather in her lap. 'We sold it. We had to. Dad found out. He wanted his share. He found us,' she says that simply. That short, emotionless way old pain sometimes sounds when spoken. 'The leak . . . I don't know, I guess he got wind of it. He found out about the house. It's distinctive. My grandad – his dad – lied and said he'd sold it to pay off business debt, but really, he signed it over to Mum before he died. He was always so apologetic for Dad and everything he did. Dad went to a solicitor, he had an inheritance claim, and . . . that was it. We had to sell it to pay him off.'

Shit. The list – the list is practically ash now. Because how could she have been behind the leak? It's one thing upending my life, but upending her own?

She fiddles more with the silky white feather in her hands. She looks so sad. I think of the beams behind her as we'd video chat. The way her face was always lit by warm, brandy-coloured light. All those weird plants behind her. All the things she told me about her mom. The way her mother had wanted it to be a kind of retreat; free rooms for families who needed it. I loved the idea. Hated how sad and tired her sister's vision of it seemed to make Allie.

'God, Allie. I'm sorry—'

'And I know you think that's what I wanted. I talked about it a lot, I know. I'm sure you feel like the leak was a . . . *blessing* in some way to me.'

'Allie, I would never—'

'And I thought it's what I wanted. To be free of it. June House was just . . . It became a sad place to be after Mum.' She clears her throat, shakes her head. Anger glistens in her eyes. 'But now I just feel like I failed her. I should've got over my grief enough to find a way to make it work, somehow, for all of us. I should've made it a success. Told him, up front, found a way to pay him off. Kept it.'

'You were grieving, Allie—'

'At least Sian tried though,' she continues. 'However misguided. I just – *sulked*. Moaned about it all. And now it's gone completely. And if I thought we didn't talk before, now it's . . . so much worse.'

I feel like I've been kneed in the gut.

'Allie, I'm really sorry.' And before I even consider what I'm doing, my hand lands on hers and I hold it. She freezes, like someone turned her to stone all of a sudden. I retract it. Stupid. That was really stupid. I look at her. 'Allie . . . You . . . Do you really – *really* – think I leaked the phones?' I want to ask her if she did it, but she looks so sad, I can't possibly put her under the spotlight of that question. And sitting here with her, I think I feel sure that . . . she didn't do it. Jeez. Am I saying that? Really? So, now what? If it wasn't Allie, how did it happen?

She doesn't speak. She hesitates and does the tiniest shake of a nod.

'I didn't,' I say. 'I didn't.'

Allie stares at me.

I can barely breathe.

'The day we completed the sale,' she says, shakily, 'was the day your magazine cover came out. The *XN Mag* cover.'

I close my eyes.

The cover. The topless one with the damn roses. The viral cover that finally got me clean. Seeing it staring back at me at a bodega as I bought beer. In the line for the register, a stray tuxedo cat at my feet, I stared at my own face on the rack, and suddenly, I wanted to die. It was like my chest had been hollowed out. I missed Allie. I missed myself – whoever that even was. I put the beer back and called Jameson outside, in the pouring rain. Nobody but him knows about it.

'Allie, I'm . . . I'm sorry, but I was not good, I—'

'And also, on Instagram,' she cuts in again. She's talking like she's a faucet, finally twisted open. 'Posting photos of the stupid memes of our messages.'

'I know,' I say. 'I was . . . screwed, Allie. I was hurt.'

'You seemed just fine,' she says. 'You know, even if I was to suspend my disbelief and believe somehow you didn't do it, I just kept coming back to those things. If he was innocent, a victim, he would not do those things. And you did. And you *seemed just fine.*'

'I wasn't.'

'From what I saw—'

'From what you *saw.* But that's not real, Allie. It's TV. It isn't who I am or *was.* And you – you talked to a live audience. What about that?'

'I'm sorry,' she says. 'I . . . I felt I couldn't walk out. And I didn't think I wanted to be heard, but I realised I did. I *did.* Because I didn't do it.'

'Neither did I!'

And then her eyes widen even more, and she stares past me. Ugh, I shouldn't have said that. She now looks like she might actually kill me – but then she stands.

'Down!' she shouts below.

And a huge bang erupts.

Chapter Fourteen

Allie

Milo and I are not talking.

We tried.

We really tried.

But it seems to always ends up the same. And ever since our latest conversation came to its dramatic close – since I fired a flare into the sky to frighten off a polar bear that turned out to be, in my stress and hypervigilance, a distant weirdly shaped mound of snow – it's safe to say, things have been pretty awful between us. The atmosphere so thick, it is basically slime.

Just moments ago, Jameson and Iris decided to turn back to camp with samples they'd collected, and it was time to check in on my auks. And Milo, no longer speaking to me, has no choice but to come with me.

First, because, as demonstrated, we must travel in pairs. (See: near bear miss.)

Second, because neither of us particularly wants to show the rest of the team we're arguing. Even if Iris and Jameson would be unsurprised if we were back to being bickering enemies, Polly and Lars don't appear to have a clue about anything that's ever happened between us, so, it's a stand-off, I suppose you'd call it. Of who can look the most normal and the most professional and the most grown-up. And all while we begin to slowly ascend the cliff, heading for a closer look at my little auks, who are oblivious to the fact that drama has arrived on their little islet. We came. We swore. We accused. And then I fired a flare to stop us all getting killed (although I'm sure Milo thinks it was a dramatic way to stop the conversation entirely, and maybe it was, but only in a very subconscious way).

Now we crunch across the slippery melting terrain together, mutedly. The wind has picked up a little, oohing like a distant choir, but everything else is so silent, I can hear my own pulse. Milo is doing everything he can to avoid looking at me.

Good. *Good*. The feeling is mutual. *Very* mutual. I can't wait for these days with him to be over. How dare he compare his endless interviews and memes to my singular podcast episode that was meant to be about *puffins*?

'It gets a bit tighter up here,' I say instead, keeping things professional.

We stop.

I glance up the side of the cliff. 'There's a vague path,' I say, turning back to him. 'So, it's fine. It's just steep for a little while.'

'You sure you don't just need some balls?' he asks, humourlessly, but his voice wobbles, his lips pale.

'Milo, are you OK?'

'Dandy.'

I ignore him.

'Are you . . .' I start but stop myself. 'I'd say you don't have to come with me but—'

'But you have the gun. I know.'

'Yes. I have the gun.' I stand back, look up at the cliff, assess.

'And you'd rather I didn't die by bear attack, right?' he asks.

'I'm concentrating.'

'Because if you're ambivalent, just say. I'll wait here. Take my chances.'

I sigh again. I knew he wouldn't be able to keep up with leaving the silences silent for long. He just can't help himself. His brain is like an overflow car park.

'Right.' I slip off my backpack. I fish out a paracord I packed to tie down equipment. 'Let's try something. I might have something that helps . . . those who prefer being on the ground . . .'

'You mean, those with a fear of heights?'

'Yes.' And I feel slightly guilty now, about the impatience (and the balls comment). I hadn't realised he was really afraid.

He sighs, eyes closing, deflating with a huff of 'fuck' under his breath. 'I'm chicken shit, right? That's what you're thinking.'

I steady myself on the cliffside, slip my bag back on my back, the cord in my hand. 'Nope. I think you're normal.'

'Bold statement.'

'From an evolutionary standpoint,' I explain. 'Acrophobia means you'd have been most likely to survive way back when.'

Milo's eyebrows knit together. His wavy brown hair is wild today with the sea air. Perfectly messily tangled and twisted. It's annoying how handsome he is. And it's annoying how much I notice, too, even though I feel I shouldn't. Although, that moment on the cliff – the *'I didn't'*. I keep thinking about it. Because right then, I really think I did believe him. And if I did, what does that even mean now for us? That there's another person out there who did this?

'So, what, I'd have been a smart caveman?' snorts Milo.

'Yes,' I tell him, holding out one end of the cord. 'Anyway. We'll hold this. It's a paracord. Walking together, holding onto something like this, me in front, helps with balance—'

'I have balance.'

'It'll make you feel safer, though,' I tell him. 'It'll give you stability.'

'I have stability,' he says. 'I had to climb, like, *ten* ladders in my last job—'

'Milo.' I stop wrapping the cord around my hand. 'Just – be a good caveman and take the cord. OK?'

He says nothing and just follows me, all cocky, I've-got-better-places-to-be attitude.

He is as good as stomping up the steep path behind me . . .

'Shit!' Milo growls.

'Are you OK?'

'I just . . . slipped,' he grunts. 'I'm fine.'

'The ground is looser up here, but we're almost there. Just go slowly—'

'I am.'

'You're stomping like a toddler.' My muttered words are lost on the wind.

'What did you just say?'

'Just – be more careful,' I say, and he does nothing more than huff.

We carry on walking, steadily, carefully, both of our hands holding the purple cord, tight and taut. I hear him sigh heavily behind me, like I'm pulling him up a cliff to a mountain-jail.

I've been counting down the *weeks* to this, to checking in on my colonies, filling the well in my chest with *good,* and now, I have a sulker behind me—

'God!'

From beneath my foot, scree and pebbles shift and cascade and it's my turn now. I slip backwards. Pointlessly, I grip onto the cord. A strangled, pathetic yelp bursts out of me. I shoot out a hand to steady myself on the rock, but . . .

Milo is there.

Right behind me.

Grabs me.

Solid.

I'm pressed against him, and through the padding of our coats, I can still feel his chest hard and strong against my shoulder blades. His arms cocoon me, like a bear hug. We stand still, against each other, on the narrow cliff path. Our chests rise and fall in unison. You slip a lot out here – it's inevitable. But for a second, this time, I don't want to move.

'You all right?' he asks, breathlessly. He's so close, mouth against my ear. Warm breath tickles my cheek. And . . . We just stay there, pressed against each other, his face next to mine, mere inches away, his body enveloping mine. Waves roar in the distance. Wind blows around us. Stones skitter, skydiving down to the ground. Something churns in me. Familiarity. A warm shiver . . .

I nod. 'Yes. I . . . I slipped too.'

'No shit.'

I reach a hand out to the damp rock, pull myself to steadiness. Milo doesn't move behind me. I can smell him. He smells like salt. He smells like whatever deep, spiced deodorant spray he used this morning. His wobbliness – his caveman fear – seems to have disappeared. And I suddenly want to say too much. Sometimes everything that happened boils and boils down until it is just one thing: *Why did you take the trust I tentatively held in my hands and hurl it against a brick wall? If not the leak itself, then everything else. Why did the world come before me? Before us?*

But then, is it actually true that he didn't do anything at all?

I tentatively ease myself out of Milo's hold and start walking again. Moments later, we reach where we need to get to. It's safer up here. More flat ground, more space.

Little auks are scattered everywhere on this cliffside. It always makes me smile to see them. Fluffy in their beautiful breeding plumage. Rows and rows of them, matching white chests and black feathery heads, like tiny birds wearing tiny white tabards. Some have little orange coils on their legs from last year's tagging.

'Hey, guys. How are we?' I beam. 'Ah. So many of you!'

Milo watches me, says nothing.

A group take flight at the sight of us, then slowly, tentatively, resettle. Sometimes I wonder whether they recognise me. The multiple pecking scars on my hand tell me probably not. Or, if they do, I'm more the strange village idiot they see about sometimes. Harmless, weird, but all bets are off if she tries to touch you. And I get it. I'd be the same if I was an auk and a woman kept showing up to put meaningless anklets on me.

'I'm just going to check these burrows,' I tell Milo, who nods, sits down slowly, rests his forearms on his bent knees.

I find one – a crevice in the cliffside. I once told Iris checking burrows was my very own advent calendar. Instead of chocolate, you look for bird eggs, or, even more exciting: little fluffy babies. Signs of hope, instead of chocolate. She'd held my face then, and said, 'Oh, mate. If nobody else marries you, I will simply have to.'

'You have to be quiet here,' I tell Milo.

'I am quiet,' he replies. 'Or is it that I'm breathing too loudly?'

He's still sulking a little, despite our moment on the cliff. He's in full-blown Yeah-I-caught-you-and-everything-but-I'd-still-rather-be-anywhere-else mode. It does not surprise me that Milo Ford sulks. I would've laid money on him being a sulker. Of *course* he's a sulker.

I bend, looking into the pokey burrow of the nest. It's murky and deep. So much so, it seems . . . black. I need to get closer.

'Here,' I say, taking out my field pack. Dictaphone, infrared camera, scales. I hand Milo my bag. 'Could you just hold this?'

'Sure.' He takes it, but I sense a sigh being held back. 'What're we doing here?'

I bend and get closer to the burrow. 'Checking in on the breeding pairs.'

'And how do you know who's who?'

'Tags,' I say. 'They've been tagged on their legs. Numbered. We tagged some last year, some the year before, and so on.' I insert the camera gently, slowly pushing my arm into the crevice. It's tight and uncomfortable, a blood pressure-cuff tightness around the top of my arm, but I'm in. I hold the small screen in my hand and watch what's happening inside the burrow.

'Is there a bird in there?' asks Milo.

'Yes.'

'Won't they be pissed? Or scared? Your arm going in like that. The camera . . .'

'The camera's infrared,' I tell him. 'They can't see it. But yeah, they probably will be a little *pissed*, but we'll try to go as gently as . . .' A bird blinks more clearly now onto the screen. It's the male. Male no. 32. And . . . Oh my goodness. *Oh my goodness*. He's keeping an egg warm. There it is. A slice of solid egg, like a ceramic bauble, beneath a puff of feathers. My heart blossoms, expands, like a sponge in water. 'Oh well done, guys,' I say to myself. 'Well done.'

'What's happening in there? They just graduated or something?' Milo speaks deadpan, his voice deep and croaky the way it is when you're tired and grumpy. But even his moodiness can't spoil this moment.

'She laid one,' I say. 'She laid an egg. This is amazing news. Bless her.'

And Milo's face softens. Because of course it does. I could've laid money on that too. Milo is a *feeler*. Emotional. A tortured poet type. He once admitted that even if a novel he reads or movie he sees is boring, if it makes his eyes mist over just once, he rates it five out of five. 'I feel like you need to appreciate being made to feel something you weren't expecting,' he said once, and I think about it every time I watch TV, which is more than I used to since coming here and having more time to pass.

There are many things I stop and think about since Milo actually. Gratitude for one. I don't keep a list, but I think about the small things, every morning with my cup of tea. I stop and take photos too now – bubbles on the surface of drinks, a tiny rainbow on my bathroom cabinet on a sunny day. Art gets me as well. I used to think it was stupid. Frivolous. Sian and her old telephones for light fittings, gnomes and taxidermy. But now, when I see something like Milo's big bear, like Sian's gnome, I think, well, if this *thing* does nothing except bring someone a bit of joy, then it's served its purpose. And isn't that what all humans are searching for anyway? Joy? So how could that strange but funny picture in a charity shop, that predictable but compelling movie, that overpriced coffee that tastes like Christmas and takes a good picture ever be meaningless if it hands you something that, in that moment, makes you feel like your life is your own. Three weeks, and Milo showed me that. I held onto it. A consolation prize.

'So, a baby's on the way?' Milo asks. 'Could I, um – take a look? Like, inside?'

I nod and Milo crouches beside me, close, and moves in near to the burrow, his eyes at the slit.

'You may need to wait for your eyes to adjust a little,' I say. 'Their nests are really deep—'

'Oh, *hey*. Ha. Wow. Hello. Hey, you.' And now *I* soften. Grumpy Milo has left the building. He turns back to look at me. His eyes are all stars. Wide and caramel and wild. 'She's beautiful, isn't she?'

'That's the male.'

'Seriously? So, what, the male sits on the egg?'

I nod. 'Yup. Male 32. That's his name.'

'*Male 32*,' he repeats, turning back to the slit in the rock. 'What do you know? Me too, dude.' I laugh as he carries on chatting. 'I'm Milo. Also male. Also 32. Looks like you're over all that toxic masculinity that seems to be around. No flies on you, eh, man? Just sitting there, keeping your baby warm. Good job. Good boy.'

My heart.

It's melting, like butter in sunshine.

'A true fuckin' provider,' he says.

'Well, yes,' I say. 'He's using his . . .'

'Ass.'

'Familiar to you, is it?'

Despite myself, I laugh, and so does he. Loudly. Both of us, giggling. Proper, true laughter.

'So, where's the mom at?' asks Milo.

'Mum is out there right now, sourcing them food.'

Then he glances around at me, eyes still wild and glistening with excitement. 'What's her name? Is she like . . . Mother 32 or something?'

I take a breath. 'Female, 33,' I say.

He smiles. It's a warm, delicious sort of smile. It's one of those smiles that slowly, slowly spreads, and I have to fight to stop myself smiling too. (I fail. Miserably.)

'So. Male 32.' He holds a hand flat to his chest. 'And Female 33, huh?'

I nod.

He gestures at me. 'And look at that. She's out there hunting and gathering and saving everyone's ass. Bet she can be a little stick-up-her-ass, too, pretending she doesn't need anyone.'

'She actually doesn't really need anyone—'

'She needs people like you,' he says. 'Right? People who look out for her. People who care about her?'

I swallow. 'I suppose.'

'And she needs him. For a time, anyway . . .'

I nod. 'I guess.'

He looks back into the burrow. 'And what, you think you've got it all together too?' he says, as if to the bird. 'Like, *look at my ass, it's doing such a great job, I don't need nobody either*. But I dunno,' Milo carries on, 'he's sort of lost without her. You can tell just by looking at his pissed-off little face.' He looks back at me and something flutters in my stomach. 'He's waiting for her.' He stands slowly, boots scrunching on cold gravel.

Silence. Wild winds. Auks squawking. The sounds of home. And Milo. Milo amidst it all. Both of us, and nothing but sky.

'I'm sorry about earlier,' Milo says.

'I'm . . . Me too—'

'The June House thing, the interview, I just . . .' He deflates a little.

'I know.'

'Allie, I've missed you.' He moves so he's opposite me.

Something gives up in me almost instantly. A resolve, once concrete, now a rag that's whipped off by the wind. My heart stills. I sometimes fantasised about a moment like this; about a parallel universe where the leak hadn't happened, where Milo hadn't betrayed me, where things were just simple. This feels dangerous. This feels too good to be true. Because what if he really didn't do it? What happens then?

'And I know this goes against our rules,' he says. 'Being professional. Being normal. And I know it's a really, really big mess, and I know we're both angry, and the trust is just . . . But – I have. And *I do*. Miss you. Every day.'

I open my mouth to speak. At first, nothing comes out. I feel like I've been speared in the chest.

'You don't have to say anything. That's not why I said it. But standing up here with you, not saying it felt harder than saying it.' Then he straightens, chuckles, a hand at his mouth. 'Anyway. Male 32 has said his piece.'

Like she sensed I really needed her, the little auk, Female 33, returns, bursting through us, drawing an invisible line between our bodies, and disappears into the darkness of the burrow.

'There she is,' says Milo. 'Right on time.'

Chapter Fifteen

Milo

It's 2 a.m. and I've just slunk out of the tent to sit with Iris, who's on bear watch. I'd have nominated myself to do anything – to be whale bait – rather than stay in the tent, staring at the ceiling, listening to Jameson breathe heavily, and Lars snore, knowing there's not even an inch between Allie and me.

Not that I *don't* want to be near her. No. That's not it. Not anymore. It's suddenly worse than that. The more I'm with her, the more I want . . . more. The more I want her.

And that's bad. Right?

For a lot of reasons. Reasons that go a little like this: We start talking, we get stuck in the same loop, and even when I feel like we've cracked through something, we circle all the way back to distrust. And then I keep thinking, well, all right, let's say we truly let go of blaming each other – can we let it go without knowing how it happened? I feel I can. I feel Allie can't. She needs to know who did this – how the leak happened. And if there was the tiniest chance for Allie and me, what the hell would that even look like? Allie lives *here*. At the end of the world. And me? My life? How does that fit? She treats a slice of limelight – messages, comments, fans – that lasted for a blink in time and space, as the moment her life was exploded. That shit is standard for me. She's here because she likes the quiet. I can never offer her the quiet. My past is not unassuming like hers. I can't even bring myself to tell her the extent of rehab or addiction. How it didn't end after that one visit she knew about, and how I was starting to struggle again when we first met. One drink with the crew, then two, then more. Wouldn't it be a shameful stain on her quiet, simple life? Regardless, looking at her this afternoon, up on that cliff, I knew. It's all still there, everything I felt for her. She *is* something to me. But when we make progress, we argue – literal flares get fired into the sky.

'Sleep evading you?' Iris slips out an earphone. They're wired to a phone which appears to be playing an audio-book. She presses pause on the screen.

I take a seat next to her, on the waterproof mat. A fire burns nearby, a gun nestled next to Iris's thigh. This whole guns and bears and wilderness thing is strangely starting to feel more normal. 'Pretty much. Cold. Hungry. Ten billion thoughts.'

Iris nods over at me; quirks a tiny smile. Like Jameson, Iris always has this little glint in her eye. We've not spoken much. We haven't had the chance, but the glint is always present. A level of cool I always aim for and miss. 'It gets to everyone,' she says. 'The quiet. The wild. Boredom. It's a lot.'

And while I nod to agree, nothing bores me about being here, which, for someone who always needs something to do – cooking, collecting, seventy-five million half-finished craft projects – is a surprise to no-one more than me. I like Allie's world. I like how it makes me feel. I wanted to freeze the moment today with Male 32 and Female 33, and stay in it with her forever. Which is . . . new for me. (And sort of scary.)

'You've brought your camera,' she whispers.

'Yeah.' I size it up in my hands. 'Thought 2 a.m. in the polar summer might be cool to get. Even though . . .'

'It looks like 2 p.m., and it could be *any time*.'

'Right.' I laugh. 'Dinner may as well be breakfast.'

'And cheers for dinner by the way,' she says. Lars, Jameson and I fished earlier, standing in a nearby lake, in dry suits and boots, Lars caught dinner. I caught one small char we threw back, although I still felt like a total hero. 'I admit, it was creasing me up watching you both. Stars forced to be in wading boots . . .'

'Hey, I've done plenty of wading boots shit in my time.'

Iris laughs, hides it behind her hand so to muffle the sound. Her gloves are fingerless and covered in leopard print. '*Sure you have*. Mr Giant Orange Coat. You look like the inside of a Jaffa Cake.'

'Whatever that is,' I say. 'And I did wilderness movies, you know.'

'Mm.' She smirks. Then she leans and picks up a rock, smooths a thumb over it.

Water sloshes behind us. Daylight endlessly beats down on us. It's weird. It's like sleeping with the bedroom light on or something. Your body gets tired, starts its usual wind down, but the sky's all wrong. And damn I miss the nighttime. I never thought I would. The nighttime is something I have to stare down until the sun comes up. But I miss the reliability of it. I miss darkness.

LIA LOUIS

'So, how was today?' Iris asks. 'Up that cliff?'

It has not escaped me that Iris will of course know everything about what happened back then. It'll be Iris who was there on the other end of a phone, when we were talking. It will be Iris who picked up every piece when it all went to shit. Just like Jameson did, I guess. Friends. The unspoken heroes of break-ups. Well. Not that Allie and I were a *break-up*. We'd have to have been together for that and we never got the chance.

She's been quiet since my heart came flying out of my throat and exploded in front of us up on the cliff with the auks. I sort of wish I hadn't said it, but it felt like a cleansing thing to do. A clean, squeaky truth in amongst all the goddamn grit of arguing about the leak. And maybe this is just blind stupidity or optimism, but we seem to have moved to a weird place, since then. The blame we directed at each other, slowly being diluted by doubt, and . . . maybe redirected somewhere else. To *someone* else who leaked our phones?

'It was good,' I tell Iris. 'I'm kinda fascinated.'

'By?' she asks, her voice sounding like two syllables from the music of it.

I laugh. She gives me a sideways look. Half eye-roll and half *'weeell?'* I love that she's exactly how Allie described her. Easy come, easy go. Part-labrador. Like Jameson but female.

'Everything,' I say. 'I think what you guys do is just . . . awesome. I feel kind of . . . touched by the bug of it or something. Like I want to hear about bacteria?'

Iris gives a dazzling smile – it's a victorious smile. Like she's succeeded in her mission. 'Yeah, I love the gaff,' she

224

says. 'I love the work, I love the team. I don't know. It seems like a lonely place out here, but it's the only time I'm with the people who make me feel less alone. And that's . . . bloody nice. You know?' Iris smiles over at me, tipping her head to one side, and her smooth, jet-black ponytail follows. If Jameson and Iris don't become at least long-distance friends after this, I really, truly will never understand the world. 'God, why am I getting all gooey and telling you soft shit?'

I grin at her. 'I have that face.'

'Is that right?'

'Yeah,' I shrug. 'People tell me things.'

Iris smiles, leans for another rock. She's made a perfect v-shape on the ground with them. 'Has Allie?'

I look over at her. 'Has Allie . . .?'

'Told you things,' she says sweetly. Then she drops her voice. 'Since you arrived. I mean, she says everything's fine, but . . .' She gives a heavy one-shouldered shrug. 'I'm her best friend. I can tell she isn't really just vibing along with everything. Even if she's putting on the whole hard bastard thing. She does that.'

A noisy sigh hefts out of me. 'I think, mostly, she wants me gone.'

'I think so too,' says Iris. '*But* I also think— Oh!' She reaches over, grabs my arm. 'Look!' Her arm points way over into the distance, and for a moment, I think she's going to say it's a bear. But it's not. It's an Arctic fox. White, fluffy, snout down, trotting along the cliffside.

'Oh, whoa,' I say. 'Beautiful.' Together, we watch, trace it across the cliff, silently. 'But, also, it sort of makes me worry for the eggs. The kittiwakes. The babies . . .'

Iris turns and looks at me. 'The kittiwakes,' she repeats. 'The babies. Hmm.'

I laugh. 'I . . . I'm kind of into my birds now.'

Iris quirks an eyebrow. 'I can see that,' she says, smiling. 'And what I was going to say was, I think Allie does want you gone, yeah. But I also think she wants you to stay all at once. Because I think, deep down, she wants to fix this. This whole messy thing with you, as . . . *fleeting* as it was. It's been a big deal for her.'

'It was a big deal for me too,' I confess, quietly.

'But after years of knowing that woman,' Iris shakes her head. 'What Allie wants isn't what she always goes for. She has to weigh it up. The risks. And, to Allie, it's already happened, her worst nightmare. It's all out there. I know you know that, but I think she thinks there's no way back.' From beneath her coat, her shoulders sag and she pulls her face into a grimace. 'Why did you do it, dude?' she groans. 'Seriously, *why*? The interviews, the piss taking. I was so bloody invested in you two. You just seemed like you had it, you know? Still do. Annoyingly.'

'I know.' As I said, measurable by science, this atmosphere, this something between me and Allie. 'Wait, you don't believe I did it? Like, you don't believe the story she does?'

Iris smiles sadly. 'I did,' she says. 'But not for long. I mean, I believed you looked guilty as shit, don't get me wrong, but – no. I don't think you did. It never added up.'

I nod. 'Thanks, Iris. Seriously.'

'And do you really believe she did it?' she asks.

Waves bubble rhythmically, calmly, at the shore. The fire crackles. 'Same answer as you. Did. Guilty as shit. Doesn't add up now.'

'Guilty as shit?' I can sense a hard shield of loyalty behind her words.

I swallow. 'The Bermuda project,' I say. 'It was unfunded, then funded—'

'It was an anonymous donor. After the leak. Sometimes I used to think it might've been you.'

'What? N-no. It wasn't me. I always thought she got paid for it.'

Iris shrugs. 'Not being funny, but thousands of pounds for your romantic one-liners?' Her serious face breaks into a smile. 'But, seriously, Milo, it wasn't Allie. She would never do that.'

I nod. I was so sure back then. From getting blocked out of nowhere, to finding out the research project was suddenly going ahead. It made perfect sense to me. To two-years-ago-Milo. But now. Now, the list is nothing but embers.

'Anything else you want to know?' Iris asks.

'I . . . I'm actually not supposed to be discussing this,' I say. 'Allie said. We have an agreement.'

'What a good boy,' she grins. '*Obedient*.'

'I'm just trying to do the right thing,' I laugh. 'I mean – she fired a *flare* earlier.' And at that, Iris throws her head back and laughs hysterically into her hand.

'Mate, there was a *polar bear*,' she says, gasping for air.

'It was snow! I didn't see no bear.'

Iris giggles so loudly, and it's so infectious, it's not long before we're both laughing our asses off, trying our hardest to muffle it behind our hands.

Iris's giggles taper off, eventually, and we just watch the distant waves in companiable silence. I wonder how right she is, about Allie wanting, deep down, to heal this. I feel like I'm at the line, weighing up whether I'm ready to say 'fuck it', leave it all behind. Allie, as far as I can see, is metres away, arms crossed, refusing to move another step.

'You know what I think?' asks Iris quietly, going back to her pebble shape on the ground.

'What do you think?'

'Regardless of what happened – and you can't tell her I said this or, you know, *flares*. But she's never got over you. She was . . . almost *there* with you, I think. Falling for you. And watching her with you, since you got here, I think she still is in some way.'

Something deep in my chest clenches, something raw. And out here, in the wilderness, Iris like a connector between me and the trust Allie holds dear to her; trust that feels so far from my grasp, it feels right to say it as the truth bobs to the surface like a message in a bottle.

'I think I was already there,' I say. 'I tried not to be, but – I was there. Falling.'

Iris gazes at me, big brown eyes shining. Her throat contracts. 'Yeah,' she says, sadly. 'And I think it's clear there's something *still* there. For both of you. And I think it's been sitting, waiting patiently, for you to both find your way back to it.'

And as rain begins to spit, as thick, smoky cloud fills the sky, Iris adds a final pebble to her shape.

The letter A.

I thought I might've moved past this point, but the truth still is that I haven't been able to come close to anything like love since Allie Lake.

And maybe that's because all the love is still waiting, for her.

Then

Extract from _THE_ magazine: An Interview with Milo Ford by Laura-Lee Lamb

It's raining when Ford and I exit the dive, fingers shiny with pizza grease, cheeks hot from cranked-too-high heating. Ford thanks me for dinner. I remind him that he paid.

'What, a guy can't thank a writer for an interview?' he asks.

'But shouldn't I be thanking you?' I throw back to him. 'For answering all my questions. For all the wisdom.'

At the word wisdom, he scrunches his face up and laughs. Brow, deep grooves, nose wrinkled, like a cartoon cat. (Can neither confirm nor deny whether I actually said this to him as well as, 'Call Pixar! Seriously!' What can I say? I, unlike Milo, did not order the ginger tea.)

'Some wisdom?' he mulls.

'I recently got dumped,' I confess. 'By a one-line text. I keep driving myself insane with why.' (Hi Jeff, if you're reading. Never fear, I have nothing bad to say about you. My dad, however, thinks you're a bag of assholes.)

'Oh, man. Sorry. That sucks,' Milo says, then he thinks silently for so long, I wonder if he's zoned out, forgotten, or is thinking of a way to exit without coming across as rude. I wouldn't blame him. I've just turned him into an agony uncle while in the rain, stinking of oregano. 'I think you've got to accept not every question has an answer,' he says. 'And stopping looking for one is a gift you have to give yourself. You may never know what happened. Like, ever. But, equally, maybe one day, you'll find out exactly why and how it happened. And maybe that will bring you peace. But, at the same time, maybe you'll wish you never knew . . .'

Chapter Sixteen

Allie

'This isn't a prank coffee, is it?'

I've just emerged from getting ready for the day and Milo has greeted me outside the tent with a steaming mug of strong coffee. We're going to see my puffins on the other side of the island today. We have a *long* drizzling hike ahead of us and although he's barely slept, Milo has insisted on fetching me coffee. Things have been . . . slightly different, since our moment on the cliff with the little auks, and I'm not sure what to do with it. So I've been doing what I do best with things that fall into this category: keep quiet and avoid. Because do we just pretend he didn't say his missed me? Do I acknowledge it, or bring it up? Do we continue obeying the bloody note? Do I tell him I think I believe him? The 'I didn't.'

'A *prank* coffee?' Milo eye-rolls. 'Tried to make you a bootleg Bunty's using little things of Canderel.'

I sip, almost choke on a mouthful.

He laughs. 'And I take it I screwed it up.'

'It's . . . sweet,' I manage, although the gesture of a bootleg Bunty's warms me through more than a coffee could. This is precisely what I mean. Different. Things are different.

'Hey, you two. You setting off?' Iris crunches over to us, hands us each a cereal bar. 'I am so desperate for toast and butter that I added a little salt and tried eating these with my eyes closed this morning.'

'Did it work?' asks Milo, turning it over in his hand, clearly already considering it.

'Hell no. Made me feel a lot worse. Totally vile.'

'Oh, fantastic, Iris. Happy for you.' He laughs, and so does Iris. '*Yes*.' He places a hand on her shoulder. 'Look at that, my British sarcasm is coming the hell *on*.'

I woke to them both whispering outside the tent last night, both giggling. I tried to listen, but couldn't make anything out over the waves and the crackling fire and, then, the rain. Something about it, the quiet giggling, the muted sounds of agreements, made me feel strangely proud. My best friend chatting to the man I spent hours talking to, back then, when she would get far too excitable about it, blowing my phone up with messages asking if I fancied him, saying how ridiculous it was for me, Allie, to spend three hours talking to a man I'd never met. Now there they were, together, and for a moment, I had closed my eyes and revelled in the comfort of both of their voices.

'We're leaving soon, I think,' carries on Milo. 'Unless, we want to wait a little. How's the foot, Allie? From the slip?'

'What slip?' asks Iris quickly.

'Oh, it's fine,' I say. And it is, and isn't. It's slightly stiff, but I'm sure walking will help it. 'It was nothing. And yes, we'll set off in a minute. It'll take a good three or four to get over there, so I'd rather get going sooner rather than later—'

'Wait, what, three or *four*?' Milo splutters. 'As in . . . four *hours*?'

Jameson, who has joined us, and is fiddling with his GoPro, bursts out laughing. 'No, four cheeseburgers, mate. Four *sunloungers*. Of course, hours, dude. Too much for you?'

Milo clears his throat, a lopsided grin stretching into his cheeks. He and Jameson exchange a knowing look – a look I know well; a look Iris and I usually throw each other, full of the sort of deep understanding that can only be accumulated through years of late-night talking and swapping parts of your soul, bravely. A friend who knows you better than you know yourself and already knows what you're thinking before you've said it.

'No,' says Milo. 'Four hours is nothing for little puffins, dudes.'

'And four hours back,' I say, and Milo pulls on his hat.

'Yup. I'm aware. Anything for puffins, Cap.' He smiles over at me as Jameson reaches across and ruffles his head.

'This your emotional support hat?'

Milo shakes him off, like a teasing older brother.

'It's a nice hat, to be fair to the guy,' calls over Lars. He's stoking the fire with a big stick. 'Is it Chanel or something? Sent from space?' Lars keeps making jokes about Jameson and Milo's coats. He's already pretended to use Jameson's as a space hopper, and also as a life raft, and executed a skit where he pretended Milo's coat was a newly discovered alien life form.

'Nah.' Milo looks down at his feet.

'He made it,' says Jameson, proudly. 'Crocheted.'

'Did you?' I ask, and my heart warms, like it's just been soaked in warm sugar syrup. He always introduced things like crochet, jokingly, on our calls, as if it gave him the freedom, if I laughed or scoffed, to take it back, pretend he was kidding. The hat is impressive too. Thick and khaki green, a neat white line around the seam.

'Um, *hello*,' says Iris. 'That is seriously cool, Milo Ford.'

Milo gives a childlike smile. 'I just . . . keeps my hands busy. I know it's like . . . not exactly cool, but . . .' He laughs – self-deprecating and self-conscious.

'I want one,' says Iris.

Lars calls over, 'I hate people like you. Those people who're just good at shit,' and we all laugh, with Iris asking Milo if he could make her one with cat ears.

A moment later, Milo ducks inside to get his bag and a 'handheld'. Jameson wants him to take some footage while we're travelling today, and I've of course agreed. Mostly because Polly was staring at me with laser-beam eyes. Also, because Milo has promised that footage of me will be at a minimum. It'll be the landscape, he vowed, and him taking some 'talking selfie shots'.

'I'd leave as soon as poss if I were you,' Iris says to me, squirting toothpaste onto a toothbrush. She holds a sports-capped bottle of water in her other hand. 'The weather should hold, but I'm just thinking, later on, I'm not so sure . . .' She starts brushing. 'Make hay while the sun shines and all that.' Then she smiles a big, foamy smile. 'Plus, if you don't get back in time, there's always the *ccufnsns*.'

'There's always what?' I ask, laughing.

She holds a finger up in the air, gargles water and spits it into her empty coffee cup.

'I was saying, there're a few *cabins* up there.' She waggles her eyebrows. 'The old miner places. If ya know what I mean . . .'

'What?'

'*Cabins,* Allie.'

'No, I know there're cabins, but I was "whatting" about your face when you said it.'

'What?' says Iris. 'What about my face? I don't know what on earth you're talking about.'

'I don't believe you,' I smile.

'So is it maybe that you would prefer I say *something* then.'

'About what exactly? About cabins?'

Iris sidles up to me. 'About you and Milo,' she whispers, then she hesitates and leans close to me. 'I really like him, Allie.'

'OK?' I stare at her. A silent 'and?'

'No, I'm just saying, he's lovely. I do really like him. And the way he looks at you and the way you are together. And today, you have this little smile . . .'

And with that, my face is on fire. I may as well be headfirst in a cauldron of soup. Handstanding in one.

'Iris . . .'

Her face – her pretty, soft features wilt. Like a story-book princess, suddenly all romance and fluttering lashes. 'It's true, though. Feels like a no-brainer to me.'

'It's not that simple—'

'No, I get that, amigo, I do,' she says, softly. She's close to me, speaking low and hushed. I can smell spearmint on her breath. 'But I just . . . I don't know what I'm saying, except maybe . . . maybe you both just move through this whole thing and take a second to really listen to your feelings. If neither of you leaked the phones—'

Then Milo appears, poking his head through the tent entrance, bag packed and on his back, camera in his hand.

'What's all this then?' he says, southern British accent totally, effortlessly perfect. 'That's what the Brits say right? *What's all this then?*'

'Nothing,' we say together, which makes him laugh. '*OK*,' he says. 'Don't believe you, though,' and I pretend not to see the meaningful sideways look Iris gives me.

We walk away, slipping on bags and zipping up additional layers.

'Oh, what's the one below a captain?' asks Milo. 'Because I'm happy to take that rank—'

'Your lace,' I say, stopping.

'Your *lace*? What's that, like "your grace" but for ships?'

'No. Your shoelace,' I say, laughing at the ridiculousness of 'your grace but for ships'. 'It's undone.'

'Oh.' He laughs. 'Right.'

And I'm not quite sure why I do it. Time probably. We need to get moving, cover ground before the rain gets too bad like it's set to much later, plus Milo's hands are full, still fiddling with the tiny handheld camera. But I drop to the ground and tie it for him.

'Uh. Thanks.'

'You're welcome.' I stand again, in front of him. Face to face. His eyes hold mine. 'And I think it's officer,' I tell him. 'The one below the captain is officer.'

Milo's amused mouth twitches. 'I see. So, I can be Officer Ford . . .'

'You can be whatever you like,' I shrug. 'But you listen to me. Your captain. Understood?'

And I can't help but smile to myself when I see his Adam's apple bob, just a little, in his throat.

Chapter Seventeen

Milo

Must remember this is work. Must remember this is work. *Must remember this is work.*

And God, I'm trying. But things are shifting by what feels like the minute. So damn fast, that I keep getting carried away. Daydreaming about what this weird, intangible change of vibe – yes, Allie, *vibe* – might mean. Could it be something again, us two? And just as I start playing that tune, I'm reminded that there are actually only two days. Two more days, then it's over. No more Allie Lake. No more Captain Lake with her authority and expertise and confidence. She's so damn smart, too, and why was it *hot* when she called me Officer; looked me deep in the eyes and told me to listen to her? It's not like I can even distract myself from all these thoughts. Because it's just us, and nothing for miles. Total, icy wilderness.

No phones.

No stores.

No hotels. (*Haha.*)

Nowhere to escape to.

She's all I'm thinking about, but she's also all I can see.

And to think when I first landed at the station, the days ahead felt like a horrible, stretching, dark forever. Now it doesn't feel like anywhere near enough time.

'Slow down,' she barks at me. She keeps doing that too, says we shouldn't rush because the ground is slippery, but there's something about the endlessness, the sameness, that makes me want to just get it over with; get to the next new thing. I'd give anything to stumble upon some sort of event right now – a lame thought, I know. What would it even be? Polar bears with boomboxes? Geese with blunts? But – something. That's what I want. Maybe some loud music, hundreds of chattering voices to drown out everything. If I was at home now, in my apartment, I'd go straight to Yio's for pizza. Nobody bothers me there. I'd sing karaoke – 'Perfect Day', Lou Reed, *obviously* – and drink full-fat Coke with the regulars who are always too focused on singing to remember my name. Maybe I'd even start Iris's hat. Place an order for new yarn. She said she wants purple . . .

'Did you hear me?' asks Allie. 'It's really icy.'

'I am slowing down,' I say. '*Captain*. Plus, aren't you the one with the bad foot?'

'It's fine.' She shrugs. 'You're the one acting as though we're late for something. As if speeding on, will get us there quicker. *Officer*.'

I laugh. 'Allie, unless I'm once again missing out on some super important science thing, usually the faster you go, the quicker you do happen to get somewhere, no?'

'Not if you fall,' she says. 'I keep telling you. If you fall, or slip. Or, you know, die, then we're screwed.'

'You're sort of obsessed with me dying out here,' I say, and she rolls her eyes, although I can sense a little laughter behind them now.

We walk and walk.

The clouds have started to darken now. It's as close to night as we have experienced since I got here. I keep seeing Allie look up at them – as if they're an unwelcome guest. As if the doorbell just rang and we weren't expecting anyone. I can imagine that's how Allie Lake looks toward the door when guests arrive. Allie likes quiet. She likes peace and organisation. Allie likes the things she likes and the things that fill her up. She *knows* what fills her up too. Whereas I have no idea. I'm learning, sure, and I'm making progress, but I'm like a fountain that takes coins, but also tyres and shopping carts and perhaps toads and also maybe old power tools. And I love unexpected guests. Anyone to help me take a break from my busy, noisy mind. And I can't help it. As we traipse across the hard, cold ground, as the clouds turn indigo, as the wind starts to pick up, as my brain scrabbles around for something to squeeze in its palm, absentmindedly like putty, I think of us. Allie and I, living in a cottage or something. Green going for miles out of the windows, dogs everywhere, always one to walk. Allie moving around in those pyjama shorts she wore once on FaceTime, with the cactuses on. Me, a paperback open on my thigh. The doorbell chiming. Sunlight on her face. Hot drinks steaming on the coffee table, our own place . . . jeez. I'm almost winded by the vision. But how would that even *work*? She lives here a lot. In nowhereness. I live in New York, I work everywhere. My life is loud and busy and under the magnifying glass. Allie's life is quiet and anonymous.

And this is why we were doomed, I guess. But then what is it Jameson says: The coolest things in life are the things that work even though they shouldn't. And maybe that's us—

A scream cracks through my thoughts, followed by a thump.

She's fallen.

Ah, shit, she is *down.*

Ass planted firmly on the ground; face all winces and hard lines.

'*Fuck*. Allie.'

She groans, clasps a hand around her ankle. 'Oh my God,' she's saying. 'Shit.'

It's not the foot. It's not the pain. More than anything, she's angry at herself. It's written all over her face.

I drop to her side. My own shoes slip, but I manage not to fall alongside her.

'Are you all right?' I rush out.

'My . . . my ankle – I . . . Argh, it hurts.'

'Was it me?' I ask breathlessly. 'W-was I moving too fast, was I—'

'No. No, it was me, I— Jesus. Oh. That hurts so much.'

'OK. OK, let's . . . let's just take a second.'

'I'm . . . just . . . I can't get up, Milo.'

'Your ankle's a little stuck. Sort of . . . jammed between the rocks.' I slip off my backpack. 'All right, I'm going to put my hands under your arms, is that OK?'

'Um . . . just hang on a minute.' Her voice is strangled, croaking at the edges. She's in pain. It's so clear she's in pain and pretending she isn't. God, the stubborn *ass* on this woman.

She tries to move – of course she does – groans. Her ankle is totally jammed.

'Allie, would you just—'

'Sorry, I . . .' She nods, almost despite herself. 'It just hurts so much.'

'I know. It's all good. We can take our time. We'll go slow. We'll go gently.' I bend behind her, and put my hands under her arms. 'I'm going to just lift you, OK?'

And I lift her. She's light, and I can feel she's shaking a little, which kind of breaks my heart.

'OK – if you can, and only if you can, slowly lift your ankle – that's it. That's right. Good.' It's out. I hold her there, her weight against me, her hair bristling against my face. Watermelon. Always watermelon. We haven't had access to proper showers, and she smells like water-melon – *how?* 'All right, I'm going to lower you now. There we go.'

'OK,' she breathes shakily.

I lower her, so she's sitting on a rock again. Water has seeped through, staining her pants. I move around to her foot. She hisses through her teeth, trying to lift it and bend her leg towards her.

'Allie, let me—'

'I'm OK,' she says.

'Will you let me take a look?'

'*I'm* going to look,' she insists, voice still shaky.

'I'm first-aid trained, Allie. As hard as that might be for you to believe. I'm not a total jackass.'

'I know lots of jackasses who also know first aid,' she remarks. She lifts her foot and groans, tries to stifle it.

'Allie, just—' I sigh. 'Just let me look at your goddamn ankle.'

And she gets it then. My stern Officer Ford voice worked.

'Fine,' she sighs. 'OK.'

I peel back the cuff of her pants, and edge down the thick ridge of her sock. It's fuchsia pink – the letter A in white on the side. And there it is. The wound. An angry dark cut through the skin of her ankle. The skin around it, a cloud of red.

'There be the culprit,' I say.

'There be?' she asks breathlessly.

'We're at sea aren't we, captain? Well. Kinda.'

She's pale. I guess she's in shock. But it gets a tiny smile. Sugar. I'll get her some sugar, that'll help.

'First aid kit in my backpack,' she says, and I grab it, finding a zip loc bag full of energy bars too. 'Hey. Can I use this?'

'The cereal bars?' She looks worried now. Like some sort of barbarian is in charge of fixing her up. A dog who's been given human powers for the afternoon, and he's going to fix up her wound using . . . oats.

'No the . . . zip loc.' I smile. 'It's just – I have an idea.'

'For my ankle?'

'No, for a game,' I say, laughing. 'Seriously, Allie, what do you take me for? Yes, for your ankle.' I break off some ice still thawing on the rocks, and put that in the bag. 'DIY ice pack.' I grin as I crouch down. And I see it. This tiny little glimmer of warmth. A look of *OK, I'm impressed.* 'I'm going to lift your foot now. OK?'

She nods and, slowly, I place her foot on my thigh, fingers grasping the warm skin. I roll down her sock a little more, and freeze when my finger touches a chain – an ankle chain. I don't know why. But it feels intimate. This part of her, hidden beneath clothes.

'All right-y then.' I have never said that before in my life but I have to admit, I feel a little discombobulated. I place an antibacterial wipe down first, then the ice pack on her ankle. 'That feel OK?'

She nods. 'Yeah. It does. Thanks.'

Water trickles around us, finding its way down to the ocean, and salty, iced wind picks up. Her hair blows into her face and she pushes it away.

'I'm going to just rest this here, then I'll fix up the cut. We should be all good in no time.'

She says nothing, then softly, I hear, 'Thanks, Milo.'

'Officer Ford to you.'

She smiles, watching me. Despite the temperature, I feel a small torrent of warmth.

I start to take things out of the kit – more disinfectant wipes, band-aids. There is something weirdly meditative about this, and a little voice in my head says, 'I could get used to this.' And I guess that little voice means looking after Allie. I want to look after her. I want to take care of her.

'Sorry,' she says.

'Sorry? For what?'

'Just – maybe we shouldn't have come out here. Iris said about the distance and weather last night. And my foot was hurting.'

'Allie, you're just trying to work.'

I gently remove the ice pack, brush a new wipe across her cut. Her perfect skin, cut like this, makes something harden in my chest.

'I feel like I wanted to prove a point, though,' she says, and there's something about the way she's talking that's different this time. Her words are looser. Without edge. No longer tightly packed in a jar. It's like the lid's been loosened. 'I *did* want to prove a point. That this is important. That *this* is what matters.'

'Prove a point to who?'

'You.'

I look up to meet her eyes. She looks sad. She looks tired.

'Allie, you have nothing to prove to me.'

She laughs then; a real, ironic laugh. 'I think that is the most untrue statement you've ever made. I feel like so much of my time since you arrived has been spent trying to justify myself to you.'

'And me to you,' I admit. 'Because you believe I leaked our phones.'

'You believe *I* leaked our phones.'

'I don't,' I say. 'Not anymore, Allie.'

She swallows. 'I don't think you did it, either,' she says, and the relief that rolls through my body almost winds me.

Silence again. And I want to ask so many questions, run headlong and reckless into the sunset with it, talk and talk and talk, but her eyes are watery and she looks so small that I step back from the metaphorical door that just cracked open. She's injured. She's emotional. Vulnerable. And all I want to do is hold her and keep her safe.

'OK, then,' I say, pulling out a small coil of bandage from plastic wrap. 'Let's get this wrapped up.'

'I'm sorry I keep stopping you from filming,' she says, watching me. 'I know this is your work, too.'

'If I'm honest, Allie, I keep forgetting I'm here for work.'

She cringes. 'Gosh, really?'

'No, no, I don't mean it like that. I just mean . . . I like it here.' I look up at her. *And being with you*, says that voice in my head again.

'Do you really?' she asks, and I love that I know she's smiling before I've even looked up. It's in the raspiness of her voice.

'Totally,' I tell her. 'I keep thinking about the way the sky out here is the actual goddamn *sky*, you know? And how everything feels like . . . the centre of the earth but also, somehow, nothing, all at once. It feels like being on another planet. Another planet where birds are the daddy. And also, polar bears. And the legends who are Male 32, and Female 33. And Male 32's magical ass.'

She laughs. It's music.

'And you're here. And I never thought I would ever get the chance to ever talk to you again. And OK, I thought for a while I didn't ever want to but . . .'

She gazes at me, and I see her swallow. And all she says is, 'I see.'

Silently, I bandage her foot. Allie watches me, then the sky. And like she was expecting it, rain begins to spit.

I hold out a hand to her, and she takes it this time. No hesitation.

Slowly, she stands, steadies herself on me, hands on my forearms, and I wait for her to move them, although

247

I never want her to move them. I want this weight of her body against mine. Again and again, I find myself wanting to freeze time and keep the moment under a glass cloche I can watch from the outside, whenever I want to.

'Sorry,' she says again. 'Just a sec.'

'Take your time,' I say. 'We can stay like this all day. All night, if you want to. All . . . I mean, whatever, I'm down for all week.'

She laughs, but again says nothing, and I wonder – I hope – she's just holding it all back, as Allie does, like a dam. Because surely she feels this? Surely she is *feeling* this and wondering, like I am? Because I can't hide it any longer. How I feel, I'm sure, is starting to seep out of my veins, through my skin, covering me, like tattoo ink.

Allie says my name. Then, 'I thought of this every day, back then. Just being with you somewhere,' she continues, raindrops growing steadier, heavier. 'Somewhere like this. Just us. And I wondered how on earth we would do it. I fought it for ages.' She pauses, gives a watery smile. 'Because it felt impossible, the idea of me and you. And the thing is – it wasn't.'

'It never was,' I agree.

'But it is now, Milo,' she says sadly. 'Too much has happened. It's too complicated.'

'What if it doesn't matter?' I say. 'What if . . . what if we just pretend it never happened? The note's working well, right? We can just do that. Over and over.'

'It's not that simple.'

'Why not? Because you need the answers? The details of how?' And now it feels like she's somehow slipping away from me, and I feel desperate to hold on to her.

'Yes,' says Allie.

'Then – then we can try to get them—'

'But it's already done,' she says. 'We've already been judged and discussed and picked apart and watched—'

'So what?' I jump in. 'Seriously. I don't care what other people who don't even know us might say. What are they even going to say, anyway? Milo wears stupid crocheted hats and Allie cares too much about puffins?'

'But we've not even spent a real, proper moment together, in the real world, and yet my life has already been on display. The level of exposure, Milo, it was—'

'I know,' I say. 'But none of that shit is real, Allie. We are. Like, what's this even all about, if it's not meant to be something? Couldn't we just – try? Pretend we don't come with this big, stupid, dramatic backstory?'

And she laughs and simply says, 'Milo . . .' in a wistful breath.

And there is so much in the way she says my name. Regret. Sadness. A wordless, 'As if it could be that simple.' A sigh that could also be a tentative, 'Could we?' A sigh that says, 'Because we have go back to our real lives and say goodbye soon. And your life is a life I never want.'

Then she leans and says close to my ear, 'And I should've said that I missed you too. Every day.'

Chapter Eighteen

Allie

We have an hour until we get to the puffins and it is *pouring down*. We are so wet, Milo and me, that every time we take a step, our feet squelch. And my ankle hurts too, which blooms and blooms with bruising and desperation to sit down, to have the pressure taken off.

Iris keeps radioing. When Lars' stern but comforting voice didn't work in convincing us to take shelter, she's now resigned herself to radioing us constantly. 'Seriously, R2, I think you guys should consider other options,' she's said more than once. And, of course, she means the cabins. The cabins she joked about this morning. There's one near the puffins, who, ironically, will all be likely sheltering in their deep, little self-dug burrows. I've just been hoping the rain might stop in time. In time for us to not need our *own* burrow . . .

Because the thought of sharing a cabin with Milo after what has passed between us today feels almost too . . . dangerous.

'Well, Captain, this is . . . well. Yeah,' trails off Milo beside me. Water streaks his face. Raindrops dot his eyelashes, run off the tip of his nose. He would never say it, of course, but he thinks it's crazy to continue on in this rain.

'I know.'

'I mean – is it OK?'

'What? It's rain. Of course it's OK—'

'I didn't say is *it* OK,' he says, over the loud white noise of the rain. 'I said, are *you* OK?'

'Oh. Um . . . yes. I'm fine.'

'It's just you're hobbling a little.'

'Am I?'

I swallow. I am. And the thought of hobbling anymore makes me want to cry.

My walkie-talkie crackles. Iris's voice comes through once again. Let's hope she says it's stopped raining where she is, or at least that the wind has slowed from these rageful gusts to a manageable breeze. It can be like this sometimes, here. Extremes. Sudden extremes. As if here is where earth lets out all its bad moods. Beats its proverbial pillows.

'Hey, R2 crew,' she says, 'Still breathing? Over. Still ignoring my advice to find a cabin and chill for the rest of the day?'

'We're OK,' I respond, but even I want to roll my eyes at myself. We aren't OK. Not at all. My ankle being the first thing that isn't. My bag is heavy on my back. Our clothes are soaked and sticking to our skin. Our faces are shining with water, as if we've had buckets of it thrown over us.

'Did you hear the thunder?' she asks. 'Over.'

'No,' I radio back. 'How's it on your side? Clearing up?'

'Oh, completely *dreadful*,' she says. 'We're all in the tents. Battened down the hatches. Please do the same.'

I feel Milo's eyes flick over to me. I don't meet his gaze.

'And how's the ankle?'

I turn then, glare at him. He gives a heavy shrug. So Milo had told Iris earlier, even though I told him not to. 'What?' he says under his breath. 'We all promised to keep each other – *abreast* – so that was me. Just. Abreasting.'

I speak into the radio. 'It's . . . fine, it's . . .' Thunder rumbles in the distance. A gust of wind halts us in our tracks. Milo puts his arm out to steady me. 'It hurts,' I say with a big sigh. 'OK, it . . . it really hurts actually. This day's been a bloody disaster, from start to finish.' I let out a breath and give myself over to it.

'Oh, mate,' comes Iris's voice.

'OK. Where do I go?' I turn to Milo, who stands, arms folded, face being pelted with rain. It's obscene how he looks as though he's posing for an artsy, wet photoshoot. His cheeks, pink, eyes wild, his slick, soaked hair dangling over his face. 'Are you OK with this? Going to a cabin. Maybe until morning. We have enough supplies.'

Milo smiles with relief. 'Hell yeah,' he says, blowing out a long breath. 'I am super down for a cabin. I am *beat.*'

Iris gives me extremely rough directions of the cabin near the puffins. 'You'll see the rusty mine tracks first and then the old wagons,' she explains. 'Just keep going north, then you know you're near.'

And Milo leans his head back, smiles, as if someone has just handed him the top prize. It makes me smile. There's something about doing fieldwork that does it. It highlights what's really important. When I'm home, I suddenly care too much. I get wound up about temporary traffic lights, about finding the right wallpaper. Yet here. It reminds you that the little things are the big things. A sunset. Rainfall. A log fire. A comfortable bed. A warm meal.

'We'll let you know once we're there,' I say, and when I look over at Milo, as we walk – those caramel brown eyes, the tiny kink on the bridge of his nose, I think about what he said about pretending, and realise in this moment, even if it feels dangerous, being in a cabin in the wilderness with him is all I want, and I don't need to pretend about that. Not at all.

Chapter Nineteen

Milo

A cabin, she said.

A cabin is . . . a slight reach?

Not that I'd dare complain. I am definitely *not* complaining. I'm frozen to my very soul. I feel like I have walked the entire circumference of the globe with Allie today, my thighs are taut, my feet are aching. But this is more a – shack? Yeah, a shack is what it is. But right now, this shack is a slice of heaven. Heat. Shelter. Rest. Allie. Sign me up.

It's also pretty beautiful in here too, in a kind of industrial, rustic way. Like an immersive museum or something. I remember working in a place like this in New York when I was seventeen. An interiors museum, where I got stationed in the 1950s room, had to dress as a 1950s businessman and stay in character. The only thing Dad ever approved of. I still remember how he brightened, standing at the kitchen counter, looking up from the coffee percolator, in shirt and cargos and beard, at the sentence, 'I have a job at a museum.' Not exactly what he wanted but a real honest job, like his. Then he scoffed at the low hours and the performance part of it. But nothing is ever good enough for the man. I tried. Made him the plus-one to all my premieres and events (he never came). Luxury retirement homes. Paid off every dime of his debt. Bought the old carpentry workshop so my cousin, Markus, never had to worry about rent and it would always be in the family like Dad wanted. Drove him two hours to Uncle Tony's every Wednesday when I was home last summer. (He just whined about my driving.) There is no combination for his approval. I know that now. It's like my friend Julia said once, 'Actors are seeking love from everyone because they didn't get it from the people who mattered most.' I have spent my life waiting for Dad's I love you, looking for it, in those brightening coffee percolator moments, as if it might be written somewhere, in code. Healing was realising it's never coming.

'There're three beds,' says Allie now, as we both creak across the shack's floor, and the relief in her voice makes me smile.

'Cool,' I say.

'What? What's with the smile?'

'Nothing. Just – three. Room for one more.'

Allie rolls her eyes, sits down gently on the end of one. It creaks. But she allows herself a smile.

It's murky in here. Like the inside of a cartoon tool shed. Dark wood. Dust. Everything slatted. A time capsule. Just outside the window is a rusty track, a genuine, old miner's wagon on it, and everything inside is made from wood and nails, with thick pencil markings still visible on home-made furniture, from people here before us.

I sit at the wonky, clunky wooden table, shrug off my bag. The surface is covered in papers weighed down with an old, rusty, but probably still sharp, axe.

'You seen these old maps?' I ask. 'I feel like I'm a pirate or something. But the only treasure I'm interested in is ramen noodles. I'm *starved*.'

Allie smiles, shifts herself up the bed, lifts her bad ankle up onto the old mattress. She props herself against the wall behind her. No pillows or turn-down service here. 'This area used to be all mines up until about sixty years ago. Something like that.'

'Really?'

She nods, sleepily. 'The miners lived here. And it's open to whoever sort of, passes by, which is not very often, as you can probably imagine. But everyone keeps it how they found it. They're maps of the area. All different ages.'

'Wow. They're sort of—'

'Dusty?' offers Allie. 'Smelly?'

'Beautiful,' I say instead. 'This one looks . . . I don't know. Hand etched? Man, I love maps. I have this old one of Hoboken on my wall at home. Reminds me of my mom. Sometimes I run my finger along the streets, track the routes we used to take, pretend I'm planning another route for us . . .' I pause. 'Ah, it's dumb, I know.'

'No, it's not. That's nice,' she smiles, her eyes heavy. 'I sometimes do similar. Less these days, but sometimes I listen to Mum's voice notes, pretend she's just left them for me, close my eyes and . . .' Her eyelids flutter closed. 'It's almost real.'

Something has shifted again, a little, since Allie hurt her ankle. Another pivot. I don't know where this is headed, but it feels good, to have the pressure between us relieved just that little more. Another little pin in a balloon; the atmosphere, softer.

I leaf through the different pages. Rain hammers harder and harder, wind thunders, and the four walls containing us creak. Allie closes her eyes. It might not be getting dark, but it's getting *cold*.

I stand up; the squeak of my chair makes her open her eyes. 'Where're you going?'

'I'm going to start a fire,' I say. 'There's a little stack of wood over there.'

She starts to get up. 'D-do you know how?'

This woman . . . 'You mean, don't I have a Hollywood assistant who starts all my fires? Washes me in a bathtub with sponges like a dude from *Bridgerton* or something?'

'Well. I . . . Yes,' she says. 'Yes, actually.'

'Nah, I can fire up the shit out of this thing,' I say.

'Can you venture out and hunt and gather, too?' she asks.

'Sure thing.'

'And dressed in a five hundred-dollar coat the whole of Instagram just *loved* doesn't count.'

'If you wanted to see me in bear skins, Allie,' I laugh, 'you just had to ask nicely.'

Chapter Twenty

Allie

I am woken up by . . . cooking smells. Oh my God, cooking smells? In a cabin. In the middle of Cote Rock. Burning. Is something burning? Although, it smells like soup. Garlic, *onions* . . . ?

I jump up. For a microsecond, I have no idea where I am. It's that familiar disorientation you get after a nap, or the first day waking up in a new hotel room. But then it comes back to me. My ankle, the cabin, Milo, bear skins. The cabin is in darkness, except for a long, tapered candle flickering on the table, and the air is warm. Milo's coat is over me, like a blanket, and he sits at the mapley glow of the wood-burning stove, the flames flickering his face amber. The wooden covers of the windows have been shut for faux nighttime. He's stirring something, and wearing a dusky pink T-shirt, biceps lean and snug against the sleeve hems. It's the first time I've seen him like this. Casual. Like someone who could simply be at home. It reminds me of his sleepy form on video calls. The naked, taut chest, the bedhead, the shorts . . . For a second, I'm breathless at the memory, followed by a strange, sudden tickle of butterflies.

'Milo?'

'Oh. Hey. You fell asleep. Are you warm?'

I nod. 'Very.'

'Asshole designers and their duck feathers,' he says with a lopsided grin. 'Asshole actors and their fires.'

I sit up in the bed. This feels . . . cosy. Safe. Warmth and cooking and roaring fires. And Milo, safe and calming.

'Are you actually cooking?'

'All right, so don't, like, scold me or anything,' he laughs, 'but I got a little creative. I used one of the metal dish things we eat out of, and I'm making us ramen on the stove top. It gets real hot. We used to have one of these. My mom used to make fondue on it for some reason. But we seem to only have one bowl.' He winces. 'I forgot to pack mine, so I'm using yours. Anyway. We'll have to share.'

'Share ramen?'

'Well, share a bowl. There's enough ramen for two.' He stares at me, waiting, fire dancing in his eyes. 'Allie, you're not supposed to look haunted. Like . . . this is a nice gesture.'

'I'm not haunted.' But I am a little. Waking to Milo Ford – *Milo Ford* – cooking for me in a tiny cabin, in the middle of the Arctic. I'm half expecting to be shaken awake soon, and realise, that, of *course*, I'm dreaming, because that would make the most sense. 'I'm just . . . I can't believe I fell asleep.'

'Don't forget that we walked a gazillion miles today. And the skies pissed all over us.'

'I know.' I watch him stir slowly. 'Still. We've not even done a full day.'

He laughs to himself and shakes his head. 'Let yourself off the hook, Allie,' he says. 'Hey, I was also thinking – well, there's this big-ass metal bucket thing over there. Like it's huge. We have snow . . .'

'Right?'

'Well, you said you wanted a bath.'

My face flashes with heat. 'Milo, I'm not bathing in a bucket.'

'I'm not saying *that*, Cap.' He stirs, chuckling. 'I was thinking for your ankle. You could soak it. Warm water, I don't know. It would help? I'm not an expert obviously, but I read some Bear Grylls before I came here and—'

'Did you? *Bear Grylls*?'

He carries on speaking but now through a smile. A look on his face that says, *I will finish this sentence, thanks.* 'And you can melt snow and ice, boil to purify, filter and use it. And I have this stuff I brought with me. It's like pocket soap? You can use it on hands and your body, or even on, like, laundry.'

A smile takes over my face at the sound of 'laundry'. 'You were going to do laundry in the Arctic?'

'You never know, Allie Lake, what things might arise.' He meets my eyes, still stirring the noodles. This is – nice. This cosy, candle-flickered bubble. Are we pretending? Being professional? Good camp mates? It doesn't feel like it. But even if it is, this sleepy haze makes me feel like I, uncharacteristically, for once, don't care. 'Anyway. I guess I just thought – I could whip you up a sort of bath? For the ankle. It says on the box you can dilute it to clean cuts and stuff.'

Something warm unseals in my chest now, trickles, pours, floods it. I freeze as if with the shock of it; the force of my own feelings. Sian and I would watch

How The Grinch Stole Christmas when we were kids, in pyjamas, the sound of Mum ironing, and this feels like that moment – when the Grinch believes something awful is happening to him but for the first time, he feels love. I used to hide my face at that scene; swallow tears down behind my hands. I was nine. But I feel like I might cry now. And like I also might run away. That's if it wasn't torrential out there. But, psychologically, I am equal parts on a boat with Lars, screaming 'Go go go! To the horizon!' and curled up here, despite it all, with Milo. And then I realise what this is. I'm being looked after. I have never been looked after.

'No?' Milo asks. 'No pressure, I just thought it might help—'

'No,' I blurt. 'No, I'd . . . I'd like that. I think it's . . . smart.'

'Shit, she's calling me *smart*, someone call the authorities,' he says, standing and flashing a smile. 'Also, the noodles are ready. Do you want to go first?'

'Or we can just share? Eat together,' and I can hardly look at him when I say that. It's that word. *Together.* Because this all feels a little dangerous. I made a pact with myself that I would never be stupid enough to let anyone in this close again because of him. And now not only am I letting someone in, but it's *the person* who necessitated that pact. The perpetrator himself. Yet it feels utterly ridiculous that Milo could ever be the perpetrator— gosh. I mean that. The soft, wild hair. The warm caramel eyes. The slow way he walks, holding our dinner, like it isn't a camping bowl full of cheap ramen noodles. And what now? What if we say we both just made mistakes? Say, like Milo insists, it doesn't matter? What would that mean then? What does it mean to accept someone else was behind the leak?

Milo sits down next to me on the bed. I swivel, fold the coat neatly behind us, watch as it puffs up again, like an inflating balloon. Candlelight strobes our faces. He holds the bowl between us and hands me a fork.

'Captain,' he says, huskily.

'Thanks. Officer.'

We eat in silence; just the scrape and twists of forks against metal. The atmosphere, like smoke. The wind battering the cabin. Wood in the log burner, spitting.

'This is . . . nice, right?' he says, voice soft and low. 'An actual hot meal eaten inside. Today was cold. *Is* cold.'

'And wet,' I add.

'And pretty fucking wild.'

'Pretty fucking wild,' I repeat and, meeting my eyes, we both smile, and my stomach backflips. A full spring backwards. I can barely swallow. I feel alight, like if he touched me, he'd get some sort of shock – gaze down at his fingertips, see the ends glowing. And I'm terrified. Truly. I never used to understand, really, when Iris would just happily wander on back to someone who had dicked her around, caused so many tears, and yet – I can't help this pull. I can't help but want to fall into him . . .

'What is it?' Milo asks.

'Mm?'

He smiles, lopsided and gradual. 'Something happened just then. Just – I don't know, I felt a vibe.'

I scoff. 'A *vibe. Really?*'

'There was a vibe.'

'There was not a vibe. Also, a vibe is not a thing. Neither is prana or sixth sense or— what?'

He places a hand to his chest, fork still hovering. 'With respect, Allie. Those are all totally things.'

'Where's your proof?'

'I have *a shit ton* of proof,' he carries on, fork back into the bowl.

'Do you now?'

Our hands, at the bowl, twisting noodles, touch. Neither of us move them. And I'm glad. It feels nice to be close to him. I *want* to be close to him.

'OK, you want proof?' he remarks, both of us twisting, then eating. 'Um. OK, when my meditation teacher, Wish, was pregnant . . .'

'Wish?'

'*Wish*. When Wish had said *nothing* to me about babies or pregnancy or any of that shit, no sign of babies or bumps, I knew. She walked in and I just – knew. Purely from just energy, from vi—'

'*Meditation teacher?*'

Milo quirks another smile.

'And I repeat – Wish?'

'Got a problem?' he asks, the flick of an eyebrow.

I smile. 'No. And what about the spirituality coach? Still seeing him? What was his name again? Dave wasn't it? Kev? Roy! It was Roy.'

Milo laughs. 'As I said. Got a problem?' He leans in now, touches his arm to mine. The bare skin of our forearms pressed together. I used to spend time wondering about this; whether I would ever be the sort of person

263

who would find someone they wanted to sit this closely with. And perhaps it's the tiredness, or the vulnerability of being here, in the cold, alone, or that we're untouchable here, with nobody else to disturb us. But I just let it arrive, inevitably, like a sunset. I want Milo to draw closer. I want to be near him, and it feels *right* that I am.

'No. No problem, but,' I say quietly, 'vibes don't scientifically exist.'

'Well, *all* I'm saying,' he replies, low and slow. 'You thought something and I saw it in your eyes. Felt it. A little . . . *something*.'

Yes, I want to say. *I was thinking about how much I like you, even though I shouldn't. I was thinking how I was mere moments away from falling in love with you once.*

Instead, I say, 'Nope, t-there was no something.'

'Right,' he says, our faces just a breath apart. He gives a tiny twitch of a smile, then slowly, the moment dissipates.

We eat noodles. I watch the fire flicker, the bowl, poised, ready for my ankle's luxury bubble bath and I let the fallen leaves of my thoughts settle. *Do* I trust him? And is it even possible, really, *truly*, that we can do it? Move past the fallout – the interviews. The laughter. The assuming the worst of each other because of our own open wounds. Forgetting it. That's what Milo suggested, wasn't it? Pretending it never happened. And maybe I can try. Even if it's just for a night.

After a while, Milo gets up. 'All noodled out. But I'll get to the ankle bath.'

'For ramen, that was good,' I smile. 'Do you still cook a lot?'

'More since I moved and got a bigger kitchen. It's awesome.'

I look up at him. 'Really? Do you still have your bear? With the hat?'

He smiles over at me, slowly, in the dark. 'You remembered,' he says.

'Of course I remember the bear. I remember . . . everything.'

A breeze rattles the old windows.

Milo turns back to the bowl. For a while I watch him as he boils water and reads instructions on a boxed filter, my eyes heavy, Finally, he swipes soap across his palms in the bowl, and walks softly, slowly across the floor towards me, with it in his hands.

'Your bath, Cap,' he says, gently.

He crouches, places it down in front of me on the floor, and slowly gets on his knees. Steam rises from it, wisping like a snuffed candle, and his eyes flick to mine. So much *everything* in those eyes. Full of the whole world and too many thoughts. Thoughts I used to want to hold in my hands, organise for him, diffuse, read, like books . . .

He smiles as if he can hear my mind chattering; a tiny warm fraction, but then it falls.

'I'm almost too scared to look,' I say softly.

'But you can hardly see me in this light.'

I laugh, reluctant at first, but then all at once.

'You know I meant my ankle,' I say. 'Dad joke.'

Milo smiles, then looks down at my foot. 'Want me to take a look?'

I nod. Not because I need him to. Not because I'm incapable, myself, of lifting my own foot. Because I want him to. Because I want Milo to touch me. I want the gentleness of Milo Ford's soft hands on my skin; I, for the first time in my life, want someone to take care of me. It makes no sense. We make no sense. I'm still mad at him. I'm disappointed in him. But – I want nothing but him . . .

He slowly folds the hem of my trouser leg, so my ankle is exposed. His hand sweeps around my calf, fingertips grazing my skin. Goosebumps prickle. Hairs on the back of my neck stand up. He grasps my ankle, like you would a wrist. 'This OK?' he asks, lifting gently.

And it does ache, but I say yes, anyway. And with two gentle, strong hands, he lowers it slowly into the warm water. At first it stings. A lot. But then it fades, and my eyes flutter with how wonderful it feels.

'Looks a little better,' he whispers, removing one hand, in a trickle of water droplets, but leaving his other hand at the skin, gently, where it's bruised, in the water with me. I nod, suddenly unable to speak.

'Thank you,' I say.

He looks up at me and swallows in the dark, candle-light glinting in his eyes. 'Always.'

And then, without a thought, the words tumble from my mouth. 'You never texted me back,' I say. 'The morning after your wrap party. You texted that night once, when you got home from the dinner, but no more. Until the next afternoon.'

We've covered so much, but never that. And it's always bothered me. The period of digital darkness before the leak happened. He'd texted to say he couldn't stop thinking about me, and then – nothing. Not until the following afternoon. Not until he was about to take off, for the UK. The leak was added to the forum that morning, reported on by Verified Insider's Instagram that afternoon.

Milo looks to the ground and takes a long, deep breath.

'I always felt like shit about that, Allie,' he says. 'But we all had dinner, I went back to my apartment late, texted when I got home to your phone, at like, 1 a.m. or something, then a group of us went to our writer's apartment. We stayed up late. Just chatting. Someone had a guitar. It was so long ago, I don't even . . . but, anyway, I fell asleep there.'

I nod. That night was something I came back to a lot, as proof he was always responsible. Just like Sue Lewis, the publicist, the interviews, the memes. My unanswered texts glaring proof I was far from his mind, my messages already making their way out of there, into the air, like thrown confetti.

'I dropped by,' he says, gently.

'Dropped by?'

He nods. 'After you blocked me. On my way to the airport. I don't know, I was worried. But you weren't home. Sian was.'

I stare at him. 'W-where was I? She – Sian never said.'

'The university. She told me you were having a meeting about Bermuda. A sudden injection of cash, or whatever.'

Ah. The donation. I remember clearly, that meeting. I hadn't eaten, nor slept. I sat opposite my awkward supervisor, equal parts overjoyed by the donation and embarrassed she had clearly read all the viral material and disapproved.

'Milo, I would never—'

'I know.' He looks up at me and smiles. Just like all the puzzle pieces I jammed together, that was one Milo had forced to fit, too. That I had leaked them for money. 'I sometimes think if you'd shown up, everything would've been different. We'd have talked. I'd have been able to really look at you.'

I nod, tearfully. He's right. He's probably completely right.

'I'm glad, though,' he says. 'Because I got to see June House. Couldn't quite see the gnome, Sian didn't let me in. But I saw the pink door. I saw your window you'd show me the sun through. The tree you said your mother loved . . .'

Something warm and true blossoms inside of me. Because those fragments of my life – he remembers them. The pink door. My home. My window. Mum's tree . . .

Without thinking, my hand gravitates towards him. That smile. Those eyes. 'Is it all the truth?' I ask, swallowing tears. 'Everything you said? Because I need to know. I need to hear you say it.' I touch the side of his beautiful face.

He looks surprised at first, eyes unblinking; almost like he thinks I've made a mistake. Then I see his Adam's apple bob in his neck. There's a long, thick pause.

'It's the truth,' he says.

I keep my hand there, our eyes on each other's, and slowly, he leans forward and lightly, like a brush of feathers, puts his warm lips to my knee and kisses.

I reach my hand around, run it through his soft hair.

Electricity races up my legs, my thighs, my stomach, my groin. Every inch of my skin clenches with goosebumps.

Then he pulls his soft lips away slowly, hand drifting down my calf, and I drop my hand, bring it back to my lap.

For a moment, we stare at each other. Eyes shining. Chests slowly rising and falling. Fire roaring. I feel it all. Everything for him builds and pushes its way through me. All I want is to touch him; to press into him.

'For the record, I remember everything too,' he says. 'I tried to forget, but . . . I remember everything. I remember every single moment of you.'

And looking at him, right now, I lean into pretending – side-stepping into that alternate world where nothing ever tore us apart. I let the world envelop me.

'Kiss me,' I whisper.

His eyes linger on mine, widening a little with surprise. Then he swallows, breathes heavily. 'You want me to kiss you?'

I can't speak, so I nod.

And then Milo moves towards me, takes my face in his hand, sweeps it down my cheek, runs a thumb along my bottom lip, parting my mouth. He leans closer, brushes his lips across mine.

'I want to hear you say it again, Allie,' he whispers.

'Kiss me,' I say against his mouth, all breath, barely any sound.

And he does. He hesitates at my mouth, gently pushes the hair away from my face, then kisses me.

Chapter Twenty-One

Milo

Allie and I kissed last night – and I can't stop thinking about it. Her mouth. The tiny gasps of breath. A slow, beautiful smile dawning across her face as we pulled away the first time.

And I want to do it again and again.

It's all I've thought about. Can't get her out of my damn head.

We kissed more after the first – the ankle bath poured away, more wood on the fire – pressed next to each other on a creaking camp bed. Her hands cradling my face, her leg bent and L-shaped over my thigh, my hand skimming the curve of her breast, the sounds in the back of her throat, her body moving into my hands . . . God. It was difficult to stay in the moment. That *woman*. I've never wanted someone more.

I got up to light more candles, to reinforce the door, the wind thrashing it angrily, and Allie fell gently to sleep, a tiny smile on her face. I kept throwing glances over at her sleeping soundly, thinking about how much like the rest of my life it felt, and how I wanted to kiss her again. The whole day was a glimpse into something that could be. And, in the camp bed next to hers, I fell asleep too. *Fast.* And yeah, I never just *fall asleep*.

But, while I'd been daydreaming, Allie had been formulating an itinerary for our final day here in Cote Rock in her sleep. She woke me up already dressed and raring to go this morning. Work mode: activated.

'We need to head to my puffins, then go back to camp,' she'd smiled from the old wooden table. 'Weather's better today.'

I wanted to take her hand, drag her over to the bed, fold her into me, put my lips all over her warm skin. But of course I didn't. I just agreed, jumped up, got dressed, pretended not to see her glance over when I took off last night's shirt. Obedient, as Iris said. That's me.

And that's where we are. The sky a clean-slate blue, the way it is after the spring clean of a storm, standing on a cliff face. Surrounded by puffins. And I am totally terrified of falling to my death, but also, like always out here, in awe. These birds, they're completely, totally awesome. Their beaks like orange windsails, their neon feet. Real-life cartoon characters. I can't stop filming them. I can't believe these things exist. The babies are called pufflings, too. *Pufflings*. The cutest shit.

Allie is in full work mode, investigating their burrows. 'Would you mind passing me my camera, please?' she asks.

I'm in charge of the bag again.

'Is that the, uh – the same one we had with the auks? The black probe? Is that what I'm looking for?' I laugh at the word 'probe', and although she would normally totally not, Captain Lake's mouth twitches. Her arm is deep into a crevice in the rock.

'That's the one.'

I want to tell her she's hot when she's in work mode. That she's hot in every mode, but when she's all badass like this – smart, that goddamn genius brain with all those polished cogs, whirring – I have to fight every urge to pull her into me . . . I wouldn't. She'd kick my ass if I did. I mean, she is currently headfirst in a hole in the side of the same mountain that's turning my legs to banana pudding. Which is just a very Allie thing for her to do. She is not thinking of last night, like I am. She is not thinking of our mouths together, like I am . . .

She emerges, takes the probe from me, and she inserts it into the burrow.

'I just . . .' Her voice is muffled, she's practically lying down on the side of this cliff. 'I need to get a good angle.'

'Jeez. Be careful, Allie.'

'It's fine.'

'But it's high up here. Like, insanely.' I've been trying not to look down. I've been pretty distracted, but I did not notice how high we were. Until, well, now. 'We were not this high before. Right?'

'Try and sit your body somewhere, if you're feeling the height,' she says, reasonably. 'It helps with grounding.' She emerges again, squints, fishing her hand deeper and deeper into the burrow. She holds a little screen, watches. 'They're nestled so far in . . . Is that . . .' She's fully in her head. Laser-focused.

'Little puffin dudes are probably wondering what the hell is going on,' I mumble, letting out a long breath. 'Kind of like I am right now. I still find it crazy we don't have a safety harness? Or like . . . I don't know. A parachute.' I laugh, but I do sort of mean it.

'Little puffin dudes are just fine,' she says. 'It's minimal disturbance for them, I assure you. At the very least, they – gosh, this is such a bloody deep burrow – they might just be raising a single proverbial eyebrow.'

'Hm,' I say, pressing my hands against the rock behind me, placing my back against it. Grounding my ass . . . 'Do puffins *have* eyebrows then?'

'I said proverbial,' she repeats with a tiny smirk. 'Oh. Oh my God. *No*. H-hang on—'

'What?'

Allie has brightened. Suddenly. Like someone has run a fingertip on the stiff end of a paintbrush, spraying stars onto a calm, still canvas. 'They're— Oh my God.' She looks up at me. 'They're back together.'

'Who – what?'

'Milo, this is . . .' She smiles, then starts to laugh. It's beautiful, her laugh. Her smile, that slightly wonky tooth, that gasped breath on her inhale. The way she says my name. All lightness and music. 'Lucky and Mart – we try not to name them normally, because you can get attached and it can get sad, but . . . well, we named these—'

'Lucky and Mart . . .'

'Yes! A researcher named them, a few years ago, can't remember the reason why. This colony's pretty small, so it's easier to get invested. But the first year I was here, they'd broken up. Like, full on broken up and switched partners.'

'That *happens*?'

'Not normally, but occasionally, yeah. I mean, like humans, anything goes sometimes. But anyway, Lucky and Mart – they were always together. And then suddenly they weren't.' She laughs. She talks fast, excitedly. It's infectious, and I'm already smiling.

'Cute shit,' I smile.

'Yep. *Well*. Lucky and Mart appear to have missed each other, because . . . they're back together.' Then she does the cutest thing. She squeaks and claps her hands together. 'They're in there, Milo! Together again.'

'What? Seriously?'

'And there's an egg too.'

'Oh, man, *really?*' and suddenly I'm invested. I am so invested in Lucky and Mart and their little puffling baby. I'm so *happy* for Lucky and Mart that I kind of want to reach on in there and take them for a pizza and karaoke. Maybe have them sing 'Perfect Day' with me, buy ice-cream on the way home . . .

'Wanna see?' she asks, sliding her arm back into the burrow. She holds the screen up to me and I take it. And I genuinely feel emotion at the sight of it. A wave of it. These two cute puffins totally snuggled together, in the dark, away from the cold and away from the world. A small egg nestled beneath them.

'Wow. They're . . . they're awesome, Allie.'

'I know.' She smiles down at me. 'Isn't it just the most perfect sight?'

'I dunno,' I say. 'I think seeing you this happy is.' Allie looks down at her feet, but a smile prods the corner of her mouth. 'If that's not too corny to say.'

'It is,' she says. 'But thank you for saying it.'

We stay there, together, watching Lucky and Mart in calm, happy silence for a while. They're so beautiful. Like creatures from a Pixar movie. They snuffle next to each other, eyes blinking, beaks occasionally clacking together. They look like they've always been this way. I wonder what made them leave. And what made them find their way back?

'How long?'

Allie looks over at me, sun in her eyes. 'How long?'

'Yeah,' I ask. 'How long have they been apart?'

And she clears her throat. 'Two years,' she says. 'They've been apart two years.'

Chapter Twenty-Two

Allie

The hike back passes quickly. It's raining again now, but the temperature has risen a little, and the winds have let up. My ankle feels a lot better, too, and the puffins are all doing so well, it's left me feeling buoyant and hopeful. So very many things happen out here that fill me with nothing but dread for the future. Melting ice, collapsing before our eyes, landing like meteors into the sea. Birds who don't breed. Finding birds we've tracked from chicks, washed up, wings tangled in plastic – but days like today make me feel as though it's working. That the world is not so bad, so long as we keep giving it what it needs, and adding only good. That there's still so much beauty, still so much hope.

And after last night, I needed the distraction of today. Because since last night, I don't know how to act. I don't know what to *do*. Was the kissing a mistake? It makes perfect, logical sense that it absolutely *was* a mistake, and so I'm attempting to act accordingly. Because, logically, it *was* silly to kiss Milo (a lot) and I shouldn't have asked him to. We should never have stayed in that cabin. He should not have bathed my foot, touched his lips to my bare knee. Because mere days ago, I was sure Milo was the man who betrayed me and upended my life. Now I'm sure he isn't, and that something else – *someone else* – did. Which means we can pick up where we left off, counting down the minutes to each other. And I can hardly imagine what that might look like. Me, here, with birds, off-grid. Him, in New York, in LA, under the world's spotlight . . .

But something totally illogical is that it doesn't feel like a mistake. Kissing Milo doesn't feel silly, not at all. In fact, Milo's mouth on mine – I shiver every time I think about it – felt like everything. Like nothing I had ever experienced, and yet, the most *right* thing. The heat of him against me. His strong, safe hand grasping my behind, pulling me into him.

So, of course, I woke up in the cabin, terrified. And thank God, fieldwork was there, waiting for me as it always is. A safe constant. So, I threw myself into it like it was a swimming pool on a hot day. Tomorrow, it'll be time to head back to the station, and I've decided everything will feel clearer then. Getting back, having dinner and going over research, a long hot shower, my own bed . . . Except, Milo will be leaving. And as much as I try to tell myself it'll all be OK, that I can scooch back to normality, as it was just a few days ago, I know it can't. Not now. But I don't even know what that *means* . . .

The rain is getting heavier and after days of fieldwork, wet clothes and no bathrooms, everyone is exhausted and has taken to their tents. There's nothing much to do in weather like this. Polly is napping and, last I saw, Jameson and Milo were sharing AirPods and looking over some of the footage. And me, I'm staring at the bowing ceiling of the tent, going over, once more, a mental checklist of everything I need to do before going back tomorrow.

Iris edges closer to me. She's bundled up in layers – a fleece, coat, Milo's hat (he's given it to her) – and she's listening to an audiobook about near-death experiences.

Rain hammers on the roof. Polly snoozes beside us.

'So,' whispers Iris, pulling out her earphone. 'Are you ready yet now Polls is asleep?'

'Mm?'

'About the last twenty-four hours,' she whispers with a grin. 'I hope you know that you're *not* going to get away with not telling me everything. What happened?'

'What do you mean?' I ask, even though I know it's utterly pointless to try to pretend. This is Iris. Iris knows everything about me. Even when I like to pretend she doesn't.

'Oh please, amigo.' We're twisted towards each other like two children at a sleepover. 'Don't start that shit with me.'

'I'm not.' I groan and pull my sleeping bag higher over my head.

'*Allie.*'

'I'm tired,' I say.

'We're *all* tired.'

I hide beneath the shiny, noisy material.

'Something happened, didn't it?' she presses. Then she leans in and squeaks with excitement beside me, into my ear.

'Maybe.'

'I swear when that man radioed me again, worrying himself sick about your ankle, I was sold. You were asleep and he was harping on about fires and making you dinner—'

'He was not worrying himself sick,' I say from beneath the sleeping bag.

'He *was*. And do you know what he said? When he radioed later?'

I pull the cover down and stare at her. Rain sprays against the tarp, like a garden sprinkler. 'What did he say?' Because of course I want to know. Because, yes, I'm terrified, but all I want is for him to kiss me again. He feels right. Milo feels right.

Iris smiles, leans in and whispers, 'He said, *hey, yeah, my girl's taking a nap.*'

'My girl?' I say.

'*My girl.*' Iris beams. 'He absolutely said *my girl.*'

'Oh, God.'

Everything rushes beneath my skin. Excitement. A static warm surge of it like I've been injected with something. And then fear. Hot, panicky fear that sounds like a panicked 'no no no' in my mind. And then a big what if? scuds in like a cloud of hope, sagging with what-could-bes.

'He is clearly falling in love with you, Allie,' whispers Iris.

'Don't be silly—'

'What?'

I pause. '*Is he*?'

'Are you?'

Then, beside me, Polly clears her throat. Polly's known for things like this: to be partial to slight theatrics. 'Are we talking about *Allo Lord*?' Polly shrugs from within her sleeping bag.

From the next tent, Lars starts laughing at something unseen. 'Yeah!' he's saying. 'I know, right?' It reminds me how close we all are, and I hold a finger to my lips.

'Sorry, darling,' Polly whispers. 'But I'm awake now and I've yet to obtain the ability to turn my ears off, so.'

'Allo Lord?' I ask.

'Yours and Milo's ship name,' says Iris with a laugh a little *too* loud for a flimsy, non-sound-proofed tent. 'Polly didn't know what a ship name was, so I schooled her and she came up with it. Pretty fast actually. The perfect blend of Allie Lake and Milo Ford, if you ask me.'

'Allo Lord is *awful*!' I whisper. 'It sounds like a . . . bad eighties sitcom or something.'

'I said this, but it's grown on me, you know.' Iris smiles at me, excitable and girlish, a sparkle in her eye. 'Plus, it's her first attempt. I think it should be celebrated.'

Despite myself, I laugh too. A touch of hysteria and giddiness, caused by tiredness. 'Some people – online people – say Mallie.'

'Nah,' says Polly simply.

'Since when has it been Allo Lord?' I ask, now trying to stifle the laughs desperate to burst out of me. If we were back at the research station, we'd all be guffawing and barking with laughter, packets of Maltesers open on the coffee table in the common room, legs folded beneath us, blankets shared. It's difficult trying to keep so quiet in what's essentially a cloth-built room.

'Since the boat moment,' Polly replies. 'When you had to go on the dinghy together to get the gear? Well. I noticed something might be off. Iris and I had a secret chat after the human knot.'

'Iris told me *off* when I got back to the tent after the human knot,' I remind her.

'She told me what had happened between you both.' Polly grins. 'I couldn't believe it was him. *The* guy. But then, crikey, did it make sense. All the sexual tension I couldn't get my noggin around.'

'There was no sexual tension,' is all I say and Polly says, as bluntly as if she was discussing funding applications, 'Yes there was.'

'There was none.'

'Oh fuck off,' says Iris and she says this in the most un-whispered voice I've ever encountered when in a tent with *material* for walls.

'Iris!'

'Sorry, sorry.' She clears her throat. 'That's just how strongly I feel about it.'

We glance at each other, three heads of wild hair and weather-beaten skin poking out of sleeping bags in a row. 'We have to remember this is a tent, not an actual brick wall. He could be listening.'

'Oh, he'll be asleep,' says Polly.

I shake my head. 'He doesn't sleep remember. He's a bit of an insomniac. He struggles with it.'

Iris makes a downward arc with her mouth. 'Is that so? And did he sleep last night? Because I'm *pretty* sure he said he slept like a log when he got back today.'

I feel my cheeks burn. 'Yeah, he, erm, did. I woke a few times and he was fast asleep. Beside me. Like on the next bed, I mean, a *separate* bed.'

'Disappointed about the separate bed deal,' mutters Iris.

Polly smiles, hair windswept and frizzy around her temples. 'He probably slept because he was with you.'

'We kissed,' I whisper. 'We kissed and it was amazing,' and beside me, Iris sinks into her sleeping bag, and Polly mouths, '*Yes*!!!!' two fists coming up to punch the air.

'Dying,' Iris utters from within the sleeping bag. 'Actually dying.' And I so want to just envelop myself in it. All this excitement. All this hope. But . . . gah.

'Oh, I don't know,' I groan.

Iris snuggles closer. 'Oh, mate, what don't you know?'

I stare at the pitched roof of the tent. It billows a little, with the cold spring breeze.

'I don't know any of it,' I whisper. 'Let's just say we somehow . . . *move forward*. Ignore all the awful stuff that happened. Forget it. How it would even work? And I feel like I still want answers, about how it happened . . .'

'I knew you felt something,' says Iris, distractedly. 'I just knew it. And he's clearly a goner. The man's eyes are all moon.'

I close my eyes. I feel like I'm inches from the top of a ladder. I'm scared to climb back down, but scared to take the final step up. 'But it could never work. Me? *Hollywood*? I don't even like a headshot being on the university's website.'

'You'd find a way,' says Polly. 'And what's the alternative, Allie? To live a life not worth watching?'

Chapter Twenty-Three

Milo

Tonight is my last night here. Tomorrow I leave, to go back to the US. But, for now, I stand on the barren edges of the island – the same Cote Rock that felt like the strangest, most uncanny dreamworld when we arrived just days ago. But now it feels like the stage upon which my life changed. I'll miss it. Everything about it. The snow. The tents. Puffins. Allie.

We're waiting for everyone to assemble onto the little dinghies to take us back to Lars, who's just moored up a few metres away, gazing up into the sky, vaping a puff and watching it disperse like the badass he is.

And although a part of me is grateful to get back to some humanity, to take a shower – *jeez*, I want a shower – I don't want to leave Allie. I can't believe I have to leave her. It's unthinkable.

So much has changed and transformed. That first boat trip to the island, we couldn't even speak without wanting to argue, to have the last, sharp, harsh, angry word. I couldn't envision, then, surviving these last few days. But now, I don't want them to end. I want them to loop and stretch and multiply. I want adventures with Allie Lake. I want to wake up with her and watch her sleep. I want to hear that laugh every day, for her laugh to be as familiar to me as birdsong. I want to kiss her lips. I want to close my eyes and listen to her breathing, let it lull me to sleep. How can I leave? *How* can I go home without her? And yet, I have to. I have to leave. I have the awards ceremony. I have a pilot to shoot. And Allie lives here, right now. Her *life* is here, and everything about my own is everything she doesn't want. And there's a part of me that's scared to show her too – my real life. Those darker parts of me, the flawed, true, gritty, real-life parts . . . A part of me is scared I'd lose her.

'Milo?'

'Uh-huh?'

I turn on the snow.

Allie laughs, hair in pigtails, each one poking out from under her hat. 'Are you getting on the boat? Or are you staying here forever with Lucky and Mart?' A sunbeam perfectly lights her face, and I wonder if I'll remember this moment, revisit the memory. Just her, skin lit by sun, close enough for me to reach out, take her hand.

And her question might be a joke, but I'm so close to saying 'Staying forever. With you.' Instead, I say, 'Oh. Yeah. Sure.'

But my feet don't want to move. It's like if they move, that's it, it's begun, a slow journey away from her. We'll leave this island. And then we'll leave Svalbard, leave Norway, leave Europe. And we'll leave her. Once again, Allie and I will be apart. Once again, we'll be something that 'was' once, in a weird blink in time. And maybe that's what Allie wants. She hasn't said much of anything, since the cabin. Maybe we just pretended for the sake of the note, and that's that. I wanted that for a day or two, to make it easier for us both. But now, one day with Allie could never be enough.

We board the boat, my chest a hollow cave. Allie talks to Lars most of the trip back, Jameson films and Iris observes, and I watch Cote Rock slowly get further and further away. I think about our cabin. I think about our kiss. And I think about those two birds, two years apart, now holed up next to each other, the rest of the world outside. And I feel sure, in a crystallised moment, that I'd leave it all behind for her.

Chapter Twenty-Four

Allie

There is something so exciting about coming back to the station after an expedition. It's the return to civilisation; the warm bed. The team who are like family. Smiling faces in the cafeteria. The download-chats over tea and our chef, Gustav's, suspicious-looking new experimental bake. It feels like coming home.

As per tradition, as soon as we all trudge inside, as much as we're all desperate for showers, clean sheets and comfortable clothes, we head into the common room – two researchers I don't recognise are already in there, sitting on the sofas chatting, and Oliver, our PI, is there with a pile of papers and reading glasses on the end of his nose.

He grins, eyes lighting up at the sight of Milo and Jameson. 'They've returned!' he says. 'And with an Oscar-worthy movie, I hope . . .'

Jameson smiles, tiredly. 'Oh, it will be eventually, dude. Right now, though, it's a mess. Like us.'

'Everyone is very excited, though. I had no idea you had so many followers . . .'

And it's weird to think about Milo and Jameson in that way – how they are to the rest of the world. Followers. Clout. Reach. *Stars*. To know people stop them for selfies, take covert pictures of them, write about them, for people who really want to *read* about them. Something about it makes them feel further from me. I almost can't think about who they are back on earth – how it changes things.

For now, we all arrange ourselves on the slightly tatty grey sofa, all but politely scramble to the coffee table, pouring tea and coffee, placing cookies onto napkins. The common room is spotless. Carpets vacuumed. A haze of pine air freshener. There's a single PC on a computer table in the corner. It'll be time for a radio silence break soon. On Tuesdays and Sundays, the ban on internet use is lifted. Jameson is already talking about how excited he is to sync the GoPro footage to his cloud, to check his emails and subscriber count.

Milo sits on the bend of the sofa, beside Jameson, his arm thrown back behind him, a lazy hand through his hair, and I watch him as he takes everything in. He was quiet on the journey back. I wondered what he was feeling. Did he want to leave? Was he dreading it?

Around me, everyone catches up, others appearing in the doorway just to say hi, Polly setting up her iPad, ready to go over a few things for Oliver.

Over the din, Milo looks over at me. 'Hi,' he mouths. 'Hi,' I smile, and slowly his mouth breaks into a smile too, and we're both laughing at nothing. Oh, I don't want him to leave. I know there are worse things in the world, but right now, I can hardly bear to consider it. I keep thinking about what Polly said last night: finding a way. Could we? Could I really just, what? *Date . . . date* Milo Ford?

Jameson plays him something on his camera. Milo smiles. Genuine. Glassy-eyed. He's so beautiful. His soul – and I can't believe I'm even saying such a thing because I didn't think I even believed in souls, not like Milo does – is golden. Wholesome. Is that really something you think about someone you're going to just happily let go?

Moments later, Polly has her iPad connected to the large screen on the wall, and she's showing Oliver photos and various notes; things she and Lars worked on. It's strange seeing pictures of day one, day two, day three . . . I'd been oblivious to it. All this going on while I was losing my mind. Iris joins in, talks to Oliver about pH and salinity and Jameson comes to unexpected life when Polly starts to talk about nitrates and the nutrient levels. It makes me smile.

Milo gestures with a cock of his head towards the screen. His eyes are tired but glinting. 'Concentrate,' he mouths.

'No,' I mouth back.

'Do as you're told,' he mimes slowly, and we both start laughing silently, pressing our lips together to try to stifle it. I feel tired and giddy and giggly, and it feels nice. It feels so nice to be here, and not where we were, days ago.

'Oh, and Allie – Oliver you won't believe what Allie discovered. This cheered us all up. Allie—' Polly turns to me, all pink cheeks and excitement. 'Tell him about the puffins . . .'

I talk about them. About Lucky and Mart. And it's nice, to once more feel that full, warm feeling of hope.

More photos are shown, more notes are taken, more tea is poured from lukewarm, town-hall-like teapots.

Then: there it is.

And I don't know why exactly it stops me in my tracks, but it does.

A photo on the screen.

Milo, at the sight of it, smiles at me, across the busy room.

In the photo, Milo and I are on the mound. The mound upon which we sat looking at kittiwakes. Us, silhouetted against the blinding, endless sun. The dome of the sky. We're looking at each other. We're smiling. And we look . . . exactly how I always hoped I'd look someday, with someone.

But as people slowly turn their heads towards it, then back at us, heads bobbing as if watching a slow tennis match, something drags hard inside my chest. My hand lands there. I feel exposed. If I don't let Milo go, if I *find a way*, photos like that . . . they won't just be for our eyes. They'll be accessible everywhere. *We* will be. Immortalised in print forever, *again*, regardless of how we end up. I can't help thinking about how the leak really happened too. What if it happens again? Another breach of our privacy, beyond our control.

The rest of the catch-up session blurs. People leave, Lars and Polly, and I go to follow. I need a break to think. I need space.

'Um. Can we just – Allie?' It's Jameson. But he's looking at both me and Milo.

'You going to make one of your speeches?' jokes Milo. 'Because I'm feeling sort of emotional today and that might push me *right* over the edge.'

'No,' Jameson laughs. 'But I was thinking, when we're off the whole radio silence thing later, could we all

LIA LOUIS

meet in the computer room?' He looks over at Iris, as if
for backup or something. 'Us four?'

'A look over the footage,' affirms Iris.

I nod. 'Oh. Sure.'

'We can have a farewell,' says Milo with a sad smile.
'Before we leave.'

And for a second, there's a blink of relief to this uneasy,
scared feeling pooling hot in my gut. I want him to stay,
and I want him to leave all at once.

Chapter Twenty-Five

Allie

After dinner, I take what feels like the longest, steamiest, soapiest shower I have ever taken. And the whole time in the glass cubicle, a watermelon and coconut scent washing away the salt and sulphur, I think of Milo. I think of that moment in the common room, the way he'd said, softly, 'Before we leave.' I think about the last few days. I think about the way he kissed me and how it felt like home. The way he read to me back then. Bunty's. Ice packs. Ankle baths. Holding me on a cliffside. All of it amalgamates into one glowing orb. And I don't know what on earth to do with it.

I take myself to my room, and although I am now lying down in my bed, soft mattress and clean, brushed cotton sheets, I feel rigid. Uncomfortable. Like I'm a magnet walking the wrong way from the thing I am most drawn to in the world.

I stare at the ceiling.

Is this it?

Is this . . . falling *in love*? How do people continue to walk around like sane human beings while this is happening to them? *You're telling me*, I want to say to some sort of authority, *that people experience this and then have to go into work?* They have to get an eyebrow wax,

291

go and do a food shop while they feel like they're being reborn and tortured all at once? There should be some sort of law against it. You should be allowed to pace in agony and talk for hours to your friends, unencumbered and without responsibility. You should be able to play Spotify Love playlists and look for philosophical answers. They should give you annual leave for falling in love.

I sit up in bed.

Milo is leaving tomorrow.

Milo's leaving.

He's leaving, and once he has, there're no more planes until next week.

He's leaving, and I have to stay.

And when he leaves, do I really – *really* – want it to be forever?

I know he didn't leak the messages. Don't I?

I know he did the stupid TV show and magazine covers and memes because, like me, he was heartbroken. He wanted his say; a reclaiming of control over a situation he had no part in. Like I did.

Maybe the real *us* doesn't look like I think it does. Who says it has to be photos and spotlights?

I know the real Milo *is* the Milo who looked after me in that cabin. The real Milo kisses me like he's savouring every second, folding it away, slotting it like a note, in his memory. The real Milo reads to me until I fall asleep. The real Milo celebrates what I do. He remembers it all, retains it, has made it important to him. *He's here.*

What's the alternative? To live a life not worth watching?

I jump up and push through my bedroom door, walk fast down the corridor towards his and Jameson's room. A text message sound dings distantly somewhere – ah. It's six. The internet can be used and radio silence, lifted, just for two hours. The mad clamour for a little digital respite.

We'll have to meet Iris and Jameson in the computer room soon, but until then, there's still time.

I knock on the door.

Three hard knocks.

'Hold up,' comes Milo's voice. 'I'm just . . . getting some pants on.'

It makes me smile. It makes me blush. It makes excited heat zip through me. This makes no sense. This makes *no* sense. At all. But, somehow, it makes all the sense in the world. What I *feel* makes sense. And I can't have him leave forever. I cannot let this be the last time I see Milo Ford.

Milo throws opens the door. His long wavy hair clumps in wet chunks, like thick blades of grass. He's topless and wearing grey jogging bottoms, with a black cord of a necklace around his tanned neck, the sort a surfer wears. He is – objectively – gorgeous.

'Hey.' He smiles widely. 'Sorry, I . . . just showered and I'm enjoying some kinda naked heater action? It's good. Really recommend.'

I say nothing. I now feel totally frozen by the sight of him. And by a knowing that regardless, Milo is . . . that person. My person. A person that will forever be a story of mine. These are the moments people write love stories about. Tragedies. Agony aunt letters. Love songs. Heartbreak songs for that matter. And I'm not even sure what comes next for me. A tragedy or love story. But right in this moment, not finding out is simply not an option.

'Wanna come in?' he asks.

I nod. 'Yes, please.'

He whips away a T-shirt and a wet towel from his bed.

'Take a seat,' he says. 'And I'll, um . . .' He looks around. 'Fix us absolutely nothing.'

I laugh, slowly sit down. Beneath me, the mattress springs squeak.

'From the man who made me dinner and an ankle bath out of nothing but sheer will?'

He smiles, a wonky boyish smile. ''Fraid so, Captain. I can only work with what I've got, and what I've got here is . . . less than minimal.'

The air is thick between our bodies, like heavy static. I fidget on the bed. Stiff limbs and tight breaths. Milo stands, eyes on me, hands on lean, tanned hips.

'So. Tomorrow.'

He releases a long breath, and it ruffles his hair. 'Tomorrow,' he says. His voice is low and croaky again, and there's something sexy about it. I think it reminds me of his bedtime voice. That deep, gruff, familiar sound that kept me company, through the phone . . .

Milo carefully lowers himself down next to me. He draws a big, heavy breath in and I meet his eyes. His Adam's apple contracts in his neck. I can smell him, and the man smells incredible. Apples. That spicy, intense deodorant. That smell that is totally Milo's warm, shower-dappled skin . . .

'Allie, I don't want to leave you,' he says, finally.

My entire body stiffens.

'You might not want to hear this, or you might be apprehensive or suspicious that I'm saying this,' he speaks carefully, 'but – I mean it. I don't want to leave you. *Can't*. And the truth is. I've never been the same. Since you. Like . . .' He laughs. 'After all of it. The mess, the stupid mistakes, the different versions of myself I've had to shed since . . . what hasn't changed is that I have never, ever gotten over you.' He looks up at me. 'Come with me.'

'Leave with you?' I feel disorientated. I came here to tell him how I feel and hadn't quite expected this – a solid, clear proposition.

'Yeah. Just – come with me tomorrow.'

I laugh. 'I would love to, Milo, but I can't. I . . . have things to do here for the next three weeks . . .'

'Then meet me in three weeks,' he says, softly. He takes my hand, gently, envelops it between his. 'I've actually got an awards thing? I'm up for one. Best Male Lead. For a play I was in on Broadway. They say there's a good chance I'll get it which . . .' He looks up and meets my eyes. 'Come with me.'

'Milo, that's amazing.'

'Be there with me,' he says, almost whispering. 'Please.'

The beat after the please feels heavy. A 'what if' balancing in my palm. Me. At an awards ceremony? Crowds and cameras and social media and thousands of judging eyes. With Milo. Could I? *Could I?* Right here, in an arctic research station, it feels absurd such a thing awaits him.

'Really? God, I don't know. What would I . . . How does it all work? Where?'

He shrugs. 'Manhattan, Four Seasons. The fourteenth, 4 p.m. All the fours. Only reason I remembered.' He gives a low, almost bashful laugh. 'It's black tie, but, personally, I'm requesting these pyjamas . . .' He thumbs the fabric of my sleeve, fingers resting at the skin on my wrist.

'I . . . I don't know what to say.'

'I know.' He swallows. 'And listen, there's no pressure. You know that. But – this can't end here.'

'Milo—'

'I know you want to say I'm crazy and too much shit has happened. But today I had this realisation.'

'Milo . . .'

'That I am mostly always something to everyone,' he says. 'I'm so rarely just *me* to someone. Someone who sees me as just Milo. I can be a meal-ticket. An ass. A story. A commodity. An ass*hole*. But so rarely just me to someone. But I am with you, Allie. With you, I'm not something, I'm me.'

'Milo.'

'Don't say it.'

'No.' I shake my head. 'I was going to say I don't know how this will work, or what will come next, or what I'm even *doing*.'

'No and I neither do I, but—'

'*I don't care.*' And we both say that at the exact same time. In perfect synchrony. And then we laugh. A laugh that means 'are we really doing this?' and 'what're we even doing?' and 'I've missed you' and 'I'm falling in love with you' and 'I've never been so scared' and 'I've never been so hopeful'.

Then our lips are colliding.

And we're kissing.

It's hotter, hungrier, than that night in the cabin, but slow, like he's savouring me; remembering me. His hand holds the side of my face, thumb hovering at my chin. I pull myself closer to him, lay a hand on his hard, shower-damp chest.

'God, Allie . . .' he whispers into my mouth, hot and wet, his tongue touching mine, slow and deft, and I feel everything. I pull back and hold his face. His beautiful face. And I drink it in. This Milo is real. He has to be.

'Don't ever stop kissing me,' I whisper to him, before pressing my mouth against his again.

'Now or ever?' he smiles into my mouth.

And I take the last step, to fly or fall.

'Ever,' I say.

Chapter Twenty-Six

Milo

Leaving this woman, even for three weeks, even for a moment, is going to kill me.

Leaving her is going to single-handedly destroy me. And kissing her like this, on this bed . . . I've never wanted time to stop more. I want every part of her. I want every bit, every inch, skin, heart, soul, every day . . .

She twists her hands in my hair, tugs a little. Her lips taste so sweet, her bottom lip so soft. I've been replaying this over in my mind since we first kissed, have had to snap myself out of it, like *Come on, man. Head in the game.* But now it's happening, it's *real*, I'm trying to take it slow. I want to embody every second I'm with her; want to bury every moment deep within me, never forget it. I want to be stuck in a time loop of Allie Lake, on this bed, forever. My mouth on her soft, warm lips, my hand under her shirt . . .

'Milo,' she whispers against my mouth, pulling back but lips still touching mine.

Milo. Milo. I love the way she says my fucking name. She makes it sound new.

She moves closer to me, a hand sliding around my neck, a tiny hum at the back of her throat. This woman is heaven. I've got to keep my cool. Keep it slow. But all I can think about is where my hands are desperate to be . . .

There's a knock on the door.

No. No, *surely* not.

There's another. Seriously?

'Shit.'

Allie pulls back, wide-eyed. She starts to laugh, embarrassed. Colour floods to her cheek, a hand flies to her mouth.

'*Hello?*' comes a voice.

'Is that Polly?' I whisper. I lean, dive for Allie's mouth and she kisses back but leans away. Pushes a finger against my lips. A wordless 'hold on'.

'Um. Hello?' she calls huskily. 'Y-Yes?!'

We listen.

'So sorry, Allie,' calls Polly, 'But could I just . . . I couldn't locate you.'

'Of course!' she replies, flustered and pink-cheeked. 'I'll, um, just get the door!'

I look at her – *seriously?* She's straight up just inviting people in? I'm in pants. I'm half-naked. I'm hard.

Surprising me, though, she slowly kisses me. 'Why can't I stop doing that?' She laughs. 'Honestly, what on earth is wrong with me?'

I am on fire for this woman. I will worship the ground she walks on for the rest of my life. Captain, officer, asshole, *whatever.* I'll be whatever Allie wants me to be.

I quickly drag a towel over my lap. That's not obvious. Not obvious at all.

Allie opens the door. Polly stands there.

'Oh. Hello. Ha. Iris and Jameson wanted to know if you'd join them in the computer room. They worry you've got distracted.'

Chapter Twenty-Seven

Allie

I'm not sure what I expect when I enter the computer room. Fanfare maybe. Some relief we're together. But, instead, it's like walking into – *something*. Something we aren't yet privy to. Iris is standing excitedly, straight-backed, hands behind her back, and Jameson is nibbling on a fingernail, his eyes wide and eager.

'Well, hello, you two.' Iris beams. 'Take a seat.'

She's arranged two computer chairs beside each other. This place always feels like a classroom, but it feels even more like it now. A teacher's classroom before a scolding. Or before they tell you you've won a maths competition and get to watch a DVD on the TV on wheels as a prize. I'm not quite sure right now.

Milo and I sit down next to each other. Milo, like a schoolboy, is already laughing. Jameson starts giggling too, but he seems nervous, both hands in a prayer at his lips. Jameson's computer, I notice, is connected to a larger screen on the wall. I admit, it's quite difficult to focus. My body feels as though it's still in the bedroom, pressed against Milo.

Iris looks at me and wrinkles her nose. I *know* that look. It's a knowing sort of look. I've seen it a lot in our friendship, ever since we met in our second university year. Birthdays. Got-the-gossip coffee dates. Post-date rundowns. And I suddenly feel wobbly and uneasy. Exposed. There's something in the atmosphere of the room. They're smiling, but there's a strange foreboding. Something . . . isn't right. Or is that just anxiety? I'm not well acquainted with it, but it's been a strange few days, and I *am* exhausted. Fieldwork like Cote Rock leaves most feeling emotional.

Milo and I look at each other, and Milo leans in. 'Oh dear,' he whispers. 'Are we about to get the talk?'

Jameson guffaws. 'Waaay too late for that, I'd say, eh, mate? For you.'

Milo's clearly amused, but I feel glued to the seat. There's something weird going on – like the sudden change in the air that happens the seconds before the lights go down at a gig.

Then, there it is.

Jameson types.

And on the screen blinks a web page.

It's our leak. It's all our messages. Muscle memory means at the sight of them, my body instantly reacts as if it's that time again. My limbs stiffen, my heart plummets . . .

Jameson stands and folds his arms. He blows a long breath that ruffles his hair. Iris joins him. 'I guess . . . We've got something to tell you. Right?'

'Right,' says Iris. 'Do, erm, you want to start?'

Six Months Ago

To: Iris Deveaux
From: Jameson Merritt
Subject: Milo and Allie

Hey!

So nice to make your acquaintance and I'm looking forward to our video chat later. Here's a rough plan I drew up that I thought you could glance over beforehand, but the short version is: I'd hope to come over to Norway with Milo in April or May, when he has breaks between projects, but I want it to be beneficial to you guys, so if there's a better or more active or important time of year for your work, let me know and I can rethink. Most important is getting a lot of eyes on you and your amazing work, and I know Milo and I can do that for you.

Equally as important, though, is our love story. Man, I'm so excited for this!!! But it's what I'm most interested in hearing your thoughts on. I hear you on the wanting to shake them!! Me too. Milo cannot move on. He says he has, but the dude is still hooked on Allie. I think there's so much unfinished, it ended so abruptly, that he can't put it to bed, you know? I mean, they never once stood in front of each other. I've always said standing in front of each other would've fixed this whole thing ages ago. They let their wounds write the story. Like, it's never made sense to me that Allie leaked the phones. I mean, did she? Milo did not do this. He's a self-sabotaging motherfucker when he wants to be, he has his demons, but he would *not* do something like this.

That's why I'm so ready to do something.

What do you think? Can we do it? Get them together? Maybe (if they're cool with it) make the doc interspersed with the real story of the leak? Of them? Of how it happened? But all the while, most importantly, shining a light on your work. Something bigger than them. It'll be the ultimate gift to them both. A gift that will at first feel like a forfeit or something, but will ultimately get them their answers.

I know you say Allie won't be into being filmed and I get that. But if worst comes to worst and she doesn't want to talk about the leak, or Milo, we'll have a gorgeous doc to show for it. Whether their story is on camera, or off, it deserves its proper ending. Ahhhh, I'm kinda nervous! Where do we start?

Speak later.
Jameson x

Chapter Twenty-Eight

Milo

'We brought you both here,' says Jameson, nervously. 'Together. On purpose.'

Beside me, I feel Allie freeze. It's like I'm suddenly next to an ice sculpture. I can feel the coldness like you do when you step outside into the snow and the cold hovers in front of your skin like a ghost.

'This,' says Jameson. 'This trip. This film. We organised it.'

I stand up. A complete kneejerk reaction. 'So, you knew Allie was here?'

Jameson nods softly, and while I want to laugh, shout something like, 'What the hell, you crazy asshole,' because this *is* crazy and I had no idea, and shouldn't I have because this is totally Jameson? I don't. Because Allie, sitting down, beside me, lets out a small, but noisy breath. Her face is pale and expressionless.

'It's not exactly how it sounds,' jumps in Iris. She isn't looking at me. Not at all. She's looking at Allie, all wild eyes and unblinking. She looks like a mother or something. Like a mother who's suddenly realised her toddler's about to either burst into tears or flip out. 'I . . . I got an email a few months ago, from Jameson. He said he was looking to film a documentary; help a cause. And he'd been donating to us for a couple of years.'

'To the funding agency?' Allie asks, all whispers.

Jameson shrugs bashfully. 'This dude here got all dick-hard about donating to causes when he was talking to you,' he says. 'Told a bunch of us to put our money where our mouths were. I just *happened* to choose My Planet from his list. Then one day, few days before Christmas, I open a newsletter, and Iris is on it. Iris Deveaux.'

'Recognised my name.'

'It's a nice one,' Jameson grins.

'So he emailed via My Planet,' explains Iris, 'and it got to me, eventually. He asked about you, Allie, and then we video-chatted.'

'A lot like the phone swap actually,' chuckles Jameson. 'Video called to confirm we were who we said we were.' He's buzzing with this – *luminous* with it. Pulsating in a cloud of crackling, golden electricity. *Fuck.* This is insane. But it's genius. It's totally genius. Totally Jameson Merritt. I want to bear hug him to the ground. (And kick his ass.)

'Oh my God,' mutters Allie next to me. 'This is—'

'And then we just talked,' Iris rushes out. She's talking like she's against the clock – like an egg timer has been wound to sixty seconds and it's tick-tick-ticking down. 'At first, we talked about telling you both. Organising a meet-up . . .'

'But then I knew I'd never get him over here. He's too chicken shit.' Jameson laughs. And he's right. Of course, he's right. And now I can't stop replaying it all – every scene, like a home video in my mind, of everything lead-ing up to this point. I can read Jameson well; I know when he's feeling low, or when he's lying, but I had *no idea*. He asked me to do it, he showed me the place online, he booked in our medicals, and I just obediently watched documentaries for research and bought huge, stupid neon coats. Of course he knew he'd get away with it.

'The other team in Skomer had just had that movie made and go wild on TikTok, Oliver was talking about something similar anyway and . . . it was like two birds and one stone. Because I just knew how much you needed this too. Even if you felt you didn't.' Iris smiles, but her eyebrows knit together. And now we're all looking at Allie, breaths held tightly in our throats.

'Allie?' Iris asks, worriedly.

Allie clears her throat. 'Sorry, I just . . . You want to make a film? About us? The whole reason this blew up like it did . . .' She looks at me, sadly. Her pink lips still slightly swollen from all the kissing we were doing, just moments ago. I reach and push hair behind her ear. 'A film just feels—'

'No,' jumps in Jameson. 'Nothing has to happen without you being OK with it. Of course your work is the star. Ideally, you'd be a sort of . . . amazing B-story. A subplot. Like – it'd be: two guys turn up to film in the arctic to shine a light on something important for the world, and all while solving a matter of the heart.'

'But you don't have to do anything,' adds Iris. 'You're in control.'

'God . . .' Allie breathes.

'And, at first, I really didn't think it was a good idea, either. Did I, Jameson?'

He nods.

'But, amigo, I've told you for forever that I wanted this for you. Closure of some sort. For you to work through it. For *both* of you to. I knew you wouldn't ever do this if it wasn't about your work, which I *love* about you.'

'Same,' Jameson smiles at Milo.

'And I know you're happy here,' carries on Iris, 'but – you *miss* Bermuda.'

Allie looks up at Iris then, with huge blue eyes, and those eyes say so much, are full of words. Reams of them, unravelling into the room. I want to take Lars' boat over to Bermuda for her with nothing but a jet-skiing licence and my own idiocy.

'And when Jameson told me that Milo hadn't been the same since you, Allie, and I knew that the hows and whys keep nagging at you both, I just thought . . . we could use the awareness for this place. And Allie could use this. Needs it, even. And maybe we can even solve it all, together. Find out what really happened.'

I'm relieved when Allie smiles slowly. The air in the room calms a little, like dust suddenly kicked up in a beam of sunlight and settling. I know now, how tough this must be for her; how much strength it's taken her to hold just a little trust after everything. I now can't believe I *ever* thought it was her.

'When you say solve it,' mulls Allie, slowly, quietly. 'What do you mean?'

'Well, I've been starting to reach out to people. To see if they might talk to me,' Jameson is all arm gestures and enthusiasm. How has he kept all this shit from me? I'm filled to the brim with held-back happy, delirious, jack-ass laughter. 'I've heard back from someone at Verified

Insider, for example. Someone there says a journalist gave them the tip – that the leaked messages were on the forum. No money exchanged hands. I've reached out to some people in Romania, from the crew on the *Sharp Hearts* movie, too. Oh, and Iris has been talking to Sian.' At that, Allie's chest caves. A breath held, released. 'We want to build a picture of how it happened. So you can both move on. *Properly*. Be happy again. Because I feel like you were happiest in those days before the leak, mate. Allie made you happy. And clearly, it's no longer past tense. Seeing you both together . . .'

'I feel the same,' Iris says quietly.

Allie says nothing. And if she wasn't looking so terrified, I'd be launching myself onto Jameson right now, hugging his gangly-ass body. This is a stone-cold act of love from them both. But Allie looks shell-shocked again. It's the film. I could see how she felt about the photo on the screen earlier. Both of us up there 'in lights', multiple faces turned towards it. I wonder with Allie, how much of this has to go back to her Dad. I know it still plagues her – *being seen*. The way they had to move away without telling him. Lay low. *Of course* this is hard for her.

'Guys,' I say, standing. 'This is – this is amazing. I . . . I'm speechless.'

'Allie?' presses Iris.

'Do you want to take five?' I ask her. 'We can leave. Or we can talk. Or *I* can leave and leave you two to talk—'

'I'm OK,' she wobbles, looking up to meet Iris's eyes. 'Just . . . the Sian thing threw me.'

'I know. But she wants to help,' says Iris and I can tell that means something huge to Allie.

She brightens. Then she gives a laugh, that seems to relax all of us in the room. 'This is just . . . slightly insane. You . . . you were shocked when I woke you up, Iris. When they first landed and I woke you up, you were so shocked Milo and Jameson were here.' And now it's like she's processing it all slowly, in a classic aligned, organised Allie way.

'I *was*,' Iris laughs. 'They were meant to come the following morning! I went to bed because I was a nervous wreck and kept feeling guilty looking at you. Then they decided to land early and shit me right up. Originally Polly was meant to bring them to Cote Rock. Just for like, a day or two.'

'It wasn't our fault!'

'Polly knew?' Allie exclaims.

'To be honest, I was pumped that I got to use my new am-dram skills.'

And now we're all laughing and, somehow, hugging, and I feel so deeply *happy*. Can it really just end like this? Can we really just reunite, put out a movie, questions (hopefully) answered, and just – be?

Jameson clicks through some emails, shows us one from the Verified Insider contact, another from someone who might know someone who worked for them two years ago, another from someone at the *airline* we flew with.

'Whoa,' I keep saying. 'Seriously, J. *Wow*.'

'At first, we thought we might only be able to get you both to drop your pistols on each other by finding out what happened,' says Jameson. 'But I still think we need to know. Or at least, try? Like, can you imagine how

impactful that could be, getting the answers? And if –
and *only* if, Allie – you guys were OK with us weaving
in your story, I've got visions of it being like *Catfish*. You
know, the original doc? You think it's about one thing,
but it's about so much more?'

Catfish. He's mentioned that more than once since we
got here. Now I know why . . .

Allie's eyes slide over to me, definitely still at *least*
half-terror, but her mouth quirks a tiny, tiny smile. My
heart – it feels weightless. For everything these two
people, our friends, have tried to do for us.

Jameson's email bleeps – the sound for a new email.

He's in his full creative zone now, all shining-eyes and
energy.

'Holy shit,' says Jameson. 'Julia – remember Julia,
from *Sharp Hearts*?'

'Julia Noto?'

'Yeah! I reached out to her.'

'Why?'

I hate even thinking back to *Sharp Hearts* and
Romania. The shame about that time is still there. I
thought I was healing, really recovering – new phone,
new number, new project, four months out of rehab –
but I wasn't. Not at all. The only good and pure thing
about that time was Allie. Everything else – I was a
slow-burning trainwreck. I was clean off the benzos,
but had started on wine watered down with tonic
water, as if that meant anything *like* recovery. I was
still lost. Even J didn't know the extent of it at the time.
He was the only one I've ever said it aloud to. Nobody
else knows about the addiction that seeped in after

Day Falls, slowly during Romania, so slowly that it looked like progress – one or two drinks that turned down the volume in my brain, that slowly turned into more, and even *more* after the leak. But I haven't known how to say it aloud to Allie. I don't want her to see me as anything other than what she does now.

'Well, we thought it would be cool to talk to people who were around back then,' says Jameson, standing but hunched over the computer. He taps away. A heater rumbles into life on the wall. 'Who remember what you guys were like, you know? The whole phone swap thing. Julia knew everything about you two.'

Allie's eyes slide over to me. She knew Jameson and Ben knew about the phone swap, but we agreed we'd keep it to us, keep the circle small and tight. I did talk about her, though. A lot, and to . . . more people than I should've. Breached that trust – acting before thinking, even when totally lucid and sober. Tried not to, but I can never keep my mouth shut. I don't know why. Wanted people to know, I guess. Fill my stupid, hollow, wounded self-esteem cup with temporary admiration. *This cool, amazing woman likes me. We're going to meet. Look how completely wholesome and good we are. Tell me you believe I'm a good person. I wouldn't have this woman to talk about if I wasn't, right?* I owe her an apology for that. 'Iris even got hold of some dude named Clive,' Jameson carries on. 'Oh, hold on. Julia's sent a video!'

Then it all happens in slow motion.

Jameson's email account appears on the big screen. Julia's name in bold.

Hey! So, I've attached a complete buttload of photos and videos of the mountains if that's of any use. And then there's also some videos of the party after. Good times (and wild times I'd probably choose not to regale my eventual grandbabies with!! LOL). I hope I've helped in some way. It all sounds so romantic, Jameson. Saving the planet. Saving broken hearts! I'm excited for you – and for M! And always kind of wondered what happened with them, in the end. He seemed so sweet on her. He'd show us her messages and we were hooked! Like we were alllll jealous!! A few of us donated that night too. Had us over a barrel! Ha.

Julia

Shit. Sort of wish she hadn't mentioned the showing messages thing. Jameson is grinning, clicking on photos. Dense, thick forest we filmed in. Dim, fuzzy, out-of-focus trailers, Julia and I hugging in full 1940s costume, both our faces stretched into mocking grins. Me bleeding fake blood from my throat. I remember that night. We were bone-tired. Freezing. I'd been trying to stop myself from texting Allie, I could feel I was getting in deeper and I knew, somewhere inside, I was falling – no, *plunging*.

And then Jameson clicks. The video starts playing. And I know, no matter how unfamiliar the scene is to me, or how much like a lost, years-old bad dream it looks, that everything is about to change.

Chapter Twenty-Nine

Allie

The video on the screen is blurred and grainy. But, all the same, it's clear to see. It's a bar. Dark, with strobed red lights. The music, loud and fast, and there's a long table in the murk. Chairs and chairs of people surround it, some people stand, leaning over, talking into ears, some people dance. It's a party that would've, just hours before, been dinner and drinks. Now, it's a sticky, glass-littered mess.

Julia laughs from behind the camera, tells everyone to wave. Some do. Milo doesn't. He sits at the table, squashed next to a woman with a high, blonde pony-tail. He's talking in huge gestures and over-the-top facial expressions. His light grey shirt is open at the collar, his hair a wreck, all over his face. The blonde is nodding and smiling. She then holds her hand out and . . .

The camera pans out.

'God, dude, you're partying hard,' Jameson laughs, but I can see regret on his face.

I can't look away. Nobody speaks.

Back on the screen, Julia pans. The room is just fuzz, like a frame full of black sand art. Dark, shadowed fig-ures, a distant bar, is that? I'm not sure, but there are low hanging lights that are just smudges on the screen.

I find myself considering how far camera quality has come in just two years, despite the fact that something about this scene is making me feel shaken. Uneasy. Because Milo is clearly *inebriated*. I recognise it the way anyone would, but I see it on a deeper, bedrock-dwelling level. Dad. Dad would show up looking that way. Hooded eyes. Spaghetti limbs, too heavy-seeming for his body . . .

Then the camera seems to linger on Milo. And . . . there it is. My phone – it's in his hand. Why on earth does he have my phone at a party? It's lit up, and he's grasping it. He's leaning into the blonde, he's . . . showing her something.

I turn rigidly to the side. Milo is watching the screen, statuesque and serious. He doesn't appear to be breathing. 'Who is that? The blonde?'

'A . . . I . . . a journalist. She came over. They . . . ran a piece on Tilly? The director?'

I remember that.

I remember Sierra, the assistant, going to collect her from the airport. She was meant to bring my phone that day. We were meant to switch back. Then the data outage. We set up the whole phone secretary arrangement, not wanting to wait for the journalist to get another flight, two days later.

I'm sure I remember this party being mentioned in one of Milo's interviews too. The pizza restaurant one. Is that the same journalist? Didn't she mention a party in Romania, losing her shoes?

'Milooooo,' Julia laughs on the other side of the phone. 'Helloooo.'

'Juliaaaaa,' he slurs, and . . . he is wasted. Totally wasted. He said he didn't drink. I specifically remember him telling me he didn't. 'Make sure you're recording this,' he grins into the camera. 'Crazy shit, but I feel like I'm in love with this woman. Seriously.' He bursts out laughing. At first, I think he's talking about the journalist, or Julia. But . . . my phone. It's hanging from his hand. Lit up. Unlocked. My photo is on the screen. My coffee selfie. The blonde next to him waves at the screen and laughs. 'This . . . this is my gesture!' He laughs. 'This is my gesture for you, Allie Lake. It's— Oh, hold on.' He turns the phone over in his hand. 'This is her work. Her beautiful work . . .' He drops the phone. Everyone cheers. He stands up and stretches his arms high. Everyone cheers and laughs. My phone is on the table. Its light still on.

Oh, God.

He's a mess.

Unrecognisable.

I feel like my chest is caving in. Why is my phone out with him too?

Julia moves away, Milo picks up the phone, and now someone else is next to him. 'Helene!' he shouts. 'Come join us.'

Helene. The writer. The one who wrote the film's screenplay. I remember now, all these names. Julia played his wife on the movie. Helene was the writer who used to drive Milo insane. 'I've got an ego, but this woman, Allie,' he'd laugh down the line. 'Seriously, if someone told her to give a kidney for an award nomination, mine would currently be on the black market. Well, after she's had my lines out of me.'

On the screen, Julia is talking, panning the camera to other people. I find myself craning my neck, to see around her body, as if that would ever work.

My eyes are glued to the phone on the table. My phone. A bright blob in the background. Constantly lighting up. I wonder if my messages are coming through now. My excited messages about seeing him tomorrow.

He told me he'd missed me when he got back from the dinner, that he found himself wanting to talk about me. I remember that. Then he disappeared for a bit. Popped up the next day – just after noon. Then the leak went live.

He told me he went home, left my phone at his apartment, as we'd always agreed.

The camera swoops past Milo again, and she – the writer woman – was *she* holding it? I don't know. I *will* with everything the camera to go back.

'Say bye!' squeals Julia and then – darkness.

The room falls silent. The light of the computer screen, back on Jameson's emails, casts us all in a pale, frightened blue colour.

I feel nauseous. I feel like I'm going to be sick. Because my phone was right there, for everyone to see, for everyone to take and look at and snoop. Because of Milo.

'Fuck,' Milo is saying. 'Oh. God. I . . . No,' and his hands come up and over his head. 'Allie,' I hear him say. 'Allie, can we . . .'

But I'm already in the corridor. I'm already walking away.

Chapter Thirty

Allie

In my dorm, I feel like I'm going to pass out. The only time I've felt like this was when the leak happened – when Iris called me, told me to do a sweep of social media. I feel like I've just stepped off a rollercoaster that has spent the last ten minutes throwing me upside down.

My hands are trembling.

I glance around at my room, my head rushing with blood. The walls seem to pulse. I can't seem to get a breath.

Why was my phone there, with him?

He was so drunk. Why didn't he tell me?

And why did he lie?

He didn't talk about a party, like the one in the video. He said he went back to someone's cabin after dinner. Made it sound like chats and soft drinks and a – guitar, was it? He told me he didn't tell anyone about us too. 'Keep the circle small,' we always said. Did drink fool him into telling them? Did drink tell him taking my phone out with him was a good idea? He always seemed sober when we talked. He always seemed OK . . .

I bend, place my palms against the wall, let out a groan. Those weird, animalistic things you do when you are nothing but adrenaline and panic.

So, it was him? He was the one behind the leak?

On that screen, I didn't recognise him. And that image of him throwing my phone around to anyone who'd look, eyes slits, limbs heavy and flopping, sidles into my mind and I feel it – a rush of anger and sadness red-hot under my skin. Sadness for us both and what I saw on the screen. Anger that even after all I just saw, he so easily blamed me for everything . . .

This is why this can't work.

It can never be as simple as that photo of us on that hill in Cote Rock.

This could never work. Too much has happened.

Milo bursts into my dorm room.

'Please just leave,' I say.

'No. Allie . . .'

'I need to think, Milo.'

'Please talk to me.'

He gazes at me – his caramel brown eyes are liquid pain, pain I feel sear across my own heart. My hands were on his chest, moments ago, my mouth on his mouth. I was ready. I was *ready* to let it go, whatever the risk. I was ready to drop the armour. And now we're . . . here. How can there be trust now? How, when Milo has definitely been keeping things from me?

'Allie,' his voice cracks and he steps towards me. I don't move. 'I'm so ashamed of what I just watched . . .'

And I don't even react. I just stand, my heart, still, like metal in my chest, although Milo uttering the word 'ashamed', still, despite my own heartache, makes me sad. 'This – none of it makes sense . . .'

'I was an addict, Allie. I was in trouble—'

'I – I don't know where to even begin, Milo—'

'—And I *was* recovering. In Romania, I *was* clean,' Milo's deep voice cracks again. 'But then like, I – started drinking. It was just one. I had like, one after about a week of shooting, and it helped. To get into the scene, to wind down my mind. But that night . . . clearly, you can see what happened that night. A relapse, a – that wasn't me.'

'Do you remember?' I ask him.

'Remember that night? No. No, I promise. They feel like blurs. Blackouts. Bad dreams you remember a feeling of, but not a scene, or something—'

'I meant everything else,' I say. My voice sounds devoid of life. Of warmth. 'Not that night. Everything else.'

Milo steps towards me. 'God, Allie,' he utters. 'I remember everything. I was *sober*. I was *awake* with you.'

'Why did you show everyone my phone? Why had you told people—'

'I – I was . . . We both just saw how I was in that video—'

'No,' I say. 'It's clear even before that night, you'd ignored what I asked you. My terms. To keep it private because that made me feel comfortable. When you were sober. When you were . . . *awake*.'

His eyes drop sadly to the floor. 'I . . . I guess I wanted to tell the world about you,' he says.

'But I didn't want you to. I asked you not to.'

And there's something heartbreaking about this. The contrast of it. The way it feels almost right. But it's actually made up of so much wrong. And I hate that it chimes in, a disloyal voice that reminds me tauntingly, of Sara, Milo's ex, and what she said about him. Smoke and mirrors, she said. Self-conscious. Cares only about himself.

'I know. I'm sorry. My stupid ego, I guess? I just – I had so much pain. All this shit to prove to the world. I was selfish.'

Milo steps forward, brings his hand to my face. 'I don't remember what happened that night, Allie.'

'I know,' I sniff. 'But even before that, you were telling people . . .'

'I know.'

'And I asked you in the cabin. I looked right at you and I asked you. I asked you "is that the truth?" You could've said no. You could've said . . . something. *Anything.* Starting with, *OK, Allie, I may have told some co-workers about us and about your phone.* Or there were things you may not remember. I wasn't expecting everything. You *know* I understand how hard that might be.'

'But I thought – I thought that you would, I don't know. *Break it off*? I didn't want people to think – for *you* to think badly of me, for you to decide that actually, no, screw this guy.'

My eyes close.

Because that's it, isn't it? He is more concerned with how he is perceived than who he really is. And who he really is is who I was ready to love.

'If we are going to really do this, Milo,' I whisper. 'You can't pick and choose the parts of yourself that you let me see.'

He swallows, hard and thick, his eyes lifting to the ceiling. 'But I told you about rehab,' he utters. 'On a video call one night. Do you remember?'

I say nothing.

'I told you about *Day Falls*. About breaking up with Sara. And you looked . . . haunted, Allie. And I got it. You know? Your dad. Everything rehab represented. But I remembered how you looked at me. Replayed it—'

'No.' I shake my head. 'But that's up to me, Milo. You don't get to control how I feel.'

Everything rushes back to me now, like a movie on fast-forward and rewind all at once. Every phone call. The cabin and my ankle bath. The first kiss, his lips against my knee. The awards in three weeks. All the hope of what we *could* be . . . and now this. This stark truth. I was right, trying to stay safe, and stay an 'I'. I was right to be scared of being a 'we'. Because they always lie. They always leave. It is never, ever simple.

'Allie, I'm so sorry,' Milo says. His eyes shine with water. His voice like shattering glass. 'Things are *different* now. I'm better. Healthier than I've ever been in my life. That was then.'

'It's not the addiction, Milo,' I tell him. My words shake. 'God, I understand that. I would never wish it on *anyone*. I know, believe me, I do, what it does to someone. But I *asked you*. I asked you in the cabin, in a moment that felt like the between of us before and us after. And you didn't even try. I wasn't asking you to tell me every single shred of your life, but you could've started with the fact my phone wasn't always where you said it was. That you messed up, boasted to people you shouldn't have . . . That there are parts of that time, the days before *our* leak, that are unclear in your memory. That you were struggling.'

'I didn't want to lose you.'

'You don't trust me with who you are.' The words burst from me. '*That's* what this is. You're . . . you're still trying to show the world only what you want them to see.'

He swallows. And I want, so much, to reach out and hold him. Because despite everything, what I felt for him was real, which makes the lie so much more damaging.

'You're right,' he says, breathlessly. 'You're right. But God, Allie, I did show you who I was. And all right, maybe not every morsel, but . . . you saw me, back then. And *knowing me*, you still jumped straight to blaming me. One phone call from a publicist, one *single call*, and that was me – toast.'

'Oh, so it's my fault, is it?'

'No.' He pauses then. Too long. 'No. No, it's not. I'm sorry, I just . . . This is a total mess.'

I step back. It's too much. My head hurts with it, like someone's plugged in fifty radios and turned them all up to full volume.

'I don't know what to do,' I say to him. My voice sounds so tiny, so pathetic, it hardly sounds like me at all. 'Was it . . . was it actually real?'

Milo looks up at me. 'Of *course* it was real,' he croaks. 'Everything I felt with you, *for* you, was real. It's me. I'm standing here. Right in front of you.'

He steps forwards and takes my hands. I can't look at him. I'm afraid that if I do that'll be it. There'll be no turning back. I need to keep my head. I need to remember myself, protect myself. Because nobody else will. Milo's just proven that. Even when someone looks you in the eye and says they will, they don't.

'It was real for me,' I say. 'There is nothing that you don't know. I'm concealing nothing from you.'

'It was real. *It is* real.' Milo moves towards me again, folds his hand around mine, presses it to his chest. 'Do you think we'd be standing here if it wasn't? And Jameson wouldn't want to do this, both Jameson and Iris wouldn't have wanted to pick this story back up if—'

'But my life is not a story, Milo. This is my *heart*.' I'm surprised when those last few words burst out of me angrily.

Milo sinks down onto the bed, head in his hands. 'Fuck,' he mutters.

'Do you know how long I've spent preparing myself to trust even just a little bit? I was even beating myself up for not trusting you more tonight. Actions,' I say. 'I told you that's what was important to me.'

'I know. I know, and maybe that's what I was trying to do, Allie,' Milo says almost desperately. A clamour. 'Back then, I wanted to tell the world. Shout it from the literal mountains. And I know I did it in a total asshole way, my stupid-ass ego in the driving seat, but at least I wasn't ashamed.'

'I have never been ashamed.'

'But even when I got here – I followed you *everywhere*, even though I was scared too, Allie. I told you I missed you. I told you I wanted to try this with you. That was all me. You talk about trust, about concealing nothing, but you go through life not wholly believing a word people say.'

'It's been proven that I'm right to. Over and over.'

Milo looks up at me, his eyes watery, his face pained. 'And you say you aren't ashamed,' he croaks. 'But if we're talking about actions. I saw your face when we were in that picture together today. You couldn't wait to get out of that room. And I know you said in my dorm that you didn't care but – your face in that moment. It told me everything I needed to know. I don't think I'll ever be who you wish I was. The things that frighten you are a part of me. And maybe that's why I was afraid to tell you the things I believe are the unlovable parts of me.'

I shake my head. 'That isn't true.'

'I think that it is.'

Laughter sounds behind the door and I feel stupid. I feel like the world is laughing at me, like they did before. Like Milo did on *The Really Late Show*. That audience. The comments all over social media after. The emails to the Count Your Chicks address. And everything now feels devastating. That this was my place. That my heart was guarded. And now it's like everything I left behind and ran from has infiltrated this safe space: Milo Ford has tarred and muddied it. *We* have. I will never be able to return here without thinking about him – about how this is where we broke apart. Again.

I am inches from falling in love with him. That's the truth. And yet I suddenly know this will be the last time I stand here like this, with Milo Ford.

'The whole thing's done,' I say, pushing the heels of my hands into my eyes. 'Always has been. We never made it because we were never meant to. The end.'

Milo then laughs – a harsh, sad sound that hurts me. 'Then looks like we're right back to where we started.' He stands and walks across the room. The soles of his trainers scraping the floor heavily. 'Goodnight, Allie,' he says.

Behind me, he closes the door.

Chapter Thirty-One

Allie

I don't sleep all night. Not for a single, hazy moment. I cry, my skin sticking to my pillow, my cheeks stinging, as if they're covered with a thousand little cuts, and I'm both relieved and heartbroken when I smell toast wafting through the corridors from the kitchen.

Breakfast.

The day is here. Milo is leaving and it means everything can go back to normal. But . . . who am I even kidding? Will I ever, ever feel normal again?

He can leave, but I will still be me. I will still be Allie Lake who is in love with Milo Ford. Because, in spite of everything, that is the truth – I love him.

Right now, my heart aches like it's been stabbed, like it'll never survive the day.

There's a tap on the door.

It's Polly, whose soft voice says, 'Allie, love, are you all right?' and then, 'The helicopter is here.'

*

Milo

When I was a teenager, I watched this TV show. This kind, warm father saying to his son, 'Oh, you'll know when it's love. Trust me, you'll know.' I remembered it. Partly because the dad was the kind of dad I wanted. But, mostly, because I wanted to know. Would I know when love finally arrived for me?

And is this it? Should it feel this bad? Because I'm in actual physical pain here, sitting on the edge of the dorm bed in the station. Bed made, sheets tucked tightly. Jameson did it as I got dressed. He's in grovelling mode. Feels like shit about just pressing play on that video without checking. He said he got too excited when we first landed too; that he hoped by the time we both saw what they'd hoped to do, he and Iris, we'd have reconnected, and any apprehension would've melted away. He and Iris knew it was a stretch that Allie would happily be filmed, published on tape, but he'd hoped I might let him edit me in, as his B-story. 'Slowly coming to the realisation you were wrong about her,' he said. 'And in love.'

'It was inevitable to us,' he also said, 'that the only way this trip would end would be for you two to be together.'

I think Allie and I thought the same, eventually.

And God, how wrong can four people be?

I drop my head in my hands, dressed in the coat Allie wrapped herself in in the cabin. It smells like her. I pick up my phone to a new message. A message that arrived just before we had to switch off again, from my new publicist, Ella. A message that feels like it's from the past. 'I am so happy for you!' it says. 'I've got Allie on the list for the ceremony, as your guest.' And at the end is a heart. Unpunctured and unbroken. Full and red and

327

whole. Like it's taunting me. I messed it up, didn't I? We were *so close*. I just wish I had talked to her, that night in the cabin. I wish, so hard.

Jameson pushes open the door. 'Hey, man. You good?'

'Yeah.'

'Chopper's here,' he says sadly. 'Time to leave.'

Chapter Thirty-Two

Allie

I have tried to continue on as normal since Milo left three days ago. I've written up research. I've chatted at mealtimes. I've showered. I even joined a few new arrivals tonight at dinner – talked, joined in on card games, playing the role of someone whose heart isn't breaking.

Inside, I feel like my chest is caving in.

I know it'll pass with time.

But here, in the silent, dim computer room, where it all happened, the screen painting my skin indigo, I realise . . . it feels like there is a hole in my chest because there is. You are not supposed to fall in love and then walk in the opposite direction. That is not the natural order of things. You're supposed to fall *in*. It's like my heart is a little lost auk and it's flying away from its nest – away from its mate and safe, perfect little egg.

I swallow down a tornado of tears forming in my throat.

I stare at my computer screen.

Everything seems so quiet now Milo and Jameson have gone. Lars has even gone home for a couple of weeks. A beer festival and to meet his new grandchild (in that order). Polly and Iris are still here, which is a comfort, but it all feels so quiet and bleak. A new team assembling in the cafeteria, Milo and Jameson's dorm room now dark, the beds stripped.

I click onto my emails. Nothing. I keep typing an email to Sian, but I just end up deleting the words. Even Count Your Chicks is quiet and that's usually a cosy source of home for me. Grey offline dots next to my regular users, SunshineGirl23, Magic_Garrett, AcerSpark make new dread settle in my stomach. It feels like since Milo left, my world is slowly coming to a close. A pair of curtains slowly drawing on a casket, marking our denouement. Gah. That's dramatic especially for me. Bet Milo would love that word. Denouement. I take out my phone and type it down. Maybe I'll add it to the Word! app later. I can't imagine, though, doing anything that isn't just surviving right now. Even opening an app feels like effort.

Work.

I'll do some work.

I open up a Word document. The world doesn't stop for heartbreak. I learned that a long time ago. Too long ago, and too young. Dad begging Mum in tears. The tears turning to rage. Mum walking away, double locking the front door and opening a box of fish fingers while drying her eyes, making our dinner with oven timers and novelty plates, smiling at us through watery eyes as we told her what was on Nickelodeon. Gosh, I miss her. Being here, in the arctic, has helped me grieve Mum. The quietness away from the real world really allowed me to process – well, start to, anyway – losing her. But I miss her. With more warmth now, with more gratitude at having known what it was to be loved by her, than anger and injustice, but, I miss her with the same ferocity. Especially in moments like this. I'd give anything to bury my face into her jumpered shoulder now, have her cradle the back of my head like she used to, sway me gently. She always, always knew what to say.

I type. *Upon arrival at Cote Rock, Colony 1, we . . .*

I stop.

I think about that day with Lucky and Mart. I think about Milo and that smile. That feeling I had, fleetingly, of knowing he was what I wanted. I wanted to share these moments with him. The puffins getting back together. The true joy on his face. Nobody has ever cared that much for my joy. Pure second-hand joy.

'*Isn't it just the most perfect sight?*'

'*I think seeing you this happy is.*'

Tears push their way through my eyes. Why didn't he just tell me the truth? It isn't the addiction. He might not believe it, but I felt ready to love all those parts of him, even the ones he was too afraid to show me. Heights and pink shirts. Crochet. His word-nerding. The struggles he faced; the ones he's ashamed of. I wish I could've been there. I hate knowing he might've been in emotional pain when we spoke back then and had nowhere to release it. But my phone – sober, awake, lucid Milo would've made the decision to take my phone with him that night before the horrid claws of addiction dragged him back into its lair. Milo knew he'd betrayed my trust in that way – Julia said they all knew about us, were all jealous – and he didn't tell me. Even when I asked him. I wish he had. I wish he had said *something* in the cabin. Just *tried* to say something. *Anything.* I might've found it hard, but I would've understood.

Two knocks tap on the computer room door. I clear my throat, turn my face away, but before I can call out for them to come in, they do anyway. It's Iris.

I don't feel comfortable crying in front of even myself, but Iris is an exception. She's seen me cry. A lot, after the Milo leak. A lot, after June House went up for sale and Mum, Sian and I, three people who had grown together within those walls – late-night kitchen conversations, bringing towels to the bathroom door for each other, folding each other's clothes – were suddenly nothing but boxes. And at the sight of her, I feel like I could cry again.

'Oh, mate.'

Iris crosses the floor. She's wearing pyjamas, as ever, and has her hair in what she calls her 'heatless curl sausage'. Iris cried with me when their chopper left. 'I'm sorry,' she kept saying. 'We really wanted this to work. I know you're angry at me. I know. I deserve it.'

I am still mad. Just a little, knowing I was kept in the dark. Especially now it's ended like this. But I understand why she wanted to do it. I'm so stubborn, Iris would've never been able to talk me into even a single conversation with Milo. Her heart was, of course, in the very best of places. Which ironically, put mine in the worst.

'I'm still so sorry,' she says. 'I feel like . . . I had this vision, this hope for it—'

'It's fine,' I say flatly, even though nothing is fine.

'It's not.' She pauses, breathes heavily. 'It's been a fuck-ton, my friend. And I feel responsible.'

'Iris,' I say. 'I promise. I understand.'

She doesn't put the lights on and I'm grateful for it. It's just the glow of my computer screen illuminating the room, and the polar night, bright as ever, shut behind roller blinds. She pulls up a chair and sits next to me. She rests her chin on my shoulder and reads the first line on the screen – the only line. The room smells like warm computer towers and the sweet cherry of Iris's hand cream.

For a while, we sit in silence. I've never needed an anchor. Not really. I've always been my own anchor. But a mate, I need, definitely. And that's what Iris is. I sail my ship, but it's nice to have a mate next to me. Mum was a shipmate too. I always wanted Sian to be, and although she'd get on board, I always felt she had other places she'd rather be. I'm sure Sian would say the same about me. We're different, I suppose. She'd say I was serious and analytical, best-foot-forward at all costs. I'd say she was artistic, running before she could walk into her whole life. A marketer's dream.

'I think I might love him,' I say, and the words come out of nowhere. Something about this safe dimly lit room, with Iris, makes me feel I'm cocooned in a safe moment I can say anything in.

Iris nods. No fanfare. No squealing.

'What am I going to do, Iris?'

'Do you want to know what I really think?'

I nod, and she takes my hand and folds it into hers, at her waist. It feels safe. The smell of her laundry detergent, her weird hair-sausage, her glittering eyes, her pyjamas covered in snowmen.

'I think you've been hiding. I know this place is safety, and I know it's served such an important purpose, and in return, so have you. But you've been hiding, amigo. You build all these walls around you, and so high that you convince yourself the world is just that small, and that small world is perfect, cheers very much.'

She gives me the warmest smile, then. A smile that tells me she loves me for that, for every wall I've built, even the ones she'd rather crumbled.

'When, in reality,' Iris continues, 'the real world is still there, you've just blocked it out. And, eventually, shutting yourself away, to keep yourself safe, harms you anyway, in the end.'

I look up at her, a warm tear trickles down my face.

'I think you need to go home,' she says. 'I think you need a break. And I think you need to finally speak to Sian. She needs you too. I know you don't think she does. But she wanted to help. She said she could help, with the leak stuff. The answers.'

'But we already know the answers.'

She takes a deep breath, and I can tell by the way her eyes drop to her lap that she's nervous to say her next sentence. I'm so wrung out, I hardly react.

'She said she knows something about your diary.'

'My diary?' I ask. 'That she read it? I know she read it. Everyone read it—'

'No.' Iris shakes her head slowly. I hear her swallow in the gloom. 'No,' she says. 'She . . . she sort of says she knows how they were leaked.'

'But we know someone from that night did—'

'But we always said the diaries weren't easily accessible on your phone. Plus, you moved them to a new drive, anyway. Remember? To be safe.'

I stare at Iris.

'I think she did something,' she says, solidly and confidently, like she's had a lot of time to mull this over and to make a good guess, and she's confident to press forward accordingly.

'Do you really?' Even though I know what Iris is hinting at, I feel so numb, it doesn't really hit me. *Sian.* Really? Why would Sian leak my diaries?

'Yes,' says Iris. 'And I think you need to go home and find out. Start closing the chapter on this, Allie. So when your heart's mended, you can finally start another. Don't you think, whatever happens, that it's time?'

Part Three

Part Three

*[Research Port // Excerpt saved by: Allie Lake]
Analysing data from 5,500 people across eight coun-
tries, Dr Tyler Rossiter and his team concluded that
the process of addressing mistakes in a relationship
can solidify trust more effectively than relationships
that have never faced challenges. 'In theory,' said Dr
Rossiter, 'things have to sometimes get worse before
they get better. Only when we accept our flaws, can we
heal them. And nothing shows us more of what we need
to fix, as humans, than falling in love does.' – Rossiter,
Tyler (2025, May 25) The Science of Falling in Love*

Chapter Thirty-Three

Milo

I hear Jameson in the dark before I see him: a large crunch of an apple. A 'wakey-wakey, my brother,' and the sound of electric blinds winding upwards. I'm in my bedroom in Brooklyn, feeling sure it wasn't just a week ago I was with Allie, but a lifetime ago. Another world. A parallel universe.

'Get lost, dude,' I say into my pillow.

'No can do, motherfucker. It's 2 p.m. You need to shower, you've got a pre-interview at four, the awards ceremony to attend tomorrow.'

I groan. I don't *want* to go anywhere. Ever.

We got back from Norway three days ago and I have rotted in my bed ever since. Fermented like an old bell pepper stuck at the back of the refrigerator.

I stayed up the whole night thinking about Allie last night, missing Allie, and running over and over in my head every single mistake I've ever made. I texted my sponsor, Adam. I used to be so snobby about AA and meetings. Preferred to white-knuckle through it alone. Something about the tired strangers waiting to go inside, smoking – always smoking – and being too scared to admit I belonged with them, because if I did, my problem was real. That was until I walked into one in Manhattan one Wednesday morning, sleep-deprived and fresh out of rehab. A church with a broken window sandwiched between an apartment building and a dental office. A church full of people who understood me. Mothers. Teachers. Diplomats. Models. Their nods, their listening ears. Short, skinny Adam's warm unexpected hug in the snow outside.

'You are not who you were, but you are who you are, remember, Milo,' he texted back, and although I sometimes wonder if he gets his quotes from, like, *Karate Kid* or something, it helped. And I know the dude's telling the truth. But that moment, with the video from Julia, it sent me hurtling backwards, like I was in one of those centrifuges NASA use to train astronauts. Because I feel the leak is my fault; that it was me who destroyed what I had with Allie. *Again.* And just talking to her could've saved it.

I've had to work my ass off to keep my thoughts in check, which has taken a lot of energy. And when I'm not doing that, I'm thinking about Allie. It feels physically painful to be away from her. I feel like my chest is filled with cement. I wonder what she's doing every hour of every day, if she's OK, if she hates me. She wouldn't even come out of her room to say goodbye.

'We need to sort you out, bro. Shower. Shave, unless you want to keep this whole beardy, stubble situation. Stylists will be here in an hour. Final measurements for the suit for tomorrow, then—'

'I haven't written my speech,' I say. 'I haven't slept, I can't think of anything to say, I don't want to talk to anyone.'

Jameson pauses, sits down on the bed. He takes another bite from his apple. 'Not like you, man,' he says. 'Speeches. You like that shit. Can't normally shut you up. Whether it be through your mouth or keyboard or pen.'

I groan, press a pillow to my face, then stuff it behind my head. Jameson passes me a juice bottle.

'You've got to get a motor on, man. I hear you, I do, but you can't just stay in bed for days. I *worry* about you.' He means he's worried I'll relapse. It's hard to explain to someone that you never would. I've really meant it before and still gone back and done it. But that video – had I seen that video back then, it wouldn't have been the magazine in the bodega that threw me over the edge into changing – it would've been that. Months before. I keep thinking about it. Taunting myself with it like scenes from a horror movie. 'Seriously,' Jameson carries on. 'Do you know why I'm here?'

'To stop me from dissolving into my bed?'

'Because you are one of the most beautiful bloody souls I've ever known,' he says. 'Seriously.'

'You on shrooms again?'

Jameson laughs, a hard hand landing on my chest. 'No,' he says. 'I'm being serious. For someone always searching, you've got *so much love* in you to give. Do you know that? Like – I knew you'd just accept the whole you-and-Allie-being-in-Norway as a coincidence. You know why?'

'Why?'

'Because you wanted to,' he says, softly. 'Because you believe in fate, Milo. In all that shit. True love and love at first sight and poetry and – everything. All the *romance* of that stuff.'

'I think I'm just a lost cause,' I say with a dark laugh.

'No.' Jameson shakes his head, curls springing around his forehead. 'It's just who you are. You're all love. Like, you wrote to me every week without a *hitch* when I was at boarding school. You always made sure I had a Christmas gift because you knew my mom hated Christmas . . .'

I smile, despite myself. 'You're not about to tell me you're dying or something, are you?'

Jameson ignores me and carries on. 'When I bought the farm, you were the one there, first thing moving day, even though you were totally messed up from all the *Day Falls* stuff, and you'd made me a *fruit basket*. Somehow. Like. What? Who does that?'

'It was fruit, Jameson.'

'*Colour co-ordinated* fruit, you jackass. And OK – your poem. You wrote me a poem when we were twelve and it was like the first time I'd actually felt like, wow, this poetic guy from New Jersey really likes who I am.'

'Oh my God, the poem,' I exclaim, sitting up in bed. 'I . . . I wrote that poem under my covers at, like, midnight, before your flight home. I remember thinking it was really bad.'

'It was awesome,' says Jameson. 'Still got it.' Then he looks at me intently. 'This is what I'm saying. You don't show people who you are, Milo. You hide parts, downplay parts, amplify others. And it's like, *why* do you do that? Just – stop. Allie didn't let you leave because of who you are. Allie left you because you hid it.'

Outside, somewhere down on the street, a car horn is pressed long and hard. It stops.

'Go get your award,' Jameson tells me, bringing his forehead to touch mine. 'Milo *earned* that award. Real, talented, weirdo Milo earned it.' He draws back, ruffles my hair.

Damn. I can't cry now. He won't let me forget it.

'Thanks,' I tell him, and I slap him on his forearm affectionately. 'Seriously. I love you, man. Thank you.'

'Thank me in your speech,' he says. 'Which you need to be writing, like, yesterday.'

'I know. And I used to have a speech. I wrote one, way, way back then, after *Day Falls*. Part of the Programme. Planning for your future. I kept a list of things I wanted to say . . .'

'Oh yeah?'

'On my old phone.' *The* old phone. The one I've not been able to properly look at since Allie. Since Sierra picked it up from Allie, who proceeded to block me.

Jameson nods, jumping up. 'Want me to get it? Where is it?' He smells amazing, the guy. Always does. Bet he's already showered, gymmed, meditated . . .

'Sure. Thanks. In that drawer over there. Cord should be in the junk drawer somewhere. Along with all the other mystery cords.'

'Heard,' Jameson salutes, and he starts searching.

I leave him in the kitchen, take a shower, and when I come back out, Jameson is slumped on the couch, a laptop balancing on his chest.

'Looking fresh, Mildred,' he smiles over at me.

It's weird, but I feel sad for Jameson too, about this whole movie thing. It was always a risk, this venture of his, but I can't help but feel grief for what could've been. The documentary. The love story. The whole thing. All of us in it together. Me and Allie, Jameson and Iris. I miss it. I miss Cote Rock. I even miss the salami and Lars making fun of my clothes. I miss all of it. But I can't even begin to think about editing that footage . . .

I find the phone plugged in on the kitchen counter. I start the coffee machine, swipe up, punch in the code. There it is.

The background I had back then – tagliatelle. It was my first proper meal after my first rehab. An old-school New Jersey Italian restaurant. It tasted so amazing with a sober mouth, a sober mind, I wanted to remember it.

The phone tells me there's no SIM inserted. The notes app should still work, though.

I scroll my apps – I stop on Bunty's. A smile creeps onto my mouth. Ah, Bunty's. Allie trying the coffee, sending me a selfie. My drink. Hated by all, except us two.

I scroll more, not looking for my notes now, but just for memories. My Word! app. This is why I couldn't take using this phone back then. It was too painful. Everything reminded me of Allie. Of when I'd trusted too much, had my ass handed to me on a silver platter. Plus, once it'd been leaked, it felt weird using it. This tainted phone, from a stranger's palm. A part of me worried for some time after Allie, if it had actually been *bugged*, but that felt crazy. I was drunk a lot then. Watering down beer and calling it a win.

I press a thumb to the Word! App. It springs open. 'Welcome, back, Milo,' floats onto the screen.

Why am I doing this?

I'm supposed to be finding my notes to help write my speech. But it's too close, too tantalising. I almost want the sting of the memory. I want to feel the pain of losing her, so I know she was at least real.

There it is. Milo's word list. I smile. But, equally, I feel like I've been kneed in the balls. Last updated, it says, along with an ellipsis. I press my thumb against it, wait for a date frozen in time, from two years ago, when we both added words to it every day. I used to get so excited when the word count increased and I knew she was over in the UK, adding them.

But – huh. Updated . . . three days ago?

Allie added: Denouement.

Seven weeks ago,

Allie added: Harlequin.

Twelve weeks ago,

Allie added: Superfluous.

My heart jump-starts.

Allie has been adding words. For years. For two whole years. Reams of them – beautiful, unusual, amazing, cool words. Some that look like art. Some that sound like songs. She's added words to my list. My stupid quirk, my hobby, that part of who I am. Allie's just been watering it, like a seed. I didn't even know. It's just been here, kept in the dark, where I left it. She never stopped.

'Jameson?'

Then I stop. No. Jameson was the one who organised me getting to her. This has to be me – something I do on my own. But first.

'Could you do something for me?'

Chapter Thirty-Four

Allie

Norfolk is cold today – the sort of cold you try to fool yourself with in that classically British way. A refusal to take a coat and just a cardigan, because it *is* May after all, and cardigans like this were made for early summer.

And I'm surprised that Sian hugs me tight when she meets me in the restaurant for breakfast. She seems different. Happy to see me. Grown up. There was a lethargy in her voice when I called her. A voice of surrender. The voice of someone who was tired of fighting. 'I've been waiting for you to call,' she said on the line, and I knew, then, Iris was right. I know what she's about to tell me.

We sit at a small round table. Faux ivy covers one of the walls and a neon-pink light spells, 'Sit Back and Relax.' Sian chose the place. She said she can't really hang out at the holiday park in the restaurants there, as she's part of the staff. 'If they see me sitting down,' she texted, 'they'll more than likely shove me in a mascot bunny suit and you'll never see me again.'

Menus are placed in front of us, and it feels like we're just dancing around broken glass.

'How are you?' she asks softly. 'You look . . .' She pauses. 'Different.'

'Better different?'

'I'm not sure yet,' she says, but she smiles kindly and runs a finger along a large letter C on the menu. I used to paint those square, neat fingernails when we were kids. I felt like I carried the weight of everything back then; would clock, somehow, that Sian was asking where Dad was, age six and totally oblivious, and I'd whisk her upstairs, aged eight, paint her fingernails, trace pictures from book covers for her to colour in. And I realise I've missed her. Regardless of all of it, I have missed my sister. We knew how to be kids together. That dynamic worked when we were little. Protective older sister who always knew too much, who knew how to fix things, distract and divert; little sister, artsy and hopeful, always up for a fun task. But when we became adults, it no longer worked. And I realise now that you can be beside someone and still miss them like they're not in the same room. I have missed her most of my adult life.

Sian and I make more small talk – we talk about the weather, about her job, about how she's been practising yoga and how she's dating a man named Jake, who's a karate instructor. She asks about my research, she asks about Iris and asks what my plans are later.

'Are you staying near Stought?' she asks. 'Because you're welcome to stay here. We could have dinner in my van. That's if they *let* me actually have my shift off tonight.'

I smile. 'That might be nice,' I tell her.

It's Milo's award's ceremony tonight. There's another version of me, somewhere, flying there to be with him right now, instead of ordering scrambled eggs and hash browns. Maybe that version is already waking up in New York with him. My heart hurts. I miss him.

Everything aside, I feel awful about how things were left between us both. For him. For me. It's like I have all these loose ends, fraying, in my mind, that I have no idea what on earth to do with, or where to start. Ignore them? Try to tie them up? Hope they simply disappear, disintegrate over time, like an old T-shirt?

Oliver has been in contact already. He sent a round-robin email to all the researchers and workers with the team in Svalbard and, also, the rest of My Planet, our funding agency, saying that it went 'very well'. Already, both Milo and Jameson have directed thousands of pounds in our direction, just from Jameson posting one ten-second clip on social media. Polly and Iris were in it, just the back of them, and I actually felt sadness at the lack of . . . me. The lack of evidence I was there at all. *I saw it. In your face, Allie, when we were in that picture together today.*

'Sian, I . . . Should we talk,' I start.

'Iris told me,' she says. 'About the movie. Milo and Jameson Merritt.'

'I know,' I say. 'She told me she'd been talking to you.'

Sian nods. A wordless 'figured'.

A kind, smiling waitress appears, places down our drinks. My tea. Sian's bright pink smoothie.

Her eyes drop pensively to her lap. 'How was it? Seeing him? I can't even get my head around what that must've been like for you. Knowing you. That sort of sudden surprise.'

'Ha.' I stiffen, lean back on the chair. 'God, Sian, it was . . . awful. Then it was great. And then amazing, then . . .' I laugh. 'Bloody awful again.' And I explain it to her, a short, condensed version, and Sian listens, her eyebrows inverted arcs, her lips apart, sipping her drink, never looking away. She doesn't glimmer, for a second, when I mention the diaries. She just looks over at me, drops her head to one side. Her wavy, mousy hair falls from resting on her shoulder.

'Oh, *Allie*. I'm really sorry. That sounds totally pants. Just . . . dreadful.'

'It was. Is. I mean . . . I know it was probably the right decision, but . . . it still hurts. A lot.'

Sian smiles softly. 'Rite of passage,' she says. 'I sometimes wonder why anyone bothers dating. It's painful when it goes wrong. After my last break-up, I got a rash the doctor thought *might be* meningitis. Turned out it was stress. All because Ian, that bloke I went out with who worked in Morrisons, dumped me on Christmas Day.'

'That's awful!'

She shrugs, drinks more bright pink smoothie. 'Part and parcel,' she says. 'Until you find the right one, anyway. And bloody Jake better be.'

We eat.

A tinny Phil Collins song plays from a speaker some-where in the café. And I think this is it. This is when she tells me. She looks up at me with huge eyes, and for a second I see every version of Sian. Five-year-old Sian, eyes wide, not wanting to go on stage and sing harvest festival songs, me smiling at her from the back of the hall, word-lessly urging her to be brave. Eight-year-old Sian, looking up from her diary, having written, 'sumtimes I'm scared

Dad'll never come bak,' handing me the pen and giggling through tears as I drew something funny and slightly offensive. Ten-year-old Sian, watery eyes, waiting for Dad at the window, and me making us a picnic in my bedroom instead.

'I need to talk to you,' she says finally.

'Sian, I won't be angry at you.'

'Angry?'

'I know for a while, it's been . . .' I pause, try to line my words up carefully. 'I mean, since Mum it's been tough and we've both been through a lot. But I won't be mad. I just want to understand.'

'Understand what, Allie?' Her nose wrinkles, and her splatter of freckles make her look so innocent, I almost feel like saying nothing else.

'I know. I know what you want to talk to me about.'

'Do you?'

Silently, we stare at each other.

And instead of saying anything else, she tears away her gaze from mine and reaches into her bag. 'I've wanted to tell you for so long,' she says, shakily. 'But I wanted to make sure I had everything before I did. Well, as much as I could get.'

She pulls out a thick envelope. It's brown, A5 and filled with a whole pile of bent-in-half papers. She passes it to me, crinkling in my hand.

I look at her, slide out the thick wodge. Is this it? Is this where I find out it was her – that she leaked my diaries? Is this some sort of mad written confession?

But as I open it, she smiles nervously, brings her hand to her mouth.

My heart stops. A breeze from the restaurant door opening ruffles the pages. Letters. Mum's handwriting. Mum's letters to her father-in-law. To our grandad. To Dad's dad. I glance over them. I see June House mentioned. I see Dad's name written in black ink. *'Davey woke the children again, banging on the front door.'* *'Davey has moved in with her now. He's taking her children to school. Can you believe it? My heart breaks for my girls. Little Allie takes on so much.'* Tears sting my eyes.

Sian brings a nervous fist to her mouth, butter yellow cardigan sleeve covering most of it. 'I've been in touch with cousin Victoria. Do you remember her? Grandad's brother's daughter. She reached out on Facebook. Uncle Tom was given a lot of Grandad's stuff. All the . . . stuff that wasn't really worth anything. He just put it all in the garage. Victoria let me take a look. She's nice. She's a beekeeper now, how weird is that? She lives literally, like, thirty minutes away from here, in North Walsham.'

There're so many letters.

Everything is here.

Everything about Dad.

Everything about our lives.

'I don't know what good it'll do,' she says. 'But I'm thinking these might help get back what's rightfully ours.'

'Sian, this is amazing.'

'I'm thinking if these letters prove what Dad did to us – the lying, the leaving us, over and over, the affairs, that Grandad wanted us to have that house – then, surely, we can get it back. We've never had a voice against him, and these letters – *Mum's letters* – do that.'

I meet her eyes across the table and slowly sag into myself. Relief floods me. Relief for Mum, her voice, her story, her truths set free again, in the words of those letters. I can almost feel her here with us; could close my eyes, find the scent of her perfume in the air, evidence she's here and listening. Then there's relief for Sian, too. Relief for *us*. And I laugh. A burst of giggles. '*Sian*, I . . . I mean, first, this is amazing, but – I thought you were going to tell me that you published my diaries. That you leaked them on purpose.'

Sian's whole face morphs. It's like for a moment, her face is made of plasticine. 'Erm, what?'

'My diaries. T-the ones me and Mum shared. The Lake Dock.'

'*Me?!*' She looks totally flabbergasted. Like someone's just whacked her across the face with a badminton racket. 'Allie, are you serious? Of course I didn't leak it. I can't believe you thought that.'

'But you'd read them all,' I say. 'The day it happened, you already knew everything.'

Sian crosses her arms and cocks an eyebrow. 'For someone as clever as you, you really can be a bit dim. I'd never be able to read all of them in a morning. I haven't read a book since, like, year two. I'm the slowest reader ever.'

I stare at her across the table.

'You messed around on an old iPad, moved everything over to another drive one night. Don't you remember, I came downstairs and you were sitting there, pissing about with it?'

'Yes. I . . . I do.'

I remember.

Gosh, I remember.

I'd talked to Milo on video chat for hours, and he confided about a lot. About *Day Falls* and his ex. About making bad decisions. And, in turn, so had I. I'd told him about Dad, about Sian and us not speaking, and I'd told him about the diary. I then remembered there was a file linking to it on my phone, which Milo had. When we hung up, my mind was reeling. I thought, back then, it was gut feeling or something, but I was suddenly preoccupied by the idea they might be erased or read or compromised or *something*. So I jumped up out of bed and moved everything to a new drive.

'You made them public,' Sian says, trying to stifle it, but letting out, eventually, a grimace that turns into girlish giggle. 'I was reading them way before the leak. You're pretty haphazard with technology, Allie. I mean, your drive has your full name in. And like, setting up two-factor authentication and not having anything other than your *phone* as backup?' She makes a pfft sound. 'Anyway, it was 4 a.m. when you decided to play spies and move everything. You just clicked the wrong thing. You were probably panicked and knackered.'

'Why didn't you tell me?' I asked.

'I didn't realise straight away. It was only while snooping that it landed for me. And I wanted to read it. Remotely. On my own phone.' She shrugs. 'Plus, I was angry at you.' She looks downcast then, ashamed. 'I always felt like I wasn't privy to what you and Mum had. Your little club. Your diaries. You were her favourite.'

'Sian, that isn't true.'

'Maybe not, but . . . she thought the sun shone out of your arse, Allie. And . . . it was all so unfair, because Dad was mine. Not for long, I know, and not regularly. *So* not regularly. But when he *wasn't* awful, we had football matches together. We loved *Star Wars*, laughed at the same things. You and Mum, you were all about the world and nature and I just never really got that. Still don't to be honest.' Sian shakes her head, swallows hard.

I reach over to touch her arm. 'Sian, Mum loved you.'

'Oh, I know.'

'But I'm sorry if you ever like you weren't important. It wasn't that we had a club. We just tried to protect you from all the horrible stuff. And maybe we went about it the wrong way. But it was always *our* club. The three of us. You just never wanted to join.'

Sian nods, smiles over at me, tearfully. 'Well, that's because it was all boring science stuff,' she says. 'No *Camp Rock*,' and both of us start to laugh.

And while I feel such relief, I can barely eat another thing on my plate. Because now I know the truth. It wasn't Sian, it wasn't Milo, it wasn't some journalist.

It was me. I leaked my diaries. I made them findable. All internet sleuths needed was my name and to know what they were looking for. I exposed them not because I couldn't trust Milo, but because for the first time, I realised I was vulnerable. It wasn't gut feeling. It was fear. I'd shown myself to him – my true self – and it had scared me so much that I'd leapt to protect myself. But ended up hurting myself. In trying not to be exposed, I exposed myself. Iris is right. It ends up harming you. Too much armour will eventually suffocate you.

LIA LOUIS

Sian talks about her plans for June House, for getting it back. 'Do you want to see? I'm thinking we go with Mum's vision. A place for women and children, like we were once . . .'

I listen, pleased for her, but Milo keeps barging his way into my mind. He was right. I said I trusted him, but I never did. He said he trusted me, but he never did. He concealed things from me, and I concealed things from him. All because we were afraid of being exposed in our own way – because people always leave. Right? And I see now that we didn't trust each other, because we didn't trust ourselves to be loved as we are.

'I think I need to go to New York,' I say suddenly.

Sian pauses. A Pinterest board open on her palm. She laughs, a fork hovering above her plate in her other hand. 'Is that, like, weird slang for the toilet or something?'

'No. I need to go to New York. City. I have an awards ceremony to go to.'

'Really?' she asks. 'When?'

'Tonight,' I say. 'I need to get to New York by tonight.'

Chapter Thirty-Five

Allie

I have flown and travelled to a lot of strange places in my time as a biologist. But Manhattan. There's not a call for seabird researchers here, yet here I am.

Twelve hours ago, I was in Norfolk.

Now, I'm in Manhattan.

In the air-conditioned, shiny-floored lobby of the Four Seasons hotel, teetering on heels I can hardly walk in, in a dress that I never thought would suit me, but one I have to admit I couldn't stop looking at myself in, in my hotel mirror.

This feels wild. It doesn't even feel like I'm really here. I'm nothing but a Sim – in fact, that's exactly how I've moved since this morning at the restaurant with Sian. When I realised I needed to come to New York, we both abandoned our breakfasts, paid and ran to her holiday park. Sian dashed from caravan to caravan to bloody *costume department*, collecting things I'd need, while I stood waiting on a cliff, surrounded by cabins with icing-white balconies, and sky-blue slats, gulls circling and crying, and panickily googling my life away.

I googled the Four Seasons. I googled flights. Then I clicked one that left in three hours' time, and bought it, passport still in my bag from leaving Norway. Just like that. Then I checked-in for my flight. An adventure, contained and executed on a screen on a cliff; my emails, a whole paper trail of everything to come.

And so here I am.

Sleep-deprived. My stomach a bag of snakes, with nerves and excitement. A tiny suitcase packed hastily, with nothing but jeans, T-shirts and one dress, borrowed from Sian's show-wardrobe, for when she takes part in the holiday park's stage productions. I've never worn anything like it. It's black, satin, a one-shoulder strap – it reminds me of something a bougie Tarzan might wear – and silver designer-dupe heels *also* borrowed from the holiday camp's entertainment wardrobe. I'm pretty sure nobody attending tonight is wearing anything from a holiday camp wardrobe, but it's something we spent the most time on. Me, standing in Sian's cabin bedroom, in front of a mirror, her friends in and out, ducking in, clothes and props and make-up in hand. It takes a village, apparently, to assemble a red carpet outfit at the drop of a hat. And we really pulled it off. Jake even drove me to the airport. He was in his karate instructor gear and his Labradoodle 'Terrence' kept burying his nose into the back of my trousers from the back seat.

All I remember about tonight is: Four Seasons, the fourteenth, 4 p.m. And it's almost four.

I couldn't get a room here, so I'm staying at a hotel around the corner – two-star, rated high on cleanliness, but low on bed comfortability, and full of Hollywood waxworks that look as though they've been caught in a fire for some reason.

I have no idea what to do. I'm hoping Milo will just . . . materialise somehow. A rush of a team, perhaps, him following. Is he even staying here? Or is this where everyone meets and gets ready? I have vague memories of celebrities getting ready for the Met Gala in hotel rooms, their Instagram profiles full of pictures of them squeezing past a king-sized bed and minibar covered in giant feathers, or dressed like a worm, or a walking hot water bottle, or something. I'm glad this is black tie. Although I'm sure Sian's holiday camp would've had me covered. Someone there, as I arrived, was dressed as a parsnip.

I approach the reception desk.

A man with long, ear-length curls and the sharpest jaw I've ever seen smiles at me. His jaw looks almost sculpted, like someone's run a scalpel down each side of his chin . . .

'Good afternoon, ma'am, welcome to the Four Seasons.'

'Hi,' I reply. 'Um, I'm sort of meant to be meeting someone here.' Which is the truth in a way, even if Milo doesn't *know* that he's meeting me. I've texted asking Iris for Jameson's number, so I can then get Milo's, but she won't see it until she gets a radio silence break, so for now, it's just me and 'all the fours'.

'Perfect, did you organise meeting here, or in our restaurant, or somewhere specific? And are they a guest here?'

'I don't know,' I say. 'I was meant to meet him here for the FA&C awards?'

'Ha. Yes. We have a lot of guests interested in the awards this evening.'

'Oh, I'm not interested. No, sorry. I just mean, I'm sort of meant to be going. That's if things haven't changed.'

He looks up at me slowly, in my Tarzan dress, in my heels, and, if I do say so myself, make-up that really glows (but also might be slightly too much, thanks to an overzealous Pinterest tutorial Sian sent me a screenshot of). Jaw Man makes a strange sound. One that could be 'I see' and 'how wonderful' but also, 'I just have to press 2 for security, you know, and your ass will be out of here'.

'If I give you his name, will you tell me if he's here?'

He smiles, but his eyes glaze over. 'I can only say if they've specifically requested that I can,' he says, hands at the keyboard. 'It's guest confidentiality.'

'Of course.'

'Name?'

What was it? Milo . . . He used something instead of his usual surname for hotels? I think it was a colour.

'Milo Green,' I try.

He types.

Maybe it was a season. This is going back two years now – was it a season? Something from outside. A plant?

'No, ma'am, nothing here.'

'Milo . . . Spring. Um. No. Aster?'

Oh, God, I'm losing him. His eyes are hooded now. A look of 'don't waste my fucking time'. And I'd feel the same if I were him.

'No, sorry. R-rain? Hail?' Argh, I can't remember. Now what? Maybe I'll just say his name. He did tell me to meet him here. But then, we did argue and vow to never speak again, so maybe whatever list my name is on has been amended, scrubbed off like a dirty mark. 'Sorry, I just . . . he told me to meet him here and I know he sometimes uses different names. Could you just try his name? Milo Ford.'

His hands freeze on the keyboard. But slowly he types.

'No,' he simply says.

'No that he's not here or no that he hasn't—'

'Ma'am, we cannot give out guest names, confirm, nor deny who is staying here. You are not the first person who has come here today asking for certain names of those who'll be attending the awards this evening, and while I appreciate you could be truthful, our guests are my priority. Are you a guest here?' He looks at me now, with unbridled suspicion, like I'm a crazed fan.

'No, but—'

'Then I'm afraid I can't help you, ma'am.'

Behind me, two people tut. One sighs and says, 'Unbelievable.'

'Hold on,' I say. 'Please, just . . .' And now I'm reaching into my bag. Am I really going to do this? Google myself? Tell this poor man at reception what happened? Can I do that? But I'm panicked now. It's past four. I have seen nothing except for hotel guests with suitcases.

I cannot come here and go home with nothing.

I came here for what feels like everything.

'Ma'am, if there's nothing else I can help you with, we have quite the line building up behind you.' He's trying desperately to maintain a polite façade, but there's no denying the snark in his voice.

'Look, this is going to sound wild,' I say, thrusting my phone over the counter. 'But my name is Allie Lake. Allie. Lake. See. Look—'

He leans forward to see my screen.

'Allie Lake . . .' he repeats. 'I'm afraid—'

'Look, we know each other. I'm not a crazy fan, I'm not . . . He's my . . . We are very close.' I love him actually, Glenn (according to the name tag), and I appear to have majorly messed it up. 'And if he is on your computer there, I know if you said my name to him, just, Allie Lake, I know that he would—'

'Allie?'

I swing around.

'Allie, oh my God.'

Jameson. He comes over to the desk, having just emerged from a lift. A plant sways next to him. He's wearing a baby blue tux.

'Oh. Jameson!' I say.

His face breaks into a huge grin and, almost as if it surprises us both, I swoop towards him and we hug. Tightly. He's huge this man. Soft-skinned, smells like expensive aftershave, gangly limbs. Over his shoulder, I say to a very confused-looking Glenn, 'See! See!' (And it appears that, amazingly, no, he doesn't see. Not really.)

Jameson holds me at arm's length, the way a father would, and gazes at me. 'Well, look at that. You're here.'

'I'm here.' I laugh. 'Can you believe they thought I was a stalker? I understand it, but it's stupid that a system isn't in place for things like this. A sort of guest noticeboard or something? What if it was an emergency?'

Slowly he smiles at me. 'Allie Lake,' he says. 'You look magnificent.'

I beam – so much I even twirl for the first time (probably) in my life. 'And so do you. Baby blue. Very you.'

'Ha. Sort of missing my neon coat.'

'*I* miss your neon coat. More than I've ever missed an item of clothing.'

Moments ago, I felt like I was lost in New York, with nothing but a load of stray memories and fantasies concierges scoffed at as lies. Like a forgetful grandma telling stories to her grandchildren, who all lean in and whisper, 'Just nod along and pretend, she always tells this one. She swears it's true.' And now I'm here. With Jameson.

'Is it OK?' I ask. 'For the ceremony? I haven't a clue about this stuff. Where do I have to go? I need to speak to him. I'm . . . The whole thing is a mess.'

Then his face falls. A slow dropping of his features; a slow wilt of the corners of his eyes.

'Allie,' he begins, then he gestures at me to follow him. He pulls me gently to one side, to the elevators, away from the desk and long line. It's quiet and carpeted. It smells like scented candles. 'He isn't here.'

And the way he says it tells me it's not that Milo isn't at the hotel, and he's somewhere else, and Jameson will take me to meet him. His sagged shoulders tell me it's something else.

'He left an hour ago.'

'To go where?'

He smiles proudly. 'He didn't tell me, *exactly*,' he laughs. 'But he's gone to find you. Passport's gone. And . . .' He slips a piece of paper from his jacket. 'I've got the speech. Not allowed to open this. Well. Unless he wins. *Until* he wins, if you ask me.'

'Oh my God. Do you think he's flying to Svalbard?'

Jameson laughs. 'Yup. I would guess so.'

'Well, can't you find out?'

'I've tried calling him. He won't pick up. I can get you a cab to JFK though?'

Moments later, we're standing out on the busy side-walk, beside a coffee cart that smells like melted cheese, hailing down yellow taxis.

'Just out of interest,' I say. 'In case I need to know. What's his hotel name? So I don't get treated like a stalker again.'

Jameson smiles. 'Acer Spark,' he tells me. 'His hotel room name is Acer Spark. His childhood pets.'

And I think he finds it weird when I bring my hands to my cheeks. All along, for the last two years, Milo has been there, as one of my most dedicated users, acer_spark, counting birds with me, oceans away.

Chapter Thirty-Six

Milo

My whole life I wanted this. This moment. And now, here it is. Best Lead. Best *Lead*. The odds are on me to win the thing. Exactly where I always wanted to be in my career – the shit I used to dream of. An award for *theatre*.

Except I'm – *here*. On a plane, wearing actual thermal clothing I raided the airport for, my stupid neon coat pushed into my bag.

And I'm flying coach. *Coach*. And you know what? I am so goddamn happy to be in coach. I'm in coach, on a plane to Norway. I'm not downtown, in a Louis Vuitton tux, next to Jeremy Allen White and Emma Stone. Instead, I'm beside a woman who is knitting what looks like a green-striped dog jumper (it has four holes – one for each leg, I guess) and a dude who is chewing beef jerky. He has headphones in, and he's . . . ah. He's watching the FA&Cs on his seat screen.

We're delayed. Some sort of air traffic control problem or something? I lean my head back, watch the muted awards ceremony. I wonder if my seat is empty. I wonder if Jameson made it. He keeps calling me, but I meant it when I said I wanted to do this alone this time. No help. Just me. Just Allie.

I handed my speech to him, sealed in an envelope. 'You need to ask no questions,' I told him. 'This is something I have to do alone. No you. No Iris.'

'I hear you.' He smiled like a proud father. 'Just saying, if you don't win,' said Jameson, 'I'm not promising I won't post this speech somewhere. I just know it's going to be fire.'

'Dude?'

Ah, shit, the guy next to me has seen me staring at his TV. Slowly, he unhooks a headphone.

'Can I help you with something?' he asks.

I stare at him. 'What? I . . . No.'

'Are you confused or in the wrong seat?'

'I . . . don't think so?'

'It's just, you're staring at my TV. You can always use your own. We've all *got* one.'

And he turns back, puts his headphone back in, and carries on watching the awards.

I stifle laughter. Boy, I love coach. Coach keeps me grounded. Coach doesn't give two shits about what you have to offer the world. They want to sit in their seats and they want to watch some TV and drink a tiny can of Sprite and be left the hell alone.

On screen, there are tuxedos and dresses for miles. Friends. Enemies. People I really, truly admire. The kinds of people who made want to act. Those people who expressed a part of such real humanity in their work that it made me understand myself just a little more. And there was a time that I wanted to be in that room, with them, above anything. It didn't matter that my craft had rough edges and I knew it: the overacting, the inability to

368

really get to the emotional truth of a character. The self-consciousness I pretended didn't exist, that always kept me from losing myself totally in a scene. I'd have given anything at all to be there. Even when they didn't want me – especially when they didn't want me. That meant love. That meant acceptance. And now love means one thing: it means Allie. And I want to be wherever she is.

The pilot announces we have a window of airspace. We'll be shortly preparing for take-off.

Chapter Thirty-Seven

Allie

'Please tell me it hasn't gone!' the words burst out of me like little gusts of wind as I get to the check-in desk. It's narrow and cream-coloured, an airline flag jutting from the surface. A box. What's essentially a box stands between Milo and me.

The woman behind it looks up and meets my eye. She's wearing all navy blue – skirt suit, hat, even navy-blue painted nails – and has the most uniform eyeliner I've ever seen, in long turquoise flicks. Her name tag reads, 'Kelli'.

'Excuse me, ma'am?'

'The plane to Norway. H-has it . . . gone? Oh my God, I can't breathe. I. *ran*. from the . . . thing.' In the taxi, I googled flights. Again. There are two going to Norway. One, any minute now, another, in seven hours. I bought a ticket online: a final seat, which felt like fate. Which I, of course, don't really believe in, like Milo does, but today, I'll take anything I can get.

'Ah. No, it's not left just yet, it's due to take off in eight minutes.'

'Can I get on?'

'I don't think that's going to be possible, ma'am, I'm sorry. I can call through? Give it a shot? But . . .'

'Yes. Yes, please.'

It's so frustrating knowing Milo is mere yards away, somewhere on the runway, on his way to find me. *Me*. When I'm right here.

She smiles, holds out a hand for my passport and my boarding pass, and wordlessly brings a receiver to her ear. I thrust my phone at her.

She starts talking – she calls me 'this very sweet passenger' more than once, and I find I'm staring at her, wide-eyed, like this woman holds the keys to the rest of my entire life.

'Sure,' she says. 'No, I understand.' She hangs up, tips her head to one side. 'I'm so sorry, it's too late to board you at this time'

'Oh, no. No, no, no.' This can't happen like this now. We're so close. Or – maybe Jameson finally got through to him? He said he'd been trying. Maybe he got through and Milo never even got on? Maybe he's in the airport, waiting for me? But I left Jameson my number. Surely by now he'd have passed it on to Milo, at the very least. And if he has, why hasn't he called? Messaged?

The agent behind the counter nods understandingly, but she eyes me like she's hoping I don't cry – that this shift is already a thousand hours long and she really could do without being handed a weepy customer at this time of the day. She likely wants a foot spa and a take-away. Not my tears. 'We can get your ticket transferred,' she tells me kindly. 'Maybe get you on the next flight.'

I nod. 'Could you at least check if someone's on the plane? I'd be very grateful if you could.'

Another woman approaches the counter. She's dressed in the same uniform; she eyes us both, smiling politely. She's familiar to me. Why is she familiar?

'I'm not really allowed to give that information over,' carries on Kelli. 'Is there someone on the plane that's expecting you?'

Argh, this is Glenn at the Four Seasons again. She doesn't have his jaw, but I would be unsurprised if they turned out to be do-gooding siblings who pride themselves on following every customer privacy rule by the book.

The minute changes on the digital clock behind her, and it pulses another surge of adrenaline through me. *Don't leave. Don't leave without me.*

The woman joins Kelli behind the counter. Her face. It really is familiar . . .

'He isn't expecting me on the plane,' I say. 'But he's expecting me to be in Norway. Well, in Svalbard. And he doesn't know that I'm not there. Milo thinks I'm there, but I'm *here*—'

'Oh my *goodness*.' The other woman lights up. 'Milo and Allie, right? Sorry, I didn't recognise you, you . . . well, you look totally amazing. But I think last time we met, you were dressed a little differently.'

'Y-yes?' I say slowly, and she laughs.

'Milo was here earlier,' she says. 'I helped him out.'

I stare at her blankly, first thinking is this some sort of celebrity thing. Do celebrities just call random airline workers and get on flights? Then she puts a hand to her chest.

'Heidi,' she says. 'Flight attendant. I . . .'

'You swapped us!' I exclaim, instantly remembering. 'Back then, you swapped our seats. Of course!'

That's why she seemed so familiar. She switched us, back then. I remember now, her petite, smiling face, the large hoop earrings. She'd asked if I'd mind swapping seats with someone for legroom. Milo told me, eventually, it was because someone in the row was taking covert pictures of him, so he subtly asked the flight attendant to move him and to blame legroom, so as not to shame anyone. That's why we swapped mid-flight. That's why our phones got swapped. This woman was the catalyst.

'I was contacted about the film,' she says, excitedly. 'Got the email last week. From Jameson? To see if I could add anything. Talk about what I remembered about the whole thing, about you guys on the plane . . .' She's picking up the phone now, dialling, as Kelli watches us, glittery-eyed. 'And I thought it was a scam at first.' She laughs. 'But then I showed a couple of my girlfriends and they were like, nooo, Heidi, that's the real *deal*. So I emailed back. And I don't know anything, other than having to swap you both. But when the leak was exposed, I was *so* excited to be part of it. It felt like a claim to fame. It makes such a good dinner party story, you know. *Hey, who remembers when Milo Ford switched phones with that girl? Google it! That was me! I switched them on the plane!* It always goes down a treat— Oh. Nobody's answering.'

She dials again, leans to her computer.

Kelli is watching in awe. 'Shall I try someone else?'

Heidi nods, types, a phone to her ear.

'He told us all about you,' she says.

'So he's definitely on the plane?' I ask. 'Milo is on the plane.'

'We're not supposed to say . . .' starts Kelli, but Heidi jumps in, 'Absolutely. Got him on there myself.'

I laugh. 'I need to get on it. Or stop it. Or something. I need to tell him. I need to tell him I think I'm falling in love with him.'

Both women freeze and explode into high-pitched sounds.

'Oh, it's so romantic,' says Heidi. 'Isn't it? Ugh, this is just making my *whole week* right now.'

Laughter takes over me. Sweet-tasting, hopeful giggles. Because it is romantic, isn't it? It *is* beautiful, falling in love. And I'm falling in love with a man called Milo Ford, and he cares enough about me that he is on a plane going to find me in Svalbard. On one of the most important nights of his career.

And then Heidi is chattering quickly on the phone, ushering me off, the wire of the phone stretching across the desk.

'Go straight through,' she says. 'Go. They're going to open the door.'

As I run down the galley towards the plane, I hear her say to someone on the phone, 'Thank you. And would you swap their seats so they're together?'

Chapter Thirty-Eight

Milo

'There will be a short delay, folks,' says the pilot. 'But hang tight, and we should be in the air within the next ten minutes. Thank you for your patience.'

I'm not sure what's going on. Flight attendants keep picking up the phone, talking hushed and quiet between them. Airspace problems again, maybe?

But I'll be in the sky soon, on the way to Allie. I'm at least on the plane. Just a few hours, and then, I'll be . . . I mean, I don't even *know*. I've not thought that far ahead. Jameson said he'd send me his list of contacts – helicopters, boats, all that – but warned me it isn't simple to just 'hop on one'. But I guess, failing that, I'll be bribing anyone I possibly can to somehow get to Allie at the research station. I have no idea how to swindle it. Flights only leave at certain times, on certain days. But I'll make it work. Even if I have to make a raft and sail there myself. I at least know how to use an oar now, thanks to Allie.

'You'll die out there,' I hear in my mind, in Allie's voice. Yeah, OK, maybe not.

It makes me smile. Allie lives in my head; she's lived there for two years now. Speaking to me, talking me down off the ledge, chiming in with irritating little contrary comments that Allie would definitely say in real life. Even after the leak, I don't think a day has gone by where I haven't spoken to Allie Lake in my mind. But now I don't just want her in my head. I want her in my real life. Every single day.

'Excuse me, ma'am.' A flight attendant appears in the aisle. She turns to my neighbour, the woman knitting the dog sweater. 'Could I interest you in an upgrade?' she says. 'Complimentary of course.'

She drops the knitting into her lap. 'Oh my Lord, *really*? Me? *Why*?'

I recognise that accent. It's a totally, born-and-bred, old school New Jersey accent. It makes me smile. She sort of sounds like Mom. She'd be all for this. Dad, not so much, but Mom. She was a romantic. She was untethered and adventurous. She loved a love story. The nights we sat there, watching *Roman Holiday* together. Recliners. Pizza. *An Affair to Remember. Charade.*

'Surplus seats,' the flight attendant smiles, and the woman beside me scrabbles to gather her stuff, as if, at any moment, if she doesn't move quick enough, the airline might change their mind and throw her in the cargo hold instead.

Well. Nobody ever complained about having a free seat next to them on a plane. Her elbows kind of kept nudging into me anyway, and I'm not a hundred per cent sure, but she was glancing over at me for a little longer than a stranger might.

Allie's voice chimes in again. 'Not *everyone* knows who you are, Milo. Lest you forget the man next to you simply couldn't care less about you. He doesn't even want you looking his way.'

I smirk to myself.

I flick through the TV screen in front of me. OK, I might not be there, but I do want to know if I win, hopefully watch Jameson read my speech. I didn't write Allie's name once, but a lot of my speech is about her. Not that she'll be watching anyway. She's probably got her whole body wedged in the nest of a puffin right now. I can't wait to be there with her. Then maybe we can fly back together. She can see my apartment. I can show her New York. Yio's Pizza. The kitchen bear. Or maybe she'll say she doesn't want this, and then I'll fly back alone. Who knows? Who knows how this'll work? I just know I need to find out. I need to see her again, tell her how I feel. I need to apologise, tell her I don't want to hide anymore. I want to thank her for the words – for holding that part of who I really am, gently in her hands for all that time.

And then I hear her voice again.

'Thank you,' it says. 'Thank you.'

And for a moment, my bones freeze, because while I feel sure it's in my head, as it so often is, it sounds . . .

'Is this seat free?'

And slowly, I turn my face towards her voice. A dress. Black. Hair in waves. Small, dainty fingers, that impish nose, that quirked eyebrow, those blue eyes . . . her.

'Well?' she asks.

'*Allie*?' I burst out laughing. 'Allie, oh my God, what . . . what are you doing here? I'm . . . I'm coming to find you.'

'Found me,' she says, matter-of-fact. 'Here I am.'

Chapter Thirty-Nine

Allie

Nobody has ever looked at me like Milo is now. It makes me feel like everything. It makes me feel like nobody else exists in the world except me. His slow, wide smile, those gorgeous, sleepy brown eyes . . .

'I can't believe you're here.' He stands between the seats, moves into the aisle. He's dressed in clothes I've never seen him in. A grey jumper. Khaki combats. It makes me smile. He's ready for the Arctic, I'm ready for an awards ceremony. He takes my face into his hands and cradles it. 'Hey,' he says mouth inches from mine. 'What are you doing here?'

I can feel them – eyes on us. So very many eyes on us. Phones poised. And I don't care. I just don't care. We're both steeped in it. Huge, disbelieving smiles and delirious laughter.

'Hey,' I whisper.

'This dress . . .'

'For your ceremony,' I say, and his face floods with heat. 'But I got to the hotel and you weren't there. And Jameson – he told me where you'd gone. So. Here I am. And I almost missed this flight. But I think they slowed things down for me. Felt sorry for me, or . . . I don't know? The flight attendant.'

'Heidi?'

I nod. 'She helped me. Can you believe she recognised me? *Remembered* us.'

'I know,' he laughs.

'She moved heaven and earth somehow. Like, you were meant to be taking off *now*.'

Slowly, Milo smiles at me. That pink, beautiful mouth that rendered me practically speechless on one of our first video calls. 'The world loves a romance, right?'

'I suppose,' I say. 'Told them I had to get on.'

'And what did you say?' he asks. 'Kittiwakes in trouble. Goose on the line . . .'

'No,' I tell him. 'The man I'm falling in love with is on this plane.'

He smiles slowly and deliciously. 'Say that again,' he says, and now I can feel all eyes on us. Even the man next to Milo has dragged his eyes away from the little screen in front of him.

'I said,' I laugh to myself, dizzy with it all. 'The man I'm falling in love with is on this plane.'

'What's his name?'

'You've probably not heard of him,' I grin.

'Ouch.' He laughs, nose to mine. 'I'm going to need to hear you say his name, though, Captain Lake.'

'Milo,' I say, and we both laugh, faces so close. 'Milo Ford.'

He strokes a thumb along my cheek, a smooth, gentle gesture that makes my eyes flutter closed. 'I'm falling in love with you, Allie Lake,' he says. 'The woman *I'm* in love with is on this plane.'

Then, slowly, he leans in, and presses his soft lips on mine. He kisses me tenderly, savouring me, and from one of the nearby televisions, I hear his name. The winner. Best Male Lead. Milo Ford.

And as seatbelt lights bleep on, as a round of applause bursts from a distant speaker somewhere in the plane, I realise I don't care if the world is watching. I'm in love with Milo Ford and I want the universe to know – every planet, every moon.

We settle in our seats, strap ourselves in, and the plane begins moving, rolling along to take off, and with my head on Milo's shoulder, he holds me, and I listen to the quiet, far away words from a TV, of someone who believed in us, telling the whole world that Milo Ford can't be there tonight, because he's off chasing 'love' across oceans and he hopes to find her.

Action. The most beautiful action.

And in a silent moment, with nobody else around to hear, into Milo's ear, I say, 'I love you.'

One Year Later

'Look at that *turnout*. Seriously. Lay your eyes on that shit, baby.' Jameson is beaming through the tinted windows of the taxi, hands in two arcs against the glass, face smooshed up against it. The car crawls along the bustling London street, summer sun still beating down like theatre lights. 'Like, this is all for us. All of it.'

'All for our *film*, you mean,' Iris says, smirking from beside him. She adjusts the high collar of her jumpsuit. My best friend looks *amazing* tonight. She scoured the whole of the UK for an outfit to wear, and eventually settled on this: a vintage seventies catsuit found in a charity bin that she spent weeks adjusting with needle and thread. Classic Iris. Had never sewn before, but wanted to do it, so learned, immersed herself in YouTube tutorials, and therefore, did it.

'Well, yeah obvs they're here for the film, Iris,' Jameson laughs. 'But they're here for us, too.' He looks over at us, bows his head towards Milo and me. 'And mostly to see these two. Our *transatlantic sweethearts*. What? That's what the *New Yorker* called you, Allie, don't be giving me sexy, cross looks like that.'

I roll my eyes at him, and Milo chuckles from next to me, brings my hand to his warm lips and kisses.

'Sexy, cross looks only for me,' he says, the words against my skin, and I laugh, shoot him one too.

There are a lot of people out there. A *lot*, Jameson is right. I can see them all on the street. Fans and photographers waiting excitedly behind metal barriers, and crawling along in cars like ours, in front, are guest after guest. Celebrities and scientists, dresses and suits making us all indistinguishable. Tonight, we're here for one thing: our short film. Our documentary filmed in the Arctic, in Cote Rock, just over a year ago. A demonstration of our important work over there, and mine and Milo's reunion, a poignant B-story. In places, it's raw – me, talking about being hunted down by the public, feeling I had to escape. Dad. Milo's addiction and my phone getting in the hands of people it shouldn't. Helene, it turns out, the writer of Milo's movie in Romania. Journalist Laura-Lee admitted Helene had talked about it to her, that night. She thought it would make a perfect companion piece to her love story of a movie they filmed in Romania. No absolute proof meant we could never fully *legally* name her, and both Milo and I agreed we wouldn't have wanted to. Not now.

Tonight, *Two Birds, One Stone*, will premiere, after twelve months of all of us editing and producing and philosophising and extracting the truth not only from our lives, but from what the world, via our amazing work in Svalbard, is trying to tell us, tell humanity.

Milo and I will also be stepping out onto the carpet – white, like snow, this time – for the very first time, at an official event, together. A couple. Partners. Boyfriend and girlfriend. We've taken that part slowly, although our relationship has been pretty public for a while now.

Milo's speech, read by Jameson, went viral – of course – and it didn't take internet sleuths long to ascertain he'd been in Svalbard, with me. It's different this time, though. We navigated it together. Slowly. Carefully. And even when it feels scary – because it does sometimes, for us both – he's right there. *I'm* right there. We return only to each other; find each other in the noise.

My phone buzzes – a message from Polly.

'Polly and Lars are there,' I tell everyone, and then laugh. 'Oh my God, Lars has spotted *Helen Mirren*.'

'Oh, *shit*,' laughs Milo.

'Polly says she is so embarrassed, she's tried to lose him twice.'

Polly sends through a photo of Lars posing on the white carpet. I have a feeling Lars is going to have a lot of fans after tonight. He looks *gorgeous*. Sunglasses and a tweed suit. A rough, grey beard. Wild salt-and-pepper hair. I smile so widely it stings my cheeks. It's so special, having us all be a part of something like this. That feather-blending of our lives and our worlds. And I'm happy. I'm so happy.

Milo laces his fingers through mine. 'You all right, Captain Lake?'

'I am,' I nod. 'And you, Officer Ford?'

'I'm perfect,' he says, leaning close to me. 'So long as I've got you next to me, I'm perfect.'

'Oh, barf, Mildred.' Jameson grins from opposite us, still gazing out of the window, and Iris jabs him in the side.

'Reminder you made a movie about them, Merritt,' says Iris. 'Mildred is allowed to be barf-y. We're only *here* because he's barf-y.'

'Thank you, Iris,' says Milo. 'Plus, who knows, there might be a sequel soon, right? Might you have a bit of barfiness in you, J?'

Jameson swoops around and looks at him then, wide-eyed and grinning. 'Stop with that.'

Iris giggles beside him. 'I think he's right,' she says, putting her hand on Jameson's knee. 'I can sense you have a lot of barfiness in there.' And Jameson smiles, places his own huge hand softly down on hers. After eleven months of heavy flirting and sticking to the story of, '*Oh, no way, we're just like, really good friends,*' Jameson and Iris kissed on Jameson's farm. They've been on three dates so far and I have never seen Iris so happy. He's also going back to the arctic with her next spring. He's going to film a series of YouTube videos while there, and from the money we've raised through the movie, My Planet have no issue with him going back.

'He can keep me company,' Iris told me. 'Since you'll be knee-deep in wallpaper and gnomes and shit.'

Sian couldn't get June House back, but she has just bought her own little place with her third of the money we got from its sale – a secluded Welsh stone cottage she's going to turn into her own B&B and she is firmly 'back on her bullshit', as Milo says. All Pinterest boards and wild plans and eBay taxidermy purchases. June House *is* up for sale, though. We've not told her yet, but Milo and I organised a viewing tomorrow. We'd talk to Sian first, of course, but Milo loved the idea of Mum's retreat – for victims of addiction and abuse – and we're hoping we can still do it. A project of our own to return home to, between movies and Bermuda and our busy lives that throw us all over the world. An actor and a scientist.

The car comes to a complete stop. A security guard sidles up to the car door. It clicks open. The hubbub and chatter of crowds leak through the crack.

Milo presses his lips to the side of my face. 'It's just us two. No one else,' he says. 'Remember?'

'Just us two,' I repeat, a mantra of ours that has helped me – helped *us* – navigate this new world together over the last year. And it has, so far, managed to feel like us two – whether we're at Milo's apartment, a slow morning of books and coffee and pyjamas, trading hopes and shadow-parts of ourselves and dinner plans, or here, in a car, the bright spotlight of the world eagerly waiting for us outside. His hand always manages to find mine, and squeeze, and that's all it takes.

The car door opens, cheers begin to slowly move through the crowds, and Milo begins to get out. 'Hand?' he says, looking back at me with a smile that turns my stomach over. I place my hand in his.

I don't know what's ahead for us. Not truly. Who does? Whether that's Arctic cliffs or red carpets. New York apartments or miner's cabins. I just know it's our story now. It's mine and Milo's, and mine and Milo's only.

As we step out of the car, Milo's hand squeezes mine, and a sea of flashing cameras illuminates our path. If I close my eyes, it could be the world's spotlight. It could be the polar sun.

*

LIA LOUIS

[Research Port // Saved by user: Milo Ford in folder: My Girl] . . . and in the case of 'Lucky' and 'Mart', Doctor Allie Lake concluded, that although the birds experienced some physical time apart, their organic reunion further demonstrates their bond had not been severed, that an interlude may have been required for growth and survival, and that the birds would 'almost definitely' 'stay together for the rest of their lives'. – Lake, Alexandra (2025, November 11) Monogamy in Seabirds, published in TLT Ecology Journal via My Planet.

386

Acknowledgements

I could not start this acknowledgement section without first thanking you, the reader. To write stories for you is such a privilege, and I hope you enjoyed the time spent with Allie and Milo. Thank you for reading, for reviewing, for picking up my books in shops, or in libraries, for recommending, and for reaching out with your beautiful messages. I am truly grateful to you all.

As ever, a massive thank you to my absolute wonder of an agent, Juliet Mushens at Mushens Entertainment and the rest of the Mushens Entertainment team. Thank you also to the brilliant Jenny Bent at The Bent Agency, New York.

Thank you to the patient and smart Melissa Cox at Zaffre, as well as the rest of the team at the brilliant Bonnier Books.

Thank you to Emily Bestler at Emily Bestler Books, and to Lara Jones as well as the whole team at Emily Bestler Books, Atria and Simon & Schuster.

I would not have been able to write this book without many talented and kind experts in their field, and what an absolute honour to listen to the fascinating words you all so generously gave over Zoom and voice notes and lunches that were worth their weight in gold!

Thank you to the master who is Giles Alderson for talking all things TV and filmmaking with me. To the amazing Rupert Graves: you really are just the coolest and most generous human being and I am so grateful for your insight, honesty and wisdom. Thank you also to Jack Ryder – yes, the very same Jack Ryder my 11-year-old self would totally freak out over – who spent a long time answering questions about acting and fame, and remained constantly open and kind when I consistently bugged him with the same question of, 'OK, and what *else* might an actor need from their phones if a woman a whole ocean away had it?'. Thank you also to the incredible Julia Whelan whose wisdom over lunch broke open a character for me. A special thanks also to CGI Catering, and to Victoria Lee for her endless chats about inheritance.

Thank you so very, very, very much to scientists, Maria Dance and Annette Fayet. These women are utterly INCREDIBLE and are saving the world. Maria, Annette, you both introduced me to a world I will never forget and one that has beguiled me ever since. (First step, bird feeders in my garden, next . . . maybe someday also having a shred of your bravery to climb cliffs to spy on puffins armed with scales and camera probes?) I will forever be in awe of you both. You are badasses.

Thank you to Amanda and Alison for always reminding me of who I am and guiding me back there when I lose my way.

I will forever be grateful to my friends. All the warmth, friendship and unconditional love in this book, is yours. A special thank you to Gilly, Beth, Grace, Sally,

Pat, Emma and Toni. Thank you for enveloping me in love and acceptance. I used to dream of friends like you.

Thank you to my family. Mum and Steve, Dad and Sue, Bubs, Vicky, and my niece and nephews. Nan, Alan, Marl, and Libby. I'm convinced that there isn't much in life that can't be solved by us simply gathering together around a table of food somewhere, being silly, and laughing at everything.

Finally, to my three beautiful children and my Ben. My whole heart. My anchors. Thank you for loving me. (And to my eldest son, thank you for the night I had my silly book-wobble. I will remember your lamp-lit, proud face holding my words forever. How lucky I am, to have you.)